*Peering back up into that tough-guy face
and those captivating eyes made her a little dizzy.*

She'd never known a guy with muscles like this. With long hair. With so many tattoos.

"No problem." He was still Mr. Unemotional, his voice flat and detached.

"You saved my life," she felt the need to add.

"I wouldn't go *that* far."

His words made her remember the whole outlaw rumor. Maybe an outlaw biker dude took that kind of statement more literally. And did this mean she should be scared? She'd been a *little* scared even *before* remembering that part.

And yet . . . even as her muscles stayed tensed, she felt a response to him in other places. Good lord—what was *that* about?

———

By Toni Blake

WHISPER FALLS
SUGAR CREEK
ONE RECKLESS SUMMER
LETTERS TO A SECRET LOVER
TEMPT ME TONIGHT
SWEPT AWAY

TONI BLAKE

WHISPER FALLS

A DESTINY NOVEL

AVON

An Imprint of HarperCollinsPublishers

This is a work of fiction. Names, characters, places, and incidents are products of the author's imagination or are used fictitiously and are not to be construed as real. Any resemblance to actual events, locales, organizations, or persons, living or dead, is entirely coincidental.

AVON BOOKS
An Imprint of HarperCollins*Publishers*.
10 East 53rd Street
New York, New York 10022–5299

First Avon Books paperback printing: January 2011

Avon Trademark Reg. U.S. Pat. Off. and in Other Countries, Marca Registrada, Hecho en U.S.A.
HarperCollins® is a registered trademark of HarperCollins Publishers.

Printed in the U.S.A.

10 9 8 7 6 5 4 3 2 1

To Lindsey Faber—
Loyal reader turned cheerleader turned publicist,
lunch/dinner companion, marketing strategist,
plotter extraordinaire, shoulder to cry on
or celebrate with, all around Girl Friday—
and, most importantly, my cherished friend.

Acknowledgments

Books are not written in a vacuum, and I rely heavily on feedback from a couple of people whose opinions I trust enormously. So huge thanks to Renee Norris for her insightful critique of the entire book (and who went above and beyond, providing this even when she was sick so I could meet my deadline). And huge thanks as well to Lindsey Faber for her painstaking help over the course of two long evenings during which we mapped out all the logistics for the action-based scenes toward the end of the book. Not to mention that she tolerates all the general plot and character stuff I bombard her with on a regular basis. I count myself very fortunate to have both of them in my life.

Additional heartfelt thanks go to Jill Purinton, Bob Frost, and Jane Ballard for their help in learning about motorcycles and what's cool in the biker world. Thanks, too, to Michelle Combs for giving me the lowdown on getting a tattoo. And thanks to the Faber family for their help narrowing down the list of names for my fictional biker gang. By the way, I've done my best to confirm that no such gang with the name I'm using exists, but if I'm wrong, it's totally coincidental—promise!

And lastly, my sincere appreciation to all the good people at Avon Books and the Rotrosen Agency for all the great stuff they do for me. I'm blessed to have you guys in my corner.

. . . I looked at his features, beautiful in their harmony,
but strangely formidable in their still severity . . .

Charlotte Brontë, *Jane Eyre*

One

"*Meow.*"

Tessa Sheridan frowned at the gray-and-white cat perched next to her on the sofa. "What do you want *now*? I put your dumb Fancy Feast out, and your special little ball with the bell inside. And your litter box is by the door."

"*Meow,*" he said again, an insistent look on his furry little face. In fact, Mr. Knightley—who didn't strike Tessa as being nearly as debonair as the Jane Austen character he was named for—stared at her as if she were . . . a cat psychic or something. But she had no idea what his problem was and didn't feel particularly tolerant. She'd agreed to cat-sit for her close friend, Amy, who was gone for the weekend with her mom seeing relatives a few hours' drive away. And she'd originally planned to do the job at Amy's place, but she wasn't feeling well, so it had just made sense to pack up the spoiled kitty and bring him here to her cabin. Only now he wouldn't leave her alone.

"What is it, you silly cat?"

"Meow."

Tessa simply rolled her eyes at him, then hugged a throw pillow to her chest. Blegh. Nausea. Not a lot. Just a little. Just enough to make her feel slightly off-kilter.

But she refused to focus on that. So she cast the pillow aside, pushed to her feet, and said to Mr. Knightley, "I'm going to check the mail. Eat your expensive food while I'm gone." She didn't bother putting on shoes because it was nice out for early March—around seventy degrees— and the sun was shining bright; the warmth of the concrete driveway would feel good beneath her feet.

The cabin's inside door already stood open, so she pushed through the screen door—only to see a flash of gray-and-white fur go darting past her feet! Oh God. "Knightley! You get back here right now!"

Of course, this went much like her previous attempts at communication—he ignored her and promptly scampered around the corner of the small log house, out of sight.

"Mr. Knightley!" She let the screen door slam shut and gave chase, soon running over cool grass instead of warm concrete, and hoped she wouldn't step on anything unpleasant as she bounded around the cabin and behind it.

And—uh-oh. Mr. K. was nowhere in sight. That fast. The realization brought on a fresh wave of nausea. This couldn't be. If she lost Amy's cat . . . well, it was unthinkable. She frequently teased her friend for her intense attachment to him, yet she could scarcely imagine Amy's life without her beloved pet. Her chest went hollow.

But don't panic. You'll find him. You have to. "Here, kitty!" she called in a high-pitched voice. "Here, kitty kitty."

Her head swam, more from fear now than anything else, as she scanned the area behind her cabin. Beyond the backyard, the land sloped upward toward a small white ranch house with a large garage to one side. Well, at least her new neighbor wasn't out and about. She hadn't seen him—or her—yet; all she knew was that the new occupant seemed to have very loud friends with very loud motorcycles and that this was no time for any awkward introductions. And given that she'd moved out here in the woods seeking peace and quiet, the frequent motorcycle noise presented yet one more problem in her life. And now she'd lost Mr. Knightley on top of everything else?

No, she couldn't have. She refused to believe it. "Knightley!" she snapped impatiently. "Where on earth are you?"

But as she padded onward through the soft spring grass, she heard no annoying meows and saw no signs of cat life. And then she started thinking about exactly where she lived. There were so many trees here. Her log cabin and the neighbor's house were the only two homes for half a mile in either direction, both built on the hilliest stretch of Whisper Falls Road. The shadowy, narrow stretch of pavement twisted past on one side of the houses and Whisper Creek ran along the other, probably fifty yards away through the trees. So many places for a cat to hide. Or get lost. Or hurt. Not that she thought Mr. Knightley would fling himself into the current or anything, but still—how would she ever find him here? "Here, kitty kitty!" Her heart was in her throat by the time she reached the side of her yard that led toward the stream and the small descent of Whisper Falls in the distance. She peered off into the woods, fairly dark already even though it was only late afternoon. "*Please*, kitty kitty."

Nothing moved in the forest, but she could hear the *shush* of the falls from where she stood. She began to walk upward, into the yard above, still staring into the trees to her right. "Mr. Knightley, if you can hear me, I'm sorry I haven't been very nice. Just come on out and let's go home. I'll feed you with a spoon if that's what it takes. I'll throw your little ball for you and scratch under your chin and all the other stuff Amy told me to do that I haven't been doing."

In the shade now, a breeze chilled her and she hugged herself. She wore only a tank top with jeans, and her bare feet had officially become cold. "Mr. Knightley, please don't do this to me," she begged, staring off into the wooded gloom. Desperation tinged her voice, but she couldn't help it. "Please come back and we'll work out our differences. We'll play and cuddle together, I promise." She knew it was silly to try to reason with him, but she felt at a loss, not sure how to proceed or what to do.

When she heard a masculine throat-clearing sound directly behind her, she nearly jumped out of her skin. Whipping around to face the noise, she found . . . Oh Lord. Surely this wasn't her neighbor. At the intimidating sight of him, she almost jumped again, but forced herself to stay on the ground this time. He stood at least six foot three, with long, dark hair that fell past broad shoulders. His black Harley Davidson T-shirt molded to his body, and his tan, muscular arms sported numerous tattoos. She sucked in her breath as her skin prickled.

"You lose somebody?" he asked, his voice as deep as she might have expected. His expression said he suspected she was a little crazy, though. Probably since she'd been staring into the woods having a conversation with someone who wasn't there. About playing and cuddling, no less.

"My friend's cat," she said. But did that make the situation any better? Given that she'd been saying dumb things about working out their differences? "He ran away. I'm cat-sitting," she added. Something about this guy's deep brown eyes on her was unnerving. He possessed . . . shockingly *pretty* eyes, framed by thick, dark lashes. Their warmth contradicted everything else about him, all of which was definitely hard, rough, and even a little scary. "His name's Mr. Knightley," she added dumbly.

"Weird name for a cat." His voice came flat, devoid of emotion.

"Yeah," she agreed. She'd considered saying more, explaining the whole Jane Austen connection, but in the end had decided to just keep it simple. "Have you seen him?" She was nervous now—suddenly speaking around a disconcerting lump in her throat.

And even as the brawny guy gave his head a shake, saying, "Nope, I just now came outside," she realized that besides looking sort of menacing, he also seemed . . . familiar in some way. Was it his voice? Those eyes? Something more subtle in his tough-guy stance? Then it occurred to her that he looked like . . . a Romo; the Romo family had roots in the town of Destiny going back half a century.

And then it hit her. Could this possibly be . . . ? Was this . . . Lucky Romo, who'd left town years ago and never been heard from again?

No, surely not. Because if Lucky was back in town, she'd know. Her friend Rachel was engaged to Mike Romo, Lucky's older brother.

Unless . . . could Lucky have come back without telling anyone? Her neighbor had moved in a couple of weeks ago, after all. And the Whisper Falls area was pretty isolated, a good place to keep to oneself—which was exactly why *she'd* chosen it.

Still, it made no sense. If Lucky had come home to Destiny, why wouldn't he contact his family? And she certainly saw Rachel and Mike often enough to know nothing monumental like that had occurred.

"Uh, you okay?" he asked, eyes narrowed slightly.

Oh crap. Not really. I've lost Amy's cat. I'm still a little woozy. I've got a big, burly biker neighbor who may or may not be the long-lost Lucky Romo. And I just keep standing here staring at him while my heart beats too fast. "No," she answered honestly—despite that his question had sounded more like *You seem odd* than *I'm concerned for you.* "If I don't find that cat, I'm dead."

He gave his head a slight tilt and spoke matter-of-factly. "Must be an important cat."

"It is. Very." Then she pointed vaguely toward the log cabin thirty yards down the hill. "I'm . . . your neighbor, by the way."

She'd started to say her name, yet somehow hadn't felt completely comfortable divulging it to this particular guy. Although she'd hoped maybe *he'd* introduce himself anyway—but instead he just said, "How'd the cat get out?"

"When I opened the door, he ran past me."

For the first time, she detected a glint of amusement in his eyes. "Doesn't sound like you're a very good cat-sitter."

Something about it softened her uneasiness a bit. "Lost my training manual," she said.

"Well, he couldn't have gotten far."

She disagreed with that assessment, but the notion propelled her to consider ways she might lure Mr. Knightley back if he *was* still nearby. Besides being the most practical thing she'd done since the cat's escape, it seemed like a better use of her time than trying to make out all the tattoos on her well-muscled neighbor. Even so, she'd instantly caught sight of an inked chain circling one biceps several times, and now couldn't help noticing some kind of orangey flames on his forearm. "Do you have any yarn?" she asked.

Her broad-shouldered neighbor blinked, back to looking at her like she was a little nuts again. "Any *what*?"

"Yarn." She swallowed nervously around that dumb lump in her throat. "Mr. Knightley likes to play with yarn. Red's his favorite." *Shut up, shut up, shut up.*

"Afraid I haven't unpacked my knitting basket yet," he said, his dry tone confirming what she already knew: Biker dudes didn't *have* yarn, red or otherwise. Only then he looked over his shoulder, toward his house. "But hang on a minute—I've got an idea."

And as he turned and walked away, toward his house, she realized his T-shirt didn't only advertise Harley Davidson. On the back, in red lettering, were the words Lucky's Custom Bike Painting.

Holy crap.

She'd been right. This was Lucky Romo! In the flesh! It was a miracle!

Because his family hadn't heard from him in so long they'd actually feared he was dead. Which was because— uh-oh, she just remembered—they'd also gotten word at some point that he'd joined an outlaw biker gang out west.

Oh boy. Bikers were one thing—*outlaw* bikers were another. Did she have some vile and dangerous criminal helping her look for Amy's cat? Should she just forget Mr. Knightley and run? Maybe the sense of danger that hung around her neighbor was what had kept her from giving him her name. And if she *didn't* run, should she tell him she knew who he was?

Before she could think further, the door on the white house opened and Lucky Romo came walking back out— carrying a small bowl of milk in one large hand. Huh.

He said nothing as he rejoined her in the yard, so she cleverly remarked, "Milk." Then cringed. *Stop with the brilliant comments already!* Lucky Romo lowered the dish to the grass halfway between Tessa and the woods, then stepped back beside her. And that's when she realized what Mr. K had wanted when he'd been meowing at her. Amy gave him a saucer of milk every night with dinner—and Tessa had forgotten. Stubborn, spoiled cat.

"Is that him?" Lucky asked.

Tessa's heart rose to her throat when she followed his pointing finger toward the edge of the yard, where the forest met the lawn—Mr. Knightley crouched there in the taller grass, peering at the milk as if it were prey. "Uh-huh," she whispered.

Both of them stayed quiet as Knightley slowly, silently inched toward the milk, his movements implying he thought he was being very sneaky about the whole thing. Once he started lapping at it, Tessa gingerly moved in to kneel beside him. He didn't flinch when she reached to stroke his fur, too caught up in the milk, and she sighed, "Thank God," giving the spotted cat an affectionate squeeze. For the first time since Knightley's escape, Tessa felt like she could breathe again. She hadn't lost Amy's cat. Life would go on.

But then she remembered the weirder part: Lucky Romo, of all people in the world, had helped her find him. She still couldn't fathom that this big, tough guy was him. He'd left town at eighteen, which was—she did the math—sixteen years ago now. But this *had* to be him. The whole motorcycle thing fit. As did the name on the back of his shirt. Sure, it *could* be somebody else's business, but he looked so much like Mike with that thick, dark hair and olive complexion.

So this was him. Lucky Romo. Home at last.

But . . . if he wasn't here to reconcile with his family, why was he in Destiny?

The second Mr. Knightley reached the bottom of the shallow bowl, Tessa anchored one arm snugly around him and pushed to her feet. "Thanks," she said. Although peering back up into that tough-guy face and those captivating eyes made her a little dizzy. She'd never known a guy with muscles like this. With long hair. With so many tattoos.

"No problem." He was still Mr. Unemotional, though, his voice flat and detached.

"You saved my life," she felt the need to add.

He gave his head a pointed tilt. "I wouldn't go *that* far."

His words made her remember the whole outlaw rumor. Maybe an outlaw biker dude took that kind of statement a lot more literally than she did. And did this mean she should be scared? She'd been a *little* scared even *before* remembering that part.

And yet . . . even as her muscles stayed tensed, she felt a response to him in other places, too. In her breasts. Between her thighs. Good Lord—what was *that* about? Or—wait. Maybe it was all just nerves, her whole body getting into the act because he was so freaking intimidating. Hopefully. She couldn't tell.

So she dropped her gaze briefly and bit her lip, her heart still pounding too hard, before forcing her eyes back to his one last time. "Well, I better get him into the house before he tries to make another break for it."

Mr. Unresponsive didn't reply, so with cat in hand, she turned to go.

That's when he said, "See ya later . . . hot stuff."

The last words halted Tessa in place. What had he just called her? Looking over her shoulder, she raised her gaze back to his—to find another tiny hint of amusement there as he said, "Your shirt."

Glancing down, Tessa wanted to die. She'd completely forgotten she wore a snug white tank with the words *Hot Stuff* written in script across it, actually half of a pajama set Rachel had given her for her birthday; the matching pants had little smiling hot peppers all over them. But the worst part was—she wasn't wearing a bra, a fact that was scandalously apparent. She even caught a hint of color through the thin cotton. Dear God in heaven.

Any portion of the lump in her throat that had receded now swelled once more, and an intense heat climbed her cheeks. "Um, see ya," she said. But she couldn't meet his eyes again—no way—so she just hightailed it briskly back down the hill through the cool carpet of grass.

With lightly clenched teeth, she glared down at the cat in her arms. "You are in *so* much trouble, mister."

Tessa had spent the evening still taken aback by the whole encounter. Not only had she found out her neighbor was the mysterious Lucky Romo—he'd seen her nipples through her shirt, too. But she'd been at home, dressed for comfort. Clearly, she wasn't yet used to having someone next door.

She'd called Rachel right after the event—eager to share the news about her fiancé's long-lost brother—yet she'd gotten voice mail. Her once Blackberry-addicted friend now frequently left her phone behind, and Tessa later remembered that Rachel and Mike had been traveling home from Florida yesterday anyway and were probably in transit at the time.

Well, now it was Monday and she was meeting Rachel and Amy for lunch, so she could fill Rachel in there. And other than some lingering embarrassment about practically having flashed the biker next door, she was in a good mood. For one thing, she felt a lot better than she had yesterday. And for another, Mr. Knightley was going home today—she was dropping him at Amy's on the way to lunch. "In you go," she told the cat as she lowered him into his deluxe cat carrier. Knightley's other belongings were already in a box in her car—although Tessa planned on telling Amy she should buy the cat a suitcase if he couldn't travel more lightly.

As she locked the cabin door and walked to her midsize sedan, she couldn't help glancing upward toward the house on the hill. All was still, no one about. She let out a sigh, wishing it would stay that way. She missed her peace and quiet.

But a glimpse down at the long, colorful skirt she wore brightened her spirits again. It had made her feel alive and energetic to put on something she enjoyed wearing, and she'd learned not to take even the smallest bit of happiness for granted over the last few years. Sometimes it was the little things in life.

Only, as her Nissan reached the end of her driveway, she caught sight of the lovely sign she'd erected above her mailbox: *Interiors by Tessa.* Oh brother. *Yeah, clever of you withholding your name that way. Very slick. He'll never figure it out.*

She bit her lip, thinking of him again. Lucky Romo. A year ahead of her in high school, he'd been the bad kid, the rough and tumble type. He'd gotten into fights, skipped school, driven a fast car, and sported long hair even then. He drank and smoked. She'd heard he did drugs.

Then, as soon as he'd graduated, he'd just . . . disappeared.

Maybe, when she added it all up, the most shocking thing about him now was that he'd actually been nice enough to help her find the cat.

And maybe the real question was . . . *Why do I start sweating a little every time I remember seeing him yesterday?*

She thought back to it, trying to recall everything she'd felt. A strange nervousness, certainly, that had bordered on fear. He was so . . . big now. She'd never have guessed Lucky Romo would end up so broad-shouldered and muscular. Plus, she'd never known any biker dudes before . . . or potential outlaws, either—a thought which made her shiver a little. She'd also suffered a certain sense of . . . naïveté with him that she'd never before experienced. Odd, because she wasn't particularly naïve. She was thirty-three years old, after all—but somehow she'd felt . . . too innocent in his presence. Like he must think she was silly for the way she'd talked to Mr. Knightley. Like she'd seemed stupid for letting him get away.

So all of that was enough to explain things like lumps in her throat and a little sweating. Except that . . . there was more. If she was completely honest with herself, she'd suffered . . . a stark, rather *brutal* attraction to him. Completely unbidden. And unwanted. Because he *did* frighten her a little. There was that whole outlaw-biker question hanging over him. And all those tattoos. Just being *around* him had felt a bit hazardous, even when he'd relaxed some and helped her lure Mr. K. back.

And ugh—again that view of her nipples came to mind. Upon getting Mr. Knightley back into the house, she'd stood in front of a mirror and—yikes. *Note to self: Now that you have a neighbor, always wear a bra. Always.*

And now . . . stop obsessing over this. Yes, that sounded like a good idea. After all, there was plenty to celebrate— the sun was shining, she was on her way to lunch with friends, and she was unloading this persnickety kitty. Conveniently, Amy lived in an apartment above her bookstore, Under the Covers, where Tessa worked part-time, so she could easily drop him off on the way to lunch.

Half an hour later, cat and cat owner had been happily reunited, and Tessa and Amy found Rachel already at a table at Dolly's Main Street Café, looking as stylish as ever in high-heeled boots, a red print scarf draped about her neck, and her shoulder-length blond hair in a chic new cut. She'd moved back to Destiny last fall to help run her grandma's apple orchard, but giving up a jet-set life in Chicago hadn't dampened her fashion sense. And a lovely tan glow from her Florida jaunt to visit Mike's parents only made her look all the more fabulous.

"Okay," Tessa said pointedly as she took a seat, "I'm not going to ask either one of you how your trips were, because I have news. Big, big news."

Rachel blinked, appearing surprised, likely because it was seldom these days that Tessa *had* news—big or otherwise. Yet Amy stopped her from sharing it by wagging a finger in her face, her strawberry blond locks bouncing with the natural curl Tessa envied. "First, I want to know how you're feeling. I felt awful making you kitty-sit, but I couldn't think of anybody else, especially with Rachel away, too."

"I'm fine now," Tessa said. "And my news is more important than that." Which was saying a lot. After several years of a mysterious digestive illness, Tessa had recently been diagnosed with Crohn's disease. The ailment had taken a huge toll on her and forced her to make major changes in her life, but she tried to be tougher than the condition—*plus* she was near to bursting with wanting to tell them about yesterday.

"Wow," Amy said, green eyes widening. "This must be *some* news."

Tessa just looked back and forth between them. "Remember I told you about my new neighbor?"

They both nodded as Amy said, "And all the motorcycles."

"Right. Well, yesterday I met him." She didn't plan to tell Amy exactly *why* she'd met him—no need to alarm her—and that wasn't the significant part anyway.

"And?" Rachel said.

Tessa let out a breath. "He's Lucky Romo."

Amy gasped and Rachel's jaw dropped. Though it was Rachel she kept her eyes on, because while Amy loved good Destiny gossip, it was Rachel's connection to Lucky that made this so relevant. Mike had suffered a lot over Lucky leaving home. To find out he was alive would be . . . enormous.

Rachel appeared too stunned to speak for a moment, but finally managed, "Are you sure?"

"Mostly," Tessa said. "I thought he looked familiar, and like a Romo—and then he turned around and his T-shirt said Lucky's Custom . . . something-or-other on it. Even before that, I was thinking it could be him, so *after* that . . . well, how could it *not* be him?"

Rachel simply shook her head, clearly still trying to absorb it. "What did he say? Why is he back? Why hasn't he contacted his family?"

"I don't know," Tessa explained, "because he didn't say *much*. And I wasn't sure I should ask him or even let him know I recognized him. I mean . . . there's that whole outlaw-motorcycle-gang issue to think about."

Now Rachel gasped, too. "Oh, you're right." Then she gritted her teeth. "God, if this is really him, should you be living next door to him? Out there in the middle of nowhere? Where no one can hear you scream?"

Tessa cast a dry look. "Thanks for giving me visions of ax murderers."

"Sorry, but . . ." Rachel appeared deadly serious. "Mike has reason to think he turned out to be a really bad guy."

"Yes, I know that. Don't remind me. Because it's not like I can just pack up and move. I bought the house. *And* I'm broke." After having to leave a lucrative career in interior design behind in Cincinnati due to her illness, she'd come home to the promise of a new, more low-key job in interiors—which had then promptly fallen through. And since then, she'd been trying to build her own small decorating business, but so far it was a failure. She'd sunk much of her savings into buying the cabin, thinking it would be smarter than renting, and she was living off the rest, supplemented only by what she made at the bookstore.

Across the table, Amy tilted her head. "Did he *seem* . . . you know . . . *bad*?"

Tessa bit her lip. It was a complicated question. "Well,

he has a lot of tattoos. Of things like chains and flames. So he *looks* kind of scary. And I felt pretty mousy when I was trying to talk to him. But . . . he was also sort of nice. In a quiet way." Then she bit her lip, remembering the worst part. "Oh, and he saw my boobs."

As Amy cringed in revulsion, Rachel made a bewildered face. "How the hell did *that* happen?"

"Well, he didn't see them *completely*. Just through the 'Hot Stuff' pajama top you gave me. But that's practically as bad. Very thin cotton. And white. And clingy."

"Nice gift, Rach," Amy scolded.

But Rachel just rolled her eyes. "I didn't intend for her to socialize in it." In fact, Tessa remembered, it had actually been meant as amusing encouragement. Tessa had felt . . . well, considerably less than hot the last few years.

"I was wearing it around the house because it's comfy, and I went outside, not expecting to meet the new neighbor. A mistake I will not make again, believe me."

Just then, their favorite blue-haired waitress, Mabel, finally arrived with menus, and they all ordered drinks. Only after she'd gone did Amy say, low and cautious, "So . . . was he, like, openly staring? At your breasts?" Amy was fairly prudish about sex, yet she always wanted to hear about it, too.

"Actually," Tessa recalled, "I had no idea he'd noticed them at all, because I'd completely forgotten what I was wearing. Until he called me 'hot stuff.'"

"So he flirted with you," Rachel said, looking none too happy. "Mike's bad-seed-biker-brother flirted with you."

Unfortunately, Tessa's more sensitive body parts chose this particular moment to flutter a bit at the reminder—but she tried to play it off. No way could she tell her friends she'd experienced an unwanted attraction to the bad seed. "I think he was just . . . trying to make a joke or something. But when I glanced down and saw . . . well, you know . . ." She stopped, shaking her head at the indignity of the memory. "I wanted to dig a hole and crawl into the ground." It wasn't so much having accidentally been seen in a too-thin top; it was being seen that way by someone she'd have to face over and over again.

After they'd placed their lunch orders, Rachel still looked glum. "I don't know how Mike's gonna take this. He has a real love-hate thing about Lucky."

Tessa nodded. "Now you see why I said it was big news."

"You have to be really careful, Tessa," Amy said, her expression fearful.

Tessa turned the warning over in her head. Despite her own unease about the situation, she'd figured the shocking fact that Lucky Romo was home would be what her friends focused on. Now, their worry made her wonder if she should be even *more* wary of him than she already was. But she tried to look on the bright side. "Well, he's been there for a couple of weeks, and other than some loud motorcycle noise, I haven't heard a peep out of him."

"Even so," Rachel said, "we don't know just how scary a guy Lucky really is."

That afternoon, Tessa returned home ready to relax and clear her head. It was still unseasonably gorgeous out— sunny and seventy-five degrees—and her deck, located at the creekside end of the cabin, was calling to her. A book, some sunbathing—it sounded like exactly what she needed.

Although as she pushed through the door, she realized, to her shock, that it felt a little weird for Mr. Knightley not to be there. She still thought he was the most spoiled brat cat she'd ever met, but maybe there had been something vaguely comforting about seeing him lying across the back of her sofa when she walked into the room, or licking his little white paw and raking it across his little cat face.

On the other hand, though, it was nice not to have to worry about him making more rebellious runaway attempts, and who liked changing kitty litter anyway? She loved her peace and quiet and was ready to bask in it. And hopefully her neighbor on the hill wouldn't have any loud visitors this afternoon to mess that up.

As Tessa moved about the house, tidying up a bit, she reflected further on her friends' fears but decided they were probably overreacting. Amy was a natural worrywart, clearly forgetting that Tessa had resided comfortably on her own in Cincinnati for ten years, first earning a degree from the University of Cincinnati, then getting a good job in her chosen field. And Rachel—still used to city life—claimed Tessa lived in the middle of nowhere, but her cabin was only a fifteen-minute drive from town. Ever since Rachel had hooked up with Mike—who was a cop—she'd started becoming more cautious. She was still bold, wild Rachel in some ways, but spending so much time with an officer of the law was definitely making her more guarded.

Glancing out the window over her kitchen sink, she peeked up toward the house above hers. All remained still, but it brought to mind more questions about Lucky Romo. She hadn't seen him coming or going very much, so what did he do up there all day? His shirt had said he had some kind of motorcycle-related business, but where *was* this business? Surely nowhere nearby or the Romos would have known his whereabouts long before now. So what had happened to the business? Had it failed and somehow brought him home? Yet, if so, how had he afforded the small ranch house?

Then a totally alarming thought struck her for the first time. Did he have a woman up there who she also hadn't seen? Did they stay inside so much because they were busy having lots of sex? Could Lucky actually be *married*?

Okay, your imagination is getting the best of you. Stop thinking. Relax and enjoy your afternoon. And, seriously, what did she care if he had a biker babe? It's not like *she* and Lucky Romo would ever fit together in any way.

Although—yikes—that thought made the idea of a biker babe a little daunting. What if Lucky's old lady—since that's what bikers called their women, right?—thought he'd flirted with Tessa and decided to beat her up for it?

Stop. Thinking. Already.

On one hand, Tessa felt a little lazy to be embarking on an afternoon of sun-worshipping, but on the other, her crazy thoughts proved she *needed* some R and R, right? It was important to take care of herself, both mentally and physically. And sure, she also needed to figure out how she was going to make a living, since apparently no one in rural Ohio needed an interior decorator—but maybe basking in the sun would allow her to . . . be inspired.

Still, as she padded down the hall to her bedroom and began to change into her bikini, more questions arose. Could Lucky Romo see her deck from his house? And if so, was it prudent to put that much of her body on display in front of him? Or in front of his surely-territorial-if-she-existed girlfriend?

But then she shook it off. She wasn't going to let her brawny new neighbor influence her activities. She *loved* the sun. She'd waited *all winter* for the sun. And she'd bought the house partially because of the deck. Besides, he was seldom outside. And if he *did* have a girl up in that house, she'd have to get over it. People wore bathing suits to pools and beaches all over the world—and he'd already seen more of her breasts than the bikini showed anyway. So she was sunbathing, damn it.

Thus she proceeded into her swimsuit—and a few

minutes later exited onto the deck with towel, book, and sunscreen in hand, immediately glad she had. Pots of colorful spring pansies situated around the deck brightened her mood as the sweet scent of fresh-blooming hyacinth wafted up from beside her front walk. And as she settled into her lounge chair, the sun's rays felt like heaven. As minutes began to pass . . . it was almost as if those rays somehow radiated through her, into her, warming her inside and out. Ah . . .

Why did the sun always make her feel . . . sensual somehow? Maybe because of the sensation that its warmth actually *touched* her skin? Or because she always felt a little prettier, sexier, with a tan? Or . . . was that feeling hitting her *now* only because big, bad Lucky Romo had called her "hot stuff" yesterday? And maybe it had been the first time in ages that she'd felt . . . remotely hot. Or even lukewarm.

She bit her lip, remembering how it felt to be . . . sexual. The sad truth was that she hadn't had sex in over four years. At first, because of her health. And even in the three years since she'd moved home to Destiny, there had still been enough bad days to keep her off balance—and though she'd dated a little in that time, she'd had no more than a goodnight kiss or two at the door. She yearned for that connection with a guy, but it had become a hope that felt very distant, almost unattainable—because it was hard to be sick and broke and sexy all at the same time.

So even if nothing much had suddenly changed here . . . maybe it had. Maybe it was huge that in this moment she finally felt sexy again. Even just lying in the sun by herself. She felt sexually aware and sexually alive, and maybe thanks to Lucky Romo, she felt . . . a little bit desirable.

That's when she blinked and caught sight of him. Up the hill, on his own deck. Watching her. The mere glimpse of him, peering down at her, stole her breath.

She never let on that she noticed him. For some reason,

she instantly wanted him to think he was stealing a secret, forbidden peek at her. Did he like her body? Did he want to . . . do things to her? It was almost difficult to breathe under the weight of the unbidden questions suddenly invading her mind, the thick sensuality rapidly filling the air around her.

Despite herself, her breasts ached. Her limbs felt heavy. She stretched out on the chair, one knee bent, arms stretched overhead, attempting to exude the natural, carefree sensuality she felt coursing through her veins right now. Oh God, it was good to feel this . . . normal, this vibrant and alive. It was as if the sun pumped life and health and energy into her flesh. Or was it just Lucky Romo's eyes doing that? She bit her lip, pondering.

Another casual glimpse upward a few minutes later revealed that her new neighbor still sat on his deck, peering unabashedly down through the tree limbs that hung in the space between them. Looked like he held a beer can in his hand. He wore some sort of dark bandana-type thing around his head, long hair falling from the back. Today's T-shirt had the sleeves ripped out, making his tattoos all the more noticeable, even from a distance.

He was still as intimidating as hell. Yet her skin tingled.

Following instincts now, Tessa reached behind her to lower the back of her chair, laying it flat. Then she turned over onto her stomach, letting the sun warm her back. Mmm, it felt good. Almost as good as those surreptitious glances from the house on the hill.

Then she thought about her favorite sundress—with a halter tie and low-cut back. Tan lines didn't look good with it. Maybe she should untie her top.

Of course, she couldn't lie to herself. She didn't want to untie the top just because of tan lines. She wanted to untie it . . . for Lucky Romo. The last guy on earth she ever could have imagined wanting to bare skin for.

God. Was this . . . dangerous? Was it asking for trouble?

She didn't know, but in that strange, heavy moment, she almost didn't care. All she knew was that she suddenly felt sexy and beautiful again. Out of nowhere. And she'd spent so much time in recent years feeling just the opposite. There were so many everyday joys she could no longer take part in, experience—but she could experience *this*, *now*. The simple act of being a sensual human being. The simple act of feeling alive, vibrant.

And if she'd learned anything since coming home to Destiny, it was not to squander good moments or take them for granted. Whether it was laughter with her friends or devouring a good book or soaking up the sun, the good moments had to be grabbed, luxuriated in. And despite her better judgment, she had to grab this one, too.

So, giving her lower lip a sensual little bite, she reached back with both hands, untying the top, then let the fabric drop casually to her sides. And somehow she felt all the more alive for having done it.

I am no bird; and no net ensnares me;
I am a free human being with an independent will.

Charlotte Brontë, *Jane Eyre*

Two

Lucky remembered her from high school—pretty, petite Tessa Sheridan. She'd hung with the popular girls, but she'd seemed more . . . mature than them or something. She hadn't bothered with being a cheerleader—instead she'd been involved in clubs and other academic stuff.

He wasn't sure why he even remembered that—especially given that he'd spent a lot of time trying to forget those years. Hell, more than just *those* years. If he could, he'd blot out most of his life before he'd turned twenty-five. And it wasn't that the last nine had been so great—only that they'd been better than the rest.

He'd recognized her immediately yesterday—but having already seen the sign over her mailbox had helped. His first reaction: surprise, that someone like her was still in this two-bit town—she'd seemed cut out for bigger things.

His second—that the slender girl with silky, long, light brown hair bordered somewhere between silly and witty, and that even though he didn't usually mind making people nervous, for some reason, he hadn't liked making *her* nervous.

And his third observation? That her breasts were gorgeous. Smallish but firm and pert. And now he could see that the rest of her body was just as nice. He focused on her back at the moment. And the sides of her boobs, which she'd just put on display by untying her top.

He should probably feel like a jerk for watching, but he didn't. He'd been innocently taking a break on his new deck when the movement from below had caught his eye. The fact that it had come from a pretty girl in a skimpy bikini wasn't his fault and he saw no reason not to enjoy it. Although he suddenly found himself wishing his deck sat a little closer to hers—he suffered a light yearning to see the sides of those breasts better, closer. He was a guy, after all.

Of course, it was high time he got back to work. There was a disassembled Harley Wide Glide in his garage right now waiting for his attention—he'd put the second base coat on yesterday, following with some clear coat, and was now ready to start airbrushing some purple flames. He'd do the gas tank first—he always liked starting with the bigger job—then proceed to the fenders. Already, his buddy Duke had sent him a number of customers—he'd have to thank him with a free custom job on the old Harley Panhead Duke had just bought, once it was rebuilt.

Well, that was at least *one* consolation about coming back to this area—Duke had relocated here years ago, over in Crestview, and it would be good to see his friend on a regular basis again. And the fact that Duke owned the only biker bar in the vicinity didn't hurt— besides helping Lucky get to know other riders, it was a good way to spread the word about his business, and he knew it wouldn't be difficult to rebuild it here. Taking into account the big motorcycle rally about an hour away in Chillicothe each Labor Day, the region had a healthy biker population. And he could do his work anywhere and was good enough at it that bikers wouldn't mind driving out into the country for it.

Taking another swig from the Bud Light can in his fist, he shifted slightly in his chair—a breeze had blown some sprouting branches into his line of vision and he found he wanted to see more of his sexy little neighbor's ass in the hot pink bikini she wore. She remained on her stomach, top undone, and now read a book.

It was still hard for Lucky to believe he was back here, but he had a good reason—about the only thing he could fathom that would bring him home.

Destiny. He sighed. For him it was . . . a place of nightmares. The only thing that made it any better was perhaps the fact that he'd found even *worse* nightmares after leaving.

Loathe to make his home here again, he'd actually looked for a house elsewhere in the area—in Crestview and beyond—but this had been the only one he'd found in the right price range with a garage big enough to accommodate his paint shop.

It located him too close to his family, though, and . . . hell, that part of the Destiny equation was a problem. He had no intention of calling them up—he'd worked hard to get over the things that had made him leave home, but he still didn't particularly figure they'd want to hear from him. Of course, they'd probably learn he was back eventually . . . and while he wasn't sure what to expect from that, he didn't look forward to finding out.

He just planned to keep to himself here for as long as he could, painting bikes and getting the house fixed up the way it should be. After that, it was only a matter of waiting until Sharon decided he was dependable—and then he'd have one *more* big change in his life, the biggest of all, the reason he'd come back.

He gave his head a quick shake and let out a breath. He wasn't sure he was *ready* for that change, but he had to be. He'd never considered himself much of a stand-up guy, but for this, he had no choice—he *had* to stand up, he *had* to get ready.

He could still remember the moment Duke had called and told him. Something inside him had transformed—in a split second, something had come to life that he hadn't even realized was there. He'd known immediately that he would close his well-established Milwaukee paint shop and head home to Ohio. He'd shown up on Duke's doorstep in Crestview around a month later, his Harley Deuce and painting supplies in tow.

Draining his beer, he crushed the can in his fist and stood up, the chair scraping loudly against the wood as he pushed it back from the rail. The noise made Tessa Sheridan flinch, raise slightly—then apparently remember her top wasn't tied, so she hugged it against herself. She looked upward toward the sound, toward him. And even over the distance that separated them, their eyes met. And something low in Lucky's gut caught fire.

"How's it goin', hot stuff?" he called down through the trees. He didn't smile, though—cute or not, he wasn't planning on getting chummy with her.

Then why the hell do you keep calling her "hot stuff"? He quickly decided it was an animal thing—he'd never been able to hold in flirtation with a woman he found attractive. But usually he was drawn to girls he had more in common with. And he knew what good, upstanding people like Tessa Sheridan thought of guys like him. Even if they didn't know everything about him. Hell, maybe some of the shit in his past shone in his eyes or something.

"Um . . . fine." She sounded nervous again. And hell,

could he really blame her? Once upon a time, he'd have been nervous having a neighbor like him, too. Or maybe it had to do with him seeing her in that untied bikini—maybe it made her even *more* uncomfortable. And he couldn't deny that the bulge in his blue jeans was a little heftier than it had been twenty minutes ago.

With that, he dropped the can in the garbage bin on his back porch, then headed back to the garage. While he could easily enjoy looking at his neighbor's ass all afternoon, he had work to do, a business to rebuild.

And still, as he walked away, he let out a sigh—one definitely tinged with arousal. *Thanks for making the view from my deck a little nicer, babe.*

"I've been thinking about skydiving." Tessa stood behind the counter at Under the Covers, watering the plants Amy kept on the windowsill.

"Thinking *what* about it?" Amy asked from where she sat on the floor unpacking a carton of books.

"About doing it," Tessa said. "What do you think?"

Amy just blinked up at her. "Um—that you're out of your mind? You don't even like climbing the ladders to reach the high shelves."

It was true—the bookstore possessed a few of the old-fashioned ladders reminiscent of antique libraries and though Tessa admired their aesthetics, she'd never been a fan of actually *using* them. But her sudden urge to throw her body out of an airplane wasn't about anything like . . . practicality. "I just feel . . . like life is passing me by."

"Well, *this* is sudden," Amy mused, clearly taken aback.

"Kind of," Tessa agreed. And she supposed it had started with Lucky Romo watching her sunbathe yesterday and making her feel so . . . aware. Of herself. Of possibilities. Then she'd seen someone skydiving on TV last night and she'd thought, *Wow, that's somebody who's really living their life, grabbing it by the horns.* "But not really. For the past few years, I've missed out on a lot, and I've . . . lost a lot." The sense of defeat she'd suffered upon leaving her job and moving home still stung. Every day. She'd *accepted* it, but she'd not gotten *over* it. "And I've just realized that when I'm feeling good, I need to get out there and . . . just *do* something." Even though she'd had less flare-ups the last year or so, the unpredictability remained daunting, and she wanted very badly to overcome that worry.

"Skydiving is pretty extreme," Amy said. "If you want to do something, how about feeding Brontë?"

Tessa glanced at the black-and-white cat who'd just peeked cautiously around the corner of a bookshelf. They'd just gotten rid of *one* stray—Shakespeare, who Rachel and Mike had adopted—when another had shown up. Amy had started feeding it at the back door, and then winter had come and the cat had turned into a resident. After Amy had found the kitty draped over an old copy of *Jane Eyre* one day, she'd started calling her Brontë. "That's a lot less excitement than I was going for," Tessa informed Amy dryly.

After putting some Meow Mix in the little bowl Amy kept behind the counter, Tessa moistened it with a splash from the bottled water she was currently drinking, then lowered it to the floor. "Come here, kitty," she said softly, stooping down, but Brontë just stared at her with big, distrusting, blue marble eyes. The cat was lanky, thin—and pretty skittish. When Tessa reached gently toward her, Brontë pulled back nervously—but at least she didn't run away, which was an improvement. "Time for lunch," she said softly, jiggling the bowl. "Mmm, yummy."

As the cat stood frozen in place, crouched down as if hiding, Tessa murmured, "What have you been through, cat?" But then she shook her head. "Never mind—I probably don't want to know."

"If you just leave it, she'll eat it," Amy said.

"I know. I just . . . want to put her at ease, show her she can trust somebody."

Amy looked over, surprised. "Since when are you all touchy feely with cats?" It wasn't that Tessa disliked cats, but she'd never felt strongly about them one way or the other. She'd been raised in more of a dog-loving family.

Now she just shrugged. "I don't like seeing *anything* be scared when it doesn't have to be."

"Speaking of being scared," Amy said, rising to her feet with an empty box in hand, "any more Lucky Romo sightings?"

Tessa's skin prickled as she stood back up, too, but she tried to act cool. "He was out on his deck yesterday."

"What was he doing?"

Watching me sunbathe. "Nothing." She fiddled with a small jar of ink pens on the counter.

"Did he talk to you?"

"Um, kind of. He sort of said hello." *I think he might have flirted with me again.* But Amy didn't need to know any of the stuff she wasn't saying. Besides not wanting to worry her friend, Tessa couldn't really explain or justify the fact that she *liked* him flirting with her. Or that she'd continued lying there scantily clad even knowing he was looking. She could scarcely explain that to *herself* at moments.

And it wasn't that she was any less wary of him or his past—it was, again, simply that he'd made her feel more attractive and *alive* than anything had in a long time. So, while it would have been a lot more handy if he were Johnny Depp or Colin Farrell, he wasn't, and she had to play the cards she'd been dealt, right?

Not that she planned to *play* with Lucky Romo at all.

The very thought of getting any more up close and personal with him than she already had made her heart rise to her throat. He was an unknown quantity and what she *did* know about him was undoubtedly troublesome. But if he wanted to admire her from afar with his eyes—well, *that* thought, on the other hand, only made her feel good and kind of warm inside.

Just then, the bell above the door jingled and Tessa's mother entered the store wearing a casual skirt and blazer, her gray frosted hair looking stylish in its short cut. She must be on her lunch break—she did part-time administrative work for the City of Destiny, and the offices were located just across the square, behind the police department.

"Mom—hi," she said with a smile.

Her mother flashed a grin. "Well, *you* must be feeling good."

Tessa blinked. "I must? I mean, actually, I am, but . . ."

"I just don't think I've seen you glowing so much, looking so vibrant, in a long time," her mom replied, clearly enthused.

Hmm, she *glowed*? And looked *vibrant*? Apparently her new neighbor possessed skills even greater than she'd realized. "Have you *ever* seen me seriously *glowing*, Mom?" she had to ask.

Her mother laughed softly. "I just mean you have some color in your cheeks. You look healthy."

Tessa simply bit her lip. Was it possible Lucky Romo had actually restored some of her health through the mere acts of ogling her and flirting with her? It sounded silly, yet . . . like it or not, maybe a big, burly biker neighbor with darkly arresting eyes had been just what the doctor ordered.

After getting off work at the bookstore late that afternoon, Tessa came home, turned on the radio, changed into jeans and a tank—with a bra this time!—and stepped out onto the deck. The sun was sinking fast, so despite the gorgeous weather, it would turn chilly soon, and she wanted to plant some seeds in a few terra-cotta pots before it did.

She'd never been a big gardener until recently—but she supposed all the major changes in her life had altered her in smaller ways, too. Maybe she was trying to get in touch with nature or something. Or—heck—maybe it was just a nice distraction from less pleasant things.

Which made her think of her brother. She'd not wanted to bring her mom down today at the bookshop, but she'd been curious. "Anything from Jeremy?" Tessa's tough baby brother had just returned to Afghanistan after a six-week furlough, and he'd been particularly short in his e-mails since then. They suspected he was being put in danger and didn't want to tell them.

"Nothing noteworthy," her mom had said, her expression changing to one Tessa had seen often the last few years: trying to act unaffected even though she was worried about one of her kids. That was one factor that had pushed Tessa to move home—with Jeremy away and Tessa ill, she knew her mother and father had *needed* to have her close, *needed* to take care of her.

"Well, I'm sure he's just busy," Tessa had fibbed. She wasn't really sure of *anything* where Jeremy was concerned. He was the strong, quiet type—always had been. And frankly, she was worried for him. Sometimes he was *too* strong, *too* quiet.

But she shoved the worries from her mind—because she, frankly, had enough worries of her own and had learned to compartmentalize such concerns. So she refocused on burying her dwarf zinnia seeds in the potting mix, feeling a little more connected to the earth as she sank her fingertips into the dirt. She knew it would be easier to buy flowers to plant from a greenhouse, but she'd wanted to see if she could grow them herself.

Next, she would plant snapdragon seeds in pots—and the other day, she'd dug up some ground and sprinkled hundreds of daisy seeds in hopes of naturalizing them out by her mailbox and along the woods beyond the deck. She liked all flowers, but daisies were her favorite. Simple and friendly, they just made her happy when she looked at them. So she'd decided the more daisies she had around her house, the better. And she was going to plant tomatoes, too. Not so much because she loved them as because they looked so bright and robust when ripe.

As she worked, she thought back on her conversation with Amy about skydiving. Okay, yeah, the idea had been pretty out of character for serene, sensible, predictable Tessa, who lived in a log cabin and dabbled in flowers and kept to herself a lot—the sole exception being the time she spent with her girlfriends, who had been a true blessing in her life since her return to Destiny. But just over the last couple of days, she'd felt something growing inside her unexpectedly—this need to break out of the ruts she'd fallen into, this need to be more bold, adventurous. She knew she had a disease, but feeling better lately made her all the more determined to fight it, to stop letting it define her life.

Finishing with her seeds, she thought ahead to her evening. She planned to heat up some chicken noodle soup her mom had made, then watch some TV—maybe the Ellen DeGeneres show she'd recorded earlier today. She'd discovered Ellen's show when she'd first grown ill—and no matter how grim things felt, Ellen's upbeat attitude and infectious personality always made her smile. The show had even motivated her to get out of bed at times when she otherwise might have just stayed there all day.

And yet, when she looked at the evening she'd just

planned, she had to sigh. *Yeah, you're adventurous, all right. You really know how to live.*

She rolled her eyes and felt torn inside. The truth was, she *wanted* to be bold and grab all life had to offer, but she wasn't sure she even knew how. Even when she'd lived in Cincinnati, working at an upscale interior design firm, no one would have ever described her as bold. Independent, maybe. Or capable. But not bold. No wonder sunbathing in front of Lucky Romo had gotten her so wound up— sadly, it was the most adventurous thing she'd done in ages.

Maybe you're just destined for a life of soup and daisies.

And if so, was that really so horrible? She liked soup. She liked daisies.

Yet right now it did feel horrible. It felt like . . . not enough. Simply not enough.

After Tessa's mom had left the bookstore, Amy had said, "If you're so anxious to do something, why don't you do something you *used* to do? Like . . . travel."

Once upon a time, Tessa and Amy had taken annual trips to Chicago when Rachel had lived there. And she'd gone to the Bahamas with friends from Cincinnati several times, along with a few other destinations. "Because I don't have the money right now. Whatever I do, it has to be right here."

"Well, you can't skydive in Destiny." Amy had nodded smartly, clearly ready to nip this in the bud.

"But there are places nearby where you can." She'd looked it up online. "And I realize this is out of the blue, but I just want to have . . . an experience. Something that makes me feel like, no matter what happens, I'll always have at least one or two exciting things to remember."

Yet . . . maybe it was a silly idea. Maybe she'd never have the courage to jump out of a plane, and maybe it was dumb to do something just to say she'd done it anyway. Maybe sunbathing in front of a guy that made her heart beat too fast was as thrilling as it was going to get.

Just then, unmistakable music from her youth pulsed out the open cabin window and onto the deck—the only radio station that reached Destiny was playing "Pour Some Sugar on Me." She'd been in middle school when she'd first heard it—she recalled Rachel, who'd always been in the know, telling her she thought it was about sex.

As Tessa stretched her hose onto the deck and sprayed a little water over her freshly planted seeds, she found herself moving to the beat, her hips swaying slightly back and forth as she hummed along, murmuring some of the words. As the sun dipped officially behind the trees billowing overhead, plummeting her into cool, deep shade, Def Leppard hit the chorus and she didn't fight the urge to sing a little louder and dance a little more. It was a good song, after all. And maybe she would have worried about a certain new neighbor spotting her, but the view was obscured at this part of the deck—there were too many branches jutting between the two houses here, already budding with new leaves. If *she* couldn't see *his* deck from here—and she couldn't—no one on the deck above could see *her*.

Glancing over the railing in the opposite direction, she spied the freshly turned soil where she'd planted her daisies. Couldn't hurt to water them a little more while she had the hose out, so—still swinging her hips back and forth—she turned the adjustable nozzle to FULL in order to reach the daisy bed from where she stood, then aimed in their direction, careful to get the whole area wet as she danced.

Just as she belted out lyrics in which she claimed to be hot and sticky sweet . . . a warm hand closed over her shoulder.

She screamed, jumped, and spun—promptly drenching Lucky Romo with the hose.

Oh Lord! She released the trigger, but it was too late—he was soaked. Her jeans and feet were sopping wet, too. Her heartbeat pounded in her head as she gazed up at him, adrenaline keeping her completely tensed.

"I said hello," he told her, sounding only slightly put out for a man who'd just been doused at close range, "but you didn't hear me."

Oh boy. Here he was, right in front of her, all tattooed and muscular again—and wet now, too. She tried to be cool, but she was pretty sure that ship had already sailed. And instead, she actually found herself snipping at him. "So you thought it would be a good idea to creep up on me and scare me to death?"

"I was trying *not* to scare you to death."

She pursed her lips, still completely on edge—about everything—and getting terse. "How'd that work out, do ya think?"

"Not very well." He looked down at himself. "Damn, hot stuff, you're quick on the draw."

She lowered her gaze to where his black T-shirt clung to his stomach, which appeared to be just as muscular and taut as the rest of him. His jeans were fairly soaked, too. "Sorry about that. Just happened." *Because not only did you scare me to death, you did it while I was singing. And dancing. Which means you saw me.*

Singing.

And dancing.

Ugh. Could this get *any worse?* Even wearing a bra this time, she still wanted to crawl in a hole.

Yet the angle of her downward glance allowed her to study his muscles a little more. She saw now that the flames she'd noticed before were accompanied by a grim reaper up above, complete with scythe. Charming. And a reminder that she remained kind of uneasy about him, for good reason. There were more tattoos on his other arm, but she'd have to stare to really see them all and she lacked the nerve.

"I'm Lucky Romo, by the way."

Oh my. Why did that take her aback? Maybe because being "pretty sure" this was Lucky and hearing it from his own mouth were two different things. It remained hard to believe the Lucky she'd once known in school had turned into this big hunka hunka burnin' biker.

"I thought so," she said, biting her lower lip uncertainly.

His dark eyes narrowed slightly, and for some reason she wished the sun hadn't gone behind the trees. It was getting too dusky all of the sudden—and he was standing awfully close. "You know who I am?"

She nodded. "Your shirt the other day—it said Lucky on the back. And you look like a Romo. Like your brother," she added, even going on to say, "Mike's engaged to one of my close friends."

That's when his eyes shifted away from hers, like it bothered him to be reminded of Mike.

"I was in school with you, a year behind," she went on. If they were doing introductions, after all, it seemed inevitable. And it had been silly not to introduce herself the first time anyway. She'd just been too caught off guard then. Not that she was exactly calm and composed now, but at least she'd gotten a little bit used to the idea of him. Even if not the *reality* of him. "I'm—"

"Tessa Sheridan," he finished before she could, then gave a light nod. "Yeah, I remember." And it truly surprised her. She'd have thought the young Lucky would have been far too busy raising hell and getting in trouble to notice she existed. And she couldn't recall ever exchanging even one word with him. His sullen angriness back then hadn't exactly encouraged conversation. Not that he was really Mr. Chatty as an adult, either.

"So," she began, still wondering what had brought him

skulking up onto her deck when she'd thought she was free to relax, "did you lose your cat or something?"

To her surprise, the corners of his mouth quirked up into a hint of a smile.

Which she felt in her panties. In a hot, tingling way. Oh dear.

"No cat to lose," he informed her. Not a big surprise. If Lucky Romo had a pet, it was probably more of the rottweiler persuasion. "But . . ."

"Yeah?" She leaned forward slightly, even though he already stood so close that she could smell the musky, manly scent of him.

"I have a proposition for you."

. . . Every nerve I have is unstrung: for a moment I am beyond my own mastery. What does it mean? I did not think I should tremble in this way when I saw him—

Charlotte Brontë, *Jane Eyre*

Three

*T*essa Sheridan's pretty gaze went wide as her cute little mouth fell open in the shape of an *O.* "Uh, what *kind* of proposition?"

And Lucky couldn't help arching one eyebrow. He really *wasn't* trying to make her nervous, but she looked like she feared he might be getting ready to suggest they have wild monkey sex on her deck. "Relax, it's nothing illegal," he assured her. "I saw your sign, about interior decorating, and I want to offer you a job."

Now she flinched as her eyebrows shot up. "*Oh.*" He'd thought this news would calm her down, but instead she appeared completely bowled over. Damn, pretty soon she was gonna start making *him* nervous.

"So, uh, why do you look so freaked out?"

She cautiously lifted her eyes to his—allowing him to

notice they were hazel with tiny gold flecks that glittered a little, even in the shade. "Because . . . you'd be my first customer."

Huh. He hadn't seen *that* coming. "Do you suck at it or something?"

She gave her head a saucy tilt—and though he'd been thinking out loud more than trying to goad her, he liked this attitude a lot better than when she was jittery. "No, I'm great at it, for your information. And I've worked my butt off trying to get this business going, taking out ads, putting flyers out all over town, and everything else I can think of. But no one in Destiny seems to need an interior decorator."

Puzzled, he lowered his chin, narrowed his gaze on hers, then asked the obvious question. "Then what the hell are you doing in Destiny, hot stuff?"

In response, she drew her eyes downward, looking sort of despairing as he took in how long and lush her lashes were, and her voice came out softer than usual. "That's a long story."

Something in his chest contracted, just a little. He knew about long stories, and he knew about despair. But he'd sure as hell never expected to see the same kind of pain in *this* girl's eyes that he saw when he looked in the mirror sometimes.

And he thought about telling her he had the time to listen if she wanted to talk, but then thought better of it. Listening to *her* story might obligate him to tell *his*. And that was something Lucky didn't do. Ever. To anybody. Only he and Duke knew about their pasts and that's how it would stay. Hell, even *they* didn't talk about the time they'd spent in California as full-patch members of the Devil's Assassins. So despite being mildly curious about what kept her here, he moved on. "Well, Destiny might not need you, but I do. What do you say?"

At first, it threw him when she acted hesitant, like she was fumbling for an answer. But then he understood, remembered. He made her nervous. And he was nothing like her. He probably scared the shit out of her. And worse yet, she was probably right to be scared.

So it almost surprised him when she finally said, "Okay."

"Yeah?"

"I'm busy in the morning, but I'll come look at the space tomorrow afternoon. You can tell me what you want done, then I'll draw up some ideas and estimates."

He gave a brief nod. "All right. I'm gonna go dry off now."

Although it hadn't been his intent, she went back to looking uncomfortable as she ran her eyes over his torso again to say, "Sorry about, um, hosing you down."

He shrugged. "I've survived worse." *A lot worse.* Then he turned to go.

Though as he made his way to the stairs at the rear of her deck, he recalled catching her singing those sexy lyrics and it set off another tiny spark of lust inside him. She was *definitely* hot—and probably sticky sweet, too. Just like the song said.

Not that he'd ever find out. Good girls like her didn't hook up with guys like him.

And it was probably best that way, he reminded himself, for both their sakes.

As for why he'd decided to tell her who he was—hell, if he was gonna have a life here, he couldn't hide. That was an ingrained habit he'd have to break. People would find out he was back sooner or later anyway. And besides, he couldn't very well ask her to work for him without giving her his name. It had hit him just this morning that while he'd never considered hiring an interior decorator in his whole life, it would take a lot of work off his hands, and help him make sure things were *right* in the house.

"Any particular time good for you?" she called behind him.

He glanced over his shoulder, catching another glimpse of her petite body in well-worn blue jeans. "Whenever. I'll either be in the house or working in my garage."

And as his boots reached the grass and he proceeded up the slope, he remembered once more the way she'd been wiggling her cute little ass to Def Leppard, and without weighing it, or even looking back at her, he said, "By the way, hot stuff—nice moves."

Mike Romo rolled out of bed late—he'd been on duty for the Destiny Police Department until midnight. And he vaguely remembered the alarm blaring, but Rachel must have turned it off. When he ambled into the kitchen in gym shorts, he found his fiancée standing at the counter eating an English muffin with one hand and scratching their fat cat, Shakespeare, behind the ear with the other.

"Rachel, you know I hate when you let that damn cat on the counter."

She looked up, her gaze surprisingly docile, and said, "You're right, I'm sorry." Then she smoothly lowered Shakespeare to the floor.

Mike just stared at her. Okay, who *was* this strange woman? Normally, she would tell him in her most superior tone that she didn't *let* the cat do anything and that she couldn't be responsible for his every action and that Mike had better get used to it. At least that's what she'd said every *other* time they'd had this discussion for the six months he and Rachel—and the cat—had been living together.

"What's *with* you?" he asked, eyes narrowed, running a hand through his messy hair. "And why didn't you wake me?" She was showered and dressed, looking all pretty and perky, clearly ready for a day at the orchard they ran with her grandma.

"Thought you could use the sleep," she said, still sounding bizarrely sweet. And she *could* be sweet sometimes, but . . . something was weird here. The topper was when she said, "What would you like for breakfast? I could make you some eggs."

He flashed another look of disbelief in her direction, but she seemed not to notice. "My normal cereal is fine, thanks." They were light breakfast eaters, both of them, except for having fallen into the habit of making pancakes each Sunday.

Without being asked, Rachel retrieved Mike's cereal from an overhead cabinet, and a moment later lowered a full bowl onto the table, complete with milk and a spoon. "Want some toast? I could make you some toast."

Okay, now he was getting mad. Something was definitely off here. "No, what I *want* is for you to tell me what the hell's going on. Start talking, woman." He sat down and began eating, since he didn't like soggy cereal—but he still shot Rachel a death stare until she took a seat at the table with him. "Talk," he said when she didn't. "I mean it."

She sighed, looking unsettled. And when she spoke, her voice came out softer than usual. "All right. Mike, I have something to tell you."

Hmm. It made him stop eating. He set down his spoon. This sounded serious. Weird thoughts blipped through his mind: *She's leaving me. She's pregnant.* But he thought neither was likely. So he just looked at her.

"You know that house on Whisper Falls Road above Tessa's?"

He nodded.

"Well, someone bought it and moved in."

"Okayyy," he said slowly, making it clear she needed to keep going.

She let out another thick sigh. "It's . . . Lucky."

All the blood drained from Mike's face. What she'd

just said was impossible. "It's who?" He'd heard her, of course, but it didn't make sense. None at all.

"Lucky. Your brother."

He took that in, analyzed it. He hadn't misheard her. But . . . Lucky had been gone for more than fifteen years. Almost half their lives. He let out his own sigh then, aware that his heartbeat was pounding in his ears now and his chest felt tight. "Are you sure?"

The woman he loved nodded. "After a conversation with him last night, Tessa called me while you were on duty and confirmed it for certain."

Shit. Mike didn't know how to feel. The flood of conflicting emotions was almost too much to take. He let out a breath, his cereal forgotten, and this time raked *both* hands through his hair. At this moment, he felt older than his thirty-six years, and tired. Tired of the drama that was his family. Always, always—even during uneventful times, the underlying, unresolved dramas remained, and right now he had the odd sensation of something yanking at his soul, pulling him down under water, making it so he couldn't breathe.

"Are you okay?" Rachel reached out beneath the table, touched his knee. Now he understood why she'd been so sweet—she'd known what a big deal this was. And thank God he had her, to ease the blow, but it was still difficult to fathom.

He blew out a long breath, tried to get hold of himself, tried to put his feelings into words. "I'm . . . glad as hell he's alive." That part was just hitting him. He'd wondered for so long. In fact, the realization was bringing tears to his eyes. And with anyone but Rachel, he'd have struggled to hide that, but with her, he didn't have to hide *anything*, so he just reached up and wiped them away. "I mean, I really thought he might be . . . gone. Dead."

Then an unexpected bolt of fury shot through him and

his teeth clenched. "But now that I know he's alive . . . I wanna fucking kill him." He met Rachel's gaze. "I mean, Jesus Christ, he let us go all these years not knowing what became of him! And now he's home? In Destiny?" He shook his head, still overwhelmed, and attempted to calm down. "What else did Tessa say? How does he look? Is he . . . healthy?" Lucky had seemed to Mike like a prime candidate for drug or alcohol addiction, and he tensed now, waiting to hear the answer.

"She said he was . . . big, like muscular—so yeah, I guess his health is okay."

Good, no drug problem. Or at least not an obvious one.

"And she said he has a lot of tattoos. And friends on loud motorcycles."

Mike let out another sigh. That part didn't surprise him at all. Not long after Lucky had left home, Mike had heard from a cop over in Crestview—via a cousin transplanted in California—that Lucky had gotten in with a bad outlaw biker gang there. He was only sorry to hear his brother was probably still hanging with those kinds of people. He'd learned at police academy that once you were in a criminal gang it was hard to get out, not a lifestyle you could easily break away from.

And then the bigger picture hit him: Did the Destiny Police now have to worry about an outlaw biker element in town because his brother had just brought it here? There was a small biker community in Crestview, but Mike wasn't aware of any criminal happenings surrounding it.

Well, as for whatever Lucky had brought to town with him, Mike would have to contemplate that later. This was just . . . too fucking much to swallow at once.

"What the hell is he doing here?" he wondered aloud. "Since apparently he didn't come home to make any damn amends or I'd have heard from him."

Rachel replied with a small head shake, her voice quiet. "I don't know. But . . . maybe Tessa can find out."

Mike's jaw went rigid as fresh anger mixed with a cop's caution inside him. "*No.* You tell Tessa to stay away from him. He's dangerous, and she shouldn't have anything to do with him. Got it?"

His fiancée nodded, then admitted, "I was kinda worried for her, too, living out there in the woods next door to him."

Mike went quiet then, thinking, still trying to absorb it all. Lucky was home. His rebellious, wayward little brother who he hadn't seen since the age of eighteen had truly come back. He'd never felt so conflicted—he wanted to weep with joy; he wanted to pound the selfish, thoughtless bastard into the ground. He also wanted to punch his fist through a door right now, but for Rachel's sake, he tried his damnedest to calm his breathing and get control of himself.

"What are you gonna do?" Rachel asked. "Are you gonna go see him?"

Mike let out another heavy breath. "I don't know yet. If I saw him right now, I might slam him into the nearest wall."

The little spot between Rachel's eyes scrunched and he knew what she was thinking: If Lucky was as dangerous as Mike feared, slamming him into the wall might not be the wisest move.

"So I'll wait," he told her. "I'll wait a while and figure out the best way to approach him." *I'll try to get my head screwed on straight about this.*

I'll try to remember I loved him once.

I'll try not to hate him for what he put us through.

Tessa handed LeeAnn Turner her change, thanking her for her business, then listened as the bell above the bookstore door signaled her departure. Then she joined Rachel and Amy in the overstuffed easy chairs that sat in a grouping near the door.

Rachel peered over the big yellow coffee mug she held in two hands, asking, "Where's this cat you guys keep talking about? I'm starting to think you just made her up."

"She's really shy," Amy replied. "She hides if anyone other than Tessa and I are here."

"Here, kitty kitty," Tessa called, peeking over her shoulder to look between the rows of bookshelves. But she didn't see Brontë anywhere. "Well, maybe if we just talk quietly, she'll decide to venture out."

"So . . ." Rachel began, "I told Mike about Lucky this morning."

Tessa hissed in her breath in worry. She knew how much Lucky's departure had wounded a family that had already suffered one major tragedy by the time he'd left. Lucky and Mike's little sister had disappeared on a family camping trip when they were kids and no trace of her had ever been found. So when Lucky had left home without warning, it had only heaped misery upon misery. "How'd he take it?"

"Hard," Rachel said, looking sad. "In one sense, he was relieved, but in another, I think it upset him in a whole new way—it reminded him how long Lucky's stayed away without ever contacting them."

Amy sighed. "Did he call their mom and dad? Are they coming up from Florida? I mean, wow—this has to be *huge* for them."

"They're on a month-long cruise of the Grecian isles right now," Rachel said. "They left on Sunday, the same day we came home from seeing them. Mike isn't sure they can be reached, and even if they can, he'd rather wait until they're back."

Tessa and Amy nodded in understanding. When Anna

had vanished—over twenty years ago—it had rocked the whole town, and it had shaken Mike and Lucky's family right off its very foundation. And probably, it occurred to Tessa now, it had a lot to do with how Lucky had turned out.

"So . . ." Then Rachel put on a smile, clearly trying to focus on something besides Mike's pain. She looked to Tessa. "What else were you getting ready to tell us when LeeAnn came in?"

Oh yeah, that's right. She'd been ready to share just when the door had opened. "Well, I have some good news," she said. *She* thought it was good anyway. Now that she'd moved past the shock of it. Mostly. "I might have a client. And my first decorating job since leaving Posh." Posh Designs was her old firm in Cincinnati.

Rachel's eyes lit with happiness for her, and Amy—Destiny's poster child for cheerfulness—clapped her hands together excitedly. "Oh Tessa, that's so great!"

"And it's about time someone around here started appreciating your talents," Rachel added. "So who's the lucky Destiny-ite who finally got wise?"

"Welllll . . ." she began, "it's Lucky Romo."

As her friends' faces both froze in horror, she could have heard a pin drop. She'd had a feeling they might not be crazy about the idea, but . . . she'd probably made Lucky sound pretty scary. Because he *was* pretty scary. Yet . . . in other ways, maybe he wasn't—he'd helped her locate a missing cat, after all.

"Are you crazy?" Amy finally asked.

"Mike said to tell you to stay away from him," Rachel announced. "Mike said he's dangerous."

Tessa sat up a little straighter, ready to defend herself. "Wait a minute. Mike doesn't know anything about him now. So Mike only *thinks* he's dangerous. And—" She stopped, a sudden off-topic thought striking her. "What's with you calling him Mike lately anyway? What happened to Romo? And Romeo?" Rachel had been in the habit of calling Mike by his last name more often than his first, along with a few other choice nicknames that had come to seem like a weird mating call between them.

Rachel sighed. "It was making him mad."

And Amy made a face. "It's *always* made him mad and that never stopped you before."

"Yeah, but I'm marrying him now, you know?" She tilted her head, shrugged. "If I'm gonna spend the next fifty years with him, I really have to start being nicer." Then she narrowed her gaze on Tessa. "Now quit trying to change the subject. Back to you working for Lucky. Seriously, what are you *thinking*?"

Tessa felt it was fairly obvious. "Um, that I need the money? And that he's the first person to offer me work in my field of expertise since I came home?"

"What have I missed here?" Rachel asked. "A couple of days ago you were smart enough to be nervous about him. Why aren't you *still* nervous?"

Tessa let out a breath and was honest. "Look, even if I'm a little nervous, I've been struggling to get this business off the ground, and now someone has offered me a job. I don't see how I can pass it up." The part she left out was: *And I like the way he makes me feel. When he looks at me. When he says those flirtatious little things. Scary or not, I'm weirdly drawn to him.*

"I don't like it," Rachel said staunchly.

In response, Tessa just crossed her arms and flashed a pointed look. "You're becoming the female version of Mike." As Rachel gasped, her blue eyes blazing, Tessa went on. "And I'm sure this will be fine—and maybe it'll even give me a chance to . . . learn more about him. For Mike," she added. Even though she was completely curious on her own behalf, too. "Speaking of which, is Mike going to . . . go see him or anything?"

"He's not sure." Rachel sounded a little down again. "I

mean, Lucky just disappearing the way he did, after them losing their sister, left Mike an only child and devastated his family all the more. He doesn't seem inclined to forgive him."

Tessa nodded. It was a complex situation.

"And he's wondering what Lucky's doing here," Rachel continued, "if he didn't come home to reconnect with his family. And . . ." Suddenly looking perplexed, she went silent and squinted at Tessa over her mug. "Stop. Wait. Lucky Romo needs an *interior decorator*?"

Tessa could only hold out her hands, palms up, and shrug. "Yeah—I didn't see that coming, either."

But no matter what Mike thought about Lucky, she wasn't changing her decision. Because, as she'd told Amy yesterday, she *needed* to do something. *Anything*. And sure, getting a peek into Lucky Romo's life probably wouldn't sound that exciting to most people, but for her, right now, it *was* a little exciting. And who knew? Maybe feeling a little fearful of him even made it more appealing. Yet she'd never been the kind of girl to go after the bad boy—this wasn't about that. This was about having lost so much time on illness and defeat that now she simply wanted to feel something else. Even a little danger, if that's what it took.

Tessa stepped out the back door of her cabin, sketch tablet and pencil in hand, and looked up at Lucky's house. Simple white clapboard, black shutters, evergreen shrubbery around the front—no flowers. Clean, simple lines. Neat and tidy without being homey. Taking a deep breath, she started up the hill.

At a glance, no one would ever know a big, bad biker lived here. Of course, they would know it if they'd heard an amazingly loud motorcycle come rumbling up the hill to Lucky's place after dark last night. But she tried not to think about that—about the type of people he might hang out with . . . or the type of person he himself might be. Rachel's words echoed in Tessa's mind. *Mike said he's dangerous.*

Maybe it was stupid to be coming up here, acting like he was any other guy, ready to take him on as a client, ready to spend time working in his home. And maybe it was even stupider that she hadn't changed clothes after leaving the bookstore. She glanced down at herself—she wore one of her favorite long, colorful, bohemian-inspired skirts with a couple of coordinated, layered tanks, belted just below the waist. There wasn't anything *wrong* with what she'd worn, but she realized now that maybe she'd left it on because she'd wanted to look pretty when he saw her. Even if, realistically, the braless Hot Stuff top was probably more his style.

Yikes. What did this mean? Was she hoping something would happen? Between them? That his sexy little flirtations would go further?

She'd decided it was doubtful a woman lived here with him or he would have mentioned it by now. And he probably wouldn't have so openly spied on her in her bikini and wouldn't keep calling her "hot stuff." Unless he was a jerk, of course. Which, now that she thought about it, was entirely possible. But whether he had a woman or not, was she seriously hoping to fool around with Lucky Romo?

She sucked in her breath when the very question made her feel tingly all over. Lord, was that really what she wanted? Sex—or something similar—with a big, scary guy she really knew nothing about?

Then she bit her lip. Oh God. Maybe it was.

But stop it already. You're thinking too far ahead. You're here to evaluate his decorating needs, not get naked with him. Just do your job. And act normal. As normal as you can, anyway. So far, acting normal hadn't exactly been her strong suit with Lucky. But maybe this was her chance to redeem herself.

She was about to knock on his front door when she caught the faint sound of music coming from the large garage to one side of the house. Walking in that direction, she could hear it better—something in the Southern rock vein.

Rounding the corner to peek into the open garage, she found Lucky bent over part of a motorcycle, spraying something onto it from some kind of nozzle. Peering closer, she realized it was a small airbrushing gun, with which he was creating an intricate design. Ah, *that* was what his shirt had said that first day they'd met— he painted motorcycles. And it looked like wherever his business *had* been, now it was here.

Twisting the gun this way and that, he used his free hand to hold various flat, shaped objects—oh, wait, they were templates—at different angles as he worked to create curves and angles as he sprayed. He did it all so quickly and fluidly that she couldn't help thinking it was like a flowing . . . ballet of the hands. Not that Lucky Romo would probably appreciate anything he did being compared with ballet, but within seconds, she was captivated by watching him. It took a minute before she understood he was crafting flames—yellow and orange on a dark red background. Apparently flames were big in the biker world, be it on skin or motorcycles.

As he worked, the muscles in his arms flexed—the chain tattooed around his biceps appeared to tighten, then loosen, then tighten again. Like the other day, he wore a black bandana around his head, and he appeared completely absorbed in his task, his art. She hadn't thought about what "custom bike painting" would be like when she'd seen it on the back of his shirt—heck, she hadn't even remembered exactly what it was he did—but she never would have expected it to be this: *art*.

Around him stood six other motorcycles, all in various states of being painted—some were dismantled, with various parts appearing to be sanded down, no paint at all; other pieces had coats of solid color on them. A couple were fully assembled and looked more complete—one displaying an artistically perfect pair of dice and the words SNAKE EYES up above.

That's when she finally understood. The motorcycles she'd heard roaring up here at all hours—they weren't necessarily Lucky's friends; they were his customers. At least some of them.

And then his arm—the one closest to her—flexed again and she had the opportunity to make out another of his tattoos. Below the chain, on his forearm: playing cards. Aces over eights. The legendary dead man's hand.

And for some reason, it gave her the shivers. Of course, they were only cards, but added to the grim reaper on his other arm, she had to wonder . . . was Lucky Romo obsessed with death? Had he been . . . near it or something? Or was it about losing his sister so tragically all those years ago?

She swallowed uncomfortably at the dark thoughts, and—once more—at the recollection that he had a mysterious and potentially frightening past. And that . . . well, if she was honest with herself, his present was really *just* as mysterious and potentially frightening. Wasn't it?

It was suddenly easy to forget about that as she watched him making art on bikes, running a respectable-looking business. And it was easy to tell herself he was misunderstood just because he'd deigned to flirt with her a couple of times and had helped her find Mr. Knightley. But the harsh reality, for some reason hitting her hard right now, was that she *didn't* know any more about him than Mike did, and that almost everything about him was a question mark.

Maybe Mike was right—maybe she should stay away from him.

Knowing what he'd been through in his youth, wondering what he'd been through as an adult—she felt suddenly, undeniably, torn. Between being safe and taking a risk. Between choosing to believe he was . . . good, somehow reformed—or accepting what she'd been avoiding: the fact that Mike was probably a better judge of his own brother than she was, even all these years later.

"What's up, hot stuff?"

The greeting shook her from her reverie with a flinch. Swell. Every single time she saw him, she acted like a basket case. So she made a fresh effort to appear very together and at ease. But when she met his alluring gaze, it became more difficult. "I'm here for our appointment."

"Thought maybe you just came to watch me paint."

Great—he'd known she was there the whole time. "This time *I* was trying not to scare *you*. Didn't want to mess you up."

He'd stooped down now, on eye level with what he'd just painted, inspecting his work. He didn't bother looking her way as he said, "Takes more than a pretty girl to mess me up, babe."

Oh. My. She was a pretty girl. And he was calling her babe. And most times in her life she would have found that way too familiar from a guy she barely knew, but just like so much with Lucky, it somehow made her tingle in all the right—or would that be the wrong?—places.

She stepped closer to him, still nervous as usual but trying very hard to, at last, be bold. Or at least normal. "I liked watching you work," she told him. "I had no idea motorcycle paint could be so elaborate."

He still didn't smile, but he did glance up at her now, looking quietly pleased by the compliment. "Thanks."

And, as always, finding it hard to meet his eyes for long, she drew hers away, and they landed on another tattoo— this one an emblem of sorts, above the chain. Inside the emblem were inked words: Ride To Live, Live To Ride. She bit her lip, pleased this tattoo wasn't about death, and also intrigued. "It's that great, huh?" she asked, pointing at the shape near his shoulder.

Lucky rose back up to tower over her, the move reminding her how big he was. "Yep."

"Why?" she asked simply. She really wanted to know.

"When you're on a bike," he said without a moment's hesitation, "nothing matters but the wind and the view and the machine underneath you. It's the perfect combination of *freedom* and *power* and *speed*. And . . ." He stopped, squinting slightly, appearing to think it over. "And a little bit of danger. Just enough to make you feel . . . alive, ya know?"

Something about the way he'd described riding made Tessa pull in her breath, and it wasn't just the unexpected eloquence or the fact that this was by far the greatest number of words she'd ever heard him utter at one time. For most of her life, she would have had no idea what he was talking about, about a bit of danger making you feel alive. But now she did. Just since meeting Lucky.

Maybe *that* was the fascination he held for her. Every time she was around him, that little bit of danger hovering about him kept her on edge, kept her blood racing, her muscles tensed. So she said, softly, "Yeah. Yeah, I *do* know."

He gave his head an inquisitive tilt. "You ever rode a motorcycle, hot stuff?"

She shook her head, blushing a little. "No. I just . . . know what you mean. Another way."

Thankfully, he didn't ask what way. But her heart nearly stopped when, instead, he said, "Wanna go for a ride with me, babe?"

It was not without a certain wild pleasure I ran before the wind . . .

Charlotte Brontë, *Jane Eyre*

Four

Everything inside Tessa went warm as her heart began to pound. At any other time in her life, she'd have turned him down. She'd never particularly had the urge to ride a motorcycle. And if forced into a discussion on the topic, she'd have likely said she thought they were kind of dangerous.

But right now, she just swallowed nervously.

Then heard herself say, "Um, yeah. Sure."

Of course, Rachel and Amy would think she was crazy. And maybe she was. But it was only a ride, right? And not like he was going to kidnap her or anything. And just like everything else about this guy, something about the notion of riding a motorcycle with him excited her—probably more than it should.

In response, Lucky's eyes slid down her body and all the way back up, making her tingle anew. "You'll have to lose the skirt, though."

Her eyebrows shot up and her cheeks went as hot as the rest of her. "Huh?"

Lucky just gave a low chuckle. "You'll have to change into something else, hot stuff," he clarified. "Like blue jeans. And some boots if you have them."

"Oh," she said, nodding, trying to act all cool about it after the fact. God, why did she behave like such a dolt around him? "I'll, um, go do that."

She set down the portfolio that held her sketch pad and mechanical pencil on a nearby table before turning to go. But then she stopped and looked back at him. "Um, before I do this, you don't have . . . a girlfriend or anything in the house, do you?" She pointed in that direction. "Or a . . . Mrs. Romo?"

The way he lowered his chin told her he found the question ludicrous. "A Mrs. Romo? Not me, babe. No way."

"I just wouldn't want anyone to beat me up or anything," she said before weighing it.

He arched one brow. "You figure any woman with me would be the type to beat you up?"

Maybe she should have felt bad, or embarrassed, but she simply shrugged. "Well, look at you. You're . . ."

"What?"

Dangerous. Hot. A little scary. "A tough guy. And I'm . . ."

"What?" he asked again.

Nothing like you. And more delicate than I want to be. She settled on, "I'm kind of small."

"Well, you got nothin' to worry about, hot stuff," he said with a quick wink she felt all the way to her toes.

And as for what he'd just said, she wished that were true. But at least there *wasn't* a biker babe inside ready to claw her eyes out. Which meant at least one worry abated when it came to Lucky Romo.

Ten minutes later she was re-ascending the hill in jeans tucked into her one pair of boots—simple, black, with heels. She feared she looked a bit like a pirate, but again, tried to act confident when she met back up with Lucky outside the garage.

"All set?" he asked.

Her eyes were drawn instantly to the bike he'd pulled out into his driveway. "I think." She was no motorcycle connoisseur, but this one struck her as attractive, the sleek body black with simple red flames painted on, the under-carriage parts done in bright, shiny chrome accentuated with two long, curving pipes.

Without another word, Lucky turned to her, lowering a helmet smoothly onto her head and buckling a strap beneath her chin—so that now she felt like an *alien* pirate. And her head suddenly grew heavy from the added weight. Then he slid a black helmet painted with more intricate red and orange flames onto his own head and situated himself on the bike. Upon starting it up, a loud and familiar sound—*plm, plm, plm, plm, plm*—vibrated from the pipes as Lucky yelled over top of the noise, "Climb on."

It was awkward hoisting her leg over the seat, especially since it was curved in such a way as to push their bodies instantly together, her front against his warm, broad back. The contact shocked her and she automatically tried to lean away, but it didn't make much difference—she was now officially stuck like glue to Lucky Romo.

"Um, what do I hold onto?" she asked loudly over his shoulder.

He turned his head just enough that she could see his eyes within the helmet. "Me." Then he faced forward again, instructing her, "Wrap your arms around my waist."

A *whoosh* of breath escaped her at the very notion. Plus she was close enough to smell him now—he gave off a clean yet musky scent that instantly appealed. She slid her hands gingerly around his torso, unable not to press her breasts into his back. And when everything inside her vibrated madly, she wasn't sure if it was from the rumbling machine between her legs or the big, sexy man she was plastered against.

Lucky casually reached down on both sides of the bike, hooking his big hands behind her calves, lifting them until her feet were balanced on pegs. "Don't move 'em," he said, then asked, "Ready?"

"As I'll ever be," she replied. Although her legs now officially felt as tingly hot as the rest of her.

And then the bike was easing down his driveway until he turned out onto Whisper Falls Road—and within seconds, they were racing through the twists and turns that had never seemed quite so twisty and turny to Tessa before. She held on to Lucky tight out of sheer instinct and wondered if he could feel the beat of her heart against the back of his rib cage. She suddenly heard the Foo Fighters singing about a new day rising, a brand new sky, and she realized the motorcycle had a sound system—the music encased her, her and Lucky both, as much as the wind that whipped around them now.

As they sped up on a straight stretch, Tessa sensed the power of the motorcycle beneath them yet at the same time felt as if they were flying, happy to take in the rough breeze on her face, the spring air buffeting her skin. Then the bike dipped into the shade—tree limbs bursting with new leaves arced heavy across the road to create a canopy, leaving the pavement dappled with sunlight. She found the ride at once frightening and exhilarating, and the motorcycle's heavy vibrations echoed all through her to leave her both aroused and alert, peeking over Lucky's shoulder as he took each bend in the road.

Latching on to him, she couldn't help feeling as if she was . . . in his care, somehow under his protection. And normally, Tessa didn't like letting anyone take care of her, but this felt different. Like holding on to Lucky provided . . . a little safety amidst the danger. And like, in some small way, she was doing exactly what the Foo Fighters' song said: learning to live again.

Lucky pulled his bike back into the garage, away from his work area, next to his weight bench. He focused on kicking the sidestand down and then putting the helmets away. They weren't tasks that particularly *required* focus, but he needed to concentrate on something besides Tessa in those sexy jeans that showed off all her petite curves.

Because what the hell was he doing? What had he been thinking—asking her to take a ride? She wasn't a fender bunny, and this wasn't Milwaukee. He was home now and everything here was different.

And it wasn't just about him, either. His past in California was ten years and two thousand miles away—but sometimes he was forced to remember that a few threats still technically hung over his head. So it had been one thing to pick up a girl in a biker bar in Milwaukee and spend the night with her, or even a couple of weeks if that's what he felt like. But it was another to be flirting with his dainty, delicate, good-girl neighbor, someone who would probably be a presence in his life for a while, quite possibly a *long* while. Enough time had passed that he felt it was mostly safe to be near his family—but it still felt risky somehow to contemplate getting even remotely close to a woman. Or to even give the appearance that he was.

"Thanks for the ride," Tessa said, standing behind him. When he turned to face her, her cheeks were flushed prettily and her eyes bright—she looked more relaxed with him than he'd ever seen her. Shit. Now his focus was squarely back on *her*, like it or not.

"So you had a good time," he said quietly—more of a statement than a question.

She nodded. "It was kind of scary . . . but cool, too."

Double shit. That made him like her. That she could *get* what was great about riding a Harley. And that she wasn't afraid to face her fears. "Um, you wanna go inside, look at the rooms I want fixed up?" It seemed best to move things along here.

Still, as he let her in the side door of the adjoining house, then led her down the hall, he couldn't avoid acknowledging that his jeans had gotten tighter. Around his groin. Hell. He'd been trying to ignore that fact, hoping it would go away, especially now that she was no longer wrapped around him. But nope, he remained hard. Just from feeling her body up against his, her firm breasts against his back. Just from having her slender arms around his waist.

Damn. She was cute as hell, and all kinds of sexy, but he still hadn't seen that coming—that he'd get *that* worked up, *that* easily. Maybe if he had, he'd have been smart enough not to suggest that ride. As the hallway opened into the living room, he tried to shake it off and get back to business. "I want this room and the kitchen redone," he said. Because he had a lot more important stuff going on in his life right now than getting a hard-on from a ride with his pretty little neighbor. *Think about the future here. Think about what matters.*

She stood next to him, studying the space—the two rooms connected by a bar counter—and nodding. And he could tell already that she saw the rooms in a different way than he did, with some sort of decorator's eye. She appeared deep in concentration, like she was analyzing every piece of furniture, every wall and window. "What sort of look are you going for?"

Damn, how did he answer this? "Something . . . normal," he finally said.

She drew her gaze from the built-in cabinetry in one corner of the living room to peer up at him. "Normal?"

He squinted lightly. "Like . . . normal, average people live here. Not like a biker lives here."

She blinked and asked, "Why?"

Aw, hell. He hadn't expected her to question it. He'd actually figured it would make her job easier and that she'd just go with it.

"Because, I mean, you *are* a biker," she went on. "And your home should reflect your personal taste."

And normally he might have agreed with that statement, but not right now. "I just want it to be a place where . . . anybody would be comfortable. I want it to be . . . homey," he finally concluded—even if he had no idea where he'd plucked that word from, since it wasn't in his usual vocabulary.

"Homey," she repeated.

He just pressed his lips together and nodded, not quite meeting her eyes. She'd probably find out why soon enough, but he just wasn't ready to share something so big and personal yet.

"You know, there's such a thing as blending styles. I'm completely confident I can make this a comfortable room for the average person and still reflect *you*."

He wasn't sure he bought that, so he said, "How?"

"You just leave that to me." She opened her leather binder and looked up at him. "What colors do you like having in your home?"

"Um—black?" he suggested.

She gave a short nod, clearly not surprised, and seemed to be writing it down. "What else?"

Hmm. Even as a custom painter who appreciated color, he wasn't a guy who sat around thinking about which ones he liked for "home decor." "Uh, I guess I like red."

Another short nod. "Any others?"

"Gray is okay."

She pursed her lips slightly, but then scribbled some more and said, "I think I can work with those."

"And make it look normal?"

She laughed at him then—which prompted him to say, "*What*?"

Giving her head a pretty tilt, she replied, "You just look like the last guy in the world who would be concerned with *normal*. You seem like a guy who would . . . you know, go your own way, do your own thing. So what's with all the normal?"

Shit—she was going to pry about this? He kept it as simple as possible. "It's just what I want, that's all." And he hoped it hadn't come out too brusque.

Next, they moved to the kitchen and had a similar conversation. They discussed how much money he wanted to spend on the whole project and she said it sounded feasible if they used some of his current furniture, which she assured him would work fine.

Once she'd finished making notes, she said, "Anything else? Any other spaces you'd like changes to?"

He hadn't thought too deeply into this—he had a lot of other stuff on his mind these days—but said, "Maybe my bedroom. Not right now, but maybe down the road."

"Can I see it?" she asked. And her tone was perfectly professional, ordinary—but he didn't miss the slight blush staining her cheeks after she spoke. At just the mere mention of his bedroom. And hell—he started getting hard again. That had almost faded away as they'd talked business—but that quick, it returned.

As he led her back down the hall, past a couple of open doorways—the bathroom and laundry room—she peeked into both, then followed him into his room. And then it felt awkward even to him—a guy who didn't usually *do* awkward. Because she was blushing again and he was straining behind his zipper, and it would have been too damn easy to just lay her down on the bed they were both staring at and give her a *reason* to blush. But instead he cleared his throat and said, "This is it."

"Okay . . . um . . ." God, she sounded all breathy, sexy. "What would you like to do in here?"

And he couldn't help it—he grinned. Probably wolfishly. Because there were a *lot* of things he'd like to do in here—with her.

Her skin flushed brighter in response, her complexion beginning to look dewy now, like maybe she'd begun to sweat a little. "I mean, what look are you interested in for the room?"

Get back to business, *Romo*. "Uh, normal," he said again, trying to lose the wolf look. "More normal."

But as their gazes met and she bit her lush lower lip, Lucky thought she was having as hard a time concentrating as he was. His body tensed with awareness as his dick went a little stiffer in his jeans.

"Um, once we square away designs for the other rooms, I'll draw up some ideas for this one," she finally replied, her voice still just as soft. Soft and . . . ready, he thought. She sounded like a woman who was as ready as he was.

But then she turned and left the room, and he thought, *Good*. Since it hadn't been twenty minutes earlier that he'd reminded himself he couldn't get involved with this girl—no matter how cute and hot she might be.

"What's *this* door lead to?" she asked as he stepped out behind her—and as she reached to turn the knob to the only room in the house she hadn't seen, he instinctively closed his hand around her wrist.

"You can't go in there." And that time he *knew* it had come out too brusque. He could feel it in his throat and he could see it in her eyes.

She drew back, both from the door and him. "Why not?"

He had no good answer. It hadn't occurred to him that she'd have reason to be anywhere other than the living room and kitchen, or that she'd be nosy enough to go opening doors in his house—but then they'd ended up coming in a different door than he'd expected, and he'd had to go saying he might want his bedroom done, and . . . hell, he hadn't thought this through well enough. *You'd think by now you'd be more careful about thinking shit through.*

"Just . . . storage. Room's packed. You can't even get in the door," he lied. It was a fucking weak explanation, but it was all he had.

And she just nodded, now looking wary, on her guard. So they were back to that, huh?

Well, as much as he didn't like it, maybe that was best in the long run. For both of them.

Tessa walked back down the hill—no easy feat in heels that wanted to sink into the soft spring earth beneath them. She didn't glance back over her shoulder, but wondered if Lucky was watching her go. And she suffered the strange, sudden urge to run—to just get out of sight and into her own house as quickly as possible—so she could process all that had happened in privacy. She just wasn't used to being around guys she found attractive anymore, let alone one that completely intimidated her, too—and it made her nervous, and now, eager to be alone so she could quit worrying about how she looked and how she acted and whether or not she was blushing like a maniac.

So after she stepped in the back door and shut it behind her, she rested against it and let out a long breath, relieved to be back in her quiet little cocoon. Wow. She barely knew how to feel about him after today.

For one thing, what the heck was inside that room he'd refused to let her see? She'd begun to feel pretty comfortable around him by that point—even if undeniably aroused, too—but the bite in his voice when he'd grabbed her arm had brought back to mind how little she knew about him and how many question marks surrounded his existence. And now there were new ones. Like what the hell was he hiding behind that door?

She hugged her portfolio to her chest and bit her lip. What did bikers deal in illegally? Drugs? Guns? Oh boy. In either case—yikes! Her stomach churned at the very possibilities. Blegh.

And that aside, there were other odd questions, too. Why did he of all people want a "homey" house? Was he planning on inviting the Romo clan over or something? And even if so, would someone re-do their home to suit their visitors? No, of course not. So what the hell was Lucky Romo's secret? Or *secrets*—plural. Since she'd begun to have a feeling he possessed a lot of them.

Lowering her portfolio to a table near the door, she moved to a window and peeked out the curtains, back up the hill. She saw nothing amiss at his house—but even just that view now, of the house, moved something inside her. It filled her with equal parts fascination and trepidation. Then she clenched her teeth lightly—that seemed like a bad combination.

And all of Lucky's secrets probably *should* be making her run madly in the other direction away from him, and away from this job—but instead, she found herself more intrigued than ever.

Maybe because it had felt so good to be pressed against him on that motorcycle. If she'd thought the sun made her feel sensual, or that Lucky's eyes on her made her feel sexy—well, those were nothing compared to how she'd felt by the time that ride was over.

The honest, brutal truth was, she'd wanted to rip his clothes off. She'd never do such a thing, of course—but it was what she'd desired, the urge tearing through her body like a wild storm. *This is the hazard of not having sex in a really long time. You start getting all heated up over guys you shouldn't.*

Well, cool down, sister. It was only a motorcycle ride. And you acting like a dope at the mere mention of the man's bedroom. You can turn all that off long enough to work on his house.

And she still had every intention of doing so—despite cringing again when she remembered the door he wouldn't let her open. Because she needed the money. And the work itself—to keep her head in the game so she'd be ready if any *other* interior work came along. In fact, the moment she'd stepped into the simple living room, her mind had raced with possibilities and she'd experienced yet another way of feeling alive again—in the invigorating wave of creativity that had come rushing over her.

In fact, she'd decided the project would be a fun challenge. In her old job, she'd worked mostly for wealthy people who lived in mansions, and the occasional business that wanted a high-priced look in a lobby or office. She'd never worked in a simple one-story home before.

And Lucky's space was functional. He already owned a black leather sofa and chairs she could use. And his coffee and end tables were a bit beat up, but they could be cheaply refinished. She even liked the challenge of making his house feel "homey" yet biker-like—as weird a request as she still found the "homey" part. So this truly seemed like a good project for her—it would revive her in so many ways.

Of course, if she wasn't mistaken, Lucky Romo was attracted to her as well. *Don't think about that part.*

And he had something hidden behind that door—and it could be *anything*. Another possibility struck her: dead bodies. Ugh.

But wait, no—those would smell bad. So, okay, at least it wasn't bodies.

Of course, it still might be guns or drugs—but she wasn't going to think about that, either. Or about how adamant he'd seemed regarding the room.

That's how badly she wanted this job, how badly she wanted some professional fulfillment, how badly she wanted to make some money and feel she was at last taking a first step on the road back to financial security.

Or was it also . . . because that was just how much Lucky Romo turned her on?

She sighed and plopped down on the couch. One more thing to push from her mind.

The following afternoon, Tessa sat curled on her couch beneath a quilt her grandmother had made. The beautiful spring weather had suddenly grown overcast and chilly, and a light drizzle fell outside. She'd felt a bit unwell all day, and the pastel colors and lumpy, bumpy texture of the quilt provided an inexplicable yet serene comfort— the kind of comfort she'd forgotten all about during her career-building years in Cincinnati but which she'd re-discovered upon returning home. Sometimes it was the simple things in life that held you together.

She took still more comfort in watching today's episode of *Ellen*. As Tessa smiled at Ellen's jokes and let herself become absorbed in the show, it took her away from her troubles. When Ellen talked, as she sometimes did, about Dory, the character whose voice she'd provided in *Finding Nemo*, Tessa found herself reaching for the pretty journaling book on her coffee table. Amy had given it to her, and somewhere along the way, she'd taken to recording uplifting and inspiring quotes she came across. Now, she wrote down the one Ellen had just reminded her of:

Just keep swimming.
    Dory, Finding Nemo

Because it was good, simple advice. And because some days, that's all you could do. And on those days, it was enough. *Just keep swimming.*

When the phone rang, she almost didn't answer, not in the mood to talk. But then she hit the PAUSE button on her remote—to find her mom on the line. She could fool most people, yet as soon as her mother heard her voice, she knew Tessa was feeling yucky, so Tessa admitted as much.

"Want me to come over?"

"No, I'm fine, really."

"You just said you weren't," her mother pointed out.

And Tessa took a deep breath. She appreciated how much her mom cared, and some days, especially when she'd first moved home, she'd really *needed* her mother's help. But she didn't like leaning on people—it made her feel . . . as if the disease was getting the best of her, and she refused to let that happen. And generally speaking, she just didn't like people seeing her when she was sick, or even making them aware of it—even her mom, when she could help it. "I love you, Mom," she said, "but please don't hover." They'd had this talk before, and Tessa had asked her mom to try to ease up on the caregiving a little—Tessa was committed to dealing with the Crohn's on her own whenever possible.

After finishing the conversation and then her TV program, Tessa considered lying back on the couch and taking a nap. She was certainly entitled to that on a day like today, and the weather encouraged it.

But then her eyes fell on her portfolio on the coffee table. And her hands felt a little . . . itchy, uneasy—but in a good way, a way she recognized. They were telling her to pick up her pencil and start making notes and working up some sketches for Lucky's house. And the very urge to do so—running so strongly through her ever since seeing the place—shot a little rush of adrenaline through her body, a little burst of energy, that overrode every other feeling just then. She could nap later. Right now, she wanted to work, to create.

To her surprise, it was three hours later before she set down her pencil, and she couldn't have been more pleased—or more fulfilled. Looking at the sheets of paper spread around her on the table and couch, she realized she'd become so absorbed in design that she'd forgotten everything else for a while, even the fact that her stomach ached and that she hovered on the edge of nausea.

She still had more work to do to pull it all together, but the most important parts were in place and this had been among the most satisfying afternoons she'd spent in a long time—she hadn't felt so accomplished in years. All because Lucky Romo had asked her to redecorate his living room and kitchen.

In that moment, in spite of everything, she quit asking questions about him in her mind and just felt glad he'd become her neighbor. Because without *that*, she wouldn't feel like *this*. And feeling like *this* was priceless.

Two days later, Tessa took a deep breath and walked up the hill to Lucky's house. Despite herself, she was nervous about seeing him again. Or was she still nervous about whatever he was hiding inside? Well, either way, she was excited to show him the plans she'd drawn up for his rooms—so she tried to focus on her enthusiasm, along with reminding herself again that she had a real, live, paying job here, a notion which still thrilled her, for reasons both creative and practical. Of course, Lucky could hate her ideas and decide not to hire her, but she really had no fear of that—she knew almost instinctively that he'd like what she'd come up with.

No music echoed from the garage today—and with a peek to her left, she found the garage door was even closed. So she knocked on his door and—despite herself—hoped she looked pretty, though she wore only jeans and a zip-up hoodie sweater. To her relief, she felt much better than yesterday.

The door opened to reveal her large neighbor looking much as when she'd first seen him: His long dark hair fell loose around his face, and he wore faded blue jeans with a black T-shirt—today's sporting an AC/DC logo. And also like the first time she'd seen him, she immediately noticed his eyes, warm and brown and sliding quickly down her body before they returned to her face—so fast that maybe he didn't even realize he was doing it. And normally, she wouldn't appreciate being ogled by some burly biker dude, but when Lucky did it, something tightened deliciously in her stomach.

His eyes softened as he said, "Hey, hot stuff."

She couldn't help smiling bashfully at the nickname. "Hey." She bit her lip, that strange, unbidden desire rippling through her again—but then reminded herself she was here on business and tried to get down to it. "I have some room designs to show you. If you're not busy."

"Come on in," he said, standing back while holding the door open.

Whatever weird tension she'd felt from him regarding that mysterious unopened door the other day appeared to have faded. And of course she still wanted to know what was behind it, but had continued trying to push it aside and keep her attention on the matter at hand: Lucky had asked her to do a job for him, and technically speaking, whatever lay behind that door was none of her business. That's what she was trying to tell herself anyway.

Together, they sat on his couch and Tessa showed him her drawings. The living room would incorporate all the colors he'd mentioned and be accented with framed, matted photos of bikes he'd painted. Though the colors and photos on their own might feel a bit harsh, she would soften the tone with patterned drapes and lots of texture, bringing in corduroy pillows, Berber carpet, and some additional fabrics to make it more comfortable and homey, as he'd requested. As she explained all this, she pulled out some paint and fabric samples she'd picked up at stores in Crestview yesterday, voicing her opinions on each but also wanting to give him some options.

Moving on to the kitchen, she explained that she was adding white to the palette to give the space light and keep it airy. "We'll paint the walls gray and the cabinetry, tables, and chairs black. The white countertop and appliances will offset the darkness, and in this room, the red will appear only as accents—red towels, red salt-and-pepper shakers. Oh, and we're going to use more *warm* reds than bright ones. And lots of light. Smart use of light is pivotal with a dark, bold color scheme—especially in rooms you spend a lot of time in."

From there, she proceeded to the less-detailed ideas she'd started on for his bedroom—without even blushing like a twelve-year-old as she talked about it, thank God. "For that, I'm going off the board with different colors. A simple, masculine, but rich navy for the bed and curtains will be warm and comfortable with the dark wood in there." Then she produced some more fabric samples for throw pillows, explaining that depending on which he selected, she could draw another shade from it for a wall color. "Maybe this pale sage, for instance," she said, pointing, "or this sandy beige."

Only when she finished did she finally realize she'd been talking nonstop. To her surprise, even a few years after leaving her old job, she'd instantly fallen right back into the mode of spelling out her plans with brisk clarity, something she'd learned at Posh—it was easier to lay it all out for a client, giving them the full picture before letting them respond or start asking questions.

Next to her, though, Lucky looked a little stunned. And she suddenly feared she'd gone too far—with all of this. Maybe he'd wanted . . . less. Something simpler. Maybe he'd just wanted . . . new curtains or something. She swallowed uneasily and said, "Why do you look weird?"

He blinked, then lowered his chin. "I look weird?"

No, you look good enough to eat. "I just . . . can't tell what you're thinking. And so now I'm a little nervous." Again. As usual. She sighed.

To her surprise, Lucky tilted his head and looked her in the eye, appearing oddly . . . crestfallen, she thought. "Don't be nervous," he said. "I hate making you nervous."

Oh crap—he knew he made her nervous.

So she shut her eyes for just a second, then forced herself back into the situation. She was always so adamant about being independent, handling her condition—well, she needed to handle this one, too. "If I'm nervous around you, it's only because . . . you're a lot different than me, and . . . have you looked in a mirror lately? You're a pretty intimidating guy. You have death and flames all over your arms, after all."

And then she was mentally kicking herself for just putting it out there like that—until he grinned and said, "Sorry, hot stuff—I don't mean to scare you with my tattoos."

"Well, I never said I was *scared.* I said—"

"And if I looked weird a minute ago, it's probably because . . . I'm kind of amazed."

"Why?"

"Because the rooms sound . . . perfect. And, well, you seem really good at this."

In response, she drew back. "You really *did* think I would suck at it?"

He met her gaze. "You never told me why you're trying to build a business in a place that doesn't need it. So it's not that I thought you'd suck, but—maybe I didn't expect to be so blown away."

She lifted her chin slightly, duly flattered. "Really? You're blown away?" Not that Lucky would probably know bad interior design from good—yet she still liked having impressed him.

"Yeah," he said, nodding. "Especially the bike pictures." That was her favorite part, too—she believed every room should reflect something, great or small, about the person or people who lived in it.

But then he changed gears when she least expected it, tilting his head, leaning a little closer to her. "So, why *are* you in Destiny, babe?"

"I could ask you the same thing." It seemed a natural question that had hung silently in the air between them— up to now anyway.

He didn't smile, gave nothing away. He simply pointed out, "We're talking about *you*. So tell me your long story—I've got time."

Tessa swallowed. The fact was, she didn't *want* to tell him—it was the topic she hated most. So maybe she could weasel out of it, talk her way around it. "I came home to Destiny to the promise of a job from someone I used to work with. She was setting up a small interiors shop in Crestview, mostly focusing on retail establishments since the area is growing so much—but unfortunately, the plan fell through by the time I got here. She lost her financing and never opened the shop." All of that was true, but it conveniently ignored the heart of the matter.

"Where did you come home *from*?" Lucky asked.

"Cincinnati. I went to UC and then got a job there."

"So you didn't like your job in Cincinnati?"

"No, I loved it. I—" Oh, crap. Since when did Lucky talk so much or ask so many questions?

"What?" There he went again, asking.

And Tessa sighed, feeling angry. At her whole situation in life. She hated telling people about a condition so severe it had taken away her livelihood and sent her running home like a child. Its very existence left her feeling like someone people saw as "the sick girl," making everything else about her secondary. But she supposed she had no choice now. And hell—everyone else in town knew anyway, so why not Lucky, too? "Well," she began, her spirits dropping, "I have Crohn's disease."

He instantly looked worried, alarmed. "What's that?"

"A digestive disease. Chronic inflammation of the intestinal tract. Which means, for me . . . I have a very limited diet and, um, sometimes I don't feel well."

"But you don't . . . ya know . . ." His voice softened. "Die from it?"

She shook her head, but he didn't look all that relieved. Instead, he said, "Damn, hot stuff. This a life-long thing?"

"Well, there's no cure." She said it quickly, quietly. "And though I started having symptoms several years ago, the actual condition didn't appear in my tests until recently, allowing me to be diagnosed, so at least I can take medicine for it now."

"So the medicine is helping?"

She simply nodded. But then felt forced to add, "Even before that, though, it had become a matter of flare-ups—it isn't constant, like it used to be."

"And it was bad enough to make you leave a job you loved, huh?"

A whole life *I loved.* But she only nodded once more,

again hating that she was even talking about it, hating that it would surely change the way he viewed her and probably douse whatever attraction he'd felt. Her stomach churned now, not from her condition but from one more instance of it altering her life in uncontrollable ways.

Lucky dropped his gaze briefly, then met hers again and spoke a bit more softly. "I don't like to think of you being sick."

Oh. Wow. The simple sentiment, combined with the look in his eyes, moved all through her. Who knew Lucky Romo could be so nice? Sweet, even. Especially since they barely knew each other and he sounded completely sincere. She wasn't sure how to reply—her chest grew tight with that strange mixture of desire and fear, but this time fear of . . . pity or something—so she just quietly reiterated the positive. "Well, like I said, things are a lot better than before."

His eyes shone warmly on her, and she found herself wondering about the many sides of Lucky Romo. Dark biker with death on his arm and secrets in his house. Wayward, long-lost brother and son. Sexy, cocky guy who flirted with confidence and undressed her with his eyes. And this man sitting next to her right now looking . . . truly compassionate. "You know," he said, "if you ever need anything . . . I'm right here. You can call me anytime."

The offer caught her off guard, almost stealing her breath. Not because it was such a huge thing, but because she just hadn't expected it. From him. Lucky Romo, it seemed, grew more mysterious by the day. "Thanks. That's nice." Yet . . . when had this turned into a depressing conversation about a depressing topic? She had to change that—now. "But back to the designs. Since you like them, does that mean we have a deal, that you want to hire me?"

He flinched, probably at the abrupt change in mood, but then began to nod. "Uh, yeah."

And she smiled, because it was true—she really had a job. "Great. I've put together an agreement stating the fee, including materials. I ask for half down and half upon completion." Then she drew the contract from her leather binder.

"Sounds fine," Lucky said, glancing down at it.

"And if you decide to move forward with the bedroom, just let me know."

"Great," he said, taking the pen she'd offered him.

"I can start right away. And, of course, I'll need access to your house."

"Well, I'm here pretty much all the time, so that won't be a problem."

"And if you want any other rooms done," she added, "like the bathroom, or if you want me to convert that storage room into something more functional, I'd be more than happy to add those on, too."

That's when his face hardened—instantly. "That won't be necessary. For the storage room anyway." And quick as that, he was back to sounding all stern again, his tone making her spine go rigid.

"Okay," she said calmly, quietly, taking the pen back. So much for trying to slip that by him. But it was a firm reminder that he still had something to hide, and she clearly hadn't just inflated it out of proportion in her mind.

"You remember what I said about that room, right?" he asked, meeting her eyes once more—yet all softness had fled his gaze now. "That it's off-limits?"

She nodded, still managing to sound surprisingly cool about it. "Yeah, I remember."

"That's not a problem, is it?" he asked.

"Of course not. Why *would* it be?" *Except for the fact that I'm back to being a little worried.* She let out a small sigh she hoped he didn't see. *What on earth are you hiding in there, Lucky?*

It was easy to forget he might be concealing something awful or illegal when she was drowning in those chocolaty eyes of his, or even when she was feeling embarrassed in front of him. But now it was official: She was working for Lucky Romo—in a house that harbored at least one of his secrets.

This was where the nerve was touched and teazed—
this was where the fever was sustained and fed . . .

Charlotte Brontë, *Jane Eyre*

Five

Lucky stood silently watching from one corner of the room as Tessa stood with her back to him, digging into a large shopping bag and spreading stuff out on his couch. She wore cut-off denim shorts and a tank top, and her hair was twisted up on top of her head in a messy knot. Her ass looked particularly tempting when she bent over to run her palm over a carpet sample. He thought she looked cute as hell. Then again, when *didn't* he think she looked cute as hell? This was becoming a problem.

He kept telling himself to back off and leave the girl alone—but where had that gotten him? It had started with what had seemed like harmless flirting—then the next thing he knew, he was hiring her to work for him. And if that wasn't bad enough, it had progressed to him poking into her life the other day, and even offering his help.

But damn. He'd meant what he'd said—he didn't like

to think of her being sick. He'd been pretty shocked when she'd told him about that because . . . well, it just went against everything that seemed right in the world. She was so pretty, and lively, and energetic. It just made no sense.

And maybe it had hit him harder than it should have. Why on earth did it remind him of Anna's disappearance? After all, the two things had nothing in common. And one of them had happened nearly twenty-five years ago.

But as he watched her running her fingertips across different bits of corduroy fabric almost lovingly, like . . . like a blind person might, maybe he understood why he'd connected the two things in his mind. Maybe it was because most of the shit in his life, when he traced it back, was stuff he could have avoided, could have changed, could have powered through and put behind him if he'd tried hard enough. But every now and then, something happened that was truly beyond anyone's control, wasn't anyone's fault, and just plain wasn't fair no matter how you looked at it. Those were the things that blindsided you and left you trying to make sense of life.

And when his little sister had disappeared on the camping trip to Bear Lake when he was ten, it had thrown his understanding of life into a tailspin. How the hell do you compute something like that when you're just a kid? Or— hell—*ever*, for that matter? It was the first time he'd seen how the world could slap you in the face when you least expected it.

And *this* was like *that*, in a way. After all, look at Tessa. He didn't know her well, but he felt pretty damn sure she'd never done anything to deserve some life-changing disease. It wasn't fair.

Now, he continued watching the way she touched things. Her long, tapered fingers seemed to glide across smooth surfaces almost appreciatively—and to stop on more textured materials, lingering, sometimes tracing little patterns. He'd stood here long enough now that he was beginning to feel a little like a voyeur, but he couldn't seem to pull himself away. Or make himself let her know he was here. The weird truth was, watching her touch stuff was turning him on a little. It was making him imagine how it might feel if she was touching *him*.

Not that she ever would. He knew she had the hots for him a little—but he was about as far away from being Tessa Sheridan's type as a guy could be. And even if there were moments when he wished that were different—like now, wondering if she ran her fingers across a man's flesh as softly as she ran them over the bristles of the paintbrush she now held—it remained best that they were from two different worlds. And yeah, if she ever needed his help, he'd give it to her—but help and this job were the *only* things he could give her.

In the two days she'd been here working so far, she hadn't mentioned the room down the hall again. Which was good. He hadn't exactly been smooth about reminding her it was off-limits—and he hadn't meant to sound so mean, but some habits were hard to break, and besides, he wanted her to take him seriously. That room was private for now. If she saw what was inside, she'd know why he was back in Destiny, and she'd surely tell people. He could ask her not to, but she had no reason to be loyal to him. And hadn't she said she was friends with his brother's fiancée?

Damn, Mike was getting married. In one way, it surprised him that his perfect, straight-arrow brother had waited this long—but in another, he was equally surprised Mike was letting himself get tied down period, because the straight arrow had also been a ladies' man when Lucky had last seen him. And there was a part of Lucky that wanted to ask Tessa about Mike, about his parents. But he pushed that aside. That wasn't why he'd come back. So instead he just kept watching her and enjoying every simple, sensual second of it.

Why was it sexy just to watch her spread out newspaper on the floor? Why was it hot to see her kneel before a can of paint, smoothly prying off the lid? Even watching her pour the dark red liquid into a paint tray affected his groin a little. It looked something like wet mud, or clay, like something she might stick her hands in to mold or squeeze through her fingers.

Whoa, down boy. He glanced toward his zipper and just shook his head. This was getting ridiculous. But Tessa was so different from any woman he'd ever been with. He'd never in his life gone for petite, let alone cute. And those hands of hers—most women he'd been with were the type to want things hard and fast, whether they were giving or taking. Tessa, he knew instinctively, would move more slowly, would touch more thoroughly, would make his gut clench more tightly.

Aw, shit. Now she'd wrapped her dainty little hand around a thick, fluffy roller brush—and was . . . caressing it. The same as he imagined she might caress his hard-on. And he *was* hard now. Completely. Achingly. He'd never known watching somebody prepare to paint a room could feel so much like watching porn.

He tried to calm himself down as Tessa carefully climbed a stepladder by the wall, paint tray in hand. She backed down to grab a thin paintbrush and a moment later was creating a perfectly straight line of brick-colored paint along the white doorframe without even covering the edge with tape. It made him crack a smile. *She'd* liked watching *him* paint, and now *he* liked watching *her* paint, too.

Go away now, Romo. Yeah, that was a good idea. He'd already stood here too long gaping at her. *Get to work. You have to do* your *work before you can pay her for* her *work.* But he permitted himself a last long look at her ass as she paused, set the brush in the tray, and began to climb up another step.

He saw it the instant her foot missed the rung and she began to lose her balance—and he instinctively rushed forward to catch her. Even as the pain tray stayed put, she tumbled backward, landing directly up against him, his body breaking her fall. The force nearly knocked him down, but he held them both upright as one arm automatically circled her torso, just under her breasts, the other coming to rest on her hip.

And then they froze that way. Partly because they were finding their balance, checking their footing. And partly because . . . aw God, she felt good. Warm. Soft. She smelled like . . . a sugar donut, he thought. Sweet and tasty. She must have had something sweet for breakfast.

Of course, he still had a hard-on. And it currently pressed into the center of her ass.

"Are you okay?" he asked behind her.

Her voice came out breathy. "Yeah."

And that made his arousal a little worse. Or better, depending upon how you looked at it.

But at the moment, it was worse. Because they definitely had their balance now, and he'd ensured she was all right, and he still just stood there with his arm tucked up under her chest, his hand curving firmly at her hip. He felt weirdly stuck in place—just . . . plain not ready to let her go. Every fiber in his body urged him to turn her around and push her back onto the leather couch—although it was covered with plastic right now. So maybe the floor. Yeah, the floor would work just fine. He found himself squeezing her hip lightly in his grasp and then—

He stopped. Because—shit—he had to.

He let go of her and backed away. Then let out the breath he hadn't realized he was holding.

When Tessa turned to look at him, their eyes met and neither of them spoke. And—aw, hell. He knew with certainty. She felt all the same things he did. She just didn't understand why it would be such a bad idea to fool around with him, why he'd *had* to let her go.

She bit her lip and then spewed out a few fluttery words, probably to fill the thickened air between them. "Good thing you were there."

He managed a nod. "Yeah. Good timing. I was . . . just looking in to see how things were going." He wanted to tell her the truth—that he'd been standing there watching her, wanting her. But again, he couldn't. The lie protected them both.

"Things are going well," she assured him. "If I could stay on the ladder, that is."

He just gave another short nod. It was about all he could manage with his cock threatening to burst through his zipper right now. "Okay, good. I should get back to work." He pointed vaguely over his shoulder. "Let me know if you, uh, need me for anything."

And then he walked away. Sort of praying as he did that she would call him back and say something completely naughty, like that she needed him between her legs.

But when she didn't, he reminded himself yet one more time that it was best that way. Best, best, best. *Get that through your thick head once and for all.*

Oh boy. Oh God. He'd been hard. She'd felt it.

That's all Tessa could think about even half an hour later. And she'd long since abandoned painting the wall's edges, instead focusing on the middle portions, because her hand was shaky now when she tried to paint a straight line.

Okay, so this pretty much clenched it. Falling into his arms to discover he had an erection shored up that her desires here were not one-sided. He was attracted to her. And telling him about her health hadn't ruined it! That revelation was nearly as stunning as the first.

She pulled in her breath remembering how incredibly good it had felt to be held by him for that strange, long, still moment. Every part of her body had pulsed. And she'd smelled him again—all musky and manly; the scent had practically intoxicated her. Those few seconds in time had excited her more than anything had in, literally, years.

And then her heart started beating harder, faster. She even had to stop painting, lest she mess up. *I want him. I really want him.*

And the want was no longer a distant thing, a secret yearning she planned to keep only to herself, never to act upon. That was why her heart beat so hard. Everything had just changed. She wanted something with him. For real. Sex. Not just in her head. She wanted their bodies intertwined. She wanted him inside her.

Up until now, she hadn't thought she could really, truly wish to pursue such a thing—because he was such a scary biker guy. But . . . she'd gotten to know him a little, hadn't she? And she'd seen those softer sides of him that Rachel and Amy would never believe existed. So maybe he wasn't so frightening after all. Maybe he was just . . . hot. Tattoos and all.

As he'd held her, she'd looked down to see the arm anchored around her and she'd caught sight of those flames, and to her surprise, they'd thrilled her even more. She knew anyone could get a tattoo, but somehow the flames had reminded her how tough he was, how strong. Those tattoos surely told the story of Lucky. And she longed to *explore* that story.

Still staring at the half-painted wall before her, she tilted her head, wondering: Did he have any *other* tattoos? Anywhere else?

She wanted to find out. Bad.

She wanted him to make a move on her.

If he'd done so today, she wouldn't have pushed him away.

It was a confession of epic proportions—even if the only person she'd confessed to was herself. Because it meant . . . she was ready to make something happen here. To quit lusting and wishing and aching only in her own mind. She was ready to put herself out there and reap what life had to offer again. The very idea, the decision, nearly stole her breath and left her feeling as invigorated as if she'd just taken a step off an airplane and was plummeting through the air, waiting for her parachute to open.

Except one big problem still remained. Lucky's secrets.

She blew out a long sigh and wished her heartbeat would slow down. She needed to think through this, carefully. Even if her head swam a little at the moment.

Maybe, realistically, she didn't need to know *all* his secrets. She wasn't planning on marrying the guy, after all—just . . . having some wild little affair with him that would ease her sexual aches. And yeah, she'd have to deal with the fact that he'd still be her neighbor afterward, but she was a big girl—she could handle that. The real issue was—did she want to fool around with someone who might be doing something illegal? And *was* he doing something illegal?

She glanced over her shoulder toward the hallway that led to the mysterious "storage room." If she found out *one* of his secrets—the one she had access to—maybe that would tell her . . . enough. Enough to determine if she could, *should*, try to get lucky with Lucky. She knew he was out in the garage working now, so . . . maybe she could just sneak quickly down the hall, take a peek inside that room, and the big mystery would be over. And the door must not lock from the outside or Lucky wouldn't have been so adamant about telling her not to go in.

But . . . did she really want to go prying into someone's private business when he'd asked her not to? Even if it had the power to tell her if . . . well, if Lucky was a good guy—or a bad guy? After all, she didn't like people prying into *her* business. That was part of the reason she lived out here in the woods. She let out a sigh, then got back to work.

By late that afternoon, she'd finally calmed down enough to finish painting the walls' edges. Although, while at Posh, the hands-on work had mostly been done by subcontractors, Tessa possessed a lot of home improvement skills, and doing it herself kept costs low.

And by then she'd also waffled over the mysterious door down the hall long enough to realize that, despite everything it might reveal to her about Lucky, she wasn't going to open it. She *wanted* to, for her own peace of mind, but in the end, she just couldn't.

Sometimes it was hell being a good person.

Upon finishing the first coat of paint in the living room a little after five, she decided to call it a day. Tidying up her mess so Lucky could sit in his living room tonight, she put on her shoes, headed down the hall past the Mystery Door, and peeked out into the garage. "Goodnight," she called overtop of the music still playing there.

And when he turned to face her, looking as hot as ever, the mere meeting of their eyes took her back to their little collision earlier. She could have sworn he was remembering it—*feeling* it again—too. "'Night, hot stuff," he told her.

And just from that, her heartbeat sped up yet again as she walked away.

The following day, Tessa felt Lucky keeping his distance from her. *But maybe that's good. You still don't know what's in that room and it might be something awful.*

Yet her body ached for him—so while she spent another day painting, on the inside, she was also doing more waffling, too. And it was all getting pretty exhausting. So exhausting that she was happy to knock off early. Reaching a good stopping point just after four, she grouped her supplies in one corner of the room and traded awkward, heat-charged goodbyes with Lucky once more.

It was nearly an hour later, at home, when Tessa realized she didn't have her portfolio and that she must have left it at Lucky's place. She didn't always take it there, but had today, to record some measurements. Which she needed for planning tomorrow's work.

So she trudged back up the hill and banged on Lucky's door—and got no answer. After which she walked to the garage—and was surprised to find it open yet empty of anything but painting supplies and dismantled motorcycles. But music blasted from somewhere *inside* the house now.

Opening the door that led from the garage inward, just a smidge, she yelled, "Lucky, it's me, Tessa," over the blaring Southern rock—and that's when she heard a huge thudding crash, a groan of pain, and a lot of cussing. God, what had just happened?

The sounds led her instinctively inside, and she followed them—right through the open Mystery Door without even thinking. It was only then that she realized she'd come into the room Lucky had forbidden her to enter—and it was too late to fix it.

She took everything in at once. Lucky lay on the floor at the bottom of the same ladder she'd fallen from yesterday, a ribbon of wallpaper border uncoiling across his torso. And this was not a storage room. Nearby sat a single bed, neatly made. She saw a small desk, and some shelves, empty but for a couple of model race cars. And what appeared to be a toy box, as well as a bulletin board leaning against one wall. Then she absorbed the most shocking fact: It was all done in a NASCAR theme. NASCAR comforter and sheets. NASCAR-themed lamp beside the bed. Even the wallpaper border featured stock cars. What the hell *was* this?

But as quickly as she asked herself the question, she realized it was obvious. It was . . . a kid's room. A boy's room. In the process of being put together. And she knew *what* she was seeing, but she couldn't figure out quite *why* she was seeing it, what it was doing in Lucky's house. It was the last thing she'd expected. Not exactly drugs or guns.

That's when Lucky finally looked up at her, eyes blazing.

She quickly reached down to lower the volume on the nearby CD player plugged into the wall and said, "Are you okay?"

He answered by shoving the wallpaper border away, bolting upright, and roaring, "*What the hell are you doing in here?*"

The booming voice made her flinch, and as he rose to his feet, fists clenched, he looked positively enraged. "Did you not understand when I said you couldn't come in here? Did I not make that clear enough for you?"

This was the Lucky she'd feared in the beginning.

But . . . wait just a minute. "What I'm doing in here is making sure you didn't just break your neck, you big lug," she told him, getting a little testy herself. "For your info, I knocked, and I called for you—and when I heard a big crash, I figured I should see if you were dead or not." She finished with a terse nod as if to add, *Take that!*

Despite still looking disgusted, Lucky seemed to relax a little, just planting his fists at his sides and letting out a sigh. But he still flashed a suspicious glare. As if she'd planned this or something.

"Quit with the look," she went on. "I'm completely innocent in this." Then her gaze dropped to the unwound wallpaper border still curled on the floor. "And by the way, that's a two-person job for an amateur. No *wonder* you fell."

Yet he just kept staring at her anyway, until it became almost unnerving. "Well?" he finally growled. "Aren't you gonna ask?"

She considered the question. And decided she didn't really *have* to ask now. "No. I mean, obviously . . . you must have a child. But you don't want to talk about it for some reason. So . . . you don't have to tell me anything." Of course, even as she was sounding all calm and respectful about it, inside she was thinking: *Whoa. Lucky Romo, a father? Would wonders never cease?*

And also: *It's not drugs or guns! Thank God!*

But what does all this mean? Why is your kid such a big secret?

That's when, next to her, his shoulders slumped lightly—and he looked a little deflated. Still hot, but deflated. Until she actually felt bad for him.

"This wasn't my fault, but I'm sorry," she said. "Why don't you let me help with the border." She moved past him then, picking up the end, then climbing onto the ladder without waiting for an answer. "You can feed it up to me—just try to keep the already wet part from touching stuff, okay?" Then she got to work.

"Are you all right? From the fall?" she asked, focusing now on the corner where she was starting.

Lucky gave a brief nod in her direction even though she was no longer looking at him, grumbling, "I'll live." Then he sighed again as he lifted the border trailing over the side of the stepladder, to keep the wet part from sticking to it. The truth was, his back hurt and he'd probably have a killer bruise on his ass come tomorrow morning. But that was the least of his concerns.

He was mad as hell. But not at her. She was right—it wasn't her fault. He'd left the house open, the damn door wide open. He wanted to kick himself for it.

This room—and the reason for it—wasn't a secret he'd been ready to share yet, with anyone, but now that it was out . . . hell, the way he saw it, he really had no choice but to explain. It was really his only hope of keeping Tessa from telling all of Destiny.

"For the last ten years, I've lived in Wisconsin," Lucky unhappily volunteered. "The only reason I came home is because I found out I have a kid, a son. He lives in Crestview with his mom."

Stopping her work, she turned to peer down at him, appearing a little lost for words, until she finally said, "I told you, Lucky, you don't have to tell me if you don't want to."

"Well, maybe I want to," he snipped.

"You didn't yesterday," she pointed out. "You acted like you were guarding international secrets in here or something."

He gave his head a tilt. "Yeah, well, now that you know, I'd prefer you have the whole story rather than just half of it." *Especially if you're gonna go running to my brother's fiancée with it.*

On the ladder above him, his sexy little neighbor just shrugged. "All right. Whatever you want." Then she stuck up another small section of the border, smoothing it down with her fingertips.

Aw, hell. Now that he'd started this, he didn't know quite where to begin. But maybe if he got through it, he could talk her into keeping it to herself. "He's nine, my kid," he started. "And I, uh, passed back through this area right before I settled in Milwaukee. But I didn't stick around long—that's why I didn't know about him until now."

"How'd you find out?" she asked, eyes on the next section of border.

"From a friend of mine in Crestview. He owns a bar there—Gravediggers."

She nodded, looking vaguely aware of the biker bar.

"And this woman I was seeing the last time I was here—Sharon—she came in the bar one night and my buddy, Duke, heard her say my name to her friends. When he asked about it, she told him I was the father of her kid but that she'd never been able to find me."

"So it was that simple?"

"Duke saw a picture—said the kid looked just like me—and since the timing was right, that would've been enough for me. But Duke's kinda cautious, so he pretty much insisted on a DNA test. I got one in Milwaukee and Sharon handled the other end of it here. And that confirmed it. So . . . that's why I'm here. In Destiny."

That's when Tessa turned to face him again for the first time in a few minutes, her hazel eyes shining on him, blinking prettily. "So, then, are you, um, seeing this woman again?"

She'd tried so hard to sound nonchalant that he almost smiled. Had he actually managed to make Tessa Sheridan jealous? That easy? And for a second, he thought about stretching that out, making her suffer a little—but then decided honesty was simpler, especially since he wasn't too comfortable talking about all this anyway. "No. She has a boyfriend. And when I said I was seeing her back then . . . I really just meant I had sex with her one night."

"Ah." He caught her nervous swallow and for once didn't mind if he was making her a little uneasy. Not that he knew why he was taking pleasure in her jealousy—given that there couldn't ever really be anything between them.

"So . . . she's happy to welcome you into her child's life?" Tessa asked. And before he could reply, she added, "Don't get me wrong—it's just that most single moms usually feel pretty protective about their kids and wouldn't necessarily want the upheaval of bringing a dad into the picture this late in the game."

He shrugged. "I was surprised, too. But turns out her

father just died—about six months ago—and he helped her out a lot, with money and babysitting and stuff like that, so that's why my name came up that night—she was really wishing I was around to do my part. And she was happy when I called and told her I was moving here, but at the same time, she wants me to get settled before I meet him—guess she wants to make sure I'm a decent guy who'll stick around. That's . . . sorta why I hired *you*. To help me get settled. To get the *house* settled while *I* get settled in *here*." He pointed at his head.

"I actually knew her back before I left town after high school," he went on, "and she told Duke she always thought . . ." his voice got a little scratchy on this part, because it was weird to say, maybe even weirder to think " . . . that there was, uh, more good in me than I let on." He gave his head a short shake. "Or maybe she just wants the child support, which I'm happy to pay."

Above him, Tessa tilted her pretty head and gave him a long look. "She was right," she said. "There *is* more good in you than you used to let on. If you're willing to pack up your whole life and move across three states to be a dad to a kid you never even knew you had."

At this, he could only offer another shrug.

Yet Tessa was looking at him like . . . like he was kind of incredible. And when he didn't say anything more, she pressed the issue. "Don't take this the wrong way, but I don't really get it. You could have paid child support without moving here. And you don't seem like a guy who'd be dying to play daddy to someone."

"I'm not," he assured her. "And I have no fucking idea what I'm doing."

She shook her head then, clearly confused. "Then why are you doing it? Why did you uproot your whole existence for it?"

Lucky let out a sigh, and a small knot formed in his gut. Part of him really didn't want to go there, and God knew he wasn't used to talking about personal stuff so much, but . . . hell, maybe another part of him wanted to tell her. He was pretty sure no one in Destiny had any idea why he'd turned into a jerk growing up, and maybe he wanted someone here to finally understand.

Still, his voice dropped an octave when he said, "I don't know if you remember . . . what happened when I was a kid."

"About your sister?"

He nodded.

"Yeah," she said softly. "Of course I do."

Lucky took a deep breath. He might want to put it out there, but that didn't mean it was easy. "After Anna disappeared . . . everything changed in my family. When my parents weren't falling apart over losing Anna, they were making a fuss over Mike—since he'd been in charge of watching her when it happened and he felt guilty about it."

She nodded, as if she knew this part—and maybe she did since she was friends with Mike's fiancée.

But the part she *didn't* know was, "So from that point on, I felt . . . pretty damn invisible. Or forgotten or something. And so . . . well, I just wouldn't want any kid of mine to think I didn't care, or that I wouldn't be there for him. That's all."

She stayed quiet for a moment, finally saying, "That's really admirable, Lucky."

Yet he gave his head a short shake. "I'm not trying to be admirable. I'm just trying to keep another kid from being as miserable as I was. It's not the same situation by a long shot, but still, I figure growing up is tough enough when things are normal, let alone when they're not."

"What's your son's name?"

"She named him after me—Johnny."

Tessa raised her eyebrows. "Your real name is Johnny?"

"Jonathan. After my grandfather, Giovanni—it's John in Italian."

She smiled. "So how did you go from Jonathan to Lucky?"

Passing a little more of the wallpaper strip to her, he thought back. "When I was little, my family played a lot of board games, and I was really lucky at them. Like . . . *freaky* lucky. No matter what we played, I won." He chuckled lightly then. "I remember Mike storming out of the room when I'd beat him at Sorry, or Aggravation, or Trouble. And he started calling me Lucky. Not in a nice way—in a pissed-off way. And my parents started doing it, too, to tease Mike, and by the time Anna started talking, she called me that, too—so I guess it just stuck. Even though it's . . . pretty damn ironic."

"How so?"

He just glanced down to the carpet beneath his feet and shook his head. "Uh, I'm not too lucky in most ways, hot stuff—trust me." Then he got back to the subject. "And I don't know how to be a dad, or if any of this"—he motioned around him to the room—"is what Sharon meant by getting settled—but she seemed to like the idea when I told her about it. And I figure giving Johnny a nice place to come for a couple of days a week, if we reach that point, is as good a place to start as any. I just . . . want things right for him. I don't wanna scare him."

When she appeared surprised at that, he simply flashed a dry expression. "Come on—*you* were scared shitless of me."

She returned the look boldly, standing up a bit straighter on the ladder. "Shitless is pushing it, buster." Then she relaxed her stance. "But yeah—you can, um, be a little intimidating."

"So I just figured we'd both be more comfortable if I could give him a normal house to be in, and a normal room. Sharon says he's into NASCAR."

Tessa grinned. "I figured." Then she tilted her head.

"But why all the secrecy? Why didn't you have *me* do the room, along with the others?"

At this, Lucky could only sigh. Maybe it seemed silly, but . . . "I just wasn't ready to let anybody know. I'm still trying to get used to the idea myself and, to be honest, it just feels . . . really weird to me. Not weird enough to ignore it—but weird enough that I'm just . . . working my way toward it slowly, to make sure I don't fuck it up."

"You'll be fine," she told him. All confidence. Like she really knew him, like she really believed it.

"Why do you sound so sure?"

She smiled. "Anybody who would go to so much trouble and worry over this is *bound* to be a great dad."

His face grew warm for some reason and he found himself lowering his gaze, back to the carpet, to the work boots he wore. Hell. Was he . . . blushing? Jesus Christ, what was the world coming to when rough, tough Lucky Romo's face turned red? All because someone . . . believed in him a little.

"Now that I know about the room," she said, "do you want me to help with the rest of it, too?"

He just shrugged. "Might as well."

And she was back to smiling at him again. "Tell you what—anything I do in here is for free. On one condition."

He cocked a hesitant grin in her direction. "What's that, hot stuff?"

She pointed to the wall directly in front of the bed. "You do *that* wall. As a mural. The same way you paint motorcycles, but something . . . NASCAR-ish. It'll be perfect."

Lucky just looked at the wall. Damn—he'd never thought of that. But he *could* paint it. Easily. It was a good idea, and he couldn't help liking that she appreciated his talent. "All right, babe—you got yourself a deal." Then he looked back at her. "But, uh, listen."

"Yeah?"

This was the important part, the whole reason he'd confided in her—even if he hadn't meant to confide quite so much, damn it. "Can you do me a favor? Can you not tell my brother's girlfriend I have a kid?" He sighed. "I mean, I'm sure before all is said and done, I'll end up having to see my family, and I'll tell them about Johnny—but I just need to do this my own way."

She gave a solemn nod. "Fair enough."

Okay. Good. And to his surprise . . . damn, for a guy who wasn't usually so talkative, it felt . . . *not bad* to have gotten all that off his chest. Although he couldn't help teasing her. "And can you do a better job of *this*," he said, "than you did of not coming in the room?"

"I told you before—that wasn't my fault. I heard you fall and thought you might need me to rescue you."

He just looked up at her for a second—and then they both burst out laughing at the idea that petite little Tessa could ever rescue a big guy like him.

In one sense, he couldn't believe all he'd just told her, but on the other hand, he was actually laughing with her. And he hadn't laughed like this in a long while. So—hell—maybe in a some small way, she *had* rescued him. Maybe she'd reminded him that sometimes it was okay to open yourself up to somebody else—just a little.

The following day, Tessa worked at the bookstore by herself until lunchtime. The morning was quiet, giving her . . . well, too much time to think. About Lucky. She remained stunned at what she'd discovered about him yesterday. And finding out what had brought Lucky home changed . . . everything. Wow, he had a kid! And he'd moved back here just *for* that kid, no questions asked. And if he was nervous about meeting him . . . well, even *that* she found weirdly charming and sort of sweet. She'd never dreamed Lucky's big secret would be so . . . endearing.

But she couldn't help feeling a little depressed, too. Although she'd never in her life had sex for the sheer sake of sex—it had always been about emotion for her, about being with a guy she cared about—she thought it would be okay to change that now. After all, four years without sex was . . . four years too many. And yet, at a point in time when she felt nearly overcome with the need to live her life to the fullest, when she was ready and willing to indulge in wild, devil-may-care casual sex, the man she wanted to do it with wasn't making a move on her. Because if he was going to try to have his way with her, wouldn't the other day, when he'd kept her from falling, have been the time and the place to do it?

Clearly, something had held him back. And Lucky didn't seem like a guy who'd hesitate to go for what he wanted. So if he'd really desired her, wouldn't he have let her know it? She'd been all excited and giddy over her admission to herself that she wanted him—but now it was hitting her that wanting and having were two different things. And maybe he flirted with every woman he met. Or, when it came to seduction, well . . . maybe he was only into biker chicks—maybe she was too sedate for him. Or . . . maybe finding out about her health condition *had* changed the way he saw her. Yuck.

She didn't know the answer, but given that she was starting to think he was a more complex guy than she'd realized, she didn't anticipate figuring it out. Besides, who *knew* what drove guys to do the things they did—or didn't do? All she knew was that her hope for hot sex with Lucky seemed as if it were over almost as soon as it had begun.

As a result, she felt all the more at loose ends, still eager to do something that would make her feel alive. And despite herself, she found her thoughts returning to things like skydiving. And—again—sex. And, oddly, even Lucky's tattoos. They'd grown on her, and now she liked the way they sort of . . . defined him. It was as if he literally wore his heart on his sleeve—or his arm in this case. What, she wondered, defined *her*?

After leaving the bookstore when Amy took over at noon, Tessa found herself driving across the old stone bridge that led to the Farris Family Apple Orchard. She was attending a bunko party at Caroline Meeks's house with the girls tonight and wanted to try an apple crumb cake recipe her mother had given her.

As she pulled up to the house that served as both home to Rachel's grandmother and office to the orchard, Rachel came out to greet her, and together they walked to the root cellar where apples were stored after each fall harvest. "Coming to bunko tonight?" Tessa asked.

Rachel sneered slightly. "Mike thinks I should. So I guess I will." Half a year after leaving Chicago, Rachel was still having a hard time appreciating what most Destiny ladies considered a fun night out. And at the moment, it hardly matched sex or skydiving in Tessa's mind, either, but at least it provided time with her friends.

"Don't bring one of Edna's apple pies, though," Tessa warned as they descended into the cellar. "It'll put my crumb cake to shame."

"All right," Rachel said as she loaded a few apples from the cellar shelves into a basket looped over her arm. "I'll pick up some cookies or something at the bakery." Then she glanced over at Tessa in the dimly lit space. "So, dare I ask how the job for your new neighbor is going?" She still looked skeptical about the whole situation, but that was to be expected.

What Tessa *hadn't* expected was to feel a little quivery inside at the mere mention of Lucky. "It's going . . . well. Lucky likes my designs and the work is really satisfying."

"Good," Rachel said. "About the work, I know you really miss it."

A moment later, they climbed the rock steps that led

back out into daylight. Pretty spring weather had returned and, all around them, white apple blossoms fluttered like lace in the breeze. As they walked back toward the house beneath a soft blue sky, Tessa said, "So what's going on with Mike? About Lucky, I mean? Any change?"

Rachel shook her head. "He hasn't mentioned Lucky again. But he's been extra snippy lately—so I know it's still on his mind." They stopped at the little red barn behind the house so Rachel could weigh the apples and transfer them into a bag. "Any new insights about Lucky on *your* end?" she asked. "I mean—what's he like? Does he talk much? Are you still convinced he's not so bad? Because, frankly, I'm still not crazy about you living next door to him."

Oh, if Rachel only knew. And that's when Tessa realized she was going to spill her guts. Not about what Lucky had asked her to keep to herself, but the rest of it. "Actually," she said as they took a seat at one of the picnic tables outside the barn, "he *does* talk. Sometimes, anyway. And I really *am* convinced he's not so bad at all."

"Hmm," Rachel said, still sounding doubtful—but also maybe as if she was willing to be swayed now that Tessa had actually spent some time with him.

"And . . . there's more," Tessa began slowly. On one hand, maybe it was stupid to share this, but she wanted to talk to someone about it, and better skeptical Rachel than worrywart Amy.

"More what?" Rachel asked.

"About Lucky."

Sitting next to her on the redwood picnic bench, Rachel blinked, looking worried all over again. "What about him, Tessa?"

Tessa swallowed back her trepidation and admitted, "I'm wildly attracted to him and I want to have sex with him."

"Holy Mother of God," Rachel said, her jaw dropping. "You're not serious? Tell me you're not serious."

Tessa gave her friend a look. "Listen, you know how long it's been. And once you get past all the tattoos, the man is hot. Really hot. And the more I get to know him, the more I think he would be the perfect guy for me to have a fling with—just something fun and casual."

"Um, since when do you do fun and casual? That's *my* department. Or, I mean, it was until Mike."

"Yeah, well, that was then, this is now. Sometimes desperate times call for desperate measures. And I *need* to have sex, Rach—*you know this*." Tessa had confided in Rachel on the topic on many occasions.

"But with Lucky Romo? Of every guy in the world?"

"No, with Lucky Romo of every guy I have access to right now," she replied. "Which is not exactly the whole world." She refrained from saying, however, that at the moment, she couldn't think of a single man she would be more attracted to.

That's when Rachel's face suddenly changed, brightened. "What about Logan? Or Adam Becker?"

And Tessa simply rolled her eyes. People had been trying to fix her up with Mike's handsome friends for ages, but she just wasn't into it. "We've been down this road before. They're great guys, but they're not for me."

"And Lucky Romo *is*?"

Tessa just nodded. That simple. Lucky Romo was the guy for her. Right now anyway. "And whatever you do," Tessa said, "you can't tell Mike I feel this way."

Rachel gritted her teeth lightly. "But I'm marrying him, Tessa. And we have this honesty thing going."

"But this is about *me*—not about him or you." Then Tessa leaned her head back and let out a sigh. "And besides, I doubt anything will *really* happen between us anyway. There was a moment when I *thought* something might happen, but he didn't make a move. So . . . I just wanted to tell you about it, to get it off my chest."

"Well, if you're so sure you want him," Rachel said, looking as if she couldn't quite believe she was actually suggesting this, "why aren't *you* making a move?"

"Because *he* didn't," Tessa explained. "That's kind of like getting turned down—without having to get turned down. Saves the embarrassment."

After leaving the orchard, Tessa drove over to Crestview. She stopped at The Home Depot for more paint and supplies, and then she stopped at a deli to grab a quick lunch before heading home to bake her crumb cake.

Glancing across the highway as she exited the sandwich shop, lunch in hand, Tessa caught sight of Gravediggers, the bar Lucky had mentioned. She'd seen it before, but had never looked at it closely. Now, she thought it rather stood out in the rows of strip malls that lined the road in this particular area. A flat cinderblock building painted a dull black, it featured neon beer logos in the windows— although not currently lit at midday—and a large sign with the bar's name in jagged red lettering, accented with a shovel at the end. So did Lucky hang out here? Seemed likely. And it reminded her that for all she was beginning to know and appreciate about him, they were still very different people.

Then her gaze dropped to the small building next door to the bar. *Its* neon lights glowed, despite the early afternoon hour. Mother's Tattoo Parlor was open for business.

Her car was parked facing both places, and as she sat inside, eating her sandwich, she watched a typical-looking middle-aged woman exit the tattoo shop with a broom to begin sweeping the front stoop. Hmm, tidy. And she looked like a nice enough lady. And Tessa thought again, for some reason, of Lucky's tattoos.

After finishing her quick meal, she started the car and pulled out—only instead of turning toward Destiny, she . . . found herself crossing the highway and parking in front of the tattoo place. She wasn't sure why—curiosity, she supposed. And she then even found herself getting out and walking up to the front window, where myriad designs were displayed. Some were unappealing to her: dragons, swords, cartoon characters. But then she noticed some clearly meant for girls: butterflies, hearts, a palm tree. And . . . she thought about daisies. *Yeah, if I were gonna get a tattoo, I might get a daisy. Or . . . even more than one.*

Not that she was going to get a tattoo. She was about as much of a tattoo girl as she was a motorcycle girl.

But then she was forced to remember how much she'd actually *enjoyed* riding Lucky's motorcycle with him, how exciting and exhilarating it had been. And that's when the door opened again, and the lady from before came out, this time with a lightbulb in her hand. She said hello, proceeding to unscrew the bulb from a light next to the door, then twist in the new one. She smiled at Tessa as she began to go back inside, then paused to say, "Can I help you with anything? Answer any questions?"

"Oh—no," Tessa replied quickly. And then she heard herself say, "But . . . would it be possible to get a daisy chain? Like, around my ankle?"

"Sure," the nice woman said. "Come on inside and I'll show you some pictures."

"Okay," Tessa said, her heart in her throat. And then she followed the woman through the door at the same time as she asked herself, *Oh God, what am I doing?*

And then she answered herself. *You're living. You're being devil-may-care.*

You're getting a tattoo!

... yet I dare not show you where I am vulnerable ...

Charlotte Brontë, *Jane Eyre*

Six

*T*essa drove home in a state of shock. A chain of ink daisies now circled her ankle. It was a little swollen at the moment, and getting the tattoo had felt like having shards of glass scraped over her skin, but somehow she'd clenched her teeth, stayed very still, and not shed even one tear. Her head swam with the reality that she'd actually just gotten a tattoo!

She'd never before even considered such a thing—it had truly been an impulsive decision. And she'd already decided to keep it hidden for a little while, under jeans or her usual long skirts—because she had to contemplate how to share this with her friends and family. Her mother would probably have a heart attack. Heck, *Amy* would probably have a heart attack.

As she pulled into her driveway, she glanced up toward Lucky's house, but didn't see any movement. Then she grimaced in his general direction. *This is all* your *fault*.

Yet as she exited the car and walked around to open the

trunk, she pulled up the hem of the gauzy skirt she wore and glanced down. Five white-petaled daisies with yellow centers were joined by thin green stems and leaves. And then . . . she smiled. She wasn't at all used to the idea of having it, or even wanting it, but . . . she liked it. And it *did* make her feel the way she'd yearned to: alive, and filled with daring.

Only, just as quickly, another revelation hit her as well.

That she might like it and be glad she'd done it, but already she knew—it wasn't enough. She still wanted more. Of something. Maybe she'd thought such a devil-may-care act would take the edge off her desire for Lucky. But it hadn't.

So she dropped the edge of her skirt and sighed.

Mike sat in his living room, flipping through an old photo album. His parents had taken most of the family albums when they'd moved to Florida, but he'd found one in a bookcase after they'd gone and never bothered to give it back to them. Maybe on purpose. Not that he looked at it a lot. But occasionally.

It was filled with snapshots of him and Lucky. Anna was in a few of the pictures, too, as were his mom and dad, but mostly it was him and his little brother, when Mike was around ten or eleven, which would have made Lucky eight or nine at the time. They were in Boy Scout uniforms, and in swim trunks chasing each other around the yard with a hose. They were riding bikes, or playing baseball at Grandma Romo's house. Damn, it seemed so long ago. A lifetime. Those had been good days—only he'd had no clue at the time just *how* good; he'd had nothing to weigh them against yet.

He'd never held himself responsible for any of Lucky's decisions or the ways he'd gone wrong over time. Nope, he blamed himself for losing Anna, but losing Lucky— that one wasn't on him. Except now, as he studied his

little brother's face in these pictures, it forced him to remember just how much Lucky had looked up to him back
then. They'd done everything together as kids, and even
when Mike had wanted to get away from his brother, he
couldn't, because Lucky had always followed him around.

Mike had done better in school than Lucky—but when
Lucky had struggled, Mike had helped him, every night,
with math and spelling. Later, probably around the sev-
enth or eighth grade, Lucky had quit trying, yet at the
time this album had been put together, Lucky had tried
hard, at everything. Thinking back, Mike could almost
still see the frustration in his brother's eyes as they sat at
the kitchen table, toiling over short division. Lucky had
been smart but impatient, easily defeated. He'd wanted
everything to come to him as easily as it had to Mike.

And maybe . . . maybe Mike hadn't been very nice to
Lucky about that sometimes. Despite knowing Lucky
looked up to him and wished to be like him, he'd never
made things easy for his brother. He'd helped him in math,
but he'd never given him the answers, not even once. In
baseball, when Lucky had struggled with batting, Mike
never threw him an easy pitch. Mike was naturally com-
petitive—to a fault, Rachel had recently informed him—
and he'd always had to be the fastest, the smartest, the
best. And when Lucky had beat him at something—like
the board games that had given him his nickname—Mike
had been pissed, stomping away mad.

And now, for the first time ever, Mike asked himself:
Was that *my fault, too? Did I do something to make my
little brother turn out the way he did?*

He let out a heavy breath. Part of him couldn't believe
he knew Lucky was right on the other side of town and
he still hadn't gone to see him. But a bigger part of him
still couldn't believe Lucky had run away in the first place
and let them suffer all these years when they'd already

had *enough* to suffer over. He couldn't get past that. He couldn't make himself let Lucky off the hook.

When the front door opened, he glanced up to see Rachel walk in. As always, she looked gorgeous, even after a day at the orchard, especially when she flashed a sexy smile. "My, my, officer—still in uniform, I see."

He glanced down at himself. Shit, how long had he been sitting here? As much as he liked being a cop, he wasn't crazy about his confining uniform, so he usually changed as soon as he got home—which had been over an hour ago. Damn, he'd been sitting here thinking about Lucky that long?

Apparently, Rachel read the look on his face and re-alized the uniform didn't mean he was planning any naughty cop games—which they had indulged in on occasion. Their gazes met as she crossed the room toward him. And as she sat down on the couch beside him, peering down at the open book, she said, "You should go see your brother, Mike."

His voice came out low, resolute. "Maybe my brother should come see *me*."

She let out a sigh, and he understood why even before she spoke. "Could you be any more childish? I know you're a stubborn guy, Officer Romo, but maybe, this once, you should be the bigger man and make the first move."

He stayed quiet, realizing his muscles were tensed. Maybe they'd been that way for a while now. Maybe ever since he'd found out Lucky was in Destiny. He was start-ing to get a headache behind his eyes. "Maybe I *should*. But that doesn't mean I *can*."

Lucky sat at the bar at Gravediggers, nursing a beer. It was Saturday night and the place was packed, but his mind was somewhere else.

He still couldn't believe how open he'd been with Tessa

when she'd found out his secret a couple of days ago. He wasn't in the habit of spilling his guts to anyone, and he'd especially thought he wasn't ready to talk about suddenly having a kid—but looked like he *had* been ready, more than he'd realized.

Despite himself, it really *had* felt good to share the news with someone besides Duke. Maybe it was just good to have someone in his *life* here besides Duke. He'd been through hell and back with Duke Dawson, and the dude was like a brother to him. And Lucky was glad to be living near his best friend again for the first time since they'd made their escape from California, but . . . maybe the time had come when he needed something more. Maybe being a loner was finally getting old.

"Somethin' wrong with that beer, compadre?" Duke stepped up behind the bar to ask.

It jerked Lucky from his thoughts, forced his eyes from the bottle in front of him up to his friend's face. He gave his head a short shake, and took a light stab at a smile that didn't work. "Beer's fine. Just not thirsty, I guess."

"Maybe I oughta kick your ass outta here then." Despite that he was joking, Duke *didn't* smile—that was just his way; Lucky always thought Duke must reserve smiles for special occasions.

Scanning the bar, Lucky found it filled with denim and black leather—the guys mostly big and bearded, the women scantily clad. Metallica blared from speakers overhead, vying with the *clack* of pool balls from the two tables in the corner. "Don't you have enough to keep you busy here without hounding *me*?"

Duke just planted his hands on the low counter behind the bar, narrowing steely gray eyes on Lucky. A shadow of stubble surrounded his dark brown goatee. "What's the problem, brother? The kid or the chick?"

Duke knew how uneasy Lucky was about stepping into the dad role. And he knew about Tessa, too, but not as much. Only that she was his cute neighbor, that he'd gladly make a move on her if he could—and that he'd now hired her to work on his house. The part Duke didn't know was, "I'm really starting to be . . . into her."

"Damn," Duke said offhandedly. "I'd have laid money on it being the kid."

Lucky shrugged, trying not to feel too overwhelmed by all the changes in his life. "Oh, I'm still worried about that, too. But she's . . . on my mind lately. She knows about Johnny," he added.

And Duke raised his eyebrows. "Shit, you turning into one of those sensitive types who's gotta bare his soul?"

Lucky cast Duke a look that said, *Watch it*, informing him, "She found his room. And maybe it's for the best. I think it made her a little less scared of me."

Duke's brow knit, just slightly, and everything they'd shared, everything they knew about each other, hung in the air around him. "You tell her she *should* be scared of you?"

Hell. Maybe he *should* be telling her even more than he already had—enough to let her know why things couldn't go any further between them, enough that she wouldn't want them to. Seeing Duke tonight . . . there was something about being face-to-face with the man who'd come through hell with him that reminded him of the cold, hard truth in a way nothing else could. Time and distance helped, but there were some things you couldn't outrun. What was done was done and he couldn't change the outcome, or the fact that he feared any woman in his life might always have to watch her back. And maybe when he was by himself in that quiet house on Whisper Falls Road, that truth began to elude him, and normal life and all that came with it began to seem possible—but Duke had just stated it plain and simple: It wasn't. Not for Lucky.

Now, Lucky sucked in his breath, remembering—and

trying to ward off—the blatant desire he'd suffered when Tessa had fallen into his arms. The lust had almost paralyzed him. And if it had been only *that*, simple lust, it would have been okay. If she was some chick like the ones decorating Gravediggers tonight—someone looking to get horizontal for a few hours—it wouldn't have mattered. It was the fact that he felt *more* than just lust for her that created a problem. For both of him.

When he finally replied to Duke, he got straight to the heart of the matter. "I get hard just thinking about her."

"So party with her a little. Get it out of your system. It's not like you're celibate, brother," he said on a laugh.

Yet Lucky just shook his head. Duke didn't understand. "Trouble is—it's not like that. I wouldn't want to do her and just be done with her. I wouldn't want to treat her that way."

At this, Duke lowered his chin, looking surprised and a little skeptical. It wasn't that either of them went around trying to use women for sex—it was that most of the women who crossed their paths weren't into more than that, either. And if they *were* into more . . . well, Lucky usually made it real clear up front that he liked things fast and easy. "This must be some chick," Duke said.

"She's just . . . different. Than any woman I've been with."

Duke looked matter-of-fact. "Then maybe you'd be wise to get back to some women who *aren't* so different." He glanced down the bar to a girl Lucky had noticed—the kind you couldn't *not* notice. She wore a tiny purple dress that hugged her from chest to thigh, with tall black boots the same color as the wild mane that hung to her ass. "There. That chick's been flirting with me all night. She's definitely ready for a good time."

Lucky arched one brow. "Then why aren't you having it with her?"

Duke only shrugged. "Was thinking about it for later,

if she's still here at closing time. But she's all yours if it'll get the little neighbor babe outta your head."

That's how it was with the women they'd known—they were . . . almost interchangeable. And Lucky had no doubt the woman down the bar could rock his world—but he just shook his head. "Naw, dude, wouldn't work."

"Why not?"

"I'd still be thinking about Tessa afterward."

Lucky waited for Duke to lecture him—or push him harder toward the dark-haired chick—and when he didn't, Lucky glanced up to find his buddy staring past him, toward the door across the room. "Holy shit," Duke whispered.

When Lucky turned to look, he swore softly, too. Even ten years later, it was easy to recognize Red Thornton. He was a little older—probably in his forties now, and sporting a little less hair, but it was definitely him. He looked more grizzled than before, like maybe life hadn't been too kind since they'd last seen him. And his shocking red hair had started to lighten—so much that the spotty beard he now wore was pale gray and so unkempt that Lucky decided the guy was just too lazy to shave. If there was anything comforting in his appearance at all, it was that his eyes looked a little less crazy. Still, every nerve in Lucky's body went on alert.

"How the hell is this even possible?" Duke muttered, his gaze going dark.

Lucky's chest tightened as he observed the worse-for-wear biker. He was striking up a conversation with someone at a pool table, maybe looking to get into the game. "I always hoped," Lucky said to Duke, "that we'd gone far enough away. But looks like we didn't."

The two men exchanged wary looks until Duke said, "On the other hand, maybe we shouldn't jump to conclusions."

True enough. Red had gone from being a hang-around

to a prospect during Lucky and Duke's last year with the Devil's Assassins, but he wasn't even a full member when they'd left—and now that Lucky thought about it, it was hard to imagine Red ever achieving high-ranking status in the club. He'd worshipped the Assassins' bad-ass president at the time, Wild Bill Murphy, but Bill had treated Red like dirt. "Red always just seemed like one of those guys who was wandering around looking to fit somewhere," Lucky mused.

"Like us?" Duke asked frankly.

Lucky met his friend's stare and answered just as honestly. "Maybe, but for all our faults, we were both smarter than him—and, God knows, not as needy. The dude was like a puppy dog yapping around Wild Bill's feet."

Duke agreed with a short nod. "Guy never knew when to shut up. Think he drove Bill nuts."

"So the question is," Lucky said, "what's he doing in Ohio?"

"Looks like we're about to find out," Duke said under his breath, and Lucky shifted his gaze in time to see Red Thornton ambling up to the bar, right next to Lucky's stool.

Lucky watched Red closely as he made eye contact with Duke—who never blinked. Duke had a way of looking right through you when he wanted to, and Lucky had seen more than one person caught in the invisible web of his stern gaze. At first, Red just appeared a little guarded, maybe a little worried—but then his eyes began to change, to widen, until he said, "Duke? Duke Dawson? 'S that you?"

As usual, Duke refrained from smiling—just kept Red pinned in place with his unwavering glare. "What the hell you doin' in my place, Red?"

At the threat in Duke's voice, Red physically leaned back from the bar. "This is *your* place, Duke? Shit, man . . . I was just passin' through. Had no idea I'd see my old buddy from the Dev—"

"Don't say those words in this bar, Red, or I'll cut your tongue out."

The warning stopped Red cold. The older man froze in place for a second, until he recovered the ability to speak again. "Sorry, Duke—I didn't mean nothin' by it."

Duke relaxed his stance a little—so little, though, that probably only Lucky could tell. "Those days are long behind me. And I don't like to be reminded of my past. Understand?"

Red nodded vigorously. "Sorry about that, Duke, really. And listen, man"—he was shaking his head now—"I'm not into that life anymore, either. Haven't been for a long time. Turns out it wasn't for me—no sir."

"That so?" Duke said, crossing his arms. Lucky knew Duke was aware it made him look taller, and his shoulders even broader than they already were.

Again Red nodded, assuring him in a lower, conspiratorial tone, "That Wild Bill—he was psycho, man."

Duke replied dryly. "Yeah, I picked up on that back in the day." Then he flicked a brief glance in Lucky's direction—which made Red look over at him, as well.

Lucky met the man's eyes. Thankfully, they really *were* a little more normal now.

"Why, I'll be damned—is that you, Lucky?"

Lucky just gave a short nod, and Red let out a too-big laugh. "Well, what do you know? It's like old home week or somethin'."

And Lucky just stared. This was surely the first time anyone had described a chance meeting between old members of the Devil's Assassins Motorcycle Club that way. Red was smiling now—blind to the less than warm welcome, and it reminded Lucky that Red never *had* caught on that Wild Bill didn't really like him. The only reason Red had ever advanced from hang-around to prospect was because he was gullible enough to do anything Bill told him without blinking, and it was always to a club's advantage to have a few guys like that around, whether it was because they were fearless or because they were stupid.

"Man, it's good to see you guys," Red said, climbing up on a stool now. "Sure didn't expect to find any of my old buddies this far east. Whadda y'all been up to since you left the—" He caught himself in response to the warning looks they both cast. "Since you left Cali," he corrected himself.

"Why don't you tell us what *you* been up to first, Red?" Lucky suggested, still in tough-guy mode, same as Duke. Red was starting to seem innocent enough, even if annoying, but neither Lucky nor Duke trusted easily, especially when it came to something like this.

At the request, Red seemed a little downcast, like maybe he didn't have much going for him. Big surprise. "I got outta there 'bout five years ago." Then he shook his head and offered a conspiring look. "Man, I hate those guys—they're bad dudes."

"Since then," Duke said firmly, cutting in on Red. "What have you been up to *since then*?" He hated talking about the Devil's Assassins as much as Lucky did—nothing got him in a bad mood faster.

It took a second for Red to catch his breath—it was clear Duke had made him nervous, but that he was trying to bounce back. "Aw, you know, just ridin' here and there, pickin' up a little work where I can." Then his spirits lifted as he pointed in a generally northern direction. "Headin' up to Chillicothe right now," he said cheerfully. "Heard my sister's shacked up with some guy there—thought I'd look her up. How 'bout that? Us both from Texas but crossin' paths *here*."

Probably he was looking up his sister in hopes of a handout, Lucky decided.

"Real nice place ya got here, Duke," Red said then, smiling. "Looks like ya done well for yourself."

"I do all right," Duke replied.

"Need any help? I could . . . sweep up, wash dishes— 'bout anything you want."

There was actually a part of Lucky starting to feel sorry for Red. Lucky and Duke had both been young when they'd gotten themselves into so much trouble out west—and then they'd cleaned up their acts and gone on to do more productive things. Red, on the other hand, was clearly just floating through life, aimlessly, and at the moment he looked sort of pitiful—like a lost, hungry dog.

"'Fraid I'm full up on help, Red."

Red began nodding. "All right then, Duke. Well, thanks anyway."

"Chillicothe's less than another hour," Lucky supplied.

Red acted like he didn't know, his eyebrows shooting up as if happily surprised. "'S that right? Well, uh, I best get headed that way then, huh?"

"Yeah," Duke said, relaxing more now even as his voice stayed firm. He actually went so far as to take his eyes off Red, reaching for a rag to wipe down the bar. "You'd best do that."

Red climbed down from the bar stool. "Sure was good seein' you two."

"You take care of yourself now, Red," Lucky said, still sounding none too kind.

And as he walked away, Duke added under his breath, "On your way outta town."

Once Gravediggers' door closed behind Red, Lucky looked back at his friend. "What do you think?"

Duke made a sizing-up face, then said, "Harmless. But . . ." He tilted his head, peered at Lucky. "You want that gun back?"

Lucky had owned a pistol when he'd come to town— he'd owned one for most of his adult life; it was part of

who he was, and it was protection. But when he'd been
staying with Duke before buying his house, he'd handed
his Glock 19 nine millimeter over to his friend. "Dude,
I'm about to bring a kid into my life, into my house. No."

"Still back there in the safe," Duke said, motioning
vaguely over his shoulder toward his office. "Whenever
you want it. You know the combination." And it was easy
to remember: 36–24–36, the mythical perfect measurements on a woman.

Lucky understood that Duke didn't like the idea of
either one of them being defenseless—it was a habit that
went back a long way. And he'd felt the same himself up to
now—but given why he'd come back to Destiny, this had
seemed like a smart time to change that mode of thinking
and get comfortable being without it. And so far, he'd felt
fine. Even now, with Red Thornton suddenly showing up.

So Lucky just gave his head a short shake, then looked
over his shoulder, back toward the door. "Weird, though—
about him. Just when I almost thought it was safe . . ."

"To go getting yourself a girl?" Duke asked. Then he
shrugged. "Hell, man, who knows—maybe it *is* safe. If
numbnuts there is the worst thing to cross our paths in
ten years, maybe it's okay to consider the past the past.
Maybe it's time. Maybe you can do whatever you want
with your little neighbor chick—ride off into the sunset
with her if you want."

The fact was, though, even if Red was kind of pathetic,
his appearance had still sent a chill down Lucky's spine.
It was a reminder that pretty much anybody could walk
through that door on any given night. Anybody could ride
their hog into Crestview or Destiny. It made Wild Bill
and the Devil's Assassins feel . . . not nearly as far away
as they had an hour ago. "I don't know, man," Lucky said,
taking the first pull on his beer since Red had darkened
their door. "Red just reminded me that, when all's said
and done, we're still pretty damn easy to find if anybody's

looking. And when I think of Vicki . . ." He stopped then, sighed, and tried to banish old images from his head.

"Don't think of Vicki, brother," Duke advised him. "Just don't."

But when the two men's eyes met again, Lucky knew they were *both* thinking about her, about what had happened to her. And Lucky knew with clarity what he had to do. Keep his hands off Tessa. Just like he'd told himself in the beginning with her: *You can look, but you can't touch.*

And once Tessa finished working in his house, things would get easier. He wouldn't see her so much. And maybe he'd get her off his mind. And maybe hooking up with the chick in purple would actually sound like fun to him. Under normal circumstances, she'd be just his type. For now, though, Duke had it wrong—for now, looked like he *was* celibate.

And it wasn't like he owed Tessa anything. Hell, he barely knew her. He could be with every girl in this bar if he wanted to without having done anything wrong.

He just . . . *liked* her, damn it.

And she'd been pretty cool to him, too. Considering what people in Destiny had thought of him by the time he'd left town, she'd given him . . . more than a fair shake, and besides being attracted to her, he almost actually considered her . . . a friend. And that was a rare commodity in his life.

And somehow the idea of getting down and dirty with some other chick right now just . . . bothered him.

Besides, he had enough to worry about already without bringing sex into the picture, didn't he? Like focusing on getting his house ready for his son's arrival. And showing Sharon he was dependable. And getting past the desire to get into his pretty interior decorator neighbor's pants. Plus he still had to deal with his family at some point.

Once all that was accomplished, *then* he'd worry about having a sex life. For now, he'd just have to take care of it himself, just like he used to . . . hell, the *last* time he'd lived in Destiny. Shit—the more things changed, the more they stayed the same.

"So," Tessa ventured cautiously as she joined Rachel and Amy in the bookstore chairs, "would you guys ever consider getting a tattoo?"

In response, Amy gasped. "Why?"

And Rachel said, "I considered it once in my twenties, but then decided it was impractical. Styles change, after all. I can change my jewelry or clothes on a whim, but you can't change a tattoo."

"And when you're seventy, it'll sag," Amy said, as if she were a tattoo expert.

"Let's be realistic," Rachel added. "When you're fifty, it'll sag. Maybe when you're forty."

Okay, so clearly Tessa shouldn't show them her tattoo just yet. "You guys are *not* making me feel any less like life is passing me by," she informed them.

"You think a tattoo will slow down the passage of time?" Amy asked, shaking her head. "First skydiving and now this? What's gotten into you?"

"*Skydiving*?" Rachel snapped, her blue eyes bolting open wide. "Who's going *skydiving*?"

"Tessa," Amy said. "Maybe. If we don't talk her out of it."

As her friends yammered on, not even noticing how little she was adding to a conversation about *her*, Tessa caught a glimpse of little Brontë slowly, quietly padding up beside her chair. She thought the cat had begun to seem a little less frightened lately, but to walk out among them, especially when anyone was here besides her and Amy, was monumental. Tessa watched from the corner of her eye as Brontë stood frozen in place, clearly ready to dart away at the first sign of trouble, and felt the need to put the kitty at ease.

With one swift but gentle move, she scooped the cat up in her hand and lifted it onto her lap. Brontë struggled, ready to run, but Tessa held her firmly, using her free hand to stroke the cat's head and back. "You're okay," she said soothingly. "Nothing bad's happening. You're just going to sit here and let me pet you."

"Where did *she* come from?" Amy asked, looking over.

"She's getting a little more trusting," Tessa replied, still holding the cat in place against her will, "and I'm helping her along, whether she likes it or not." She continued running her fingertips over Brontë's smooth fur, murmuring down to her, "Calm down, kitty. Learn to relax." After a moment, the cat finally went still, and another minute later, Tessa felt some of the tension leave her lanky little body. "There, that's better," she cooed, still petting. And soon, Brontë even began to purr a little.

"Hmm," Rachel mused. "Cat whisperer."

And Amy actually looked a little jealous—being the chief cat lover in the group. "How'd you do that?"

Tessa just shrugged, and Rachel said, "Maybe you could come over and talk to Shakespeare. Tell him to stop getting on the counter and eating Mike's food while he's still fixing it—before Mike kills him."

But Tessa had a feeling that wouldn't work—she just felt an odd little attachment to shy, skittish Brontë and was compelled to help the cat live a more enjoyable life.

On Sunday, Tessa took the day off. No work at the bookstore, no work at Lucky's. She suspected he was probably home if she'd wanted to do some painting, maybe choose a wall color for his son's room—but it felt like a good idea to put a little space between them, and the weekend was providing just that space.

The fact was, the more she thought about Lucky not making a move on her, not trying to kiss her, or *something*—the more it bothered her. It would be one thing if he just wasn't into her, but that hadn't been a banana in his pocket when she'd fallen back against him—and besides, sometimes you could just sense when you had chemistry with a guy. It was like . . . electricity in the air, a strange sizzle and pop even when you were both completely still. It crackled through your whole body, and part of that was because you could physically sense it crackling through his, too. And she'd sensed the crackling. And she'd wanted to use all that sizzling and crackling to . . . build a fire or something. So why hadn't Lucky accepted that silent invitation?

She found herself curled up on the couch in a cami and gray jogging pants, hugging a throw pillow, and selecting the most recent *Ellen* show from the offerings on her DVR. She had a tattoo she was too embarrassed to show anyone, she still felt life was passing her by, and she was even more sexually frustrated than usual—it seemed like a good time to let Ellen cheer her up.

And it worked. Ellen's monologue made her smile, and when Ellen talked about positive thinking, it reminded Tessa to try to do that—think positive, look on the bright side. In totally practical ways, life really *was* looking up lately—she'd been feeling better *and* she had a paying job. And if the past few years had taught her anything, it was not to take things for granted.

Then Ellen began to dance. She danced on the show almost every day and sometimes spoke about why, noting that it was great exercise and just made you feel good. Hmm. Tessa thought she could probably *use* some exercise. And back in her college years, she'd *loved* to go dancing—she just hadn't done it lately. Well, except for that day Def Leppard had come on the radio. That *had* made her feel kind of good—until Lucky showed up, that is.

So as Ellen moved up and down the aisles of her studio audience to Rick James's "Give it to me, Baby," Tessa made a split decision—to cast aside her pillow and get to her feet. Then she danced along with Ellen in her living room.

She glanced toward the windows, of course—just to make sure Lucky wasn't going to sneak up on her again—but all was clear. And the truth was—even if it felt a little wacky to dance by herself, she also immediately felt . . . uplifted. Like her problems were surmountable. Her health was manageable. And she had a job. And even if Lucky didn't want her, well . . . maybe someone would eventually, maybe even someone she would want in return.

That last part was the hardest to talk herself into believing—but she did it. And she kept dancing along with Ellen until, soon, she wasn't thinking about anything *except* dancing. And it was . . . fun. Wow. Still a little weird by herself—but she felt far better when she finished dancing than she had when she'd started.

By the time Ellen's show was over, she felt all-around energized, ready to make her day more than just one of sitting around pouting. The sun had risen high in the sky, creating another pretty spring day that beckoned her outdoors.

Slipping on shoes and a long cardigan sweater, she ventured onto her deck to check her seed containers and was thrilled to see the first little bits of green growth poking up through the soil in several pots. She found herself running her fingertips gingerly through the dirt surrounding the first zinnia sprouts, then gliding them over the rim of the clay pot, the terra-cotta warm from the sun.

Leaving the deck, she stooped to drink in the fragrance of her hyacinth and admire the pretty pink tulips that grew in friendly clumps alongside them. Then she headed to her daisy seed bed at the edge of the woods. Like in the pots, the first hints of green had appeared in the dark, rich soil, and thinking of the daisies she'd have here for years to come made her smile.

The gentle shushing sound of the waterfall back in the trees led her to glance in that direction, the sound soothing to her. Despite the soft spot she'd developed for her new neighbor, she felt thankful he hadn't had any customers on motorcycles this weekend—at least not when she'd been home. The cadence of the rushing water delivered exactly what she'd moved out here to find—a sense of peace and nature.

Without really planning it, she walked into the woods, toward Whisper Falls. The trees overhead made the air cooler, so she hugged her sweater around her, tying the sash in front. She'd come to sit by the falls many times since buying the cabin, but not since last autumn. The crashing water grew louder as she approached, until finally she reached her favorite spot—she lowered herself onto a large, wide rock near the base of the falls that always seemed to her as if it had been placed here on purpose, like it was God's park bench.

Shards of sunlight sifted through the trees to cast a vague glow on the small waterfall. The cascade descended only ten feet or so, but the rocky shelf it flowed over stretched across a wide part of the stream, spanning probably twenty feet. Sometimes she climbed the short, steep hill next to the falls to the top, to look across the smooth, placid water there, but today she felt like watching the crash and swirl of Whisper Falls from below. Both views were peaceful to her in different ways, but this one felt . . . well, somehow comforting yet turbulent, like a slightly wilder part of the gentle setting here—and it suited her mood lately, her need to reach out and grab life, to no longer sit sedentary here in the woods by herself.

"Hey."

She flinched at the sound and glanced up—to find Lucky standing a few feet away. Clearly the rush of the falls had masked the noise of his steps through the trees. And—oh God. As usual, he looked ferociously sexy, the breeze coming off the falls blowing his long, dark hair back from his face. And despite the dim light and the shadows cast by the trees, she was reminded of something she'd noticed the first time she'd met him—what amazing eyes he had. Her heartbeat kicked up. "Hey."

"Sorry to sneak up on you."

Oh crap—did that mean she looked nervous again? "You didn't. I mean . . . no problem."

"I was getting ready to mow the lawn and decided to finally check out these falls."

For some reason, she liked thinking of Lucky doing something as ordinary as mowing the lawn. It made him seem . . . all the more safe, all the more like her and everyone else she knew. Even if he wasn't in a lot of ways. She motioned to Whisper Falls and confided, "This has become one of my favorite places."

He nodded. "It's nice. Kind of just . . . hidden back here."

She slid over on her rock bench, making more room, and said, "Even comes with a built-in seat."

Please, please sit next to me. She'd been trying to get him off her mind, trying to not want him anymore, but now that he was this close again, it was impossible. That spark that moved between them was already sizzling once more and Whisper Falls instantly became the most seductive place she'd ever been. The fresh green leaves bursting forth suddenly felt lush and sensual, the shade created a deep, dense privacy, and the sound of the tumbling water rushed over her in an intoxicating way.

So when Lucky sat down, his muscular body taking up all the space she'd freed and more, she didn't scoot away. Their arms touched, and their thighs, too. She could smell that musky scent of his mingling with the aroma of new growth all around them.

They sat quietly for a moment, Lucky taking in the falls, Tessa watching him in her peripheral vision and hoping he couldn't tell. He wore ripped blue jeans and a puffy down vest over a hooded sweatshirt, and everything about him exuded warmth right now. Although it surprised her to discover she missed seeing his tattoos— they were such a large part of his identity in her mind. Then she smiled quietly to herself, wondering if Lucky would like the daisy chain around her ankle, and it hit her that he was perhaps the one person she knew who would understand why she'd gotten it.

"So why is it called Whisper Falls?" he asked.

Most people in Destiny knew this already, but apparently Lucky had never heard it when growing up here. She pointed to the top. "The story goes that if you stand up there on one side and whisper something, someone standing on the other side will hear you, even over the noise of the water."

He glanced down at her, clearly intrigued. "Ever try it?"

She shook her head. "It's an old story. Years ago, people used to come out here more, up an old trail by the bridge." She pointed over her shoulder toward a stretch of Whisper Falls Road that curved across the creek—just before the ascent that led to their homes. Then she laughed softly. "My mom tried it when she was young and said it didn't work. Or maybe you both have to be standing at just the right spot, or maybe the wind has to be blowing the right way or something nutty like that. Or maybe it's just an old legend someone made up."

Next to her, he shrugged. "It's a nice story anyway."

They sat in companionable silence for a moment—until Tessa's palms began to sweat. Suddenly, every part of her body felt highly sensitized, yearning for touch. She realized she wanted to kiss him so badly she could barely breathe— and it was all she could do not to reach out to his arm, or his shoulder. So instead she spoke—just to break the tension building within her. "If you're going to be around tomorrow, I'll start working in Johnny's room."

He nodded, then glanced down slightly. "I'll be around." His voice had come out lower than usual, though, and when their eyes met, she caught it in his gaze—the knowledge, once again, that this went both ways. Oh. My. Her stomach fluttered and her breasts tingled. And maybe all this meant she should just do it, just kiss him herself—but whatever mysterious thing was holding him back made *her* hold back, too. She didn't want to be pushed away.

So she just bit her lip and wished she could banish the sensuous ache at the small of her back—and tried for more conversation. "Do you forgive me?" she heard herself ask. "For coming into the room and finding out about your son?"

When he looked down at her now, their faces came closer together, and for the first time, she saw true vulnerability in big, bad Lucky Romo's eyes. His voice dropped even further, to a low, raspy timbre. "Yeah. As long as you haven't told anybody."

She didn't break the gaze—she couldn't. She just shook her head. "I haven't. I won't." Her whole body rippled with want.

And he whispered, "Thank you"—and then his eyes drifted . . . to her lips.

She sucked in her breath, let it back out—but it came slow, thready. She went a little lightheaded. She'd never been so drawn toward a man, physically, so much as if her body had taken over her brain.

That's why she found herself leaning just a little nearer to him, aware that he'd moved closer now, too. That's why the whole world stopped in that moment, and why it felt as if nothing else existed but them.

"Lucky," she murmured, knowing that, at last, he was going to kiss her.

... with my veins running fire, and my heart beating faster than I can count its throbs.

Charlotte Brontë, *Jane Eyre*

Seven

*H*is breath mingled with hers, warming her lips, as she closed her eyes, anticipating heaven. The ache, the need, roared all through her, desperate and hungry—and thank God he was finally going to *ease* that ache.

"I should go," he said then, pushing to his feet—and Tessa nearly fell over sideways since, somewhere along the way, she'd begun leaning against him.

She simply stared up at him, wide-eyed, her mouth hanging open. "Huh?"

"I . . . have stuff I gotta do," he said, eyes resolute even if slightly troubled as he started to depart. But then he stopped, met her gaze, and spoke low. "Sorry, hot stuff," he told her, sounding . . . almost a little ashamed, she thought.

And then he was gone, tramping off through the spring green woods back toward his house to leave her sitting there feeling far more alone than she had before he'd shown up.

Whoa. What the hell had just happened here? He'd come so close to kissing her—she knew it. She couldn't have invented something like that. And she certainly hadn't invented that erection a few days ago, either.

She had no idea what had sent him dashing off through the trees away from her. All she knew was that she hadn't felt this deflated in a long time.

On Tuesday, Tessa painted three walls of Johnny's room a warm shade of blue pulled from the NASCAR wallpaper border. Blue was soothing, and that was good, since she *needed* to be soothed after Lucky's disappearing act at the falls on Sunday.

She'd worked in the house the previous day, too—but mostly, he'd avoided her, staying out in the garage. And yet, every moment they *had* been in each other's presence, she'd still felt that undeniable heat moving between them. *What's going on here, Lucky?*

It was Wednesday afternoon when she headed back up the hill, ready to work on refinishing some of Lucky's living-room furniture. Like painting and wallpaper, this was a task she could do herself to keep her expenses low and her profits high. Southern rock echoed from the garage, drawing her to it, and like when she'd found him there before, he looked deeply involved in his work—today deftly painting a white skull on a black gas tank—so she stayed quiet until he reached a stopping point.

"Hey," she said. She didn't smile, though. She couldn't. She officially felt weird around him now—and oh how quickly things had changed. Not long ago she'd been nervous because he scared her a little; now things were strange because she was dying for him to make a move on her and he wouldn't.

Lucky, however, *did* smile at her— a little anyway. It looked forced, like he was trying to get past the awkwardness, but it still made her heart beat faster. Damn it.

"Hey, hot stuff." He said it like nothing was wrong—like they hadn't come painfully close to kissing a few days ago.

But she still didn't smile. "Just wanted to let you know I'm here. I'm going to start on your end tables."

He nodded, but dropped the grin, as well—apparently deciding it wasn't working. "Thanks." And as she started toward the door that led into the house, he asked, "You mad at me?"

When she stopped and turned back to him, his eyes remained on the gas tank, not looking at her. "No," she said. "Just confused." Maybe it was time for yet more honesty here.

He still didn't look her way, though. Just kept his eyes on that skull as he began to airbrush a red glow around it. "You wouldn't be the first person to be confused by me," he informed her matter-of-factly.

Huh. *That* was a hell of an answer. Or *non*-answer, she thought. And that was *it*? All he was going to say? She was beginning to have a little more sympathy for the Romo family at this point. If Lucky had spent his whole life running so hot and cold, no wonder there'd been problems. "I can only imagine," she bit off more sharply than intended.

And when he said nothing more, she opened the side door and went inside, down the hall past Lucky's bedroom, as well as the space that would soon belong to his son. But then she stopped, backed up. Something had caught her eye in Johnny's room.

And when she walked in, she gasped. Lucky had painted the fourth wall—with a mural, as he'd promised. Just since yesterday! And what a mural it was!

A little taken aback, she lowered herself onto the bed and studied what he'd created. It was a work of airbrush art. He'd painted a scene as if viewed from a car on the racetrack, the wall showing in bright hues what a driver would see through the windshield: the asphalt track curving away before him, the infield to one side, the crowd in the stands on the other. Checkered flags and the repair pit were visible, and other cars dotted the road ahead. Any NASCAR fan would love it, and Johnny would surely see in it how much his father cared about pleasing him.

She couldn't believe Lucky had done the entire thing overnight. And then not even mentioned it just now. In fact, it compelled her to walk back out, down the hall, planning to say, *You didn't even tell me about the mural. It's amazing.*

But then she stopped—just before opening the door.

She'd sensed all along that Lucky was more complex than she knew. And for a little while, she'd thought he was letting her begin to see inside him, to understand a few of those complexities. Yet now she was forced to re-member . . . all the things Rachel and Amy had worried about. His past, possibly in a biker gang. All those missing years. The potential criminal activity. It was difficult not to revisit all that now and wonder if her friends' warnings were worth reconsidering, heeding.

Either way, one thing was becoming scathingly clear: Lucky Romo was not a simple man. And he didn't want to let her any deeper into his life than she already was.

As for asking him about the mural—it suddenly seemed like a bad idea. It implied that they were . . . close in some way, that they shared something beyond a professional relationship. And other than the fact that she knew about his son, they . . . didn't. Not really.

So maybe she just needed to accept that and move on with her life.

Lucky tried to focus on the design he was painting on Spider Conway's Harley Fatboy. Spider was an acquain-tance of Duke's, one of the many he'd sent Lucky's way lately. Not surprisingly, the large, bald guy had requested Lucky airbrush a black widow and spiderweb on his gas tank, and then echo the webbing on the fenders. Lucky had fashioned the black widow after the one tattooed on the back of Spider's head.

Using a curved template, he created tiny white swishes that would form the web—but his mind kept wandering. Because he knew he was screwing up with Tessa—bad.

He wanted her in his bed, but he couldn't have that. And so he instead wanted her to be his friend—but if he wasn't careful, he wouldn't have that, either. He just . . . hell . . . he didn't know how to be when he was with her. The more he was around her, the more he wanted her, and he'd come so damn close to kissing her by the waterfall that it had scared some sense into him. Just like Red's little visit to Gravediggers over the weekend.

Seeing Red had reminded him that it was easy to get too relaxed. Maybe that was one reason he'd settled in a sizable city after leaving California. In a city, you didn't relax. There were people coming and going—in your business, in your life—all the time. There were honking horns and sirens to help you remember that it was a trouble-filled world out there, and that you had your own fair share of that trouble.

Here, in Destiny, out here in the woods . . . it was so damn quiet sometimes that he could almost believe he'd moved into some other existence entirely—like the Devil's Assassins were some figment of his imagination.

But that's why it was good he hung out at Gravediggers—there, with Duke, much as he might want the DAs not to exist, he always remembered they did. There, surrounded by people he didn't know very well but still had a lot in common with, he couldn't forget who he was—and who he would always be.

Just then, he heard a bike in the distance, mounting the hill on Whisper Falls Road. More business—good. He'd take all he could get. He was doing fine on money, but he'd just started sending child support to Sharon, and he wanted to be sure he could give Johnny anything he might need.

When the motorcycle rumbled into his driveway, he stopped working and walked out into the sunlight. And—shit. He could scarcely believe his eyes. It was Red again. He rode an old Softtail that, like Red himself, had seen better days. What the hell was Red Thornton doing *here*?

Red killed the engine and lifted his hand in a wave. "Hey, Lucky—how ya doin'?"

Like before with Red, Lucky didn't smile. "Doing all right. Didn't expect to see you again, Red."

Unfazed, Red motioned to the bike beneath him. "My baby here needs a paint job and I heard in Chillicothe you were the man for the job."

Hmm—already word had gotten out nearly an hour away that it was worth driving here to get your bike painted? The news was great for business—but with Lucky's recently renewed worries about being too easy to find, it left him slightly unsettled, too. "No offense, Red, but can you afford it?"

Red's smile stretched from ear to ear. "Found my sister, and turns out she's doin' real well. Offered to buy me a paint job for my birthday next week—so here I am."

"You won't mind then if I ask for payment up front?" Normally Lucky didn't—he figured the bike itself served as collateral if a customer didn't pay. But he was sort of hoping to drive Red away, right back to Chillicothe—just because he was a reminder of bad times.

"Nope." Red patted his back pocket, unoffended. "Got the cash right in my wallet."

Hell.

From there, Red described to Lucky the paint job he wanted, and—finally concluding that Red's money was as good as anybody else's—Lucky pulled out a catalog of designs to show his new customer.

And the more he talked to Red . . . well, he didn't like

it, but the same as at Gravediggers, Lucky almost started feeling sorry for the guy. Red was immature for his age, and directionless, and too excited about a gift from his sister—but talking to him forced Lucky to realize Red had probably had a shitty upbringing and likely didn't have even one friend. Lucky knew what it was like to feel you had nobody, so . . . shit, no wonder Red was so amped up about finding his sister.

Once Red had selected what Lucky thought was a pretty cheesy pirate design—he even tried to talk Red out of it, pointing him toward pirate flags instead of an actual pirate, with no success—Lucky decided to broach his least favorite subject with Red. When he'd first seen Red at Duke's bar, he'd thought it meant trouble—but now it occurred to him that maybe, just maybe, talking to Red about his old biker gang wasn't a bad idea. After all, where else could he find out information about them that might prove useful? Maybe he should see Red not as an annoyance, but as more of a . . . tool.

Red even gave him an opening as he walked back over to his bike, leaning against the seat. "Still can't believe I ran into you after so damn long, Lucky," he said, shaking his head. "Man, California seems like it happened in a whole 'nother life."

Lucky could definitely relate to that. And since Red had turned the topic back to the old days, Lucky cautiously began. "Sometimes I still worry about all that shit coming back to haunt me. Know what I mean?" He made a point of meeting Red's eyes as he spoke, to gauge his sincerity.

The other man appeared weary at the question. "Well, yeah—me, too."

Lucky tilted his head, curious. "What did *you* do to be worried about?"

Red glanced at the ground, looked uneasy, then crossed his arms, shoulders slumped. "Let's just say me and Wild Bill had a bad partin' of the ways."

Huh. Lucky would be damn surprised if it was nearly as bad as *his* parting with Bill.

And he almost asked about someone else then, about Vicki—how she'd been before Red had left, if she was still putting up with Bill's crap—but he stopped himself. Wild Bill's girlfriend had been attractive, and she and Lucky had—unfortunately—shared a raging chemistry. Though he couldn't credit her with being especially smart or strong-willed when it came to taking care of herself. Hell, what had happened between them proved that. Maybe that was why he didn't really want to know. Given all that had happened back then, he hoped she was okay, but he still decided it would be better to just move on to a different topic. "Did Bill ever make any more threats against me or Duke?"

"Not that I recall," Red replied. "One good thing about Bill—he's got a short memory."

Lucky narrowed his eyes on Red. "If his memory's so short, why are you worried about those times coming back to bite you in the ass?"

Red tilted his head and looked like he was thinking it over. "With a guy like Wild Bill, it's hard *not* to worry. But on the other hand, I ain't so sure it's . . . what's the word? A *practical* worry, a thing that'd really happen—know what I'm sayin'? The more time passes, the farther away I get, I figure what are the chances? So yeah, I worry, but . . . it's probably a big waste of time." Red shifted his weight from one boot to the other, and met Lucky's gaze. "Hell, I been gone almost five years. And how long ago did you and Duke leave—nine, ten?"

"Just over ten," Lucky confirmed with a light nod.

Now it was Red who changed the subject, and Lucky didn't mind. "Seems like you two fellas are doin' all right for yourselves."

"We are," Lucky agreed.

And maybe, if Red was right about any of this—Bill's

memory, the passage of time—Lucky could be doing even *better* for himself. Maybe Red made a lot of sense. Maybe Lucky was torturing himself for nothing. Maybe. It was weirdly comforting to hear somebody else express what he'd been waffling over and wanting to feel, wanting to *believe*, for a damn long time. Especially given that Duke saw things the exact opposite way, and it was partially *his* views that kept Lucky from letting himself move on. He'd been bold enough, comfortable enough, to come to the place where his son was—and if he'd felt *that* was safe, maybe it was stupid to worry it would be any different where a woman was concerned, no matter *what* Wild Bill had said all those years ago.

"Well, I'll be seein' ya, Lucky," Red said with a wave as he climbed on his bike to go.

"Dude," Lucky informed him dryly, "you have to *leave* the bike if you want it painted. Whole process takes about a week."

Red looked just as embarrassed as Lucky thought he should. "Shit, didn't think of that."

Lucky could only sigh. "So you don't have somebody coming to pick you up?"

"Nope."

"Well, don't look at *me*," Lucky informed him. "I got work to do. Better call your sister." Then he lamented knowing he had to spend a whole additional hour with Red.

But . . . well, maybe it was worth it for the confirmation he'd gotten—the idea, the possibility, that maybe the past would stay in the past, that maybe he could slowly start letting himself accept that the nightmare that had started with the Devil's Assassins was really over, at last.

And if it was . . . well, that would change a hell of a lot.

By Friday afternoon, Tessa was back at work in Lucky's living room and kitchen. The weather was typical for

April—drizzly, with a chill in the air—forcing her back into blue jeans and making her wish for more of those warm sunny days that had come so early this year.

As she tried to mount a new curtain rod over the wide front window behind Lucky's couch, she realized she needed more than two hands. So even though she was doing her darnedest to be cool toward Lucky and not interact with him much, when he passed through the room, she was forced to ask for his help.

"Whatcha need, hot stuff?" he asked.

Standing up on his couch, she swung her head around to peer down at him—he sounded positively jovial. *For crying out loud, which way is it, Romo? Are you mysterious and brooding or hot and flirtatious?* "Could you hold this above the window while I stand back and check the length of the drapes?" The new drapery already hung from each end of the decorative rod.

"Sure thing, babe," he said—then took the last crisp bite of a juicy-looking apple, chucked the core in the kitchen garbage can, and came toward her. *Oh boy, he's calling me babe again. And since when did seeing a guy eat an apple start turning me on?* This attraction was becoming . . . painful.

As Lucky kicked off his shoes and joined her to stand on the leather sofa, they bumped slightly and his sock-covered foot ended up pressing right against hers as they executed the hand-off of the long rod. "Been meaning to tell you," he said, "Johnny's room looks great."

Crap—his smile made her stomach go hollow.

She stepped down off the couch feeling a little numb, her head swimming. *God, I just want to be under him.* The need was growing more raw and intense by the day. She was tired of this roller coaster of emotions—but at the same time, it was impossible to resist staying on the ride to see where it took her. "I've been meaning to tell *you* how great the mural is." Double crap—she hadn't planned to give him any compliments, but her appreciation of the painting apparently overrode her intentions.

He glanced down at her, his vulnerable expression surprising—and somehow more endearing on such a big, tattoo-covered guy. "You really think he'll like it?"

Tessa's stomach curled inward. He didn't realize it yet, but he was *already* being a great dad. And that made it even *harder* to be cool and aloof. "Of course he will," she told him, unable to keep the sincerity from her voice. "It's really special."

"Good," he said on a short nod. "And it was a good idea, so . . . thanks."

As she stood back to study the drapes, she instructed Lucky to lift the rod a little, then to lower it back down a smidge. Once it was where she wanted it, she said, "Perfect. Now don't move." She'd use a level before screwing anything in, but for the moment, she rushed to mark the spots for the brackets with a pencil—one mark at each end—standing up on tiptoes. "You seem in a good mood," she tossed out casually.

"Yeah, guess I am."

"Better than lately," she noted, eyes still on the wall she scored lightly.

"Maybe so," he agreed, but left it at that.

"Why?" she asked pointedly. This time she looked up at him. "And you can set that down now, on the back of the couch."

"Nothin' I need to bore you with," he said, lowering the curtains, then stepping down next to her on the floor. "Just . . . maybe starting to get rid of some old baggage that's been weighing me down."

Hmm. Her mind raced, so she followed it. This was the only way she'd ever find out anything more about Lucky Romo. "Female baggage?"

At this, her brawny neighbor grinned. "No, hot stuff, nothin' like that."

Okay, massive relief. He'd told her before that he didn't have a woman in his life, but still . . . "Then did you . . . get in touch with your family or something?"

He lowered his chin and cast a chastising look. "No. And quit being so nosy." But it came out teasingly, almost flirtatiously, making her chest ripple with fresh desire.

"Sorry," she said, not really meaning it. "I just can't help being curious about a guy who disappears for fifteen years."

"Yeah, well—I'm ready to start focusing on the present, and the future. You should, too."

And as luck would have it, she'd already been trying to do that in her own life—stop fretting over the past. So maybe she shouldn't worry about *his* past, either? And maybe she *wouldn't*—if he'd ease her present aches.

And the thought reminded her of the bigger, more *universal* ache plaguing her lately—the urge to grab onto life before she woke up one day, old and frail and alone. "Have you ever gone skydiving?" she asked him out of the blue.

He looked amused, cocking a surprised grin her way. "Nope—flying on my bike is a big enough thrill for *me*. Why?"

She bit her lip, tilted her head. "I just . . . kind of want to do it. And my friends think it's crazy. But you seem like someone who wouldn't be afraid of something like that."

"I'm not afraid of much," he stated plainly.

"So then . . . would you go with me maybe? Sometime?" Oh Lord, wait! Had she just asked him on a date? Oh brother, how had *that* happened?

And she was just about to yammer on, say something to let him off the hook—when he smoothly replied, "Sure, hot stuff—whenever you want."

Oh. Okay. He hadn't turned her down or made her feel stupid or rejected. Pure relief flooded her veins. Except, well . . . maybe she shouldn't be all *that* relieved, since it wasn't like she'd done what she'd *really* wanted to do:

throw herself on him and rip his clothes off. "Good," she managed to force out, her voice a bit too high-pitched. "We'll do that. Sometime."

He gave an easy nod. "So . . . any big weekend plans?"

Her stomach churned at the simple question. "Not really. You?"

"I've been hanging at Gravediggers a lot, over in Crestview."

"Mmm," she said, still trying to sound casual, cool, like the biker bar was just your typical friendly neighborhood pub.

"You ever been there?" he asked with a doubtful grin.

And she met his gaze, now letting her expression shift to self-deprecating honesty. "No."

"You should come by sometime," he said, still smiling. He was teasing her again, clearly sure she'd be afraid of such a place.

And even if she was, she met the challenge. "You never know, Romo, maybe I just will."

He said nothing in reply, yet that severe chemistry between them kicked up a notch simply because they stood so close to each other for no practical reason—and neither of them smiled any longer. So she went to move past him, to retrieve the curtain rod brackets from a table across the room—but he didn't step out of the way. "You need anything else, hot stuff?"

Oh Lord, quit torturing me, Lucky Romo! Because of course I need something else—your hot body— and you just torment me with it. "Nope," she said, resolute, drawing her gaze downward, to his chest. "Thanks for the help, though—now I have to get back to work."

After which she pushed past him, her arm coming into solid contact with his, and the smell of his skin, the warmth of his flesh, nearly paralyzed her—but she stayed on her feet, glad her back was to him now so he couldn't see the lust surely written all over her face.

"I'll be out in the garage working. If you need more help," he said.

Though she refused to let herself meet his gaze even one more time, certain it would be the death of her. "All righty. Happy painting. See ya later."

That night, she called Rachel and insisted they meet for dinner at Dolly's Café. Because Lucky was driving her crazy, and making her feel a little desperate. She'd tried to stop questioning why he hadn't put the moves on her, but as she drove toward town, she couldn't help pondering it further. Could it be because, like her, he realized how different they were? Or . . . maybe he thought a nice girl like her wouldn't be able to have sex without making it a big, heavy, emotional thing.

Well, once upon a time that had been true, but no more. At moments with him, in fact, she felt like sex was *all* that mattered to her. She wasn't especially proud of that, nor did she find it a particularly appealing trait, but at least she understood her mounting needs and could accept them for what they were. She only wished Lucky could see that, too, and perhaps even appreciate them.

She reached Dolly's first, happy to find it relatively quiet on a drizzly Friday night, and by the time Rachel sat down next to her at the small, round table, Tessa felt like she was about to burst with frustration.

Rachel's gaze instantly narrowed in concern. "You look crazed. What's wrong?"

"It's Lucky," she said.

And Rachel nearly flew into a rage, her eyes going wide. "What did he do to you? I'll kill him."

Tessa pressed her hand down over her friend's to calm her. "No, it's nothing like that—he didn't do anything to me. In fact . . . that's the whole problem."

Rachel blinked, looking confused. "Wait, I thought you told me about wanting him just to get it off your chest—not because you really . . . *want him*."

Tessa pursed her lips, then admitted, "Yeah, well, getting it off my chest wasn't enough. And last weekend, he nearly kissed me, but then he stopped. And then there was the time I lost my balance and fell against him and he had an erection, and . . . half the time he's sexy and nice, and the other half he's quiet and withdrawn—and today I asked him to go skydiving with me and he said yes, but I don't think I can wait for that."

Rachel just looked at her like she wasn't making sense and Tessa realized her friend was right: She *was* crazed. Officially. She grabbed onto Rachel's wrist. "See, this is what happens when a woman in the prime of her life goes this long without sex. She loses her mind."

Rachel held up her hands in a stop motion. "Wait—I'm trying to sort this out. What the hell does skydiving have to do with sex?"

Tessa tried to sort it out, too. "Well, they're both about . . . living. Feeling life."

"So you think skydiving will make you feel the same thing sex does?" Understandably, Rachel squinted her confusion. "Because I've never gone skydiving, but, uh . . ."

"No," Tessa said, exasperated—by the situation, not Rachel. "Skydiving is just . . . an extreme substitute. But I didn't call you here to talk about skydiving. I called you here to talk about Lucky."

Rachel nodded, eyes still wide, probably from the rapid pace of the conversation. "Okay—what about him? Exactly."

Tessa swallowed and tried to spit out the idea she'd come up with. She knew what she wanted to do—she knew it with clarity—and she wasn't going to let Rachel, or her own fears, stop her any longer. "I want to seduce him."

Just then, Mabel—the elderly waitress who seemed to be at Dolly's around the clock—slapped two menus down in front of them. "What can I get you girls to drink?"

"Two iced teas," Rachel said quickly, taking the liberty of ordering for them both, and the second Mabel ambled away, she turned back to Tessa. "Seduce him how?" And, of course, she looked very worried.

"Is Mike working tomorrow night?" Tessa asked.

"No—he's having a guys' night with Logan and Adam. Why?"

"Will he be out late?"

"Probably."

A rush of adrenaline shot through Tessa's body. This meant that maybe, just maybe, she could really go through with this. "Good—then you can come with me. Because I can't do it without you."

Rachel already looked apprehensive. "Come where?"

"To Gravediggers, the biker bar in Crestview—where Lucky hangs out."

"Huh?"

Tessa rushed ahead, trying to win Rachel over before she refused. "We can be biker chicks for a night! Doesn't that sound fun?" She raised her eyebrows and smiled.

While Rachel just sat there, mouth gaping. "On what planet?"

"Think of it like Halloween," Tessa suggested cheerfully. "You used to love dressing up for Halloween. This will be like that—only . . . in springtime."

"Are you out of your mind?" Rachel asked.

Tessa answered matter-of-factly. "I thought we'd already established that. But I'm also a desperate woman."

"Well, yes, you *sound* desperate. I'm not convinced you're thinking clearly here. So snap out of it."

That's when Mabel—suddenly Miss Speedy—chose to show up with two glasses of tea and her order pad. "What'll ya have?"

Neither of them had cracked a menu, but they came to Dolly's often enough to know the offerings by heart. Both placed their orders briskly, eager to get back to the matter at hand. And as soon as the waitress departed, Tessa said to Rachel, "I *am* thinking clearly, trust me. Just imagine how *you'd* feel if *you* hadn't had sex in so long. And for all of Lucky's flaws, Rach, I really believe he's a perfectly okay guy." *I think*.

But Rachel still looked uncertain. "So why do *I* have to be dragged into this?"

"Do you really want me to go sashaying into Grave-diggers by myself?" Tessa tried to look extremely innocent and vulnerable.

"That's a low move," Rachel informed her.

"And it's not like I'm gonna get Amy to go."

Rachel nodded. "She'd probably pee her pants at the very suggestion."

"And you're worldly. You know how to handle your-self."

"True," Rachel said smugly, and Tessa saw the tide beginning to turn her way.

"And furthermore, this would be a perfect opportunity for you to check out Lucky."

"Well," Rachel admitted, "I *am* curious to meet the guy. Both for your sake *and* Mike's." Yet then, just when Tessa thought it was in the bag, Rachel's gaze narrowed. "But why do we have to go to Gravediggers of all blemishes on the landscape?"

Tessa pursed her lips. "Because I know he's attracted to me, too—I know it with every molecule of my body," she insisted. "But there's *something* keeping him from pursuing it, and I really don't think my fragile ego could take it if I made a move on him and he rejected me. So my plan is—make myself irresistible to him, make it so he can't *stop* himself from making a move. And I figure the quickest way to a biker's heart is to become a biker *babe*.

I just need to show him how hot I can be, how daring. Once he sees me in biker chick mode, he'll have to have me. So what do you say? Can I count on you? Will you do this one little thing for me? Are we on for Gravediggers tomorrow night?"

Rachel looked completely uneasy, and totally torn. "Mike will kill me," she said.

"He'll never have to know."

She spoke through clenched teeth. "But we have this *honesty* thing going—*remember*?"

"And like before—this isn't about you and him, it's about me. And I *need* you, Rachel. I need you to come through for me on this. Will you do that? Will you come through for your dear old friend, Tessa, who desperately needs some passion in her life?"

Rachel sighed. "Oh hell," she muttered under her breath, rolling her eyes. "Fine. I'll go."

I have a right to get pleasure out of life:
and I will get it, cost what it may . . .

Charlotte Brontë, *Jane Eyre*

Eight

As Tessa stood before her mirror, preparing to go to Gravediggers, her stomach churned. Maybe this idea was "out there," but she was *ready* for out there, ready to do whatever it took to get Lucky in bed. And it was hard to be so daring, but the last few years had taught her she could survive a lot of things she wouldn't have thought she could, so she told herself now that this was just another one of those things. And a *better* one of those things. Which would hopefully reap grand, orgasmic rewards.

She couldn't help thinking she made a pretty good biker chick. She wore a lace-trimmed white cami with a lacy red bra underneath—and though, normally, she'd never pair clothing like that, tonight was about being daring. Below, she'd put on a short denim miniskirt she'd picked up at a thrift store to wear to an eighties theme party back in college, and the same black boots she'd worn with Lucky on their motorcycle ride.

Of course, if this didn't produce the desired result, she'd feel humiliated. She was pretty much laying it all on the line with Lucky—when she walked in there tonight, he'd know why. And if he didn't respond . . . well, she'd just have to act like she had a secret yearning to be a biker chick or something. Even so, it seemed a better risk to take than kissing him and maybe being pushed away. And besides, this was kind of like skydiving—it felt like grabbing life boldly by the horns.

Just as she was applying makeup, trying to give her eyes that smoky, sexy look, a knock came on the door. A moment later, she opened it to find Rachel on the other side in dark jeans, a red tank, and strappy red heels. Even in biker babe wear, her friend appeared long, lean, and sophisticated.

As she gave Tessa a once-over, though, she looked slightly aghast.

"What?" Tessa asked.

"You look . . ."

"Like a sexy biker girl?" Tessa asked hopefully, batting her eyelashes.

"Um, actually . . . a little like a prostitute."

Tessa refused to be daunted, however. "No, this is biker chick chic, trust me."

"But your bra is showing," Rachel informed her critically.

Tessa just rolled her eyes. "Where have you been, Rachel? *Everybody's* bra is showing these days."

"Not in Destiny," Rachel pointed out.

"Then it's a good thing we're going to Crestview."

"So," Rachel said, stepping inside, "we're really doing this, huh? Because we could always change clothes and catch a movie at the Ambassador instead."

Tessa simply flashed a dry look. "I'm pretty sure catching a movie at the Ambassador won't result in sex for me—so no." She would not be deterred at this point—her bra was showing, for heaven's sake; she'd come too far to turn back.

But Rachel still looked doubtful. "I just feel bad doing this behind Mike's back."

"Then call his cell phone and tell him where you're going. Blame it on me. Say I wouldn't take no for an answer. Because I won't."

Yet Rachel shook her head. "No, he would forbid it. And, of course, that would piss me off and then I'd *have* to do it. And besides, the guys are drinking beer and playing pool at the Dew Drop Inn, and Mike doesn't get cell reception there half the time anyway."

"If you'd go no matter *what* he says," Tessa asked, grabbing up her purse and starting to turn off a few lights, "then what's the problem?"

"The problem is that if he finds out, I might no longer be engaged. And I *like* being engaged to Mike."

"Because you get to have great sex all the time."

Rachel crossed her arms. "That's not the only reason."

"But it's certainly one ingredient—don't deny it. An ingredient I'd like to have in *my* life, too—you know?"

Rachel shrugged in concession. "I *have* gotten quite used to it. And I guess I've also gotten used to being totally honest with him, so even though I'm not really doing anything wrong, that's why this feels weird."

"See, you really *have* turned into the female Mike Romo, walking the straight and narrow all the time." Tessa actually saw Rachel's point, but she knew this would get to her.

And it did. Rachel narrowed her gaze on Tessa. "Quit saying that."

"Then quit proving it true."

Rachel sighed. "Fine. We're going. I hope you appreciate this."

* * *

Lucky sat on his usual bar stool, shooting the bull with Duke when he wasn't occupied with other customers. Saturday nights were busy, but it was early yet at Gravediggers, where the real action didn't start until around midnight, and Duke wasn't the only one tending bar tonight—a young, heavily tattooed and pierced guy named Rocker was handling the bulk of the work.

Lucky had told Duke about Red's visit, and now he said, "So what do you think, man? *Is* it time to let go of all that old worry, once and for all? Is it crazy to live your whole damn life looking over your shoulder, no matter how long the view's been clear? Or am I just . . . seeing this through rose-colored glasses?"

Duke wiped down the bar—Lucky had observed in the time he'd been home that this was what Duke did when he was thinking something through. So Lucky took a drink from the longneck before him and waited patiently as the din of music and talk blared around him. Finally, Duke said, "It's my fault the way things ended up that night." And it was the last thing Lucky expected to hear. Especially since Duke seldom brought up the grim events that had sent them running from the Devil's Assassins.

And he wasn't exactly sure *why* Duke was bringing it up, but his friend wasn't making sense. "Dude, what the hell are you talking about?"

Duke narrowed his eyes. "I could have ended it quicker. I could have had my ear to the ground better and known it was coming. We could have been ready for it. So I've . . . always felt kinda responsible. And . . . shit, man, maybe I've made us both fucking paranoid because of it."

Lucky just balked, taken aback. "Duke, you got it all wrong. I'm the one at fault." How could Duke not see that? Hell, Duke had always been protective of him in ways—and it made him feel all the more guilty. "I never wanted you to have to pay for the trouble I caused. And you *have* paid, just as much as me."

Duke spoke low, quick. "Doesn't matter who did what, brother. We were in that shit together, same way we still are." Then he resumed wiping down the bar, even though it was already spotless. "Either way, what I'm thinking is this. Even though I'm still watching my back and yours every second—hell, maybe it *is* a waste of time. Not sure I know *how* to stop looking over my shoulder, but maybe it'd be smarter to just . . . live like normal."

Lucky felt his eyebrows knit, then shared his recent revelation. "Guess maybe I already have, in a way. I mean, I came here, where my family is. I'm getting ready to be a dad. If I felt, in my gut, like it wasn't safe for them, I'd still be in Wisconsin, right?"

Duke shrugged. "I thought the same thing when you packed up and moved home. But . . ." He paused then, wiped down the bar some more. "But it's different with your family than with a woman."

"Yeah," Lucky reluctantly agreed. Because of what had happened between him and Vicki, and after that. But he decided to shake that off. "Still, it's been ten years. Ten years and not one fucking peep out of those guys."

Duke met Lucky's gaze. "Maybe you should just let yourself do what you want for a change, compadre. Maybe you should just go for it, and screw my paranoia."

Lucky grinned, then restated an old favorite line of theirs. "You know what they say—it's only paranoia if they're not really out to get ya."

Just then, Duke looked up, toward the front door, and murmured, "Interesting."

"Shit—don't tell me Red's back."

"No, it's not Red. Far from it. Just a couple of hot babes I've never seen before. Wonder where *they* came from. And which one of 'em wants to go home with me tonight."

And when Lucky turned to look—*damn*. He couldn't believe his eyes. He even blinked to make sure they weren't playing tricks on him. Then he said to Duke, "Make it the blonde. Because the other one is Tessa."

"You're shittin' me," Duke said.

"Nope." Both of them kept watching as the two women made their way through the milling crowd—though Tessa, looking shockingly hot in a way he hadn't known she could, looked straight ahead and let the blonde lead the way.

When finally Tessa looked up and their eyes met, he gave her a smile, not trying to hide his surprise at seeing her here. "What's up, hot stuff?" he asked when she reached the bar.

Her own smile appeared more shy than usual. "I told you I might show up sometime."

"Guess I didn't take you seriously," he admitted.

"Maybe you should."

"Maybe I should," he agreed. At the moment, though, he barely knew where to focus his attention: on the two curves of scalloped red lace peeking above her low-cut top, on her delectably short skirt, or on the eyes that appeared warmer, darker, in this lighting. As nice as the rest of her was to look at, he settled on her eyes and watched as she bit her soft lower lip—and felt it in his groin.

And that's when he understood. Why she was here. Why she was dressed so much . . . like the rest of the women here. She was making a play, showing him she wanted him. Which he pretty much already understood, but . . . hell, this took things a big step further.

Because he knew this wasn't a typical night out for his hot little neighbor. She was . . . putting herself out there for him, trying to . . . fit into his world. He'd never been so flattered in his life, and though he'd liked her a lot already, in that moment he began to realize . . . just how remarkable she really was.

And he also realized . . . how selfish he'd been with her, in a way.

Yeah, he'd been looking out for her by pushing aside his attraction, but the fact that she'd do this, come here for him like this, made him understand that despite good intentions, he hadn't taken the time to think much about her feelings, about the fact that maybe his resistance had been just as hard on her as it had on him.

"What can I get you ladies to drink?" Duke asked, drawing both women's attention his way.

And maybe that was good, since at the moment, Lucky couldn't keep his eyes from drifting down over Tessa's sumptuous body and . . . damn, she looked fine. Of course, it didn't hurt that he was getting to see completely new parts of her and learn new things about her—like that she owned a sexy red bra. Which she'd worn tonight for *him*. His chest tightened and he suffered the instant urge it take off her.

"Don't suppose a girl can get a glass of wine here?" Tessa asked Duke across the bar.

And Duke chuckled deeply. "Afraid not. We got beer and hard liquor, darlin'."

Tessa could scarcely believe she was pulling this off. Of course, she'd never been so glad to see Lucky before, given that it had felt like every biker in the place was ogling them when they'd walked in. And she sensed *him* giving her a solid once-over right now, too—but when *he* did it, it felt like a good thing, not a bad one. As for what to drink, her Crohn's even dictated what beverages she could consume, so she thought for a minute and said, "How about a Cape Cod?"

The goateed guy behind the bar in a muscle shirt looked doubtful. "Afraid you'll have to help me out on that one."

That's when the other bartender, sporting more inked skin than *un*-inked, came sliding over to say, "Cranberry juice and vodka," then winked at Tessa. "Right?"

Still feeling out of her element, but at the same time energized by the sensation, she smiled. "Right."

"Comin' right up," the tattooed guy said, and the bearded guy looked to Rachel. "What about you, hon?"

"I'll have a sex on the beach," she said easily, and Tessa couldn't help glaring in surprise. It was a strong drink and Rachel was driving, not to mention fulfilling her duties as "wing-woman." In reply to Tessa's look, Rachel just shrugged and murmured, "When in Rome . . ."

Walking into Gravediggers had been both scary and exciting, but the look in Lucky's eyes made it mostly just exciting. While their drinks were being mixed, she turned back to him and said, "This is my friend, Rachel Farris. Rachel, Lucky Romo."

"Hi," Lucky said, then looked like he was vaguely recalling the name. "Did we . . . go to high school together, too?"

Tessa watched carefully as Rachel gave a short nod. She wasn't being overly friendly yet, but also not disdainful. "Yeah, we did. And now I'm engaged to your brother, Mike."

Whoa. Tessa hadn't seen that coming, although it only made sense for Rachel to mention it—and clearly neither had Lucky, since he looked for a second like he'd been hit with a brick. "Wow," he finally said, then ran his hand back through his long hair before meeting Rachel's gaze again. "I didn't know if he knew I was back in town, but I guess this means he does."

Rachel nodded once more, adding in a surprisingly kind tone, "I think he's hoping you'll come see him." And Tessa realized, remembered, what a huge gap of time—and understanding—stood between Lucky and his brother. Between her own troubles and her quest for an exciting life, she'd sort of forgotten some of the issues Lucky faced—even if she still didn't know all the facts behind them. And she was glad Rachel was using this situation to try to move things along—even though she must not have planned it or she'd have mentioned it on the ride over.

Lucky looked taken aback by Rachel's words. "Really? Because . . . I didn't know if he'd want that. To see me."

Tessa watched as Rachel lowered her chin slightly, maybe a little surprised by Lucky's confiding response. "Don't get me wrong—he's angry. About not hearing from you in all this time. But I know deep down he'd like to reconnect."

"Where, um, does he live?"

Wow, it just hit Tessa that Lucky didn't know even the simplest things about Mike's life. She could have told him, of course, but she'd purposely not brought his family up very much, not sure she should intrude. She felt as if Rachel, being Mike's fiancée, somehow had more right. "He and I live in the house where you grew up."

Lucky's eyes narrowed. "Then where do my mom and dad live?"

"They moved to Florida," Rachel explained.

And Lucky looked to Tessa. "You never told me any of this."

"You never asked. I wasn't sure you wanted to know anything about them."

"You're right," he said, again letting a tad of vulnerability leak through his tough exterior. "I kinda . . . didn't want to know, I guess. It's easier for me to ignore the situation that way." He shifted his gaze back to Rachel. "Uh . . . how *is* Mike?"

Rachel tilted her head, clearly thinking through how to reply. Then she told his brother, "He's a gruff, stubborn, know-it-all cop who, deep down, still misses the family he used to have when he was a kid—but he'd never say that." Tessa knew instinctively that Rachel wouldn't have shared that with anyone but Lucky, and maybe it meant she already realized he wasn't a jerk. "But other than all that, he's doing well," she went on, concluding with a smile. "And he's got a great fiancée."

Lucky nodded, looking somber. "I'm glad. And I agree on the last part—my brother did good finding you."

Rachel appeared duly flattered, and when she glanced at Tessa, Tessa flashed an expression that said, *See? He's not so bad.*

"Only . . ." Lucky scrunched his eyebrows together, suddenly looking skeptical. "Aren't the Farrises the family mine never got along with?"

Rachel and Tessa both laughed, and Rachel said, "One in the same. And Mike and I didn't get along very well in the beginning, either. But over time, we worked all that out."

When both drinks were set on the bar, Rachel started to reach for her purse—until Lucky said, "No—they're on me." Then he looked to his friend with the goatee. "And I think *I* need a shot of whiskey." He laughed slightly as he said it, but still seemed a bit flummoxed to Tessa.

Feeling bad about it, she moved in closer to Lucky's side. "Hey, I'm sorry—when I invited Rachel, I didn't think about all that might heap on you."

But Lucky was shaking his head—as he slid his arm comfortably around her, his palm pressing into the small of her back. "No—it's fine. It's . . . maybe even good. Just caught me a little off guard."

His touch sent a hot ripple down her inner thighs and she instinctively leaned even nearer, wanting to explain more. "Still, I should have anticipated that. It's just that Rachel is my only friend who would . . ."

"What?" he asked when she trailed off.

She offered him a small smile. "Well—who would come here with me in a million years."

They both laughed, and Lucky assured her, "Don't

worry, babe—it's fine," then lifted the shot glass his bartender friend had just set before him. "Pick up your drink. What should we toast to?"

Tessa thought about the night ahead and all it might bring—to both of them. Then she suggested, "New beginnings?"

"To new beginnings," Lucky said, clinking his glass with hers.

Half an hour after Tessa had arrived at Gravediggers, Lucky had introduced her and Rachel to Duke—and he'd purposely *not* introduced Rocker, deciding he didn't like the way the younger guy flirted with Tessa.

He'd found out Rachel had moved back to Destiny from Chicago to be with Mike, and that the two of them had joined up with Rachel's grandma to run the Farris Family Apple Orchard, a piece of land that had once belonged to Lucky and Mike's grandfather—the same one Lucky had been named for. And Lucky hadn't been surprised to hear Mike was a cop. Given Lucky's past, Mike's profession wasn't the most convenient thing in the world, but he'd been getting ready to head off to the academy before Lucky had left town.

When Rachel had asked Lucky about *his* business, he'd explained he did custom paint jobs on motorcycles. He'd been getting more and more heated up ever since Tessa had walked in the door, though, and when she'd added, "You should see his work—it's *so* amazing," it made him a little harder than he already was. From a mere compliment. Damn.

Of course, the few minutes he'd spent talking to his brother's fiancée about his family had been weird, bordering between painful and . . . well, twisting his heart in a way he hadn't expected, just to be thinking about them, hearing about them. But that shot of Jack Daniels had done the trick, numbing him to nothing but the good stuff, and that included the fact that Tessa had pulled a stool up next to his now, so close that their thighs pressed together under the bar. He never consciously decided to touch her, but somewhere along the way as they all talked, he'd eased his arm around her and kept it there. Maybe the Jack had helped with that, too—made him quit measuring his every action with her so much, made him just do what came naturally. Now he could smell her perfume, and he could feel all the sexy femininity just pouring off her in waves.

When Duke said to Rachel, "You're the best looking thing to ever walk into my bar," Lucky had to break it to him that the woman was engaged to his brother.

But it spurred Tessa to ask, looking back and forth between the two guys, "How do you know each other so well? Were you friends before Lucky left Destiny?"

Lucky just exchanged a look with his best friend and said, "No, we met out in California. Duke's like a brother to me, though." Then he glanced in Rachel's direction, adding, "No offense to Mike."

"Well then, Duke," Rachel began, pausing to sip on her drink, "how did you end up living *here*, in Lucky's home area, when *Lucky* didn't even live here?" Then she turned to Lucky. "And where were *you* while Duke was *here*?"

The fact was, when they'd left the Devil's Assassins, they'd decided it would be safer to split up. As for the places they'd both settled, there were additional reasons, which would make a good enough answer now. "We were traveling together and passed through here," Lucky explained—and in fact, that was when he'd hooked up with Sharon—"and Duke liked the area."

"I've got family in eastern Indiana," Duke explained. "This is close enough without being *too close*, if you know what I mean."

"I do," Rachel said emphatically, giving Lucky the idea

that maybe more people had family issues than he realized. Of course, few could have family problems as big as his.

"And guess I was ready for . . . something quieter," Duke went on, "after living in California awhile."

Lucky picked up where Duke left off. "And *I* wasn't ready to, uh . . . be back home yet, so I ended up in Milwaukee. Back then, I liked being in a city, where it was busier." *Where it was so much easier to blend in and less people asked questions about you—like this one.* "Plus, since Harley Davidson's headquarters is there, it has a big biker population, so I figured it would be a good place to start my business—and I was right."

"Then . . . what brought you home?" Rachel asked.

Good question. Which only Duke and Tessa knew the answer to. "Just . . . time for a change," he finally said. He already liked Rachel and didn't enjoy holding back the truth, but he'd grown used to it over the years, and this wasn't the time or the way for his family to find out he had a child.

Though in response, his brother's fiancée made a teasingly suspicious face. "*That's* a mysterious answer."

And Lucky just tried to keep smiling even as he lowered his gaze. "Guess I'm just a mysterious guy."

Just then, big, bald Spider Conway marched up on the other side of Rachel, leaning in to plant his face directly before hers. "Hello, you sexy thing. If you're lookin' for a man who can take care of you right, you just found him." Sounded to Lucky like Spider had had a few too many.

Behind the bar, Duke just shook his head and said, "Rachel, this is Spider."

And Lucky waited for Rachel to cower in fear— God knew the man was intimidating, even in the biker crowd—but instead she boldly replied, "Thanks for the offer, Spider, but I *already* have a man who takes care of me right."

Only Spider didn't appear to be convinced. "Not like *I* can. Does he have one of these?" Lucky cringed, worried about what the hell he might show her, so it was a relief when the big man spun around to flash the black widow tattooed across the back of his head.

"Uh, no," Rachel said, then turned toward Tessa to mouth, *Thank God.*

"Then what's so great about this guy? What's he got that I don't?" Spider demanded, promising, "I can give you good lovin' all night long, baby."

Lucky was just about to stand up and suggest Spider move along, when Rachel replied, "Well, I love that he's a cop. A really mean, protective one, too."

Spider immediately took a step back, throwing his hands up like he'd just been attacked. "Hey now, I never laid a finger on you, so don't go threatenin' me."

"*Spider*," Duke said firmly. "Go say hi to Gypsy. She looks lonely."

A glance across the bar toward the chick everyone called Gypsy revealed that she didn't look lonely at all—but she *did* look as drunk as Spider and like someone who might welcome his advances. Spider looked Gypsy's way, then wordlessly started toward her. At least the dude was easy to distract.

"He's harmless, by the way," Duke informed Rachel, then dropped his gaze to her near-empty glass. "Another sex on the beach?"

She appeared to consider it, but then said, "I'm driving. One's probably enough."

So Duke drew his chin down slightly. "You're not leaving *already*?"

When Lucky saw Rachel glance at Tessa, as if seeking guidance, he quickly volunteered, "I can bring Tessa home, if you're ready to take off."

And as Rachel cast a calm but knowing smile to say, "That's okay—I don't mind staying awhile longer," he sensed that his brother wasn't the only protective one. Rachel was still sizing him up, still deciding if it was okay to leave Tessa here with him.

But he didn't mind—he was glad Tessa had people who cared about her.

Of course, at the same time, he was dying to get her alone, too. Though maybe . . . hell, if Rachel had no intention of giving him any private time with Tessa, maybe that was fate or God or something telling him to stick to the plan. The plan he'd always stuck to. The don't-get-involved-with-a-woman-who-could-get-hurt-because-of-you plan. He knew what he *wanted* to do. And maybe it was the shot of whiskey he'd consumed added to a couple of beers, or maybe it was the talk he'd had with Duke earlier, but he *wanted* to just forget the past and give Little Miss Hot Stuff what they both craved. He just didn't know if he *could*. If he could *let himself*.

Yet at the same time, he also wasn't sure he could resist any longer. The little bit of red lace peeking up out of her top was too tempting—teasing him, beckoning him, and every time he caught a glimpse of it, his erection stiffened further. He'd been trying to avoid getting this close to his sexy neighbor—but now that he was . . . shit, he was only human.

"Hells bells," Duke muttered, out of the blue.

"What, dude?" Lucky asked.

Duke stared toward the front door but shot Lucky a quick glance. "Red just walked in."

"I'll be damned," Lucky said. And when Duke met his gaze, longer this time, he knew what they were both thinking: It would be just like Red to come up to the bar and start spouting shit that could give Tessa and Rachel a lot more clues about their past in California.

"Who's Red?" Tessa asked, leaning into him slightly. Damn, he liked when she did that.

"Nobody important," Duke said.

But since Duke had made him *sound* important, Lucky added, "Guy we used to know. And don't like. That's all."

Duke continued eyeing Red unhappily. "Maybe I oughta just kick his ass out. I thought I'd pretty much asked him to move along the last time he showed up. I didn't think he'd be back."

But Lucky shook his head, his arm still comfortably around Tessa. "I'm painting the guy's bike, remember? I gotta deal with him some more." Then he decided *he'd* take care of it. So he reluctantly withdrew from Tessa—God, her curves were warm and sweet to hold onto—and got to his feet. "Going to the bathroom. I'll be back."

On the way there, though, he deliberately passed by Red, who just stood leaning up against the front wall of the bar. And after they exchanged greetings, Lucky said, "Uh, listen, Red, do me a favor and hang back here, huh? Don't come up to the bar."

Red's brow knit. "Why's that?"

"Thing is, Duke doesn't like you, and you'd best stay clear of him, not piss him off."

As Lucky might have predicted, Red appeared to be more hurt than angry. "Oh. Well . . . hell—don't know what I did to him, but all right. Sure don't wanna make him mad."

Lucky gave him a short nod of approval. "It's nothing personal," he lied. "You just remind him of somebody he used to know."

There. One bullet dodged. If he knew Red, he'd do exactly as Lucky had asked and not come anywhere near Duke—or Tessa and Rachel. Sometimes with a guy like Red, you just had to be blunt and spell things out.

And now that he no longer had to worry about Red spilling the beans about his life as a Devil's Assassin, he could concentrate on something much more pleasant—Tessa. But the question still remained: Would he or wouldn't he give in to the lust coursing like wildfire through his veins?

"Well?" Tessa whispered to Rachel as Lucky headed across the bar.

Rachel didn't even pretend not to know what she was asking. "Okay, yes," she said, even if she sounded none too happy about it. "He's hot. In a big, scary biker way."

"And?" Tessa prodded.

Rachel pursed her lips. "And . . . . he doesn't seem like a terrible guy."

Tessa offered a sharp, well-pleased nod. "Aha—so you admit it."

"But I'm still not leaving you here alone with him," Rachel said, her gaze intent and her voice razor sharp.

Tessa simply rolled her eyes. "I'll be fine. I'm not nervous anymore, and I completely trust Lucky to look out for me."

Rachel let out a heavy breath. "It's not that I don't trust *him*—exactly. It's that there's a whole *bar* full of questionable people here."

"And you think you can save me from *all* of them if something bad happens?"

"Safety in numbers, girlfriend," Rachel insisted.

Feeling a little giddy in response to Lucky's change in attitude toward her tonight, and maybe slightly intoxicated, Tessa glanced at Duke farther down the bar, now serving up bottles of beer to some newly arrived bikers. The arm facing them sported one small tattoo—his initials, and on the other she'd noticed a detailed motorcycle done in ink. "So, if you didn't have Mike," she ventured to Rachel, curious, "you and Duke?" She raised her eyebrows suggestively.

Her friend studied Duke a for a few long seconds, then said, "Um, potentially tempting in a dangerous way—but no. I'll leave the biker lust to you. And hope you get it out of your system soon."

Being reminded that she really *wasn't* a biker chick and really *wasn't* comfortable around most of the people here, Tessa nodded. "I will. I mean, I think." She stopped, blinked. "I mean, quit rushing me—I haven't even gotten to the good part yet."

Rachel let out a laugh. "Okay, okay, you're right. Have your fun, or your fling, or whatever, with Lucky—and then you can move on with your life."

Yes, that was exactly what Tessa wanted, and what suddenly seemed within her reach. Even more so when Lucky's warm palm closed over her shoulder as he returned from the bathroom. As she turned to look up at him, he leaned in near her ear. "Take a walk with me, hot stuff." And when he smoothly slipped his hand into hers, she felt herself melting off the stool without thought.

She peeked over her shoulder toward Rachel, who moved her lips to say, *Be careful.* But the truth was, Tessa hadn't come here to be careful—she'd come to be daring. So she just smiled, then let Lucky lead her wherever he wanted her to go.

They crossed the room amid the *clack* of billiard balls and an old Motley Crue song that pumped through the air, until Lucky drew her back a short hallway, where he tried a closed door, which didn't open. "Damn," he muttered. "Of all the nights for Duke to start locking his office."

When he tried another door, also locked, he let out a deep sigh, then simply turned around and leaned her back against the nearest wall, his face instantly close to hers. His body, too. "I just wanted to talk to you alone, babe," he explained.

Her breasts ached, and the juncture of her thighs pulsed. It was suddenly hard to catch her breath. "Okay."

"I . . . wanted to apologize," he said. "For walking away

from you. Last week. At the waterfall." Pressing one hand against the wall next to her head in a way that made her feel pleasantly trapped, he looked—felt—so big, masculine. As he peered down at her from beneath shaded lids, the warmth of his breath grazed her skin.

In response, she simply shook her head, then found a couple of words. "It's okay."

"No," he said, his voice dropping, going utterly deep and sexy, "it's not. I . . . didn't *want* to walk away."

She swallowed, every pore of her flesh seeming to throb with the strange connection that always stretched so tautly between their bodies. Now *her* voice went lower, too. "What . . . did you want to do?"

"This," he rasped. Then he lifted his other hand to cup her jaw and lowered his mouth to hers.

The kiss moved through Tessa's entire body like a slow, warm, engulfing storm. She sank into it, embraced it, let it swallow her. It was, without a doubt, the best thing she'd felt in four long years.

As Lucky's tongue pressed between her lips, she met it with her own and heat flowed strong and potent between her legs. The tang of whiskey incited her senses further. And on instinct, she lifted her hands to his chest, felt his heartbeat, the warmth of his body, all that was hard and broad and male about him, soon curling her fingers into the T-shirt he wore as the intensity of the kiss overcame her.

When finally the kiss ended, she opened her eyes and found Lucky staring back at her, looking as aroused as she felt. She heard them both breathing, felt the rise and fall of his chest as he pressed his body close to hers. "You taste good," he murmured, their mouths just an inch apart. "Like cranberries."

"You taste good, too," she managed. Though it didn't matter what the taste was—anything he tasted like right now would have pleasured her, added one more sensation. In one sense, Tessa couldn't believe a mere kiss had left her so utterly poleaxed, but on the other hand, she'd been waiting so long. For a kiss like this. From a sexy man like this.

Now they just looked at each other, and the connection of their eyes felt like enough in that heady moment; it felt like sex. The first low, provocative notes of AC/DC's "Touch Too Much" sounded over the loudspeakers and the pungently seductive lyrics only pulled her that much more deeply into the moment, into him. His dark eyes pinned her in place, so that she felt captured by him, but she liked it.

When he reached up between them to run one fingertip ever-so-gently across the top edge of her bra, visible above her cami, her breath grew ragged, her stomach tight. The sensation skittered through her, straight to the juncture of her thighs. "Want to know a secret, hot stuff?" he whispered darkly.

"Uh-huh," she mumbled.

He dropped his gaze to her breasts—which were heaving now—so she did, too. It was an admittedly sexy view and, for a second, she could scarcely believe this was her. "These little glimpses of lace," he said slowly, "have been driving me wild since you walked in the door."

She sucked in her breath, tried to hide the quiver in her voice. "I . . . remembered you like red."

A small, wicked grin made his brown eyes sparkle. "I do. But that's not why it's driving me wild."

"Why then?" she whispered.

"Because I want to get underneath it to the rest of you."

His words stole her breath and when he kissed her this time, she instantly circled her arms around his neck—she had to, or else she might have collapsed beneath the heat they generated. Each firm kiss he delivered was long and deep and swallowing, enough to make Tessa forget where they were or even who she was. She'd never been so lost to simply kissing a man.

Of course, there was nothing simple about Lucky's kisses—they were warm and utterly intoxicating, injecting an incredible energy into her veins even as they weakened her. His strong arms left her feeling all the more safe and protected—she couldn't think of any place in the world she'd rather be than in Lucky Romo's embrace.

When a large noise came directly from Tessa's right, they both stopped kissing and looked up to see an older, rather overweight biker stumbling drunkenly around the corner, probably looking for the bathroom. "Can I have some, too?" he asked.

"Back off," Lucky growled, then ushered Tessa quickly away, to the end of a short hall and through a steel door with an exit sign lit above it. Suddenly, they were outside, behind the building, where crisp night air bit at her skin and the world was much quieter—only the echo of AC/DC could be heard reverberating through the walls now.

Before she knew it, Lucky's arms were back around her and he'd resumed kissing her, whispering in between, "Too cold out here, babe?"

"No," she breathed. "I'm fine."

It *was* cold, but a blizzard couldn't have pulled her away from him.

He kissed her again and again, until she was utterly lost to him, until hot and cold didn't even register anymore, until . . . his hands eased downward, over her ass, drawing her close, so blessedly close that his erection nestled against her through the denim. Oh God, *yes*. It was the perfect union between hard and soft, and maybe the best thing she'd ever felt in her life. Until, that is, they began to move together, to grind, to seek that ultimate pleasure in each other. It was natural, it was primal, and Tessa surrendered to it without thought.

Her breath came short as his kisses dropped to her neck and she clutched at his broad shoulders. Soon he was lifting her, hands still on her bottom, up onto the hood of an old car she hadn't even noticed parked out there among crates and boxes. A dim security light shone down on them.

Their eyes met once more as Lucky smoothly drew his hands around until they were splayed across her thighs, the tips of his fingers edging beneath her skirt. She sucked in her breath. Nothing about the setting was as she'd imagined it, but seldom in her life had anything felt so powerful, so right. Everything about the moment was raw and honest and utterly intense. She didn't care where they were—she just wanted more of him.

So when he parted her legs and stepped up between them, she didn't even think about resisting. And when he used his hands to slide her rear to the edge of the car, pressing his hard-on back against her, under her skirt, right up against the lace panties she wore, she let out a low moan.

"You feel so good," he murmured deeply, moving his delicious arousal against that most sensitive part of her again.

"*You* feel *amazing*," she breathed near his ear, then kissed his cheek, letting him know she wanted still more. More kissing, more everything.

"I want to take you home with me," he whispered. "I want to be with you all . . . night . . . long."

She drew in her breath at the heady promise and bit her lip in passion as Lucky slipped his thumb beneath the straps of her cami and bra, slowly lowering them from one shoulder, baring it to the night completely.

And that's when a racket came from inside the bar, so loud they could hear it through the thick door. Something crashing. Someone yelling. She felt his muscles tense at the distraction.

He let out a disgusted sigh. "Shit—I hope Spider isn't making trouble."

And every nerve in Tessa's body went on red alert. "Rachel," she murmured in concern. In fact, it just occurred to her that she'd abandoned Rachel in there—the very thing Rachel had refused to do to her, whether she'd liked it or not.

"Duke'll look out for her," Lucky promised. But even as he eased his arms warmly back around her, he glanced uneasily toward the door—through which they could hear more yelling—and said, "Aw, damn—better go see what the hell's going on in there."

Tessa bit her lip and nodded as she reached to move her straps back onto her shoulder.

And Lucky paused, lifting his hand to her cheek. "Sorry, hot stuff."

She just shook her head. Inside, she was going crazy, her body hungering for more—but after realizing she'd left Rachel alone, she also experienced an almost frantic need to get back inside. She even took the lead, hopping down from the car and grabbing Lucky's hand to head toward the back entrance.

Lucky opened the heavy door and together they rushed in—him stepping in front of her, which was probably best. There for a moment, she'd almost forgotten where they were, but she supposed *anything* could be happening in the biker bar.

As they emerged from the hallway into the main room, Tessa tried to make sense of what she saw—which could have been far worse, but still shocked the hell out of her. A stool had been toppled, and Rachel stood between Duke and her fiancé, arms thrust to either side to keep them apart.

Oh God. How had Mike ended up here? Maybe Tessa's first thought had been wrong—maybe things *couldn't* be far worse, since Mike looked completely outraged and she knew it was, ultimately, all her fault.

She tuned in to the shouting, most of which seemed to be taking place between Mike and Rachel now, even as music continued blaring around them all. "What on earth are you even *doing* here?" Rachel was yelling.

"We decided to go to Bleachers instead of the Dew Drop, and I saw your damn car outside!" Bleachers was a nearby sports bar. "I was *sure* it couldn't be yours, but the hell if it wasn't!"

"Oh, so it's okay if *you* have a change of plans and don't let *me* know, but I can't decide where *I* want to go without running it by you first?"

"*No!* Not if it's *here*, for God's sake! Jesus Christ, woman, have you completely lost your mind?"

Tessa didn't know why Duke was even involved—maybe he'd mistakenly tried to protect Rachel from Mike. Or maybe Mike had jumped to conclusions if he'd come in and seen Rachel talking with Duke across the bar. Whatever the case, the whole scene was a mess—and she felt the overpowering need to intervene.

She marched up to where they stood arguing and held up her hands. "Stop, this is all my fault!" Then she looked to Mike. "Don't be mad at her. I made her come here—she didn't want to, but I twisted her arm."

Mike just stared at her, clearly dumbfounded—whether due to the way she was dressed or because she'd dragged Rachel to Gravediggers, she didn't know. Probably both. "Why on earth would *you* want to come here?"

Oh boy. That's when it hit her. Somewhere behind her Lucky stood watching, seeing his brother for the first time since he was eighteen years old. This wasn't exactly the family reunion she'd envisioned them having. Yet she had no choice but to answer Mike's question—even if her voice came out softer than intended. "To see your brother." And without quite meaning to, she motioned vaguely over her shoulder.

Then Mike's focus shifted from her . . . to a spot behind her. And she turned to find the two brothers gaping at each other, the gruff cop and the wayward biker face-to-face at last.

"Lucky?" Mike gasped, his expression filled with shock, anger, pain.

She heard the breath Lucky expelled from where she stood a few yards away. "Mike," he said quietly.

I wish to be a better man than I have been . . .

Charlotte Brontë, *Jane Eyre*

Nine

Lucky felt rooted in place, like he couldn't move.

And maybe that was good because his first instinct was to run away from this—to just turn around and walk out the door. He was good at running—he'd been doing it all his life. But right now, his body wouldn't let him. He had to face his brother, ready or not.

Mike's Adam's apple shifted as he swallowed, making him look uncomfortable, upset. At the same time Lucky watched his brother's expression, he tried to take in the ways he'd changed, grown up, aged. Like Lucky, he was bigger than he'd been as a young man, his shoulders broader. He appeared strong, healthy—although now he possessed small creases around his eyes. He looked, at the moment, tired.

He sensed Mike taking in the same with him—the changes. The ink, the muscles. And Lucky felt strange to realize he'd gotten a little taller, and more muscular, than his big brother.

After what felt like a long time, Mike simply began shaking his head. "What the *hell*, Lucky?" he said, clearly angry. "You couldn't pick up a fucking phone? Send a fucking letter, or e-mail? You couldn't let us know you're still alive and breathing someplace?"

His attitude pissed Lucky off. He knew Mike and their parents had plenty to be angry about, but if Mike cared so damn much, couldn't he let it show a little the first time they set eyes on each other? This was exactly why Lucky hadn't let them know he was home—not just because of the complicated awkwardness of it all, but because he'd feared this very thing; he'd almost known they wouldn't make him feel . . . missed. Or welcome. Instead Mike could only remind him what a screw-up he'd always been.

"Maybe I didn't think anybody gave a shit," Lucky bit off, his body tensing with his *own* rage now.

Mike just looked at him like he was crazy, stupid. "*What?* You didn't think your own family cared if you were dead or alive?" His tone remained filled with just as much disdain, implying Lucky was an idiot.

And despite the fact that it felt a little humiliating to admit this in front of the whole damn bar, Lucky was completely honest. "That's pretty much the size of it, yeah."

Mike just stood there shaking his head, still as if Lucky wasn't making any sense—when, in fact, he thought he was being perfectly clear. Eyes squinted and glassy, still disgusted, Mike growled, "Damn it, I don't know if I want to hug you or punch you in the mouth."

Lucky just glared at him. "Guess that's your call, big brother." Then he held his hands out to his sides, palms up.

His gaze never broke with Mike's as he came nearer, and Lucky had no idea what Mike was going to do—but he began to feel, strangely, what it might be like to get a hug from his brother after all these years. And he'd just begun to realize he wouldn't mind that, even here, even in front of all these people—when Mike drew back his fist and landed it squarely on Lucky's jaw, a hard, jolting blow that knocked him back two steps.

Everything around him went fuzzy, not from being hit, but from the surprise of it, and the surprise that it wounded him so much—inside. He felt like he and Mike were in some kind of a weird bubble—he could vaguely hear Rachel saying Mike's name, could see Tessa in his peripheral vision covering her mouth with her hand, her eyes gone wide. He sensed Duke standing back, but ready to defend Lucky if need be. Yet Lucky just kept looking at Mike.

He could hit him back; any other time in his adult life when someone had hit him, that's what he'd done, hit them back. And whether it was a short scuffle or a long, knock-down, drag-out brawl, he'd usually been the last man standing. He didn't lift weights for nothing—his muscles were one way he protected himself in this world. And given his size, he knew—he thought they *both* knew—that he could pound Mike into the ground right now if he wanted. But he just stood there.

Maybe because somewhere deep inside him, he thought Mike had the right to take a swing like that.

Or maybe because nothing that had happened when they were kids had really been Mike's fault, and he was just now beginning to see in Mike's eyes that he'd hurt him by leaving.

Or maybe . . . he just didn't want to hit his brother, didn't want to *hurt* his brother. Not anymore.

"You can hit me again if you want," Lucky said after a minute. "You can beat the hell out of me if it'll make you feel better."

Mike's expression remained cold, unforgiving.

And Lucky's heart broke a little more than it already had. Damn it. *I didn't think I felt shit like that anymore. I thought I was done caring what my family thinks of me.*

Apparently, he'd been wrong. He swallowed, hard, trying to keep the emotion from showing on his face. He didn't have much in ways, but at least he had his pride.

"It won't," Mike finally said. Then he turned his back, grabbed Rachel's hand, and said, "Let's go. We're leaving."

Lucky thought it looked like Rachel wanted to say something in response—though she held her tongue, probably wanting to just get this moment over with, which suited Lucky fine. He faced Tessa then—only to have Mike stop and look her way as well. "Come on, Tessa," his brother said.

She simply blinked, pretty and shockingly pure even in that slightly sinful outfit. "Huh?"

"You're going with us," Mike said, his jaw set. "I'm not leaving *you* here, either."

She sucked in her breath, and Lucky had half a mind to object, but the truth was, he didn't want to make any more trouble for Tessa and her friend. He was *used* to trouble—but it sucked, and he wouldn't heap it on someone who didn't deserve it. "Go," Lucky told her softly, just as Rachel made a prodding face at her to say, "Just come on already." Then she shoved Tessa's purse at her, which she must have been holding on to while Tessa and Lucky were outside.

Tessa gave him one last look and their eyes locked—right before she turned and left him there.

Upon reaching the parking lot, Mike had announced that Rachel would ride with him in his pickup and Tessa would drive Rachel's car—they'd follow her to her cabin.

But it was all Tessa could do to drive Rachel's BMW—her hands trembled for the first few minutes after leaving Gravediggers, and even after that subsided, she remained tense. *Did that really just happen?* She blinked, then let out a sigh, trying to focus on the road. She'd never seen

Mike so enraged, nor had she ever witnessed such pain in Lucky's eyes. How had the night ended this way?

It ended this way because you were selfish and dragged your friend someplace she didn't want to go.

And after this, Lucky probably wouldn't want anything more to do with her—and she couldn't blame him. Clearly, he and Mike weren't ready to see each other—and because of her, they'd had it out in public.

Tessa kept reliving the moment Mike had hit Lucky, and it upset her more each time, until she was almost as angry with Mike as she was with herself. She'd come to like Mike since his engagement to Rachel, but she hadn't liked him tonight. How could he hit his brother like that? She didn't know everything that stood between them, but it had still felt unduly harsh.

As she wound the car across the country byways, soon turning onto Whisper Falls Road, Tessa tried to wrap her head around everything else that had happened, too—but the night had felt like a whirlwind and it all came to her in a mishmash of memories and feelings.

Lucky kissing her, and kissing her, and kissing her.

Rachel had gotten in big trouble with her fiancé now, thanks to Tessa.

Lucky running his fingertip along the upper ridge of her breast.

Mike had seen her dressed like a trollop and probably thought she'd gone insane.

Lucky splaying his strong hands across her thighs, sending bursts of heat shooting to her core.

Rachel now knew Lucky wasn't an awful guy. And they'd actually gotten some tidbits about his past—even if he'd been evasive at moments.

And . . . if Mike hadn't shown up, Tessa was pretty sure she'd have had sex with Lucky right there, behind Gravediggers, on the hood of that old car!

Except then she remembered . . . he'd told her he wanted

to take her home with him. Which maybe meant . . . he thought she was worth more than just a quickie outside a bar. And the truth was, her body had been so ready, so primed, so eager, that if they hadn't been interrupted, she wouldn't have been very bothered by where they were or how sudden it all was—but she liked knowing Lucky had wanted it to last longer; she liked the idea of him wanting to take her into his bed.

By the time she pulled into her driveway, Mike's truck right behind her, her heart pounded with renewed lust. So much that she had to grit her teeth and try to will away the pulse between her legs before she could exit the car and face the matter at hand, namely the problems she'd created for Rachel with her selfishness and impatience.

Finally, she took a deep breath and opened the door—to find Rachel approaching her in the glare of Mike's headlights. Upon getting out, Tessa gave Rachel a hug and said into her ear, "I'm so, so sorry, Rach. I didn't mean to be so selfish. I never dreamed things would turn out this way."

When Rachel drew back to look at her, Tessa was surprised to see such calm understanding in her friend's blue eyes. "It's okay, Tessa, really."

Tessa just sighed. "I didn't mean to cause a rift between you and Mike. I never imagined he'd show up there."

"I know. But . . . he's a lot more upset about Lucky than mad at me. Don't worry—everything will be okay."

"Between Mike and Lucky?" Tessa asked.

Rachel gritted her teeth, her expression troubled. "Well, I meant between Mike and *me*. I don't know about Mike and Lucky—I really don't." Then she bit her lip and met Tessa's gaze. "What about *you* and Lucky?"

Tessa let out a heavy breath, her thoughts drawn back to the profound passion they'd shared—albeit briefly. She wasn't sure she'd ever experienced such intense need with a guy, such a powerful urge to simply go with it—with the moment, with the man, with everything he made her feel. "Well, things were getting really, um, *great* . . . until Mike showed up. Now, though . . ." She stopped, shook her head. "He'll probably hate me. I knew Lucky had reasons for not wanting to see his family, and it's all my fault this happened."

"He'd be crazy to blame you," Rachel said.

Yet the thought drew Tessa's eyes toward where Mike sat waiting. "But sometimes emotions clearly get the best of people."

Lucky raced through the night, probably going a little too fast on his Deuce, but having to focus on the road was a good distraction from what had just happened. Not that it wasn't all still roaring through him, but he gripped his handlebars tight and tried to feel each bend and curve in the road. He tried to let the brisk night wind rip his emotions away. All of them. The way he'd wanted Tessa. The pain of his confrontation with Mike. He wished he'd never come back here. He didn't need this shit.

But then he remembered. He had a son—a son he'd be meeting as soon as Sharon gave the okay. So he *had* to be back here.

For once in your life, you're gonna do the stand-up thing, you're gonna do something right.

Even if coming home to this backwater town kills you.

Limp Bizkit's version of "Behind Blue Eyes" played over the sound system on his bike, so he tried to focus on that, too—tried to let the somber song calm him down. But he felt the song's words too much. What a fucked-up night. And there for a while, it had seemed like such a *good* night.

But maybe . . . hell, maybe everything happened for a reason. Maybe his self-righteous brother had punched him in the mouth because he wasn't meant to be with Tessa the way he wanted; maybe this was fate's nasty way of telling him he wasn't meant to quit worrying about the past coming back to kick him in the ass. After all, this was a cruel reminder—the past *had* just come back, in a different way. To kick him in the ass—and to punch him in the mouth.

A few months ago, life had been easy. Well, wait, no—not easy. Not . . . good. But normal. He'd had a routine, and a set of rules he lived by, and everything had been on an even keel. For years, more or less. Sure, you run with a crowd of rough bikers, sometimes you had to push your weight around or even get into the occasional bar fight. But anything that had happened in the past ten years had all been petty shit for Lucky, nothing that mattered. And here, back in Destiny, it felt like *everything* mattered. He felt things here *more*. Whether it was anxiety over meeting his kid, or worry over his family, or lusting for the pretty girl next door.

Right now, all Lucky wanted was to turn it off. All of it. Even Tessa. Because tonight had reminded him in a whole new, brutal way how in small towns everything was intertwined, how everybody was a part of everybody else's life, and how fucking complicated that always made things. No wonder he preferred city living, where people kept to themselves and left other people alone.

Hell, in nearly ten years in Milwaukee few people had ever even asked him a question that had caused him to mention California. In the city, no one made him remember, or worry—at least not any more than he did on his own naturally. Here, one night out with a woman he was attracted to and he'd been forced to bring up those California days and fudge answers and feel that ugly weight of keeping ugly secrets. And all *that* forced him to ask still new and troubling questions: Could a girl like Tessa ever truly *get* him? Understand him? Accept everything about him? This whole night had just served to remind him how different they were.

He wanted to go to bed and sleep until noon tomorrow. He wanted to forget. It was the closest he could come to . . . not being here, to running away from it all . . . without running away.

As his bike rumbled into the driveway, he glanced down at Tessa's house, sitting quietly in the dark, all the lights out.

Goodnight, hot stuff.

Good*bye*, hot stuff.

Tessa lay tossing and turning—she couldn't sleep; she couldn't even relax. She'd been home for two hours and it was officially late now, but she was wide awake. And distressed.

Or was that . . . sexually frustrated?

Both, she supposed.

She wore the "Hot Stuff" pajamas with the little red peppers on the pants, but couldn't help remembering how sexy she'd felt in her lacy red bra and the matching undies Lucky would now never see. She'd truly been bold tonight, and it had worked—until her grand plan had all come crashing down around her.

She hated the way she'd left things with Lucky, that she'd left him just standing there; she hated that she'd let Mike boss her around, even if he'd had good intentions. Now, she couldn't get her big, brawny neighbor off her mind—partly because of all the making out they'd done and the sex they didn't have, but also because of everything else, too.

Like all the secrets surrounding him—those she knew and those she didn't. And because seeing him with Mike tonight, and even with his buddy Duke, had opened up all kinds of new uncertainties. From the moment she'd met him, he'd seemed like a walking contradiction—the scary, tattooed guy who helped her lure Mr. Knightley back with a bowl of milk. And the more she learned about him, the more that held true. Was he the dangerous biker

with secrets? Or the dad who wanted to give his son a
great second home he would love? Was he the big, burly
guy who could clearly snap someone in two like a twig?
Or was he the man who'd touched her so tenderly and
refused to defend himself against his brother's fist?

She let out a sigh. *You'll never know now.*

After all, he'd forgiven her for being nosy and forcing
him to come clean about having a child. But that, added
to the trouble she'd unwittingly brought his way tonight,
would surely be too much. She could easily envision
Lucky continuing to do what he'd done earlier this week:
keeping his distance from her, avoiding her when she was
working in his house. And then, when the job was over,
they'd just go back to being neighbors, the kind who casually waved when coming or going.

Just then, a loud knocking pierced her thoughts and
made her flinch—then bolt upright in bed. What the hell
was that?

When it came again, it registered that someone was
beating on her door. She had company so seldom that it
had thrown her off. Plus it was the middle of the night.

As she flipped on a light and tromped out into her living
room, she thought of ax murderers, but decided they
probably wouldn't knock. Although now seemed like a
good time to have had a peephole, and she thought briefly
of Rachel and Amy's worries about her cabin being so
far from town. The only thing that made her yank the
door open was the logical thought creeping slowly into
her brain—that there was only one person who lived anywhere near her: Lucky.

Still, even when she found him waiting on the other
side, she had no idea what to expect now. She only knew
that his dark eyes looked so wild at the moment that it
made her draw back slightly.

"I tried to stay away, tried to go home and go to sleep,"
he said.

And then—*oh*. She understood. He . . . he still wanted her.

"Why?" she breathed, stunned. Because after tonight on the hood of that car, how could he not know she wanted him, too?

He let out a breath, shook his head, swallowed visibly, and appeared wholly uncertain. "I'm not sure if . . . I'm good for you."

She simply blinked and asked the same question again. "Why?"

Pressing his lips together, he hesitated. "It's complicated. But . . . I couldn't stay away."

Tessa bit her lip, then pulled in her breath as her heart began to beat harder, warmth expanding through her chest. "Thank God," she said. "I can't sleep, either."

A small, deep sound of passion escaped Lucky's throat just before he lifted both hands to her face and kissed her with the same heat that had been building inside her for the past few hours, too. It nearly stole the breath from her lungs, left her weak, nearly collapsing into his arms.

"Are you okay?" he whispered as she slumped against his chest, pressing her palms there.

She lifted her gaze to his and felt the full measure of how large and tall and broad he was. "I just . . . want you," she whispered.

He let out a low moan, then lowered his hands to her ass through her pajama bottoms, lifted her until her legs wrapped naturally around his hips, and pressed his erection exactly where she needed to feel it. Then he took a few long steps with her in his grasp and fell with her onto her couch, pinning her there with his hard body.

Their gazes met hotly, and she could feel his breath on her lips as he asked, "Are you sure you're ready for what's coming, hot stuff?"

Come to me—come to me entirely now.

Charlotte Brontë, *Jane Eyre*

Ten

Tessa didn't even have to think. "Oh *yeah*," she practically purred. In fact, she was reasonably certain she'd never been more ready for anything in her life.

She peered up into Lucky's eyes, ran her fingertips over his stubbled cheeks. She'd seen plenty of expressions on Lucky's face—she'd seen him angry, she'd seen him hurt, she'd seen him distant and withdrawn. She'd seen him cocky, confident, teasing, and kind. But the expression he wore right now was the one she liked the best—he looked like he was going to devour her.

A second later, his kiss engulfed her once more, deep and with intent, like a man who knew what he wanted and was going to take it. He didn't hesitate to thrust his tongue into her mouth and she liked the small sense it gave of being invaded by him.

His erection remained right where she wanted it, pressing between her legs—which she'd instantly, willingly parted for him. As they kissed some more, she skimmed her palms over his strong, wide shoulders, combed her fingers through his long, silky hair. Moonlight through the window combined with the soft glow of the lamp from the bedroom to allow her to study him, and to watch the way he touched her; cupping her jaw in one hand, he let the other glide down over her neck, then pressed it flat against her chest to slide it ever-so-slowly between her aching breasts.

That's when he glanced to her chest, then back up, giving her a wolfish grin. "You're wearing my favorite shirt."

She bit her lip, met his heated gaze with her own. While she'd fantasized about Lucky seeing her—exploring her—in her racy red lingerie, now she was glad it was happening like this. Because this was *her*, the real her. The girl who wore "Hot Stuff" pajamas far more often than sexy bras. And cotton panties more frequently than lace ones. And even if he'd liked the way she'd looked earlier, he didn't seem the least bit disappointed in her late-night appearance *now*. Oh God—it hit her just then that she didn't even have on makeup. But then she calmed down, remembering once more: *He doesn't care about that.*

The realization made her reach up to kiss him again, luxuriating in the feel of his hands on her skin. He'd eased them under her top, over her ribs, and she longed for them to rise higher, higher.

"Could we go in your bedroom?" he murmured deeply.

She was unable to summon words amid her overwhelming desire. "Uh-huh."

He leaned in to lower a warm kiss to her neck, whispering, "Couch is too small. I wanna be able to take my time."

Oh my. The words fluttered through her like the best promise anyone had ever made. "Okay," she breathed.

And instead of getting up off her, he said, "Wrap your

arms and legs around me, babe," and when she did, he easily hoisted her up until he was on his feet, saying, "Down the hall?"

"Mmm-hmm." She was simply too excited to speak, and glad at least one of them was able to communicate sensibly.

Lucky found the way and soon lowered her gently to her bed—the covers already drawn back from before. Despite being dim, the lamp on the bedside table allowed her to see him better than in the living room as he gazed down on her, then kicked off his shoes and lifted one knee to the sheet alongside her. Now that she was past being intimidated by his appearance, she thought him truly beautiful—a beautiful man with olive skin, sculpted cheekbones and jaw, and muscles that felt strong and capable when they encircled her.

Feeling aggressive, she reached up, placed her palm on the rippled muscles of his stomach through his T-shirt. Then she closed her fingers around the fabric and pushed upward. "Take this off."

His warm sigh said he liked the request—just before he smoothly removed the black tee over his head and tossed it aside.

She gasped, not only at the sight of his chiseled chest and stomach—but at other things, too. A small scar near his rib cage. A larger, more angry one that slashed down his side. And yet another tattoo he'd been carrying around hidden beneath his shirt, and curving over his heart: *Anna*. He'd had his little sister's name engraved on his skin.

"What?" he whispered at her reaction—but then followed her eyes and said, somberly, "Oh."

She just nodded.

"Keep her close to my heart that way," he said soft, low, then bent over her, stretched out alongside her, and kissed her some more.

He was right—the bed was better. The bed somehow

silently meant, *We can go all night long if we want to*, just as he'd suggested back at Gravediggers.

His kisses reignited all the fire inside her until finally his mouth trailed over her jaw, down onto her neck. Sighing languidly, she bent her head to make it more accessible—her neck was one of her most sensitive areas. He lay on top of her now and slowly smoothed his warm palms down over her breasts and on to her waist. Oh God, just to have that momentary touch—there—delivered more pleasure than he could possibly know. *Oh Lucky, please. Please, more.*

He must have read her mind, or maybe her reaction, since he continued kissing her neck even as he began to roll the bottom of her tank upward over her torso, each motion painstakingly slow. And then his kisses ceased and he raised slightly, peering down, studying his movements, her body. She bit her lip and watched, too, but also lingered over his brown eyes with those long, black lashes and all the secrets that hid behind them.

But the secrets didn't matter right now. Whatever they were, in this moment she didn't care. All she cared about was being with him, connecting with him, letting him make her feel good.

When he rolled the fabric up over her breasts, a low groan escaped his throat and Tessa felt it between her legs. "You're beautiful," he whispered, and a hot spark rippled down her spine.

Then he bent to drag his tongue gently over one beaded nipple, making her shudder and expel a ragged breath. He met her gaze only for a second—before sinking his mouth fully over the peak, beginning to kiss and suckle her, using his hand to mold and caress her other breast, somehow both firm and gentle at once. Oh God, it had been so long since a man had touched her there, kissed her there—she shut her eyes and stroked Lucky's shoulders and simply basked in the wondrous sensations.

Eventually, he kissed his way down her stomach, actually making the muscles there contract, and he peered up at her as he used his teeth to slowly pull the red drawstring below her navel.

Rising to his knees, he said, "Lift up," and she elevated her bottom from the bed long enough for him to tug her pajama pants to her thighs, though he left her panties on. Then he hoisted her feet playfully high as he drew the hot pepper pants the rest of the way off, letting them drop behind him.

They both noticed her tattoo at the same time, on the one ankle still balanced in his palm, near his face. At moments, she practically forgot about it, but when he said in a low, utterly sexy rasp, "Aw, *babe*—what's this?" she was so, so glad she'd gotten it. He studied it closely then, adding, "It's perfect." And she no longer cared if it sagged when she was fifty; she didn't care if every other person in her life hated it when they finally saw it—this moment, and the look in Lucky's eyes, made it completely worth it.

"You like it?" she asked shyly. He'd just said he did, but maybe she wanted to hear it again.

"I *love* it." Then he cast a small grin. "And I'm surprised as hell by it."

And then he kissed it, her ankle, the ink there. Just a *tiny* kiss, but the sensation skittered all the way up her thigh. And then the light little kisses began to move—he kissed his way from her ankle to the inside of her knee.

She drew in her breath when he continued, his kisses moving still closer to her very center—each kiss made her wetter and wetter, made her ache madly. She found herself spreading her legs farther for him without thought or hesitation.

When he swept his hand over her feminine mound through her panties, as if gently petting it, she murmured a shaky "Ohhh." Then, just like the kisses that had traveled the length of her leg, he dropped one sweet, gentle kiss overtop of the blue flowered panties she wore.

After which he rose back to his knees, the fingers of both hands curling into the elastic at her hips. "I want these off, too."

She didn't answer, just lifted, just let him draw the fabric down.

After that, things began to run together for Tessa in a heady, ecstatic sort of blur. Lucky's mouth was between her legs, licking her, pleasuring her, and she was biting her lip, moaning deeply—and coming. That quick.

She'd needed this for so long that it took only seconds for his slow, deep ministrations to push her over the edge of orgasm and she found herself crying out, digging her fingers into the sheets on either side of her, lifting herself to his mouth as the pleasure rushed through her, as brisk and wild as the rush of Whisper Falls.

When the climax had passed and the only remaining sound was her heavy breathing, she opened her eyes to find Lucky peering up at her. Oh God, was it bad to think he looked deliciously naughty between her legs? Especially while giving her that hungry little grin?

Of course not. You have needs. And tonight, finally, this man is fulfilling them. "I want you," she murmured breathily. "Please."

And she hadn't quite planned on saying either of those things, but wasn't sorry she had when Lucky rose up and started undoing his jeans. She sat up and began to help, a little rushed now and no longer shy. A moment later, they were both pushing the denim and underwear to his thighs and Tessa let out a gasp at the sight of him. It was always such a surprise to see that part of a man—maybe in between lovers she forgot how big and hard they got, how utterly different their bodies were from hers. But like the rest of Lucky, this part was beautiful, and she automatically reached out to skim her fingers down his length, as silky to the touch as it was smooth and rigid.

She peered up at him, and as much as she didn't necessarily want to cover up the work of masculine art that was his penis, she asked, "Do you have a condom?"

He gazed down at her touching him and appeared almost unable to speak—until finally he said, "Um, yeah," his voice now scratchy. He took his jeans completely off and dug in the back pocket until he extracted a small foil square from a well-worn leather wallet.

He sat on the bed near her, ripping into it, then said, his voice still surprisingly strained, "Put it on me?" It moved her, made her stomach flinch, that a guy who'd probably had as many sexual encounters in the last few years as she'd had fantasies was so affected by this.

She took the condom from him and balanced it at the tip of his shaft, then slowly rolled downward. Her hands shook, excited and unused to being intimate like this, but she didn't care—she wasn't embarrassed or nervous with Lucky anymore. And when she was done, she followed the raw, blatant urge to wrap her hand around his solid length and gently caress, squeeze him through the thin rubber, listening as he sucked in his breath in response.

Then she lay back on her pillow, so ready she could barely breathe.

Though as Lucky moved back between her parted thighs, coming to hover over her, a matter of practicality bit at her. "I should warn you," she said, "it's . . . been awhile for me. So . . . it might be a little difficult at first."

"I don't think so," he said without hesitation. "You're completely wet." And as if to prove it, he smoothly slid two fingers into her below, the entrance jolting her body lightly and causing another moan to erupt from her throat. It had been so long since a man had been inside her in any way whatsoever that the sensation struck her powerfully.

Even so, she replied, "But *you're* so . . ."

"What?" he whispered.

She swallowed. "Big." And he was. Not scary big, but good big. She instantly remembered Rachel once describing Mike exactly that way—and now she found herself thinking that some things must run in the family.

"I'll be careful, babe," he rasped, lowering his body further over hers now. "I promise." Then he lifted one hand to her cheek. "I'd never wanna hurt you."

And with that, he pressed into her, the sensation welcome yet undeniably snug—enough that she had to grit her teeth and hold her breath for a few seconds.

Until she realized the short moment of discomfort was over, almost as soon as it had begun, and he was inside her, and . . . oh God, had anything ever felt so wonderful, so right? She peered up into his eyes and said exactly what she was thinking. "You feel *sooo* good."

He let out a heavy breath. "Aw, *damn*, babe—you, too." Then he shut his eyes, murmuring, "So warm and tight around my cock."

Tessa sucked in her breath at the words—and that's when he began to move in her. Slowly at first, but when she responded, he thrust harder, faster, more rhythmically. Each stroke connected with her deepest inner core, and she remembered that as great as orgasms were, she'd always loved this part, too—the primal movements, the sense of being filled up by a man. And she was loving it with Lucky now. She was loving the way he made every second of it more intimate by looking into her eyes the whole time, raw heat emanating from them.

Lucky was overcome with lust. But it was more than just plain lust. It was all mixed up and entangled with her passion and simple beauty. He drew back at moments— still moving in her, their pelvises still joined but their bodies otherwise apart—to study her: her face, her breasts. He molded those breasts in his hands now, exploring their shape, their weight, teasing the taut pink nipples with his thumbs. Like most guys he knew, he was generally drawn to large breasts, but Tessa's smaller ones held him entranced. Everything about her body, in fact, was so delicate—yet over time she'd begun to seem like a pretty tough chick to him, and something about the contradiction captivated him all the more.

After a while, he rolled them onto their sides. He remained buried in her tight warmth, but their movements slowed, and he kissed her some more, caressed those pretty little breasts more gently.

When she looped one leg over his hip, he reached to massage her round ass, at the same time pulling her closer, more snug against him. He was sheathed to the hilt, but he suffered the urge to somehow be even deeper inside her. And he found himself rolling onto his back, lifting her up until she straddled him and then began to grind.

"Aw, babe," he murmured, liking the rhythm she took on, the untamed way she moved her lithe, slender body. He liked gliding his hands over her breasts, waist, hips, as he watched her.

Although almost as soon as she started, he could see her getting more heated up, could hear her labored breath, could see in her half-shut eyes that she was nearing orgasm again. Damn—it hadn't been long since the first one and she was already that close? It excited the hell out of him, and he wanted to take her there.

"Bend closer," he whispered. "Let me . . ." He didn't bother finishing, just raising as much as he could, lifting his mouth toward her breasts. In response, she leaned nearer, lowering one hardened peak to his waiting tongue. He licked at it just once, then latched on and suckled her, instinctively knowing she needed to feel it harder now—to take her tumbling into ecstasy.

In response, she moaned and arched deeper and he

soaked up the pleasure of tasting that engorged nipple, hard as a pebble between his lips.

"Oh—oh God," she whimpered then, and he watched as her rhythm changed, as her head dropped back, her lips parting, her eyes falling closed. He held her hips, continued pulling on her breast with his mouth. Then she cried out, again, again, and the climax rocked her so hard he almost felt it vibrate through his *own* body.

As she slumped over onto his chest, he wrapped his arms around her, kissing her temple, whispering to her. "You okay, babe?"

"Mmm," she purred against his sweat-slick skin.

And Lucky kept moving in her. Because he couldn't *not* move in her right now. Though they weren't the deep, rougher thrusts his body urged him to deliver, but instead motions as soft as he could manage while she basked in the afterglow of pleasure.

Yet when she whispered against his neck, "I want to make you come, too, Lucky," that changed everything. It gave him permission to drive harder into her sweet moisture. And thank God, since he couldn't have held back any longer if he'd tried.

"Aw, now—now, babe," he bit off through clenched teeth, and then he was lost in the mindless pleasure of exploding inside her, plunging deep with each long burst that rushed through him and out. As he came, she cried out in response to his strokes, her hands clutching at his chest, then falling around his neck. She kissed his mouth, his jaw, then relaxed against him, clearly as spent as he was.

They lay quietly after that, and Lucky listened to the silence of the night. Only it wasn't really silence. The chirps of crickets came in through the windows and he almost thought he could make out the wild white noise of the waterfall in the woods, but he was surely imagining

that. Maybe what he heard was just . . . peace. And maybe
he didn't listen for it very often and had just missed it—or
maybe this was simply the first real time he'd felt it in a
while.

Not the peace of hiding unbothered, not the peace of
blending in so no one would know he had secrets. But
real, *true* peace. In that strange moment, every muscle
in his body was relaxed and he didn't have a care in the
world. Not Mike's disdain, not his past, not worries over
how different he was from Tessa, not even the worry over
figuring out how to be a good father for Johnny. In Tessa's
bed, in Tessa's arms, everything else went away.

By the time light filtered through the curtains on Tessa's
bedroom window, they'd had sex three times. Or was it
four? Sleep had come in between, but repeatedly Lucky
had awakened her—gently. With a kiss on her shoulder,
or fingers easing between her legs, and oh—one time
he'd simply leaned against her from behind, his rock-
hard erection nestling at the center of her ass. After one
mere welcoming sigh from her, he'd sheathed himself and
eased between her legs and gloriously up inside her.

Now Tessa felt more replete than she'd known she
could. And certainly more replete than she'd expected
upon going to bed last night. She found herself trying
to suppress a bit of giddy laughter at the realization that
Lucky had actually shown up at her door, and that finally,
finally, her long and frustrating sex drought was over!

Turning on her side, she watched him sleep. In one way,
he looked out of place here—almost too large for her bed,
and as if everything about him lay in stark contradiction
to the soft, feminine pastels she'd used in the room.

On the other hand, though, he looked . . . surprisingly
serene, and she could almost remember him as a little
boy. She hadn't really known him then—but she vaguely
recalled him from elementary school. He'd been just an

average kid back before Anna had disappeared—she remembered her mother once referring to him as "that nice little Romo boy," when he'd sold her some candy bars for his Boy Scout troop. She thought now, asleep, he was like that nice little boy—innocent. Wasn't everyone at their most pure, most innocent, when they slept?

When his eyes fluttered open, she almost wondered if he'd somehow felt her looking at him. "Hey," he rasped, eyes heavy-lidded, voice shaded with leftover lust.

She smiled softly, just as glad to see that innocence replaced with heat. "Hey yourself."

"Doin' okay, hot stuff?"

"Doing *very* well, thank you." She saw no reason to be coy—they'd had undeniably great sex and she was still wallowing in the joy of it.

He flashed one of his most wicked grins. "You have a lot of orgasms."

A small laugh escaped her since, indeed, she'd had so many she'd lost count. A first for her, certainly. And no wonder she felt equal parts joyous and exhausted now. "Like I said, it's been a while."

He cocked his head against the pillow. "And here I thought it was just *me* getting you off."

"It *was* you," she promised him, voice low. And though she'd have loved to engage in pillow talk all morning long, something more important nagged at her. "About last night, Lucky—I'm really sorry."

He narrowed his gaze on hers. "What are *you* sorry for?"

She lowered her eyes slightly as she replied. "If I hadn't come to Gravediggers with Rachel, Mike never would have shown up. And . . . none of the stuff that happened after that would have happened."

His face went a bit slack at the reminder, but then he resumed being his more usual, confident self. "Way I see it—if you hadn't shown up at Gravediggers, I wouldn't be in your bed right now. I wouldn't know how gorgeous your naked body is. I wouldn't know how warm and tight you feel when I'm inside you."

Tessa's face flushed with warmth, both from excitement and being unaccustomed to such sexy talk.

"So if I had to take a right to the jaw to get all that, don't worry, hot stuff, it was well worth it."

She bit her lip, noticing now that the flesh beneath his eye was red this morning and a little puffy. And she was flattered by his words, but . . . "Still, I know that was hard on you. You didn't have any warning it was coming. And it was my fault."

Yet Lucky just shook his head against her yellow pillowcase. "It could have happened anytime, anywhere. It was bound to."

Tessa thought he was letting her off easy. Given that Lucky didn't exactly frequent any Destiny hot spots, and probably only a few in Crestview, it really *couldn't* have happened anywhere. But she appreciated his understanding—she hadn't forgotten the pain she'd witnessed in his eyes last night.

Although he was right—if she hadn't been so bold, they wouldn't have ended up like this. "So . . ." she ventured, "why did it take me turning into a wannabe biker chick for you to make a move on me?"

Propping on his elbow, he lowered his gaze, looking surprisingly sheepish. Finally, he focused those chocolate brown eyes back on her and said, "It's hard to explain, babe, but . . . let's just say I didn't think I'd be . . . quite right for you."

"And now?" she asked.

"I decided to quit thinking so much."

She smiled in response, still trying to get used to the notion that Lucky had just spent the night with her. "Want some breakfast?"

He shrugged. "Don't usually eat it, but you *did* give me a workout. What'd you have in mind?"

She thought it over—wanting to offer him something more than the toast or muffin she usually ate. Then she remembered the waffle iron her mother had given her as a housewarming gift. "Do you like waffles?"

"Is there anybody who *doesn't* like waffles?"

She smiled. "Waffles it is."

After breakfast, they parted ways—but not for long. It was Sunday, yet since Tessa had more hours than usual scheduled at Under the Covers this coming week, she decided to put in some time on Lucky's kitchen today. After tossing on a fitted tee, denim shorts, and tennis shoes, she was out the door.

Turned out he didn't keep much of a typical work schedule, either, as she found him sanding down a motorcycle in the garage when she showed up, getting it ready for paint. He looked over and smiled when he saw her, then bent one finger toward himself, motioning her closer. When she approached, he leaned down to give her a kiss.

Mmm, it rippled all through her, just as electrifying as the very first one less than twenty-four hours ago. "I could get used to this," she said teasingly—then almost regretted it, worried he'd take it wrong and think she was implying some kind of long-term affair.

But he only cast a lusty little grin, replying, "And I could get used to giving it to you." So she decided to do exactly what Lucky had told her *he'd* done: quit thinking so much and just enjoy this.

She ended up watching Lucky work for a little while, and when she asked, he explained some of the basic steps he went through to paint a bike, and told her he also did custom painting on helmets, too. He then showed her a photo album he kept of the bikes he worked on, and they picked out a few for her framing project for the living room. Fortunately, Lucky had digital copies on his computer, and he saved them on a CD for her.

So it took a while, but she finally got busy painting his kitchen cabinets. And as she stopped to look around at how things were coming together in the house, it pleased her. It was a far cry from the expensive and luxurious rooms she'd done in the past, but she *liked* that. She liked that the changes she was making in an average home were both affordable and, in her own estimation, appealing. She thought of her design for Lucky's house as "biker chic."

Refocusing on the cabinets, she climbed onto a short stepladder, her mini-roller black with paint, and concentrated on covering all the cabinets' nooks and crannies.

She had no idea how much time had passed when she felt Lucky's palms sliding up the backs of her legs. "Ohhh . . ." she purred, stilling her roller, catching her breath. She used her spare hand to reach over to the nearby fridge for balance, and said, her voice a little thready, "If you're not careful, you're going to have black paint splotches on your appliances."

"Chance I'll have to take," he murmured behind her, then his big hands curved around her thighs and she felt his warm breath at the hem of her shorts—just before he lifted a kiss to her ass through the denim.

"*Ohhh*," she moaned again at the delightfully ticklish pleasure that permeated her.

"Those flowers on your ankle are turning me on way too much, babe," he said, low, against her rear.

Her reply came amid ragged breathing. "Too much for what?"

"Too much for me to keep my hands off you. I'm gonna have to have my way with you, hot stuff."

"Is that so?" she purred, staring into the wood grain of the cabinet she'd just covered in black, but totally caught up in the man behind her, and the promise he'd just made.

"Mmm-hmm," he said, kissing her sensitive bottom some more.

"Then you should carefully take this away from me and put it in the paint tray on the counter," she said, still breathy—but practical.

He did as she asked, and she started to back down the ladder—until he returned, his hands stilling her hips in place. "Not so fast."

"No?" she said over her shoulder.

"No," he answered, voice deeper and more commanding than usual.

Then he reached around from behind her to deftly undo the button on her shorts and ease the zipper down. Oh my. After which he began tugging the denim from her hips—along with her panties. And she was starting to suspect her new lover was a little kinky, since it never would have occurred to her to do this on a stepladder, but the daring Tessa who wanted to grab life by the horns didn't mind—she just waited to see what would happen next.

It felt weirdly exciting as the shorts dropped to her knees, and she bit her lip, one hand on the side of the fridge, the other on the hood above his stove. Lucky wasted no time reaching up to begin massaging her bottom, and as his touch echoed all through her, a hot moan escaped her throat and she arched for him without planning it—just her body's natural urge.

She let out a hot sigh as the out-of-the-ordinary foreplay aroused her still more deeply—besides feeling his touches in all the usual places, sensation raced down both her legs. Finally, he slipped two thick fingers up into her moisture—making her whimper even as she parted her legs to give him better access. After that, all was quiet but for their breathing as he plunged his fingers in and out of her warmth. Her face grew hot and something about the position made her feel the little thrusts through her whole body.

When finally he withdrew his fingertips, his voice

turned raspy behind her. "Come down one more step, babe," he said, returning his hands to her hips to help her.

"Wh-what now?" she asked, weakened with excitement.

"Brace yourself on the ladder," he instructed her. She stood on the bottom step now, bringing the top of the ladder even with the tops of her thighs, making it easy to grasp with both hands. A quick glance over her shoulder revealed the step put her at eye level with her new lover, too.

"Bend over just a little," he said, and when she did . . . oh! His erection was right there, behind her, sliding in deep and tight. Her face and hands practically pulsed from the intensity and all she could do was lean back her head and let out a well-pleased moan.

He moved in her that way for a blissfully long time, whispering into her shoulder how hot and sexy she was, and though she'd never realized she wanted or needed to hear things like that, right now, she realized it. She'd wanted and needed it for *years*—and now Lucky was giving her what she hadn't even known she was missing.

Finally, he helped her wordlessly down from the ladder—just to turn her around and lift her up onto his kitchen table, where he relieved her completely of her shorts, parted her legs, and stepped in between. Within seconds, he was in her again—thrusting hot and hard, and as she leaned back, bracing herself on the table so that she could lift to meet him, he reached down to rub his thumb over the little nub just above where their bodies were joined. The sensation forced a sob from her throat almost immediately and she knew another quick orgasm would come.

She then heard herself murmuring mindlessly. "Oh . . . oh yes . . . God . . . *God*." And then—oh Lord! Just like every other time she'd come with Lucky, it rushed over her in pulsing waves that vibrated through her whole body. And when he didn't draw his thumb away, but instead kept stroking her there—dear God, the orgasm went on and on, longer than any she could ever remember!

She was forced to shut her eyes, clenching her teeth as she cried out through the overwhelming pleasure—and it came to her as if through a fog when Lucky said, "Christ, babe, I can't stop." After which he planted his hands at her hips and plunged into her hard, hard, hard, and his climax rushed powerfully through them both even as her own was just beginning to wane.

As it ended, as Lucky bent over her, laying her back on the table to rest his head on her breast, she peered up at the ceiling, utterly fulfilled. Not just sexually, but in *every* way. Amazingly enough, sex had somehow smoothed out the rough edges between them, taking away her nervousness, dissolving his avoidance and gruffness. And as he finally rose back up, she couldn't help teasing him. "Is this how you pay *everyone* who comes to do work for you? Plumbers? Electricians?"

Unfazed, he merely arched one eyebrow in her direction. "Only the ones with sexy tattoos, babe."

... he could see that the boy had inherited his own eyes ...

Charlotte Brontë, *Jane Eyre*

Eleven

*B*y the time Tessa arrived at Under the Covers the next day, she was physically exhausted—she'd ended up staying at Lucky's place last night, and of course, there had been more orgasms. So she was tired—but utterly exhilarated, too. She even stopped at the bakery to pick up snacks for the bookstore today.

"I come bearing muffins," she announced as she stepped through the door, the bell overhead heralding her arrival. Amy and Rachel were already drinking coffee in the easy chairs.

"Yum," Amy said, plucking a blueberry one from the box Tessa opened and held down to her. "What's the occasion?"

"No occasion," she said merrily. "Just felt like some muffins."

Rachel, however, being a little more astute—or was that suspicious?—flashed a look that said she knew something was up. "Amy told me you were working today, so

I wanted to see how things are with Lucky." She helped herself to a banana nut muffin as she spoke.

Tessa took a seat in an overstuffed chair, the muffin box balanced in her lap, but before she could form a reply, Amy leaned forward, eyes widened in horror. "Rachel told me about the other night! You and Lucky Romo? And I can't believe you two went to that biker bar. Are you crazy?"

Tessa just sighed, calmly said, "No, I am *not* crazy, thank you very much," and then turned to Rachel. "Are things okay between you and Mike?" Even as busy as she'd been with Lucky and orgasms, she'd remained worried about the fight she'd caused.

Pinching off a bite of her muffin, Rachel nodded. "I couldn't believe it, but he really did let it go."

"Well, thank God. Hopefully he realized it was my fault. So—is he mad at *me*?"

Rachel popped the bit of banana muffin into her mouth. "No. He questions your judgment a little, but . . ."

"Frankly, I question *his* judgment, too," Tessa snipped, still put out by the way Mike had reacted to seeing his brother.

"I know," Rachel said, her voice thick with concern. "I told him Lucky seemed like an okay guy, but for him, it's about more than that. It's about trying to get over the past. And I'm just not sure he's willing to." She concluded with a sigh.

And they all stayed quiet and somber for a moment, until Rachel spoke up again. "You haven't answered me, though. How are things with Lucky?"

"Well, I'm still working on his house—I have a few more days to go in the kitchen, and I need to get a few photos blown up and framed. But he seems pleased with how it's turning out, and so am I."

Rachel just offered up a dry look, now ignoring the muffin in her hand. "That's not what I meant."

"Okay," Tessa relented, not really wanting to hold back

any longer anyway. "I lied—the muffins are for an occasion. They're for I-Have-a-Sex-Life-Again Day. And it's *well* worth celebrating, girls."

Amy let out a short gasp as Rachel's eyebrows shot up. "Saturday night? After you got home?"

Tessa nodded. "All night, in fact. And it went on the next day. And then again last night." It was hard to believe that what Tessa had thought might be a one-night event had become *more* than one, and what she'd been sure in the beginning would be a fling at best was beginning to feel . . . very comfortable, very quickly. She let a small smile escape her. "By my count, we've had sex around seven times since Saturday night."

"Wow," Rachel said.

And Amy murmured, "I still can't get over this—you and Lucky Romo." Then she asked, "So how was it?"

They both just looked at Amy—until Rachel replied, "Amy. They've done it seven times in less than forty-eight hours. I'm guessing it was pretty good."

And now, thinking back, Tessa actually had to fan herself. "It was more than pretty good. In fact, I'm . . . speechless."

"Hmm," Rachel responded. "Speechless. Sex has left me a lot of ways, but never speechless."

"Well, no," Amy said. "You like to spill every detail, so how could it?"

Rachel just shrugged, probably seeing the truth in Amy's words, then said to Tessa, "I'm happy for you. And you deserve some fun, that's for sure."

"Don't I know it," Tessa agreed, recalling the sexless years just past that made this feel so monumental.

"But, uh, seven times," Rachel said. "Does that mean . . . ?" She tilted her head. "Is this turning into a thing?"

"A thing?" Tessa asked.

"Like . . . more than you expected? Like a relationship thing?"

Tessa bit her lip, pondering it. And she stuck with the same answer she'd given herself yesterday. "I'm not thinking too hard about it—I'm just enjoying it. And whenever it ends, it ends—and that's cool."

Although even as she spoke the last words, her stomach pinched a little. But she decided to ignore that. She felt too good to let even one iota of doubt bring her down. Her Crohn's disease had taught her that—to appreciate the good times and not fret over the future or the past. As much as she could help it anyway. Finally plucking a muffin of her own from the bakery box—a particularly fluffy-looking lemon one—she closed the lid and set the container aside, then crossed one leg over the other and began to peel down the muffin paper.

When Amy let out yet another soft gasp, Tessa simply gave her a what's-the-problem look—but when Rachel's jaw dropped as well, as they both stared at Tessa's shoes, she paid more attention.

"What the hell is that?" Amy asked—noteworthy because Tessa wasn't sure she'd ever heard Amy cuss before.

Since they still gaped at Tessa's feet, she glanced down. And then understood what the fuss was about. "Oh. That . . . would be my tattoo." Her usual long, flowy skirts had kept it hidden up to now, but crossing her legs had lifted today's skirt just high enough to reveal it.

"Is it fake? Temporary?" Amy asked, still appearing completely stunned.

"Nope, it's there to stay." Funny, but she was feeling so happy about sex and Lucky that she no longer cared what anyone thought of the ink on her ankle.

Rachel met her gaze, looking suspicious again. "A night or two with Lucky and he has you getting tattoos already?"

And Tessa just rolled her eyes. "I got it before that. A couple of weeks ago, in fact. I just didn't tell you guys because I knew you'd react like this. I, for one, like it," she finished with a brisk, confident nod.

She watched Rachel studying it, turning her head first one way, then another. "Well," she finally admitted, "as tattoos go, it *is* nice. Even pretty. You just have to hope your ankles always stay thin."

"Best of all," Tessa informed her friends with a smile, "Lucky thinks it's hot."

A few days later, Tessa stood in Lucky's living room by herself, looking around her. Her work on his house was finished, and she personally loved what she'd done with the place. She'd just put up the finishing touches—hanging the photos she'd mounted in simple black frames, and putting up a few warm red details in the kitchen: a couple of towels, a decorative potholder hanging above the stove, a set of salt-and-pepper shakers.

So now it was time for the big unveiling. She'd just brought Lucky around from the garage and had him waiting outside the front door. "All right," she said. "You can come in."

He entered and glanced around, appearing to be taking in the new accents he hadn't seen, which she thought of like fashion accessories—the details pulled the rooms completely together. And as he walked into the kitchen, then back in the living room, he began nodding. "It looks good, hot stuff," he said with a small "tough-guy smile" that pleased her. After all, a big, burly biker could only show so much enthusiasm over home décor.

And then came the moment she'd been waiting for—when he noticed the surprise above the mantel. In addition to framing pictures of some of the bikes he'd painted, she'd taken her own photo of Lucky's beloved Harley Davidson Deuce—the gleaming black parts streaked with stylized red flames—then enlarged it more than the rest of the pictures. She'd selected a charcoal gray matting to make the blown-up print stand out further, and now, hanging over Lucky's small fireplace, it became the centerpiece of the living space. Lucky's eyes went wide when he saw it, then a happy—much bigger—grin unfurled on his tough biker's face, warming her heart.

He turned to her, arching one eyebrow, looking amused at her stealth. "When did you take that?"

"Sunday afternoon, when you went out for groceries."

Lucky rode his bike most places, but groceries meant he had to take his other vehicle, a red Jeep Wrangler. And not only had he just washed the bike that day, he'd left it in the driveway, allowing her to photograph it with a backdrop of spring green foliage.

"It's really great, babe. Really." He punctuated the sentiment by closing her hand in his and leaning down to give her a kiss. As always with Lucky's kisses, it nearly curled her toes.

"I'm glad you like it. It seemed like the perfect final touch."

He tilted his head, dark hair falling around his face, eyes seductive as ever. "You in the mood for another ride on the Deuce, hot stuff?"

She'd only ridden with Lucky once before, and now it would be much easier—she wouldn't have to feel awkward about holding onto him. And it even sounded fun, especially since it was another beautiful spring day in Ohio—a mix of sun and clouds and blue sky. "Sure," she said, and within minutes she was holding tight to her lover as they zipped up Whisper Falls Road.

She ended up enjoying the excursion even more than the last one, and by the time Lucky steered the bike back down his driveway, Tessa felt exhilarated—by the ride, and by the man in front of her.

When they'd both gotten off the motorcycle and removed their helmets, Lucky took the one he'd given her to wear and said, "This doesn't suit you." It was black, plain—and yeah, maybe it looked more like something a guy would wear, but she didn't figure it mattered. Still, he added with a wink, "I'll have to see if I can't come up with something more your style." Then he set the helmet aside on the bike's leather seat and said, "Come here," pulling her into a close embrace for another of the kisses she loved. He leaned back against the motorcycle, and *she* leaned warmly against *him*.

As his mouth moved over hers, as she sank snugly into his strong arms, she couldn't help thinking back to Rachel's and Amy's questions about her and Lucky. Where was this going? Was it turning into a thing? And she still wanted not to care—she wanted to appreciate this time with Lucky simply as . . . her way of grabbing life, and sex, and the unexpected excitement she found on the back of his motorcycle as the wind whipped past. But . . . where *was* this going? *Was* it turning into a thing?

Stop. Don't do that. Don't make this into something you care too much about, something that could then end badly.

As long as she continued to see it as only a fling, after all, it *couldn't* end badly. And besides, if she let herself see it as more . . . well, it would be far more complicated than with any other guy.

Because there was still so much she didn't know about him. So many questions about his past. *Had* he been in an outlaw gang? And if so . . . what sorts of things had he done? She suppressed a shiver—then shoved the thought away. Because it was unpleasant and Lucky was still kissing her, and she wanted to enjoy every spine-tingling bit of pleasure he delivered. She'd decided somewhere along the way that she didn't *need* to know the answers to those questions as long as what they shared was simply a mutual attraction, some good times, some hot sex. But if this ever progressed beyond that . . . well, *then* she'd need to know.

When a car turned into Lucky's driveway, they both

looked up. An old Camaro rolled to a stop right next to Lucky's bike.

"Aw, hell," Lucky muttered under his breath, and Tessa said, "Who is it?"

He shook his head. "Nobody important. Just a customer—that same dip wad that showed up at Gravediggers last week." Lucky hadn't released her from his embrace right away, but he slowly let her go as a slightly older man with reddish hair and a scraggly gray beard exited the passenger side of the car, slamming the door. "With any luck," her lover said, speaking low, "this'll be the last time I gotta deal with him."

"Hey, Lucky," the man greeted him as the car began to back away. "Can't wait to see my bike!" He sounded overly cheerful—almost to the point of coming off as childish—and was clearly oblivious to the fact that Lucky didn't like him.

"Come on in the garage, Red, and take a look," Lucky said, not bothering to introduce Tessa—and she didn't mind. Maybe she shouldn't judge this Red guy the same way she'd initially judged Lucky, but despite his upbeat demeanor, he looked like someone to stay away from.

As Tessa ducked quietly away toward the front door, deciding to wait for Lucky inside, she heard Red say, "That the same chick I saw you with at Duke's bar? Damn, reckon they don't call you Lucky for nothin'—that's a nice piece o'—"

"*Red*," Lucky snapped, cutting him off. "Don't go there or I'll have to kick your ass. Got it?"

And Tessa smiled. Lucky Romo was protecting her honor.

Once inside, she found herself walking down the hall toward Johnny's room. Now that she'd completed the other areas, she could put some finishing touches on the NASCAR-themed room as well. She fluffed the pillows and moved the desk into place against one wall. She was deciding on the best spot for a couple of storage bins when Lucky came in.

She looked up, giving him a smile. "Is the guy who thinks I'm a nice piece of ass gone?"

He offered a small hangdog grin in reply. "Sorry about that, babe. But he and his bike are *both* gone, and hopefully, I'll never see him again."

She tilted her head, suddenly curious. "So—what did he do that makes you hate him so much? I mean, *I'm* not crazy about him, but . . ."

Lucky simply shook his head. "He's just somebody me and Duke knew a long time ago—and we'd rather keep the past in the past."

Hmm—was that an opening? She kept trying to tell herself it didn't matter and that she wouldn't ask or pry, yet . . . "Are you ever gonna tell me anything about this mysterious past of yours, Mr. Romo?"

He narrowed his gaze on her and she wondered if he was considering it—until he said, "I'm more into in the present, hot stuff. In fact . . ." He walked over to the bed and sat down on it, then patted the comforter, motioning for her to join him.

"In fact, what?" she asked, taking a seat facing him.

Again wearing shorts, she stretched her legs out in front of her, and Lucky ran his hand smoothly up one calf, onto her knee. "I need to ask you something, Tessa."

Wow. Had he ever called her by her name before? She wasn't sure, couldn't remember—so hearing it now struck her. "What?" Her heart fluttered a bit and she sensed something big coming.

"I was wondering . . . if you'll go with me when I meet Johnny for the first time."

Whoa. She could scarcely believe the request. It felt . . . colossal. And like a huge compliment. And also like . . . this was officially a fling no longer. Lucky had just asked her to be with him for what was possibly the most important event of his life.

Before she could summon an answer, he went on. "Since the house was almost done, I thought it would be a good time to call Sharon. And I think hearing about the home improvement, plus the fact that we've talked pretty much now, finally has her ready to move forward with this. So we set a time. This Sunday." Which was Easter. "They have stuff with Sharon's parents during the day, but she's having me over for dinner afterward. And when I mentioned maybe bringing someone with me, she was cool with it."

Tessa blew out a breath, and stated what she thought was kind of obvious. "Are you sure bringing me is a good idea? I mean, he might be nervous enough about meeting *you* without you dragging a second stranger along."

"I know, but . . ." He sighed, looking tired as his gaze dropped to the comforter—before he lifted it back to her, wearing a profoundly honest expression. "Look at me, hot stuff. I'm afraid I'll scare the shit out of the little guy. But if I'm with you . . . you look so normal. And nice. And you're friendly. I bet you're great with kids." He stopped, swallowed, suddenly appearing a little uneasy. "I don't want it to be like I'm taking you just because you look so different than me, but . . . I just thought being with you might make me seem a little less . . . everything. I thought you might put him at ease. And I know you'll put *me* at ease." Then he reached down, squeezed her hand. "I kinda need you, babe."

Wow. Now Lucky not only wanted her—he *needed* her. "Of course I'll go with you," she said.

Lucky got a lot of ways: he got worried, he got upset, he got defensive, he got broodish, he got quiet, he got mad—and sometimes he even got even. But one thing Lucky seldom got was nervous, and that's exactly what he felt by the time Tessa showed up at his door just after five o'clock on Easter Sunday, looking pretty as spring itself in a cheerful, flowy yellow dress. She smiled and held up a small blue Easter basket filled with candy. "Have a peanut butter egg and relax," she told him.

Shit, was he that transparent? But he didn't deny feeling uptight, and . . . God, having her there helped. And to his surprise, even the peanut butter eggs helped. In fact . . . when was the last time he'd eaten Easter candy? When the was the last time someone had given it to him? Probably . . . before he'd left home. And it wasn't like he'd ever thought about that before this minute, but . . . "Damn, you're sweet," he told her as they left the house.

The two of them pulled into Sharon's driveway half an hour later.

She and his son lived in a little home a lot like Lucky's, but not as well cared for, and the cars in the driveway looked functional but like they'd seen better days. And for the first time it occurred to him that maybe his new financial support would really give Johnny a better life. Somehow it was like a balm on his fears as he grabbed Tessa's hand for support, approaching the door. *Even if he hates me, at least I can make sure he gets the things he needs.*

"You okay?" Tessa asked.

"Sure," he lied.

"Because you're about to squeeze my hand off."

"Shit," he muttered, letting go. "Is it okay?"

She nodded, then said, "Take a deep breath. And smile."

He tried, but had a feeling it looked pretty weird.

"I said smile, Romo, not grit your teeth like you're in pain," she told him on a laugh.

Which made *him* laugh, too. A little. "Maybe I'll forget the smile for now. Do I look decent?" He'd worn a black button-up shirt Tessa had picked out of his closet—probably to cover up his tattoos.

"For the fifth time, yes," she said.

God, he'd already asked her? Damn, he was even more nervous than he realized. As she'd suggested, he took a deep breath and tried to shake off his nerves, finally saying, "Hell, let's just do this. If I blow it, I blow it," as he rang the doorbell.

"You won't blow it," she whispered as they both heard movement inside, someone coming to answer. His stomach churned.

He didn't expect a guy as tall as him to open the door, but the mustached man wearing a gray Cincinnati Reds T-shirt and jeans flashed a friendly smile. "Come on in. I'm Randy, Sharon's boyfriend."

"Thanks," Lucky murmured, putting a hand to Tessa's back to usher her in. The TV was on, the sound echoing around them, and he smelled something good cooking—chicken maybe.

Sharon emerged through a doorway, looking much as she had when they'd met upon his return to Destiny. Heavier and plainer than he remembered from that fated night ten years ago—but they'd all been younger then. She wore her straight blond hair long with bangs, and had on jeans too tight for her body. Just now, it struck him that she possessed a truly kind smile and he sensed she was a good mom. "Hi, Lucky."

"Hey," he said, still nervous as hell, wondering if his kid would appear at any second, and what he'd think of his new dad. Still, he managed to introduce Tessa, who thanked Sharon for having her, and just glancing down at the woman by his side calmed him a little.

That's when he caught sight of a dark head of hair ducking past the doorway behind Sharon, and then finally coming into the room to stand next to his mother. And . . . holy shit. This was his kid. And Duke was right—he looked just like Lucky, from the olive-toned skin to his mouth and his eyes, which Lucky tried to meet as Sharon's arm fell around the boy's shoulder. She said, "Johnny, this is your dad."

"Hi," Lucky said, lifting his hand in a lame wave.

Johnny's eyes went wide, taking Lucky in. "Hi," he returned.

And though Lucky hadn't planned it, words rushed out, words that suddenly seemed all-important. "Sorry I haven't been around."

"That's okay," Johnny said, shifting from one foot to the other. "My mom explained how you didn't know about me."

"But I'm here now," Lucky offered, "and . . . I hope we can get to know each other, hang out some. If you want," he tacked on at the end. He didn't want to make the kid feel pressured, and he probably just had.

Johnny gave a little nod, and looked about as nervous as Lucky still felt. Great. He was just as scary as he thought. So Lucky played the one card he was holding—although he'd hoped he wouldn't have to use it this fast. "I hear you're a NASCAR fan."

The very words softened the boy's expression, brought a happy expression to his face. "Yeah. Are *you*?"

Shit. "Well, me, I'm into motorcycles . . . but maybe you could teach me. About racing."

This time, Johnny's nod looked more enthusiastic. "Yeah—I have a book I could show you. And lots of stuff on the Internet, too."

He pointed to an older-looking computer in one corner of the living room, as if ready to do this right now, but Sharon kept a hold on his shoulder and said, "Let's save that for after dinner." Then she looked to Lucky and Tessa. "Hope you like fried chicken."

"Smells great," Lucky said. "I haven't had any good fried chicken in ages."

That's when Johnny's eyebrows knit and he looked up at Lucky. "What should I call you?"

"You can call me Lucky. Or Dad," he added, even as

weird as that sounded to him. "Whatever feels good to you."

Yet the boy looked all the more confused. "My mom told me I'm named after you. So how come you're named Lucky and I'm not?"

"Lucky's just a nickname," Sharon said, laughing softly.

And Lucky added, "My real name's Jonathan, after my grandpa from Italy. So you were sort of named for him, too."

Johnny's eyes went wide in amazement. "Really? I'm from Italy?"

They all laughed and Randy said, "You're not from Italy, little man. Your great-grandfather is. But guess it makes you *part* Italian."

"Wow," he said. "That's cool. No wonder I like pizza so much."

Everyone laughed some more and Lucky found the kid's wonder about his ancestry both appealing and amusing. Lucky had never cared much about it as a kid, and now he wished he'd shown more interest. He used the opportunity to say, "I have some pictures I could show you sometime. Of my family. *Your* family."

"Really?" Johnny said.

And Tessa turned to look up at him, clearly surprised. "You have pictures?" she asked quietly.

He shrugged. "A few. Took 'em with me when I left." Then he peered back down at his kid. *His* kid. The idea of that was starting to feel a little less daunting. "Yeah, I could even show you where your great grandpa lived when I was growing up, over in Destiny. Sometime. If you're interested."

"And I happen to know," Tessa chimed in, "where Grandpa Romo moved when he first came to America from Italy, and that he built the house himself."

Oh, the orchard, Lucky realized. Rachel's family had owned it as long as he remembered, but he recalled something about it originally belonging to Giovanni, and how that had somehow started the problems between the Romo and Farris families. "So he built the house, huh?" Lucky asked Tessa now. He hadn't known that part.

She nodded. "According to Rachel."

Lucky refocused on Johnny even as he pointed to Tessa. "Look what a smart girlfriend I have." Then, hoping he wasn't going too far too fast, he said, "No pressure, but if you want, sometime, you could come over to my place and hang. I've got a room there for you, anytime you like."

The kid appeared excited. "Really? I already have my own room at your house?"

And Lucky laughed, thinking "really" was Johnny's favorite word. "Yeah," he said.

"And you're *so* gonna love it," Tessa added.

"Why?" the boy asked.

Leaning forward slightly as if telling him a big secret, she said, "*Well*, could be that your dad fixed it up with a bunch of NASCAR stuff."

"No way!" Johnny's jaw dropped and his eyes got even bigger.

"Way," Tessa said.

And as if he'd never been the least bit nervous about any of this, the kid then turned to his mom and said, "Can I, Mom? Can I go to my dad's house soon?"

And that's when Lucky had to push back a lump in his throat. At hearing the boy say, "my dad." And because Johnny wanted to come over, wanted to be a part of his life. Johnny wasn't scared, by Lucky's size, or his looks. Even if he'd been lured by NASCAR talk, Lucky didn't care. He automatically reached out, squeezing Tessa's hand, as he heard Sharon say, "Sure you can." Then she looked toward the kitchen. "But we'd better continue this conversation over dinner—I'm afraid my chicken is about to burn."

Lucky couldn't believe how relatively comfortable

he felt moving with the rest of the small crowd into the kitchen. Once there, Sharon started taking up the chicken from the sizzling skillet, and Tessa was soon mashing potatoes while the guys worked on getting everyone sodas from the fridge. Damn, it was strange. Like he was . . . part of a family. He didn't know most of them, but . . . it was still nice. He hadn't had a meal like this since . . . hell, since the last time he'd been in Destiny.

Tessa rode home at Lucky's side, reflecting on the evening. Things with Johnny had gone so very well! And she could see how happy Lucky was. *And* he'd called her his girlfriend—oh so casually. She wanted not to care as much about that as she did the other parts of the night, but every time she thought about it, a little *zing* shot through her chest.

At dinner, she'd had to eat lightly—but later, while Johnny showed Lucky the NASCAR-themed Easter basket he'd gotten, she explained to Sharon about her condition, and the other woman had been very understanding. Tessa had sincerely liked her and felt glad for Lucky that he'd gotten such a nice person pregnant all those years ago.

"So when Johnny comes over next weekend," Lucky said as they pulled into his driveway in the dark, "should I plan something to do or just play it by ear?"

"Um, maybe a little of both?" she suggested. "I'll help you come up with something. And . . . since you two did fine on your own, you should probably make your day next weekend one-on-one time, don't you think?"

He looked at her as he brought the Jeep to a halt in the parking spot next to the garage. "Probably, but I think the kid likes you," he pointed out, "and so do I, so we might have to mix up the one-on-one stuff with some you stuff, too."

Given that she and Lucky spent most of their nonwork-

ing hours together these days, Tessa found it easy enough
to agree.

"So," she said as they got out of the Jeep, "my place
or yours tonight?" The time they spent together extended
to sleeping, too, although it usually came with a healthy
dose of sex first. And most of their sexy encounters had
indeed taken place in a bed, but every now and then passion got the best of them, as it had last Sunday in Lucky's
kitchen—so they'd also had fun on Lucky's living room
floor and a couple of times in her shower.

"Mine," he said. "First, though, I have something to
show you." And then, rather than heading to the front entrance, he stopped next to the garage, unlocked and lifted
the heavy door, then flipped on a light.

Inside, Lucky's motorcycle sat in one corner, and three
more waited in his work area, all in various states of being
disassembled and painted. It struck her suddenly that
when Lucky's customers arrived these days, she didn't
get nearly as irritated by the loud pipes as she once had.
Maybe she'd just gotten used to it, but she more thought
it had to do with having become so immersed in Lucky's
life. Those sounds were like . . . a part of him to her now,
so she didn't mind them anymore.

Standing in the garage, he took her hands in his and
said, "I want to thank you, hot stuff."

"For . . . ?" she asked, peering up into his dark, sexy
eyes.

"For a lot of things. For making coming back to this
town better than I expected. For helping me ease into this
dad thing. And for going with me tonight. It meant a lot."

It was hard to believe this was the same scary biker she'd
met just weeks ago. He was still strong, tough—but she'd
found more softness beneath his rough exterior than she
could have imagined. "You're very welcome," she said
softly. "You've . . . helped me a lot, too. More than you
probably know."

"I've got something for you," he announced, then walked over to a shelf and took down a helmet—the sight of which made her gasp. It was a pearlized pink color with a daisy painted on each side, and her name curled across the back in feminine-looking letters.

"It's perfect," she said, stunned. Stunned to realize she was excited about having a motorcycle helmet. Stunned that one so perfect for her could exist. And stunned that Lucky knew her well enough already to *know* what was perfect. "I love it."

"Good," he said. "'Cause I really can't have my girl riding around in that scratched up old black one you've been wearing."

His girl. She bit her lip and her stomach fluttered.

But . . . wow, this made it kind of official—she was a biker babe now. "If I'm becoming a biker chick," she said, "does this mean I need to invest in some black leather?"

Lucky arched one brow, offering his usual sin-filled grin. "You can wear whatever you want. But I wouldn't mind *seeing* you in some black leather."

She flashed sexy eyes at him—but then said, "Just one thing, though. If you ever call me your old lady, I'm outta here."

Her biker guy just laughed. "It doesn't mean you're old—it's just how bikers talk."

"I don't care. I will not be anyone's old lady, even when I'm an old lady. Got it, buster?"

He winked. "Got it, hot stuff."

After that, she tried on her new helmet, even going inside to check her look in the bathroom mirror—yet as minutes began to pass, the reality of having Lucky in her life began to hit her harder. A week ago, it had been about the hot sex she'd craved for so long. But now . . . things were feeling very real. She was his girl. She had her own helmet for riding with him. And going with him to meet his son, experiencing that with him—had clinched it. They were connected way more than just physically now.

And as she saw her face in the glass peeking out from under a motorcycle helmet—definitely the last spring accessory she'd expected to be wearing—she knew this meant . . . she needed to start wondering, asking those questions again, about his past. She thought she knew Lucky—but did she? She'd never asked him about the scars she saw on his body during sex, but how had he gotten them? What would his secrets reveal about him? And would he ever tell her?

Still checking out her reflection, however, she let out a long breath and decided she'd have to shove those concerns to the back burner. For just a little longer. Because . . . there was something else Lucky had to deal with now, whether he liked it or not. And she felt compelled to push him a little, to help him through this next part of coming home, of really *being* home.

So as she took off her new helmet and turned to face him in his little bathroom, she said, "You know what comes next, don't you?"

Lucky couldn't help feeling a little arrogant at the moment, glad she liked the helmet—glad about the whole damn night. "You thank me for the helmet by ripping off my clothes?"

Tessa rewarded him with a pretty smile—yet replied, "I was thinking more in a big-picture way. About what comes next now that you've officially got Johnny in your life."

In response, he just met her gaze and let out a sigh, his good mood instantly deflating. Damn. "I know what you're thinking, but . . ." He stopped, shook his head. He knew it was shitty that he didn't want to deal with this, but maybe he still felt like the same kid he'd been at twelve, and fourteen, and sixteen. Maybe he still felt . . . unwanted.

"I happen to know your parents get home from a cruise tomorrow," Tessa said, "and that Mike plans to call and tell them you're here. Maybe . . . I could tell Mike *you're* going to call them instead."

Lucky sucked in his breath, blew it back out. And felt a little mad at her for taking a great night and putting a damper on it. If he did this, if he called them, what would happen? Would they make him feel as crappy as Mike had? Would he find out he was right and that they'd have preferred he stay away? He didn't answer her—just remained quiet.

That's when Tessa reached out and took his hand. "It's your *mom*, Lucky. I know she'd want to hear it from you, hear your voice."

Aw, hell. She was right. This was his mom. His mom and dad. And no matter what problems they'd had, he should do this. He *had* to do this. He had a son now, after all—he had to stand up, be a man. Even if it was hard as hell.

So he looked Tessa in the eye. She was so smart.

"All right. I'll do it."

And she made him a better man than he would be without her.

I had yet an aching heart. I still felt as a wanderer on the face of the earth; but I experienced firmer trust in myself and my own powers, and less withering dread of oppression.

Charlotte Brontë, *Jane Eyre*

Twelve

Tessa still had moments almost every day when she felt less than top-notch. But they'd been fewer than usual lately. And she'd long ago quit mentioning those moments to anyone, figuring it could only make her—and them—feel worse. Now, as she watched Ellen talk about the power of positive thinking on her show, she hoped Ellen would be proud of her. Since she *was* doing more and more of that lately. And dancing. And laughing. In fact, right now she wore the "laugh. dance. ellen" tank top she'd ordered online—and she danced along with Ellen on TV, at the same time straightening her living room.

Maybe, at long last, she was accepting her condition. And mostly, life was good. Too good to dwell on the bad parts.

After the show ended, Tessa turned on the radio, loud enough to hear it outside, then exited onto the deck. And it wasn't even in an effort to drown out the loud motorcycle she heard just then, either arriving at or leaving Lucky's place—it was simply because she wanted to listen to music while she worked. Her flowers and tomatoes were growing like crazy now and it was time to water.

When the first notes of "You Shook Me All Night Long" blasted through her window, she didn't hesitate to move her hips to the beat, hose in hand. And although she liked a wider variety of music than Lucky did—and had insisted just yesterday that they were going to start listening to some of *her* favorites when riding his bike in the future—she could also appreciate some good, old-fashioned AC/DC. She danced her heart out for the whole song, watering everything on the deck and also the bed of daisies by the woods, and had to admit dancing made the chore much more fun.

But when she heard a slow applause begin, it made her jump—just before she turned to face Lucky.

"Like I told you once before," he said, clearly amused, "nice moves, babe."

She simply smiled, since it was pleasant to no longer be embarrassed in front of him. "I just recently figured out that dancing is something that makes me happy," she explained.

"Well, *watching* you dance makes *me* happy," he replied. Although when he glanced deliberately down at the large bulge behind his zipper, she realized he didn't actually mean *happy*, he meant *aroused*. But that suited her fine.

"And this time I didn't even drench you with the hose," she pointed out.

He leaned against the railing across the deck from her, arms crossed. "I kept my distance, just in case."

And Tessa bit her lip, feeling a little frisky to know she

turned her biker guy on so easily. "Hose is off, mister—so you don't have to stay all the way over there."

Her big, muscular man raised his eyebrows. "You flirtin' with me, hot stuff?"

And in that moment, something in Tessa went a little wild. She'd been grabbing a lot of life lately, with few regrets, and now she wanted to grab more. "Would you consider . . . *this* flirting?" she asked, putting on an innocent voice even as she crossed her arms over herself and smoothly removed her tank top over her head. "Or *this*?" Then she reached behind her to the hook on her pale pink bra, soon flinging it aside to leave her topless before him.

Lucky's eyes went dark with lust, making her pool with moisture in her panties. "Nope," he said deeply. "I'd consider *that* downright naughty." Then he crossed the deck toward her.

Within moments, she was completely naked in his arms and Lucky's jeans were undone and he was inside her. She sat balanced on the rail in Lucky's strong grasp. And it felt just as wild and carefree and forbidden as she'd hoped—but it was also . . . more. They looked into each other's eyes beneath the green branches surrounding the deck, and she *knew* they were connecting on a deeper level. How on earth had this happened? How had dangerous Lucky Romo become such a fixture in her life? And more than that, how had he become a man she cared about?

As Lucky thrust into her, she wrapped her arms around his neck and followed the primal urges of her body, grinding against him in hot, rhythmic circles. She got lost in the mounting pleasure until, as usual with Lucky, she came quickly, moaning and whimpering in his embrace.

And it was only when the intense waves of pleasure subsided that she went still—realizing, remembering . . . things had happened so fast that he hadn't put on a condom. God. That was a first with them—other than the very first time, she'd never even had to ask; Lucky had just always been prepared and ready. Now, she sucked in her breath, hard.

"What is it, babe? What's wrong?" he murmured in her ear as she clung to him.

"We didn't use protection," she said, then lifted her head from his shoulder to meet his gaze.

Lucky didn't even sound alarmed as he assuaged her fears. "I promise you're safe, hot stuff. I wasn't the most careful guy when I was young, but I once knew a guy who got a nasty STD, and after that, I got myself checked out. And then I got careful and stayed that way. This is the first time since then . . ." Yet then his voice trailed off, and she understood that the news about the condom hadn't come as a surprise to him.

"Why?" she whispered. "Why with me?"

She looked into his eyes and saw the heat and emotion wash over his strong face. "I wanted to be closer to you. *All the way* close. Skin to skin."

"Oh," she breathed. Tessa had already had occasion to tell him she was on the pill, more for health purposes than to prevent pregnancy, but she supposed now it would get to perform its primary function. And she noticed he didn't bother asking her if *he* was safe—maybe he already knew enough about her to know the answer. She'd never played risky games with sex.

Except as their gazes stayed locked and Lucky began to move in her again, it hit her that maybe that had changed—with Lucky. From their earliest encounters, something about him had made her want to be a little risky, take some chances. All along, she'd held her health woes responsible for that, but in this moment, she wondered if maybe it was only Lucky himself that had inspired so much recklessness in her lately.

"Aw, babe," he murmured deeply as his strokes grew harder, faster.

And she whispered his name, and told him how much he excited her, and said she wanted to make him come. And then he did, pounding into her fiercely and gloriously until they finally slumped together there on the deck. And the whole world seemed warm and safe and right—so much more than before she'd met Lucky Romo.

Later that evening, after getting with Tessa on her deck, Lucky faced a much grimmer task. As dusk cast dark shadows over his newly done living room, he sat on his couch staring at the telephone on the end table next to him.

He liked the room—it felt warm yet modern, and maybe even a little tough, and he hoped Johnny would dig it, too. Damn, it was hard to fathom the changes Tessa had made in his life in such a short time. From redoing his house to . . . redoing his heart.

Was that what she'd done—made his heart over into something it hadn't been before? Well, she was softening the damn thing, that was for sure. And . . . maybe she wasn't making it into something new; maybe instead she was just peeling back all the hard layers that had grown overtop of it, helping him find . . . a little of the person he once used to be. Or . . . the person he *would* have been if life hadn't taken a particularly bad turn that day at Bear Lake when they'd lost Anna.

No matter how he sliced it, though, he couldn't deny it—he'd started to care for the woman. And it wasn't exactly a decision he'd made—but something that had happened when he'd let his guard down. And now he was calling her his girl. How the hell had that happened? He wasn't sure, and the knowledge was almost a little stifling added to everything else going on right now, but . . . damn it, the bigger truth was that he *liked* having a girl for once in his life. He liked spending time with her. He liked riding his bike with her. And God *knew* he liked sex with her. He just plain liked having her around.

Yet the thought made him lean back, rest his head on the couch, and let out a long breath. God, these were big changes. A girl. A son. All at once. So much big change was hard for a long-time loner. And he still wondered, deep down inside, if he could ever *really* be the kind of man a girl like Tessa wanted, needed—long term. If someone like him could ever meet her expectations—the built-in, lifelong kind. Maybe caring for her was dangerous.

But then . . . maybe it was just the *idea* of so much change that was difficult. Since, slowly but surely, he was doing all right with most of it. After all, no one had *made* him take responsibility for Johnny. And turned out he really liked the kid—and had experienced an immediate sense of pride that he'd helped *create* the kid. Already, he felt committed to making sure Johnny had everything he could ever want or need to make his life complete. To make his life better than Lucky's had turned out.

And certainly no one was forcing him to spend so much time with Tessa. Tonight was the first night since they'd first gotten together that they were sleeping apart, at their own houses, because Tessa had an early day at the bookstore tomorrow, helping Amy with inventory, and both of them knew they weren't getting much sleep lately because they couldn't keep their hands off each other. But as practical as it was for both of them, already he missed her.

Raising his head, he looked back toward the phone. There was one more big change that needed to come— Tessa was right, and he was glad she'd pushed him to do it. Now came the actual . . . doing it.

Finally, Lucky picked up the cordless receiver and looked at the little sticky note Tessa had given him with his parents' number in Florida. Then he shook his head at the weirdness—that he'd had to get his own parents' number from his new girlfriend. Very slowly, he keyed it in. And as it began to ring, his chest tightened painfully.

"Hello?"

God, his mother. How long it had been since he'd heard her voice? He felt numb for a second, almost paralyzed, until finally he said, "Mom?"

She was slow to respond, clearly confused by *his* voice. At length, she said, uncertainly, "Mike?"

He tried to catch his breath, but it was hard, especially given the lump that had just grown in his throat. "It's . . . Lucky, Mom."

He heard her gasp, then make a few small crying sounds that ripped his heart to pieces. Until she said, "Lucky, is it really you? Are you all right? Are you okay?" She sounded frantic.

"I'm fine, Mom, I'm fine," he rushed to assure her, hearing the stark love in her voice. He wasn't sure *what* he'd expected to hear, but he supposed it hadn't been that. Maybe if he'd expected *that*, he'd have made this call years ago.

"Wh-where are you?"

God, the irony. "I'm in Ohio. In Destiny. I'm . . . at home."

His mom continued to make stuttery, excited noises. "Oh my God, I can't believe it's you. And y-you're at home? Wh-what are you doing there? Have you seen Mike—does he know?"

It remained a struggle to talk around the swelling in his throat. "Uh—Mike knows. I . . . bought a house out on Whisper Falls Road. And . . . I have a son."

She still sounded just as stunned, understandably. "*What?*"

"That's why I came home—I just found out I have a son

in Crestview. I . . . just met him on Sunday. He's nine—turns ten later this year."

"Oh my God. My God." Her voice went lower then; she was no longer speaking directly into the phone. "John, it's Lucky! Lucky's on the phone!"

"What?" he heard his dad say in the background, and a moment later, his father picked up an extension. "Lucky? Lucky, it's your dad. Are you all right, son?"

His eyes began to ache and he had to shut them. If only . . . if only his dad had ever sounded half as concerned when Lucky was growing up. "I'm fine, Dad—I'm good." Then he relayed some of the same stuff he'd just told his mom, about being in Destiny, about having a kid. His mom had gone quiet and he sensed she was crying. He ran his free hand back through his hair and tried to stay cool, as much as he could surrounded by so much damn emotion he wasn't used to.

"Lucky, we'll be on a plane tomorrow," his father said.

But Lucky tried to stop them. "No, you don't have to do that. I don't want to put you out." God, what was he saying? "Any more than I already have, I mean."

"Nonsense," his dad said. "Of course we're coming to see you! Of course we are!"

"Nothing could keep us away," his mom insisted.

"My God, I can't believe it's really you," his dad said on a happy-sounding sigh.

"I . . . I can't wait to see you guys," Lucky heard himself say. And in one sense, it was a lie—something said out of guilt, or just to fill the air. He'd run away from them once, after all. And despite all the trouble he'd found out in the world, he'd never really missed the life at home he'd left behind. But in another very real, visceral sense—down in his gut, in a way he couldn't run from or deny—he realized it was the complete truth. Now that he finally felt their love—God, he wanted to see them more than he'd wanted anything in a long time.

Talk about big changes.

The following night, Lucky found himself riding his bike down Meadowview Highway, a road he hadn't seen since he was eighteen and headed in the opposite direction, leaving town in a fast car. And as he drove up into the gravel driveway to one side of his old home, which now belonged to Mike, he felt . . . disconnected from his own life, his own past. The house looked the same except for small things: a new mailbox, unfamiliar cars in the driveway, and the maple tree in the front yard had grown, almost seeming to dwarf the two-story farmhouse now. So it felt like coming home . . . but different, scarier. He was only thirty-four, but for the first time in his life, he began to feel . . . old. In some ways, anyway.

His stomach swam with nerves as put down his kickstand, took off his helmet, and walked in even paces toward the front door. And unlike when he'd met his boy a few days ago, this time he didn't have Tessa's hand to squeeze. She'd offered to come, but he'd said, "Don't you think I should do this one by myself, hot stuff?" Maybe if she'd been here at his side, though, stepping up onto the old front porch would have felt a little less surreal.

Everything kicked into high gear, though, when the door opened and his mother rushed out, arms flung wide. His first impression was that she looked good—pretty but older, and smaller than he remembered. Except . . . no, he'd just gotten bigger. "Lucky," she said, her eyes glassy with tears.

"Hi, Mom," he managed before she threw her arms around his neck.

He hugged her back, aware that she'd paid no attention to how scary he must appear to her—all tattoos and long hair. He'd not bothered to hide his ink tonight—not scaring his kid was different; he figured the adults in his family had to accept him as he was or not at all.

Behind her came his dad, his once dark hair now shot through with gray, his face worn—from so much loss, Lucky figured. He said nothing, just joined in the hug.

And the moment lingered strangely. Like their reaction on the phone, Lucky hadn't expected this, either—the hugging, or for it to happen so easily, so immediately. They'd never hugged him much as a kid, after all, and for him, hugging was mostly a thing he did with women—he'd just never really *learned* the hugging thing. But . . . maybe it felt good. It felt good to feel their care flowing so freely over him all of the sudden, after all these years.

Everything after that soon became a blur in Lucky's mind. He supposed he was just on overload at this point. He heard his parents asking him questions, their eyes searching his for answers. "Where have you been all this time?" "What have you been doing?" "Why didn't you call?" And then came the barrage of exclamations. "So many tattoos!" "You ride a motorcycle now!" "The grim reaper? Why would you choose the grim reaper?" "You have a boy of your own now—tell us about him!" And his dad, through a hardy chuckle: "Where the hell did you get all these muscles, son?"

He noticed Mike standing off to one side of the room, staying quiet through it all, and he couldn't help thinking, cynically: reversal of fortune. Once upon a time, Mike had been the constant center of attention, Lucky the neglected one. The big difference was—Mike was old enough to handle it, and this would be temporary. And thank God. As a kid, Lucky had hungered for such attention, but now—shit, it was a little overwhelming.

Lucky answered everything the best he could, ignoring the grim reaper question, and very purposely skirting past his biker gang years, explaining that his appreciation for souped-up cars had shifted to motorcycles after he'd left Destiny, and that he'd spent most of his time away in Milwaukee, home to a thriving biker community, building his custom painting business.

His mother sighed and said, "You always did like to draw," and Lucky was almost surprised she remembered. She'd seemed so disinterested at the time.

He realized as he spoke, though, that he felt a sting of pride telling them about his business, letting them know he was self-sufficient and successful—and an even stranger, bigger spark of pride struck when talking about his new son. "He seems smart, and funny. Speaks right up and says whatever's on his mind. He's not shy—and that's good since I was worried we wouldn't have anything to talk about. He's a NASCAR fan and . . . he looks just like me." Lucky stopped then, glancing up at his dad, and then even to Mike, who stood silently behind the chair where their father sat, to add, "Like *us*." It was odd to be back among the people who shared his looks, to realize he'd *come* from somewhere and wasn't this lone creature floating around the world by himself anymore.

Both his parents were over the moon to discover they had a grandchild, his mother gushing, "Now that Mike is finally engaged, we thought maybe we'd finally get to be a grandma and grandpa one day, but now we already are!"

"When can we meet the little guy?" his dad asked with a big grin.

"Well, we might want to wait a while—he just met *me*. But soon."

And they nodded happily, saying all sorts of *Of-course*s and *We'll-work-it-out*s.

But then, finally, came the inevitable question Lucky had dreaded, from his father. And he asked it hesitantly, like maybe he feared Lucky would get up and run right back out the door at the first negative word. "We were so damn worried, Lucky. Why didn't you ever let us know where you were?"

It was a fair question, and Lucky wasn't going to sugar-coat it. "I didn't think you'd care."

His mother gasped, and both his parents sounded horrified to learn he'd felt that way—while Mike just stayed typically quiet, crossing his arms over his chest and looking angry.

So Lucky went on. "After . . . after we lost Anna," he began, swallowing—although suddenly now, he was only able to glance quickly from his mom to his dad in between staring at the coffee table—"I felt . . . invisible. Like you didn't know I was even alive."

His mother drew in her breath, looking hurt, but if anything were to exist between them, he had to keep it real—he had to explain his side of things. "I know you probably didn't realize it or do it on purpose, but . . ."

"This is bullshit," Mike interrupted.

And Lucky lifted his gaze to his brother, snapping, "*What?*"

Mike stepped forward, his eyes burning with the same resentment Lucky had witnessed in them at Gravediggers. "You and I were in the exact same boat after Anna disappeared. We *all* lost her, we were *all* mourning. You just grew up making shitty decisions and now you want to blame Mom and Dad for it."

Lucky didn't want to start a fight here, but *shit*—he automatically shot to his feet to face Mike's accusation. "You're out of line on this," he said, trying not to let the fresh rage bubbling inside him reach the boiling point. "We weren't in the same fucking boat at all. *You* were wracked with guilt, and that's all *they* could see. I get that now. But back then, I didn't."

He took a deep breath, tried to calm down, heard himself murmur an apology for his language, then took a seat again and refocused on his parents. "I think . . . between mourning for Anna and bending over backward to make sure Mike didn't think it was his fault . . . I think I just . . .

got lost in the shuffle. And I just felt . . . alone, and like Anna and Mike were both way more important than me."

"And so you started acting out," his mother said, surprising him by shifting almost immediately into acceptance, and puzzling through the logic behind his actions in a way he'd never even bothered to do. "You were trying to get our attention any way you could—and we were too caught up in our grief to see it."

Lucky wasn't completely sure about that part, but . . . "Maybe," he said. Then he shook his head. "I know *something* turned me into a troublemaker—I never really knew what."

Mike continued looking disgusted, but Lucky just ignored him. This wasn't *about* Mike.

And then Lucky kept talking, thinking back, trying to make his parents understand how he'd felt at the time. It was strange, because he wasn't usually so good at that—just talking. Or not until lately anyway. It was as if coming back here had . . . slowly cracked away his outer shell, letting all the stuff inside him leak out. And right now, he was glad, because the more he talked, the more his parents seemed to get it. And unlike Mike, they didn't argue with him or tell him it was all his fault. And even as tense as the discussion grew at moments, at the same time, it left Lucky feeling . . . *freer*. Freer than he had just an hour earlier, like a huge weight he'd been carrying around all these years had suddenly been lifted off him.

It was only after the hard stuff had passed that his dad asked, "How long were you in Wisconsin?"

"About ten years," he said.

And he realized instantly that he probably should have lied, since he could see his mother thinking, realizing that left more than a five-year gap in his absence. "Oh—well, where were you before that?" she asked.

Hell. He'd just have to keep right on glossing over that part of his history. "I went from place to place for a while, picking up work here and there. Sold my car in Nevada and bought my first motorcycle," he said. "From there, I was in California a while. That's where I started painting bikes. But I eventually came back to the Midwest." *Where the outlaw biker presence wasn't as heavy. Where there weren't people looking to kill me for the things I'd done.*

His mom and dad seemed to accept the answer and didn't ask any more questions—thank God. And his mother moved on to telling him how excited his Grandma Romo was to hear he was home, and trying to catch him up on all his aunts, uncles, and cousins—some of whom he couldn't even remember.

Lucky nodded and replied every so often—and yet from the corner of his eye he could see the grim, distrustful expression still on Mike's face, and he could sense the narrowed, suspicious eyes glued on him the whole time.

And he remembered his brother was a cop now. With cop instincts.

Shit. Clearly, even if his parents hadn't caught on, Mike knew Lucky wasn't telling them everything.

Lucky hugged his mom and dad goodbye and left his old home, still not having reconciled with Mike. And even as good as it felt to have his parents' suddenly back in his world, the stark strangeness of it, combined with Mike's unspoken suspicions, made Lucky feel . . . a little like running. Like he just wanted to get on his bike and ride, right out of Destiny, right out of Ohio.

Maybe tonight was the tipping point, the thing that knocked him over the edge. He'd been doing pretty damn well with all these big changes . . . but now, right when he should feel great, instead he felt . . . overwhelmed. And responsible to too many people suddenly. Like being the lone rider   responsible to no one, able to shut everything out—had been easier than this.

And so he rode. Fast. Up and down highways. He concentrated on the pavement before him, the cool evening breeze cutting through the leather jacket he wore. He concentrated on the sweet country scents of earth and trees and spring grass. He listened to the music he most liked to ride to: the easy pounding beat of Molly Hatchet on "Call Me the Breeze," and the Allman Brothers going a little darker, deeper on "Midnight Rider."

He was twenty miles outside the Destiny city limits, however, when on the fringes of his mind, he found himself calculating a route back, trying to reach into his memory to recall how the country roads were all connected. It was the ultimate freedom to ride without knowing or caring where you were going—but maybe he was outgrowing that now. Because *that* kind of freedom suddenly didn't seem as important as the things he was going back to: a son, a woman.

When he pulled into his driveway, he put his bike in the garage, but didn't bother going inside—instead he walked down the hill to Tessa's. He was about to knock on her back door when he caught a hint of movement on the side deck. He climbed the stairs to find her curled up in her lounge chair, wrapped in the quilt he knew her grandmother had made.

"What are you doing?" he asked softly.

Her answer came just as quiet. "Enjoying the night." Almost May now, the late evening air remained brisk, but you could also feel the slow coming of summer in it.

Lucky grabbed a chair from her patio set and pulled it up to sit beside her. Crickets and other insects sang loudly in the trees, sounding almost as if they surrounded them.

They sat silent for a long minute, until Tessa said, "Are you going to tell me?"

Lucky thought about what to say, and finally settled on, "I feel a little like my head's gonna explode."

He felt her look in the dark. "Things didn't go well?"

"No, things went great. With my parents anyway. We talked. They . . . understood. It was good. Weird, but good. I mean, I haven't seen them for almost half my life. And they're hugging me and telling me they love me and . . ." He stopped, shook his head. "And like I said, it was good, but . . . everything's changing for me, Tessa, almost faster than I can keep up with." He let out a breath, again suffering the sensation of being overwhelmed.

"And Mike?"

"He's an asshole," Lucky bit off.

She let out a sigh. "I thought maybe he'd soften up a little once your parents were here."

"Not even close."

They stayed quiet for another moment, until she said, "Lean your head back. Look up."

He sensed her doing it, too. The sky was clear tonight, and this far out in the country . . . damn, a billion stars shone down on them. He hadn't noticed when he was riding—too much focus on the road required, too much shit in his head.

"Nights like this make me feel peaceful inside," she told him.

He kept looking, and slowly, he began to feel that way, too. Then he reached down and found her hand, squeezing it in his.

Tessa stood behind the counter at Under the Covers, copying a quote she'd just found in a book into the little journal she even carried with her in her purse—just in case she needed it.

Think of all the beauty that's still left in and around you and be happy.
Anne Frank

If Anne Frank could still appreciate beauty, inside and outside, during *her* ordeal, surely Tessa could when she was feeling less than perfect. Reading it over again made her smile.

"So Lucky finally made up with his family, huh?" Amy asked from between two bookshelves. "That's so nice."

Tessa had started to fill Amy in, but when a customer had arrived, she'd stopped. "Well, he made up with his parents, but Mike is another story."

Just then, Brontë appeared, merrily trotting out from the shelves and up behind the counter, where she actually rubbed up against Tessa's ankle. The gesture filled her with warmth—she couldn't believe Brontë was openly showing affection—and on instinct, she stooped down to scoop the black-and-white kitty into her arms. "Look at you, being all bold and friendly," she said, peering into Brontë's blue eyes.

"Meow," the cat said, as if answering her.

That's when Amy poked her head around to look. "What did she do?"

As Tessa explained, she gently hugged Brontë against her and began stroking her neck. And then . . . "Oh wow, now she's even purring," Tessa told Amy with a smile.

That's when Amy let her gaze narrow, and Tessa could almost see the wheels turning in her friend's brain. "You should adopt her."

Tessa blinked. "What?"

"Don't act like it's a crazy idea. You're getting attached to her, and she's not nuzzling and purring with *me*. And wouldn't you like having a nice kitty around the house? I can't imagine how lonely *I'd* get without Mr. Knightley."

Although Tessa liked animals, she'd never really considered getting a pet. But maybe the suggestion made sense. Though she wasn't prone to loneliness, she might enjoy having Brontë as a cabinmate. At least when she was acting fairly normal like this and not freaking out around everything that moved.

Only . . . a pet was a big responsibility, one she wouldn't take lightly. Even if she *would* take steps to make sure her own pet didn't become as spoiled and needy as Amy's.

And then a much bigger deterrent hit her, taking the wind out of her mental sails. "What about when I have flare-ups? I'm not sure I could care for a cat when I feel rotten, and I wouldn't want to neglect her."

Amy shrugged. "Cats are easy. Mr. Knightley isn't be cause I've been a smidge too indulgent with him."

A smidge? Tessa hid her smile. Then looked back down at the purring kitty still in her arms. "But this cat might *not* be easy. I mean, yeah, she's all cuddly today, but who knows how she'll be a week from now?"

Amy nodded, clearly seeing her point. "A skittish cat can be tough. But you should think about it." She gave her head a tilt. "Think about how you would feel if you came in to work one day and I told you someone *else* had adopted Brontë."

At the mere thought, Tessa's stomach pinched up. But she tried to ignore that, and said, "I'm just not sure I'd want to have to worry about *her* at times when I'm busy worrying about *me*."

The week after Lucky reconciled with his parents, he found himself on a wild roller-coaster ride of emotions.

His parents had stayed in town and he'd had dinner with them twice at Mike's—although each time, Mike had continued to be quiet and surly. The second time, Tessa and Rachel came, too, which helped, and sort of gave him that unexpected family feeling again, but Mike's suspicious gaze had constantly reminded him that he still had secrets—bad ones. And the look in Mike's eye said he was determined to figure those secrets *out*—yet the only way *that* would occur would be if Lucky told him, which wasn't gonna happen.

As planned, Johnny had come to his house, and things had gone well. He loved his room, especially the mural, and seemed as fascinated as Tessa had by Lucky's work. They'd spent time playing a NASCAR game on Lucky's computer, then Tessa had joined them for a ride past the various Romo landmarks, and they'd grabbed a quick pizza in Crestview before taking him home. "Next time I come over, Dad," he'd said, "maybe I could stay overnight in my new room." Lucky had tried to act all cool about it, but his heart had nearly crumbled in his chest.

The night after that, his mother had taken him to see his Grandma Romo, who'd made a huge tray of lasagna and kept stuffing him with it in between kissing his cheek and telling him over and over in her thick Italian accent, "It is so good to have my Jonathan back home again." It had felt weird being called that after so long—she'd been the only person in his life as a kid who'd never taken to calling him Lucky. And even if she drove him a little crazy, and had given him hell over "those terrible tattoos," he couldn't deny being glad to see her again. She'd been good to him when he was a little boy—he remembered her noticing him a little more, looking out for him a little more, than most people had after Anna's disappearance.

Once the whirlwind week of "family time" was past, though, and his parents had finally flown back to Florida, he'd found himself thinking: *Whoa*. How had all this happened so fast?

The truth was, he felt as if he'd lost control, as if everything was closing in on him—and he needed some serious downtime, needed to get some space. It was the only way to find any balance with all the damn *talking* he was doing these days, all the *relationships* he was suddenly having with people. So he just stayed home and worked.

He didn't go to Gravediggers, and he didn't even see much of Tessa.

Fortunately, the timing was good—she expected to be busy this week, putting in extra hours at the bookstore due to some kind of May Day festival in town that he was happy to avoid, and he'd also gotten her another potential job. After Duke had come over and seen what she'd done to his place, he'd approached her about making some improvements to the bar.

The problem with getting some space, though, was that it gave Lucky time to think. And when he took a big step back and looked at it all, he was forced to realized that he felt . . . torn.

What he had now was . . . well, the closest he'd ever get to having the things he'd envisioned as a boy, and the things most people wanted: the love of his family, a nice kid, work he enjoyed, and a woman who made him happy. But at the same time, it wore him out. Inside. He wasn't used to spending time with people. He wasn't used to being responsible to anyone but himself.

And he wasn't used to . . . *caring* so damn much. About *all* of them.

And at moments . . . hell, it shamed him to admit it, even to himself, but he kept suffering that itchy urge . . . to run, to leave it all behind, just like he had once before—the same as he'd felt that night after reconciling with his parents. Every time the impulse struck, he just shut his eyes, leaned back his head, and tried to will it away.

What was *wrong* with him? Why couldn't he just be grateful for all the good things in his life? Why couldn't he lose this nagging feeling that kept dogging him?

Because you're scared. Scared you won't measure up. Scared if they really knew everything about you that they'd hate you. Even Tessa.

And you're scared for *them, too. You're scared for them in the way you used to be scared for yourself—you're scared your past will somehow come back to hurt them, endanger them.*

It was funny—sometimes, the more people who came into his world, the harder it was to remember the hazards of his old life. But at strange, stark, almost surreal moments, it made it harder to *forget* the hazards, too. He wished he'd never seen Red Thornton again, wished the mere sight of the guy hadn't brought those unpleasant memories back, full force.

Finally, after the tension inside him had risen so high that he feared it might smother him, he did something he hated doing—something he'd been avoiding for weeks now even as it had floated around the back of his mind. But he had to know.

Picking up his living room phone, he dialed the number he'd used to reach Red when painting his bike. When Red answered, he sounded far too happy to hear from Lucky—which Lucky had expected, so he nipped it in the bud by saying, "Listen, Red, there's something I've been meaning to ask you." *Putting it off* was more accurate, but the question burned inside him now, making it so he couldn't dodge it for even one more minute. "I was wondering how Vicki is. Or was. When you left the club. I know it's been a while, but . . ."

Just say she was fine. Or maybe that she'd gotten smart and left Bill. Anything to put his mind at ease. But when Red hesitated a second, Lucky's stomach sank and he almost knew—even before Red said it. "Well, gosh, Lucky . . . Vicki's dead."

Lucky's gut hollowed and he pressed his lips together tight, trying to steel himself against the news. "How?" was all he could force out.

Red let out a sigh, and Lucky realized the answer was going to be as grim as the news itself. And when Red spoke, his voice came softer than usual. "Cause of death was an overdose," he said. "But she was in an alley when they found her, beat up damn bad."

"So Wild Bill killed her," Lucky said, struggling to breathe, sound normal. It felt like somebody had just loaded a pile of bricks onto his chest. "He beat the hell out of her, then he pumped her full of drugs to cover it up."

"Bill told the cops she'd been hangin' with some stoners, and that they musta shot up together and then things musta turned violent. Cops *suspected* Bill—but couldn't pin it on him."

Lucky stayed quiet after that, trying to absorb it, wrap his head around it. Vicki was dead; Bill had killed her. He began to fear he would vomit. And it wasn't that he'd cared for Vicki deeply—it was just that it was sad. And that it added to those old remnants of worry still floating around inside him.

He heard Red on the other end of the line, changing the subject, saying something about the paint job on his bike, but Lucky just said, "I gotta go, Red," and hung up.

Then he let out a long sigh and ran his hands back through his hair. Shit.

Maybe this didn't matter. Maybe it didn't affect his life even one little bit. Yet he couldn't help letting it heap new coal onto the fire of his fears. *Irrational* fears? Yeah, sure, probably. But *damn*, it made him want to run. It made him want to get on his bike and ride so fucking far away that no one could ever find him, that no one could ever, *ever* be hurt because of him. He'd done nothing to cause Vicki's death, but once upon a time, he *had* caused her to be hurt. Sort of. It all depended on how you looked at it.

Aw, hell. How long would he last like this—before he really did it one day, before he really got on his Harley and started riding and didn't come back? How long would it be before he hurt people again by running away?

* * *

It was on Thursday as he worked that he realized he hadn't talked to Tessa in a while—at least a couple of days. And maybe that was best. Even if, when he reached a good stopping point now, he found himself putting down his paint gun to walk outside. The day was warm and bright, and blooming redbud trees decorated the woods in purple. When he saw her sedan in the driveway, he knew she was home. And he wondered what she was doing. But he ignored the impulse to find out.

Because he was still just as overwhelmed by all the changes in his life as he'd been a few days ago. And because finding out Vicki was dead was still making him a little sick inside, still creating that knot of fear in his belly. He knew one thing had nothing to do with the other, that Vicki's death and Tessa were about as far apart as two things could be, yet in his mind, he couldn't stop linking them.

Probably the best thing you could do is back away from this relationship now. Keep it casual. Slow it down.

He'd decided it was safe to come here, and ultimately he'd decided it was safe to let more and more people— like Tessa—into his life. But it was all happening awful quick now, and the truth was, if something did go wrong, if something bad came back from his past, what would he do? He'd stepped up for his son, determined to protect him if it ever came to that. And then his family had entered the picture and so he'd had to step up for them, too. But hell. He couldn't protect *everybody*. Could he? So maybe Tessa—as amazing as she was—was the part he needed to back away from a little bit.

Or maybe it was about more than that, about the other part—the part about him not measuring up. With his kid, his parents—they were joined by blood, always would be. And his parents had already proven they'd be there for him, they'd already forgiven the unforgivable. But with Tessa—what really tied her to him? What really kept her from waking up one day and realizing he wasn't right for her, or good enough for her? Maybe backing away from her a little was about protecting *himself*, too.

It wasn't until later, just before dark, that he glanced out the front window toward her house once more and realized that . . . aw, crap—overwhelmed or not, he missed her. He missed her and, despite himself, he'd had enough space now. Space she didn't even know he was taking. He felt like a shit for everything in his head that she didn't even know about.

Her car was still there, and he'd seen no movement at her place all day—so despite himself, he decided to walk down and say hi. He didn't particularly like the idea that he'd suddenly become a guy who could get that caught up in a chick, but he was definitely caught up in Tessa—no point in denying it.

Yet the cabin felt . . . weirdly quiet upon Lucky's approach. He guessed he'd just grown used to seeing her out watering her flowers on the deck or checking her mail, or to hearing music waft through open windows. But everything felt strangely still tonight.

Rather than knock on the back door as he sometimes did, he walked around to the front. He pressed the doorbell and listened to the muffled sound of it ringing on the other side. Then he waited. But no one answered.

Huh. What the hell was *that* about? He shifted his weight from one work boot to the other, then pressed the bell again, longer this time, to make sure she heard it. And he experienced a definite twinge of relief when footsteps approached on the other side.

When Tessa answered, she wore her sexy little Hot Stuff shirt with a pair of cute drawstring shorts. But her hair looked messy—half of it falling out of a ponytail—and her skin pale, especially for a girl who got out in the sun a lot. Her face appeared drawn, her eyes tired. And

Lucky's heart sank to his stomach. "What's wrong?" he asked.

"Nothing." She gave her head a short shake that appeared to require more effort than it should have.

"*Something*," he protested.

She drew her gaze away and said, "Just not feeling well."

That's when it hit Lucky. "Is it your Crohn's disease?" He was aware of her limited diet because they'd eaten plenty of meals together, but he'd never seen her appear ill and had nearly forgotten about that part of her condition.

She looked uncomfortable with the question. "Yeah, but no biggie. I'll call you when I feel better," she told him—then actually moved to shut the door in his face.

He raised a hand to stop her. "I hope you don't think you're getting rid of me *that* easy, hot stuff."

She blinked, clearly caught off guard. "What do you mean?"

"I'm coming in," he told her. It wasn't a decision so much as an instinct.

And it came as a pretty damn big shock when she answered with a surprisingly adamant, "No."

What the hell? "Why not?"

"Because I don't want you here."

... a solemn passion is conceived in my heart;
it leans to you, draws you to my centre and spring of life ...

Charlotte Brontë, *Jane Eyre*

Thirteen

*T*essa didn't mean to be cruel, but she hadn't expected
Lucky to show up at her door, and she preferred being alone
when a flare-up occurred. And she felt too yucky at the
moment to mince words.

Lucky just looked at her. "What the hell is that supposed to mean?"

Geez. She hardly felt like explaining her feelings right
now, but tried anyway. "Look, I just . . . don't want you to
see me like this."

He gave his head a short shake. "I don't care how you
look right now, babe."

But it was more than that. And it wasn't just him—it
was everybody, the whole world. She let out a sigh, trying
to find the words that would make him understand. "It's
easier for me to be alone right now, okay? And I don't
like *anyone* seeing me this way. I don't like . . . being the
sick girl. I don't like it being this big part of who I am. I

don't want people to start thinking of me like it's the most important thing about me."

Lucky just lowered his chin, staring at her like she was off her rocker. "Sounds like you've thought about this a lot."

Another sigh left her as she tried to fight off a wave of nausea. "Well, yeah. In the beginning, I had far more bad days than good. I lost weight, I got weak, and . . . I *was* the sick girl for a while. It *was* the biggest part of me." God, she hated saying that, remembering it.

"I'm real sorry about that, hot stuff—I really am. But if you think it's possible for me to see this as the most important thing about you, you're fucking crazy."

Tessa blinked, taken aback. In Cincinnati, at Posh, she *had* come to be seen that way—as a liability, and as someone to be pitied. It had been as if everyone she knew forgot everything else about her: that she designed great spaces, that she loved colorful clothes, that she was smart, or funny, or kind. She'd just been struggling to survive and that had been all anyone could see. It had been the worst, most trivializing feeling of her life. Finally, she said to Lucky, "I am?"

He still looked at her like she'd lost her marbles. "Of course. You're just feeling bad right now, for God's sake. So I'm coming inside and taking care of you."

His words settled somewhere deep and warm inside her. Yet old habits—and feelings—died hard. "That's nice, Lucky, but . . ." She shook her head again, woozy. "I'm just not good at being with someone when I feel this way. I'm not very good company."

"You're not *supposed* to be good company when you're sick, dummy," he pointed out.

"Still . . ." she began, ready to argue it. But then— whoa—a thick wave of nausea passed through her, forcing her to reach out and grab the doorframe for balance.

"Still *nothing*," Lucky growled. Then he scooped her

up into his arms and carried her to her sofa before she could utter another protest.

"Ugh," she said, happy to be lying down again, then muttered to herself, "Good thing I didn't adopt that cat." Since right now it was all she could do to occasionally walk from the bed to the kitchen to the couch.

"What cat?"

Her eyes had fallen shut, but now she opened them to see Lucky's handsome face hovering over hers. He knelt next to the sofa.

She spoke softly as the nausea faded a bit. "A cat at the bookstore. She's really sweet, but kind of skittish. I sort of considered adopting her but figured that would be a bad idea, and I was right. I wouldn't be able to take care of her at times like this."

Lucky arched one brow, grimacing slightly. "A *cat*, huh? I didn't know you *liked* cats."

She shifted her head slightly on the couch pillow. What was it with guys? Every guy she'd ever known had either loved cats or hated them—no in between. "So being sick won't change how you see me, but if I like cats you're calling it quits?"

He met her gaze, his expression laced with dry amusement. "I guess I'll let it slide, but . . . what's so great about cats anyway?"

"It's not cats in general so much as this particular one," she said. "She's just nice to pet and cuddle with."

The tilt of his head came with a cocky look. "If you want something to pet and cuddle with, babe, you got me."

She couldn't hold back a small grin, but ignored his arrogance to add, "Brontë's very affectionate. I just . . . like being around her."

Yet Lucky still looked doubtful. "If you ask me, cats are . . . sneaky-looking. Like they're out to get you. That cat at Mike's house kept staring at me and I didn't like it."

His words made Tessa laugh out loud. "Oooh—big, bad Lucky Romo's afraid of a little kitty cat."

He lowered his chin, eyes chiding. "Funny, hot stuff. You should take that on the road."

"I can't," she said sardonically. "I'm sick."

"You gonna quit being silly and let me take care of you now?"

Tessa peered up at him. She couldn't have imagined a few weeks ago that her brawny neighbor would be bending over backward, insistent on caring for her. And the truth was, she still didn't like the idea of him seeing her at her worst—she wanted him to keep seeing her as his hot, sexy girlfriend. But even though he was asking her, she suspected Lucky wasn't really giving her a choice in the matter. "What if I say no?"

He shrugged. "You're stuck with me anyway."

"That's what I thought."

He gave a short nod, apparently taking that as surrender. "Now—how can I help?"

Tessa sighed, finally accepting her defeat, then glanced toward the TV. "Hand me the remote and sit down. We're watching *Ellen*."

Being a small town cop gave a man a lot of time to think. Mike figured that could be a good thing or a bad one depending upon how you looked at it. Most of the time, as he patrolled the streets of Destiny and the surrounding highways in his cruiser, he appreciated that gift of time. God knew he'd spent a hell of a lot of time thinking about Rachel behind the wheel of this car, especially when they'd first met. It had given him a chance to sort through all the complexities of their relationship, time to decipher his feelings for her.

But lately, he was thinking too much. About Lucky. About times when they were kids, and times when they were teenagers. And about more recent times, too. It was the damnedest thing. For the past fifteen years, he'd been sure that if Lucky walked through the door one day, he'd be glad to see him. And he *was* glad to finally find out Lucky was alive, and healthy—all that. But Mike never could have dreamed Lucky would come rolling back into their lives and that he wouldn't want anything to do with his little brother.

Even now, as he drove slowly up and down the small grid of residential streets that flanked Destiny's town square, his chest tightened over thoughts of Lucky.

Lucky acted decent to everyone. And hell, he had a kid, which meant Mike was an uncle now. And he truly hadn't seen his mother this happy in many years. Everybody but him, it seemed, was downright giddy about his wayward brother's homecoming.

But there was a lot Mike just couldn't get over.

The betrayal of being left alone when Lucky had taken off, for instance. One night, the summer after Lucky's high school graduation, he simply hadn't come home. So they'd called all over town, driven around all night trying to find him—but they'd figured he was raising hell somewhere and that he'd turn up the next day. And then they'd realized his clothes were gone, his underwear, his shoes. And then Mike had developed that same lump of dread in his stomach as when Anna had disappeared.

Later, old Willie Hargis had told Police Chief Tolliver that he'd seen Lucky's car leave town the day he'd gone missing. And they finally accepted that all the fights Lucky had had with his parents and the threats he'd made about "getting the hell outta here" were coming to bear. And the rest, always, had been a painful mystery.

Then there was the fact that Lucky's story had some big holes in it, and Mike wasn't finding it difficult to believe the rumor of an outlaw motorcycle gang in California was true. Now, he could barely sleep nights for wondering what sort of bad shit Lucky had been involved in. Even if it was a long time ago. Mike knew enough about MCs to know "bad shit" was a mild way of describing gang behavior. Outlaw gangs were made up of two kinds of people: the ones with no morals, and the ones who followed along. He could easily see Lucky being one of those followers, especially when he was younger, more rebellious, maybe looking for someplace to act tough and feel powerful. What kinds of heinous things might his brother have done?

And then there was the bullshit of blaming his family for the way he'd turned out. Why the hell couldn't Lucky man up and take responsibility for his actions? Mike couldn't believe Lucky had the gall to walk back into their lives and lay the blame for his troubled existence at the feet of his parents, who'd already suffered more than enough. And they'd acted like they agreed with him on it all, but he didn't remember things that way. And he figured his mom and dad were just so happy to have one of their missing kids suddenly back, grim reaper tattoo and all, that they'd have agreed with *anything*.

Rachel had been giving him a hard time for not cutting Lucky any slack, and it was true, he hadn't. The truth he hadn't admitted to anyone, though, was that he was impressed with Lucky's willingness to step up for his kid. And he was equally impressed with Lucky having built his own business. Both were more than he might have expected.

Lucky had taken their parents to his house during their visit, but Mike had conveniently had to work that night and he wouldn't have gone anyway. Yeah, he was mildly curious to see where Lucky lived, and even see the work he did—but no matter how he tried, he couldn't get past the granite wall that materialized inside him every time Lucky came to mind.

"Mike, you should see what an artist your brother is," his mom had told him afterward. "And he's put together a nice home for little Johnny."

Mike had merely grumbled something in reply.

And then his dad had spoken up. "Son, I know this is hard for you—it's a strange time for all of us. But your mother and I would appreciate it if you'd make an effort with Lucky. We all have to put the past behind us now."

Yeah, that made sense. There was no other way to move on. So, for the sake of his mom and dad, he'd said he'd try.

But he hadn't.

He'd just kept thinking, and thinking. About all the times it would have been nice to have a brother in his life over the past fifteen years. About what a hard man he'd become, and still was to many degrees, because of all the loss he'd suffered—and Lucky was a big part of that. Rachel had . . . hell, she'd softened him more than he'd have believed possible, but he supposed the way he felt about Lucky now was proof that he was still a hard-ass and probably always would be. He just didn't know how to forgive.

Just then his cell phone rang and he glanced down at the screen. Rachel. He picked it up. "Hey, baby," he said easily.

"Oh good, you're in range." His phone, she meant. "Up for late dinner?"

Sometimes, when he worked the night shift, Rachel met him at Dolly's Café on his break. It was almost that time, and he could *use* a break. Not from his work, but from the thoughts swirling in his head. Hell, it was almost enough to make him wish someone would commit a damn crime so he'd have something else to focus on. "Yeah, that sounds good. Half an hour?"

"See you then, Officer Romo."

After Mike hung up, he drove slowly around the town square—quiet at this hour, but the warmer weather was keeping people out a little later. He saw Amy watering the flowerboxes outside the bookshop, probably getting ready to close for the night, and lifted his hand in a wave.

A minute later, he turned onto Stone School Road and found himself driving past the town's old elementary school. It was no longer in use—a new school had been built in the nineties not far from Destiny High, and now the old one housed the board of education and the small community ed program. But it was where Mike and Lucky had gone to school as boys, and it conjured up a lot of memories, many of them good.

Even being two years apart, he and Lucky had been close then. Their Boy Scout troop had met in the room at the front right corner of the building, which he braked to look at now. Their classes had played kickball in the large yard out back. Lucky had once fallen down while playing tag in the gravel lot outside the small gymnasium, ripping his pants and tearing up his knee pretty bad, and Mike had come running, eventually helping Lucky limp inside to the office for first aid while he tried not to cry in front of the other kids. Something about that, the mere fact that Lucky had once been a child who cried, made a lump rise to Mike's throat as he sat in his car on the quiet road in front of the school.

And then other memories came flooding back. An art teacher—Miss Bailey. She'd been pretty, with red hair, and she'd come to Destiny Elementary one day a week, spending an hour with each grade. Lucky had had a crush on her. He'd never said so, but Mike had been able to tell and he'd teased Lucky mercilessly for it—yet he'd never mentioned it to anyone else, keeping it just between the two of them.

Mike almost smiled remembering the awe on Lucky's face one day when . . . how old were they then? It was soon after Anna was gone, so Lucky had probably been ten or eleven, Mike twelve or thirteen. And Lucky had climbed on the school bus trying to act cool but not doing a very good job of it—happy as hell because of a note Miss Bailey had written on an assigned drawing he'd done of their family, copied from a photo that hung on the wall above the TV. Mike remembered it saying in red capital letters, EXCELLENT—A+. And the note had said Lucky had real talent and should continue to develop it. It had been one of the first nice things to happen to any of them after losing Anna, one of the first moments when anyone in the family had had a reason to smile.

And when they'd walked in the door at home, Lucky had yelled out, "Mom! Dad! Look! Miss Bailey says I'm talented!"

And Mike had known from the expression on his mom's face that it wasn't a good time, but Lucky, in his excitement, had missed that and gone pulling the family portrait from his notebook. And their mother had promptly burst into tears and fled the room.

A familiar old sadness, too big for a kid to have suffered, closed around Mike now. He'd hated seeing his mom cry. He'd felt pissed at Lucky for causing it and for being too immature to see she was on edge when they'd walked in. And that overwhelming guilt from those days came roaring back to him. Another reason to be pissed at Lucky that day? Mike had been happy for a little while, distracted by something, and Lucky's actions had brought all the bad stuff back.

Mike blew out a long sigh. He hadn't had reason to think back on that day . . . probably since it had happened. And for the first time in his life, he wondered if his mom or dad had ever said anything nice to Lucky about the praise. Probably not.

Mike narrowed his eyes, still looking at the old stone building. It hadn't been long after that when Lucky had won first place in the school art contest with a painting of their house. Mike remembered hearing about it at school, being proud of his little brother and a little amazed at how good the painting was. He remembered seeing the blue ribbon in Lucky's hand, and later, hanging from a bulletin board in Lucky's room. But what he couldn't remember was . . . anyone at home making a big deal out of it. Or ever even mentioning it at all.

Shit. Was Lucky right? Had they really ignored him that much?

Whereas Mike could clearly remember feeling loved and acknowledged when *he'd* done good things. He recalled a special cake when he was named MVP of the basketball team in eighth grade. And his parents had been in the stands for every sporting event he'd ever taken part in, from Little League to high school. He remembered a special dinner at a steakhouse over in Crestview once after he'd brought his grades up from Cs to As.

Mike's achievements had always been celebrated in their house. But maybe Lucky's really *hadn't* been. And until this moment, maybe Mike had chosen to believe Lucky just hadn't excelled enough to *have* any achievements, but now he was forced to realize: He had. For a while anyway. Until he'd kind of just . . . given up and quit trying.

And maybe . . . maybe Lucky was right. Maybe Mike's accomplishments had been celebrated because he'd been in his own private, guilt-stricken hell over Anna and his parents knew it. And because *they* felt guilty, too. And since Lucky was the only one of them who didn't have anything to feel guilty about, maybe that had left him on the outside in a way. Hell.

Talk about guilt. Mike was starting to feel pretty fucking guilty right *now*.

By the time he pulled up outside Dolly's a little while later, a knot had grown in his stomach. He kept thinking back through those years after Anna's disappearance, and the more he thought, the more he realized . . . he'd never noticed Lucky was fading into the background. Because he was a kid. With his own issues. His own life. But Lucky *had* faded. Slowly but surely. And by the time he'd reached twelve or thirteen, he'd turned into a pretty bad kid.

When Mike walked into the café and sat down at a small table next to his fiancée, she looked into his eyes and immediately asked, "What is it?"

"I've been thinking about Lucky," he said. "And I'm gonna say something I hardly *ever* say. I think I was wrong."

Rachel's jaw dropped, which Mike could easily understand.

"Not about everything," he went on. "I still don't know what he was up to the whole time he was gone, and I'm still not sure I trust him or think it's smart for Tessa to be with him. But some of the stuff he said about when we were kids, about him getting neglected . . . I'm starting to think it might have been true and I just never saw it."

In reply, the woman he loved reached under the table to squeeze his hand and said, "I'm glad—relieved—to hear you're starting to see things in a new way. But . . . maybe instead of telling *me*, you should be telling your brother."

By Saturday night, Tessa still felt lousy, and it made Lucky feel like someone was reaching into his chest and squeezing his heart. She'd insisted he work Friday during the day, but otherwise, he'd hung out with her and wished he could make her feel better. The fact that he couldn't left him feeling helpless—as helpless as he had as a kid.

And what did Lucky usually do when he felt helpless, like he had no control over a situation? He ran. He'd run away from Destiny, and later, he'd run away from the Devil's Assassins. *That* move had been a smart one—but it was still running.

Yet over the last couple of days with Tessa, he'd been forced to realize that . . . well, maybe his running instinct was more of an old urge than a thing he really wanted to do. And maybe his fears for the people in his life were silly and impractical. Maybe his fears about her expectations were silly, too. This, being here with Tessa when she needed him—*that* was practical. In fact, she kept telling him to go home, so he had an out if he wanted it—but while she was sick . . . hell, he couldn't leave her. In fact, the second he'd discovered she was sick, it had washed away every thought in his head about slowing things down or staying away from her.

Now they lay on Tessa's bed, atop the covers, side by side. Lucky stroked her arm, sometimes brushed his fingers through her hair, hoping it somehow helped a little.

"What exactly do you feel when you're sick like this?" he asked her quietly.

"It varies from person to person, but for me, the main symptom is nausea. Sometimes I have a dull stomach-ache, too, or sharp pain in my lower abdomen."

"I wish I could fix it, babe," he whispered.

"I know. That's sweet," she said.

He glanced down at her—God, she looked so tired. "How long does it last?"

"Hard to say. These days, anywhere from a few hours to a week or so."

He nodded.

"Although," she went on, "I actually feel a *little bit* yucky at some point every day. I'm just used to that part."

And that took him aback. When he thought of all the time he'd spent with her, he'd never had any notion she'd felt bad, even for a minute. "I didn't know that."

She shrugged against her pillow. "No need to talk about it. And I don't like bringing other people down."

At that, Lucky reached to tilt her chin upward with one bent finger. "Tessa," he said, "don't worry about that with me. You can tell me if you feel bad. I mean, keeping it to yourself probably isn't good. I kept a lot to myself as a kid and . . . let's just say it didn't do me any favors."

Yet she shook her head. "No—it's better for me to be tough about it. Talking about it much is just . . . indulgent. I never want to wallow in self-pity. I did that in the beginning, and it didn't help."

He sighed, gave another quiet nod, and thought she *was* tough. "Will you . . . at least tell me what happened? In the beginning? You never really told me the details of how you wound up back in Destiny."

Tessa supposed she knew Lucky well enough now that she owed him an answer if he really wanted to know. And even though she'd actually been mad at him at first for forcing his company on her when she felt crappy, she was beginning to realize . . . how darn sweet it was. Pushy, but sweet. And whereas two days ago she'd been fairly horrified for him to see her like this, now she realized it was unimportant—he still liked her just as much. Nothing had changed . . . except that maybe she felt even closer to him now.

"I got sick out of the blue," she said. "Just basically woke up one day unable to digest anything. I was living on cereal for a while, and I got very weak. I couldn't go to work for a couple of months, and the doctors couldn't find anything wrong with me, even after extensive testing."

"You were in Cincinnati for all this?"

She nodded against his chest. "My mother came after about a month. By then, I was having trouble taking care of myself. I was losing lots of weight, and before long, I couldn't even think clearly. What I didn't realize was that I was eating and drinking so little that I'd become severely dehydrated. And I later learned that once you reach a certain point, your body stops absorbing what you *do* drink."

Tessa paused then, deciding how much to say. She was

willing to share it with him, but she still wasn't willing to indulge in making it as drawn-out and dramatic as it had been at the time. "At one point, I collapsed from the dehydration. My blood pressure was sixty over twenty."

She felt him flinch slightly. "Jesus, is that even possible?"

"Believe it or not, yes. So I had to start drinking gallons of Gatorade and other stuff with electrolytes to replenish everything I'd lost. It took about six weeks to fully rehydrate my body, but even after that, when you add in the poor nutrition, I was pretty weak and underweight for about a year. I underwent tons more testing without a diagnosis, and though I became able to digest a few more foods, it was still rough."

She sighed, remembering the next part. "On the occasions I did try to go to work, I'd end up with my head down on my desk or having to cut client meetings short because I was about to keel over. And I began to realize that my bosses and colleagues, even people who I'd considered real friends, were looking at me differently."

Lucky sounded puzzled when he said, "Looking at you how?"

"I know they cared about me, but at the same time . . . I was very aware that I was making their lives harder by not being dependable. That's when I felt people thinking of my condition as the biggest part of me. And after a few months, I knew they wanted to fire me and that only kindness was keeping them from it. So I quit, without a plan. Which was really scary. But it was *all* really scary, and kind of overwhelming."

"I'm really sorry you had to go through that, babe."

"Then another interior designer I knew told me she was opening a branch of her firm in Crestview of all places. She knew about my problem, and that my family was in Destiny, so she offered me a job with the understanding that I might need a lot of flexibility. Like I told you before, though, the job fell through—almost as quickly as I'd bought the cabin.

"Coming back to Destiny was the hardest thing I've ever done—because I felt like I'd failed, and it was for reasons totally beyond my control. But it seemed the only sensible choice—and it relieved my mom and dad to have me close. My little brother is in Afghanistan right now, and I think feeling like both their kids were in danger, away from home, was killing them."

"I didn't know that, about your brother," he said, his voice soft with compassion.

And Tessa sighed. The truth was, Jeremy was like her Crohn's disease: She thought of him often but tried not to. Because it came with so much worry, and left her feeling so helpless. "It's scary. He e-mails us, but he's kind of tight-lipped, so we don't really know what's going on with him."

Lucky nodded, brow knit in understanding. "So . . . you came home, you bought this place, and . . . you started feeling better?"

She gave a slight nod, still resting against him. "Slowly but surely. Though it took a long time before I felt even remotely normal. It was the strangest, darkest time of my life. And . . . the oddest thing," she said, looking back. "This all started in the winter, and other than doctor's visits and occasional stabs at going to the office, I spent a few very long months mostly in my condo, never going out at all. And when I finally felt good enough to go outside again, it was like . . . it was brand new."

"What do you mean?"

Tessa still recalled this part with a bit of wonder. "This will sound crazy, but it was like . . . the grass was greener, the sky was bluer, flowers smelled sweeter. I suddenly couldn't get enough of being outdoors. Now, I'm all into gardening and sitting outside, even at night—"

"Like the night I found you on the deck looking at the stars," he reminded her.

And she smiled softly against his chest. "Yeah, like that. I was never so into nature before, but the experience changed me in that way. And . . . I don't take as much for granted anymore. Any day I feel well is a good day. Any day I can get dressed and go out into the world, I feel fortunate. Those are . . . the few good things that came out of it all."

"You go through something tough and it gives you a whole new outlook, doesn't it?" he said as if he knew.

She raised her eyes to his. "Yeah." And she would have asked him *how* he knew—but just then, it didn't matter. All that mattered was that he was here, holding her, relating to her, making her feel better. "Thank you," she said.

"For what?"

"Being here with me. I didn't think it would help, but it does."

It was almost twenty-four hours later that Tessa lay in her bed, but no longer in Lucky's arms—now he hovered over her, holding a tray in his hands, clearly trying to figure out how to make things better. She'd slept a lot today, feeling worse than yesterday, and worry shone in his eyes.

"Feel like eating?" he asked.

"What is it?"

"Chicken soup. From your mom. And some Club crackers. She said you liked those when you aren't feeling good."

Tessa's eyes opened a little wider. "My mom?"

He gave a short nod, looking uneasy. "She dropped by a little while ago."

"Oh God."

"Yeah, I think I scared the shit out of her, answering your door."

Tessa bit her lip. Her mother had called this morning

after not hearing from her for a few days, suspecting she was unwell, and Tessa had tried to soft-pedal it. She'd also mentioned Lucky was there, looking out for her, "so you don't have to come over. I'll be fine."

"Lucky's there?" her mom had asked. Tessa had told her mother about her new neighbor—that he was Mike Romo's long-lost brother, and that they'd spent some time together. She'd been trying to ease her into the idea.

"Yeah," she'd said simply, leaving it at that.

But her mom understood what a big deal it was—she knew Tessa didn't like anyone around during these times. So she'd asked, "Is it serious?"

Good question. Since it was no longer just sex. And maybe it never really *had* been, even if that had been her original motive. All she knew was that there was much more to Lucky than met the eye, that he called her his girl, and he was here for her now. Still, she wasn't quite ready to put a label on it, so she'd just said, "I don't know."

What she *hadn't* mentioned to her mom was that Lucky was a biker with long hair and tattoos. So now, as she peered up at the man carefully lowering a tray to her lap, she asked, "What happened after you answered the door?"

Lucky's brow knit slightly. "Not much. I told her you were asleep. She gave me the soup. She seemed less freaked out after she talked to me for a few minutes."

Good. Maybe that meant her mom had seen past his appearance to the guy underneath.

After that, Lucky lay down beside her and they watched TV together while she ate. When she was done, he said, "How do you feel?"

"A little nauseous," she replied, easing back into the pillows propped behind her.

It was a few minutes later that Lucky lifted the tray away and set it aside—and then, to her surprise, he bent back over her, sliding his arms beneath her. "Wrap your arms around my neck and hold on," he said.

"What are you doing?" she asked as he scooped her up into his grasp.

"You're always talking about wanting to experience life," he replied, "and now I get why. So . . . I'm not gonna let you lay in this house not experiencing life for one minute longer tonight."

"Lucky, I'm still feeling blah," she said in protest, taken aback by the fact that he was carrying her down the hall, apparently headed for the front door.

He wore a determined look on his face as he said, "You don't have to do a thing, hot stuff—it's all on me. Trust me." And then he carried her out of the cabin into the dark of night, down the walk and to the passenger side of her Nissan, which he promptly, gently, loaded her into. "Be right back," he told her, and she waited, bewildered, until he returned carrying her keys and her iPod in his hand, her grandma's quilt draped over one arm.

After tossing the blanket and iPod in the backseat, he climbed behind the wheel, then proceeded to back out onto the road, all without saying a word.

"Lucky, where are we going?"

"You'll see."

Fifteen minutes later, they pulled into Creekside Park, but Tessa still didn't understand why. "The park is closed after dark," she said, pointing to a sign near the entrance.

And Lucky just slanted her a look, as if to remind her he was a bad biker dude and it would take more than a sign to keep him out of a park.

After he brought the car to a stop and opened his door, she did, too—only to have him say, "No, don't get out— I'm coming to get you."

Then he grabbed the quilt and iPod from the back, and

a moment later he was again carrying her in his arms, this time into the quiet solitude of the unlit park. As her eyes adjusted to the darkness, she could make out the white gazebo, and the playground in the distance on the bank above Sugar Creek. Tall, shadowy trees lined the creek's edge.

Soon Lucky lowered her to her feet, announcing quietly, "Here," then he spread the quilt on the ground and whispered, "Lie down."

It hit her only then that the night was warm, the warmest they'd had so far, and as she lay back into the quilt's softness, she drank in the sweet, lush air and heard the faint, peaceful sound of crickets in the nearby woods. As Lucky lay down beside her, he said, "Now—look up."

She did—and she saw the same thing as when she'd recently given him the same instruction: a dark velvety sky sprinkled with twinkling stars. Only . . . it was even more stunning tonight. Because tonight she needed it more. And maybe Lucky knew that. "Wow," she murmured.

"Yeah," he agreed. Then added, "Isn't this better than being stuck in the house, staring at the ceiling?"

She glanced over at him with a smile. "A *lot* better." The truth was, it was almost enough to make everything else fade away, even illness.

Just then, Lucky pushed abruptly back to his feet, though, and she said, "Where are you going?"

"I'll be right back," he promised before disappearing quickly into the darkness.

What on earth . . . ? she wondered, waiting. And she was just on the verge of feeling a little abandoned when Lucky finally arrived back beside her in the dim moonlight.

Although that faded, too, when her gaze was drawn to the bunch of daisies clutched in his fist, clearly plucked from along the creekside walk—they must have bloomed early, from the warmer-than-usual spring. She smiled up at him as he lowered himself to the quilt beside her. "I think picking flowers in the park is illegal."

"Guess my brother'll have to haul my ass to jail for all these bad crimes I'm committing tonight," he said, then held one of the daisies out to her.

For some reason, the simple gesture made her heart feel so full she feared it might burst. "Thank you," she said, taking it from his fingers into hers. Then she teased him, looking at the remaining flowers, which he'd lowered to the quilt beside him. "Keeping the rest yourself?"

He gave her a grin. "Keep it up, hot stuff, and you won't get your present."

"My present?"

"Yeah," he said. "Now close your eyes so I can make it a surprise."

Hmm. What was Lucky up to? She shut them, both touched and amused. Although when a few minutes had come and gone, she grew impatient. "When can I open my eyes?"

"Just . . . a second," he said in a way that told her he was concentrating on something. Then finally he told her, "Okay, open 'em."

When she did, she found big, masculine Lucky Romo dangling a chain of daisies from his fingers. And the sight took her breath away. Oh God, he'd just sat in the park making a daisy chain in the dark of night—for her.

"Sit up a little, and I'll put it on your head," he said.

Oh—it was a wreath. A smile stole over her as she propped herself on her elbows and let him place it in her messy hair. "Thank you, Lucky," she said.

He looked endearingly sheepish. "When I caught sight of the daisies, I just . . . thought you'd like it."

"I do," she promised him.

Lucky reclined next to her again, and they silently peered back up at the sky. And though she'd already forgotten all about the iPod, Lucky then gently inserted one earbud in her ear and the other in his, so they could both hear. Then she listened as the notes from a gently plucked guitar began Jack Johnson's "Constellations," a song about . . . the sky. She just looked at Lucky. How could he know? How could he know, even better than she did, what she'd needed right now? It was one of the most perfect moments of her life.

"Don't look at *me*, hot stuff—look at the stars," Lucky said. So she did. She let the relaxing song waft over and through her as she lost herself in everything around her: the millions of stars glittering above, the soft quilt beneath her, the man whose hand slipped warmly into hers. And she began to understand something she hadn't only a few short minutes before; she began to feel a certain, undeniable truth seeping into her skin, her muscles, her very bones.

And when the song came to its sweet, peaceful conclusion, she continued peering up at the sky even as she leaned her head over to rest it on Lucky's shoulder. And she whispered, "You love me."

He kept gazing upward, too, his answer coming softly. "Yeah. I do."

And it sounded . . . like it wasn't a surprise to him at all.

The new knowledge made Tessa's skin tingle even as her body filled with warmth. And she pulled back just slightly to peer over at him, this man who loved her. He hadn't put it into words, but he hadn't needed to—because he'd shown her, in so many sweet ways.

When his beautiful eyes met hers, she reached up, pulling their earbuds away. A minute ago, soft music had been perfect, the perfect distraction from feeling unwell. But silence suddenly seemed better—right now, she wanted nothing to dilute her focus on Lucky.

Their eyes stayed locked and she experienced a familiar pull inside. It stretched all through her—from her chest to the crux of her thighs. And, leaning forward, she brought her mouth tenderly to his. The kiss was slow, warm, gentle. It was the nicest thing she'd felt in days. When it ended, she didn't move away; she simply rested her forehead against his, felt his breath on her lips, felt the emotional connection they shared.

But when she drew back again to gaze on him, she experienced more than just an *emotional* link. And more than just a physical one, too. When those two things joined together, they created a whole greater than the sum of their parts, and it swirled through her suddenly in a bundle of need and lust and sweetness and sex. She kissed him again, and again, still slow and deep, until the sparks inside her sizzled. "Oh my God," she breathed in soft wonder.

"What?" he asked.

"You're amazing. You're so hot you actually turn me on even when I don't feel well."

A small, sweet grin made his dark eyes sparkle. "Damn, I knew I was good, but . . ."

And she giggled lightly . . . aware that her desire was truly overriding every other feeling.

But then her smile faded as she confided in him, "You have no idea how un-sexy I feel most of the time, because of . . . you know." Right now, she didn't even want to say it, didn't want to give it power over her.

And Lucky looked at her like she was crazy. "Babe," he said, soft and low and sure. "You're the sexiest girl I ever met."

She kissed him again and realized she didn't want to *stop* kissing him, ever. She never again wanted to feel anything but the way Lucky was making her feel at this moment: cherished . . . and sexy as sin, even in old jogging pants and dirty hair.

Lucky hadn't touched her anyplace intimate since he'd first found her at home sick, but now his hand slid to her breast. She sucked in her breath at the shocking pleasure. And then he began to squeeze and mold, and she tipped her head back to look at the stars once more and saw them in a whole new way: as a lovely backdrop for what was happening down here, on earth, where things really mattered.

"Lucky," she whispered.

But he misunderstood. "Sorry, babe." He drew his palm back down to her waist. "I didn't mean to do that. It just happened."

"No. I *want* that," she immediately corrected him. Reaching for his hand, she placed it right back where it had been, on her breast. Then she gazed back into his eyes. "I want *you*."

Looking up, I, with tear-dimmed eyes, saw the mighty Milky-way. Remembering what it was—what countless systems there swept space like a soft trace of light—
I felt the might and strength of God.

Charlotte Brontë, *Jane Eyre*

Fourteen

"Even now?" he asked.

"Especially now. I told you—you turn me on, Lucky. You make it all better. You make me forget the bad stuff."

Aw, hell. The truth was, she had the same effect on him, too. Completely. And . . . Jesus, had he just told her he loved her? He was pretty sure he had. He wasn't sure how it had happened—but it had just been . . . obvious. In that moment, it had been so clear that he hadn't even thought of denying it, even if, up until then, he hadn't quite known it himself. He loved her. He loved Tessa. Now, the very thought made him kiss her a little more firmly as he resumed caressing her small, pert breast, the nipple jutting into his palm through her top. A tingling sensation rippled down his spine and his breath grew labored, just from this—from the touching and kissing.

In a way, he suddenly felt big—clumsy with her—and afraid, in her current condition, he might hurt her some-how. But battling with that fear was how badly he wanted her, how driven he felt to bond his body with hers. He was suddenly so hard for her he ached.

"Are you okay?" he whispered a moment later.

"Yes—yes, I promise," she said. And the urgency in her voice, the desperation, made him finally believe her. And long to pleasure her deeply.

When he kissed her neck, she let out a pretty sigh that tightened his chest. And part of him wanted to stop going slow and being careful, but a bigger part of him longed to . . . make love to her. He'd never even used those words together: make love. Yet that was what he burned to do right now—make slow, deep love to Tessa Sheridan.

Gently, he lifted the hem of her top over her soft, slender stomach and bestowed kisses there, as well, while easing his hand tenderly between her legs. A low, feminine moan echoed up into the warm night, filling him with heat, sat-isfaction, and he began to stroke his fingertips through the sweatpants she wore. Her breath grew thready as she moved against his touch, and he heard himself whisper-ing against her skin, "You're so beautiful, babe. So damn beautiful."

Then he shifted, sliding his hand down inside her pants, her panties. At the same exact moment, he gently closed his teeth around her nipple, through her top, and the little sob that left her set him on fire.

Stretching out fully alongside her again, he kissed her some more while exploring her wetness with his fingers, somehow feeling that intimacy in a whole new way. How many women had he touched there, or had sex with? He didn't know, but it was plenty. And yet this felt completely new. He was sure Tessa had been touched this way before, too, and he suffered the sting of jealousy over it, wanting to be the only one she'd ever shared herself with.

This must be what comes with the love part. Suddenly he understood why people said sex was so much better when you were in love, because right now, every touch echoed deeper, and in every place their skin connected, he felt truly joined to her. He wanted to belong to her. He wanted her to belong to him. He wanted to give her every joy, every comfort. He wanted to take away everything that hurt her.

And he was powerless to take away her illness, a knowledge that now tortured him—but tonight anyway, he could at least make her forget about it. Make it go away for a little while. And her every moan and sigh, and every lift of her pelvis against his hand, told him how much she was feeling it, how much he *was* taking away the bad stuff in that moment. "I want to make you feel so, so good," he whispered against her lips, then kissed her yet again.

That's when her breath grew short, choppy, and it was almost as if Lucky could feel the pleasure he delivered vibrating through her, growing, mounting. "Come for me, babe," he rasped. "I wanna see you come so bad."

And that's when her body stretched, lifted, held, and then she was moving again, but crying out now, climaxing, and Lucky's face turned warm, his whole body shuddering in response. He'd given his fair share of women orgasms before, but this was the first time it had made him feel so . . . powerful. Powerful in a way that mattered, in a way that went beyond masculinity—because suddenly it *did* give him some real control, at least a little, over how she felt tonight.

"Lucky," she breathed upon finally going still. "Lucky?"

He was busy raining kisses across her forehead, cheek, mouth. "What is it, babe?"

"Please. Inside me. Now."

Aw, God. It wasn't the first time she'd issued such a demand, but this time it came so gentle, so sweet. He said nothing in reply, just extracted his hand from where it had been and pulled on the drawstring at her hips. A second later, she was lifting, helping him push her pants down. As she kicked them off, he undid his belt, his jeans, and she began reaching, trying to shove the denim away, impatient. It made his heart beat even faster. "Please," she said again.

"I'm on my way, hot stuff," he promised, and without bothering to undress either of them further, he moved between her parted legs and pressed his erection inward, listening as she sucked in her breath at the contact.

The entry was slow, wet, deep. Immersed in her as far as their bodies would allow, Lucky gazed into her eyes and said, "God, you're warm. Tight. This is . . . so good."

She only nodded, and her eyes told him she was experiencing the same sense of connection as him. And as they began to move, their rhythm *remained* slow, lingering—it was more about feeling the union of their flesh than about sensation and friction.

Lucky didn't know how long it stayed that way, but he got lost in it—lost in her eyes, in the warm night air, in the enveloping moisture between her thighs. At some point, her legs wrapped around his hips. Their foreheads touched. He could hear them both breathing

"Jesus," he whispered eventually, because after a while, he wanted to move deeper, harder. He began to sweat.

His strokes increased gradually, but she met each one, and finally he knew the time for going slow was over. Thank God. Because he had loved that—in a way he hadn't known he could—but now he needed to let himself go, to drive into her over and over, hard and fast.

And before long they were both moaning, crying out with each powerful stroke, and finally Lucky just closed his eyes and allowed the pleasure to own him. He plunged into her waiting warmth, faster, faster; he smelled fresh green grass and spring flowers mingling with the scent of her skin; he braced himself, planting his palms at either side of her head, making her sob with the hard pleasure he delivered now—and then he let go. He let go and erupted inside her, his climax explosive and swallowing and . . . so draining that when it was done, he simply lowered his weight on top of her, resting his head next to hers on the quilt.

"I meant it," he whispered, low, in her ear. "I love you."

By Tuesday, Tessa felt much better. Enough that she'd gotten up, showered, dressed, and surprised Amy by coming in to work. And it was such a relief to hear that Amy had handled the rush of the May Day festival without her!

Now, she sat on a stool, shelving new mystery novels, soaking in the lovely scents of books, old wood, and coffee, and let out a happy sigh—it was good to be out and about again. Even the sun shining in through the front windows of Under the Covers felt brighter than the last time she'd been here.

Maybe it was silly, but she could have sworn sex with Lucky had cured her flare-up. Or maybe it had been his words. When he'd agreed with what she'd said. About loving her. Her heart felt as if it swelled in her chest just remembering. Lucky loved her. And maybe that was a little scary in a sense—they were so different in ways, and there was still so much she didn't know about him. But it felt amazing, too.

They'd slept in the park all night, waking with the sun—then looking frantically around to make sure no early birds were out and about to see them wrapped, half naked, in her grandmother's quilt. Then they'd scurried back to her car and headed home, having shared so much: the sky, the night, the sex, the sleeping together beneath the stars.

She hadn't told him she loved him back—because, in truth, she hadn't allowed herself to think that far ahead.

Even as close as they'd become, it had never occurred to her that Lucky would say those words, that this would turn into *that*. And now . . . well, maybe she loved him, too, but just hadn't let herself admit it. Maybe she was afraid of the things Lucky hadn't told her about himself. There were questions to be answered, for them both, but for now, today, she just wanted to enjoy the sensation of purpose and productivity delivered by being back in the land of the living. Funny—sometimes she felt that to truly grab life, she had to seek out all sorts of radical things like skydiving or tattoos. And then, other times, it was as simple as putting books on a shelf on a sunny day.

"Hey, look who wants to see you."

Tessa glanced up to find Amy standing beside her, little Brontë in her arms. She let out a soft gasp at the sight. "She even lets *you* hold her now, too?"

Amy lifted the kitty's white mitten paw to wave it at Tessa, saying in a silly cat voice, "*Hi, Tessa. I've missed you and I'm glad you're back.*"

Tessa couldn't help smiling.

"She's still antsy around customers," Amy explained, "but yeah, with me, she's calming down a lot." And with that, she slowly handed Brontë down to Tessa, and taking the lanky kitty into her arms, provided yet another sense of comfort.

"Hi there," she whispered. "It's good to see you." She hugged the cat to her chest, running her fingertips over her fur.

"I still think you'd like having a cat at home," Amy said.

Tessa lifted her gaze back to her friend and replied honestly. "I kind of do, too—but after the week I've just had . . . well, I definitely think she's better off here where we can share kitty duties."

"I bet she gets lonely and scared at night when she's alone," Amy offered up.

But in response, Tessa just rolled her eyes. "She'd be alone at my place a lot, too."

"Not in the dark," Amy persisted.

"Knock it off," Tessa said. "I like her, but I just don't think it's in the cards." Even if she suddenly *didn't* enjoy envisioning Brontë alone here at night. Maybe they could rig her up a night light or something. "Don't you have some books to sell or plants to water or something?"

Shrugging, Amy said, "Suit yourself," before she walked away.

Tessa then lowered Brontë to her lap, fully expecting the cat to jump down and go trotting away—so when she didn't, instead curling up and lying among the folds of Tessa's skirt, Tessa smiled gently down at her, then reached over her to discover she could shelve books with a cat on her lap just as easily as without one.

A couple of nights later, Tessa cooked Lucky dinner using a simple baked chicken recipe and breaking out a bottle of wine—all to thank him for being there during her tough days. "And," she admitted over the table as they ate, "for making me *let* you be there. I'm not very good at sharing that part of my life with people."

"I wasn't *about* to take no for an answer," he told her just before forking a bite of baked potato into his mouth.

"Despite myself, I'm glad you didn't," she confessed.

"Have you talked to your mom? Did I freak her out very bad?"

In fact, Tessa *had* talked to her mom, who'd admitted it had scared the wits out of her when Lucky came to the door, but that she'd quickly seen in his eyes how much he cared about Tessa and how worried he was. To Tessa's surprise, that seemed to be enough—her mother had no qualms about Tessa seeing a guy with flames and a grim reaper on his arms. "Actually, she thought you were very sweet."

He scowled. "*Sweet?*"

And Tessa just grinned at her big, tough biker. "In fact, I think I know what kind of tattoo you should get next. A big yellow smiley face—right above Mr. Reaper there."

He arched one eyebrow. "That's not funny, hot stuff."

"Yes it is," she said on a giggle. "Just picture it."

Lucky was clearly holding back a smile now. "Well, then I think the next tattoo *you* should get is a great big skull, right in the center of your chest."

Her jaw dropped in horror at the image he'd just put in her mind. "*That's* not funny."

"See what I mean?"

The days were lengthening, the sun setting a bit later each night—and by the time they'd cleaned up the dishes, dusk fell over the cabin. It came earlier here along Whisper Falls Road for the pair of little houses nestled down among the trees. Lucky poured two more glasses of Chardonnay from the bottle Tessa had opened for dinner, confiding, "I've always been more of a beer or whiskey man, but this stuff isn't bad."

They stepped out onto Tessa's deck to enjoy the night, sitting at her patio table. When she mindlessly lifted her feet onto Lucky's thigh, using it as a stool, he began giving her a light foot massage and she wondered what she'd done right to get such a man. To *find* such a man behind that rough-and-tumble exterior.

What parts of Lucky *hadn't* she found yet, though? What parts of him didn't she know? She'd been basking in the pleasure of their affair, telling herself that part could wait—but how long? *If you don't find out the rest, then this isn't real, and it won't last.*

God, the thought of that wrenched her soul. She didn't *want* this to end. And she longed for it to be as real as it felt in her heart. So as she sat watching him, she realized she had to ask him. Even if it scared her. Even if she wasn't really sure she wanted the answers.

"Tell me about California, Lucky," she said softly, but she knew her tone underscored the seriousness of the question.

Lucky's hands went still and he raised his gaze to hers in the darkening air. His muscles tensed. And his heart felt heavy.

Maybe he should have seen this coming. Maybe he should have known you couldn't get this close to a woman without her needing to know your secrets. And . . . maybe it had been a lot easier to just not think about those secrets lately, after deciding the past really *was* behind him and that it was finally safe to let a woman into his life.

His first instinct was to lie. To sugarcoat every bit of it. He'd gotten real good at that in Wisconsin, after all. On the rare occasions he'd volunteered information about those days to friends, customers—it had been easy enough to talk in vague stories that made it sound like nothing worse than sewing some wild oats. He could do that with Tessa, too. Except that—to the very core of his soul, he didn't *want* to lie to her. He didn't think he could bear it.

So he considered just refusing to answer, point-blank. Telling her it was nothing she needed to know, that it was a long time ago and didn't matter. God knew it was his least favorite subject, and the very idea of dredging it up made his stomach churn.

But with Tessa, that wasn't good enough, either—it wasn't right. He wasn't sure *what* was right. *He* wasn't even very good at reconciling the man he'd been *then* with the man he was now—so how could he expect *her* to do it?

So finally he said what he was thinking. "You might hate me if I do."

He saw her flinch—just slightly; she'd tried to hide it. She'd clearly been hoping he'd tell her nothing really bad had happened. Which made the idea of telling her the truth all the more daunting.

"I would never hate you," she whispered. He thought her voice sounded like an angel's in the night. An angel with a daisy chain around her ankle.

"You might," he heard himself say.

"No," she insisted.

Which was sweet as hell—but she didn't know yet. And if *anything* could change the way she felt about him, it was this.

So maybe he should shut up. Just not tell her.

But again, no matter how he looked at it, he felt he owed her the truth. *It's that damn love thing.* It felt like a chain in a way, and not the daisy kind. More like a big, heavy, steel contraption that pressed on him, and pulled on him, and took away the freedom inside him, in his head—which was maybe the last freedom he'd retained after coming back here.

And yet . . . it wasn't fair to describe it that way—because it wasn't an *ugly* thing. It wasn't something he would give up if he could. It felt like something holding him tight in its grasp—but also like something warm, good. So good that . . . for Christ's sake, it had him making daisy chains in a park. He must want it. It was scary as hell in a way, but he must want it in his life to have gone there so easily.

With one hand still resting softly on her ankle, he ran the other back through his hair. He couldn't think how to begin. He couldn't think how to make sense of the things he'd done, the shit that had happened when he'd been young.

Just do it. Just tell her. Dive in. Get it out, once and for all.

"From the time I was twenty until I was twenty-three, I was in a motorcycle club called the Devil's Assassins."

He looked up at her in the dark, met her gaze. So far, she didn't look too worried. But he hadn't gotten to the heart of the matter yet. And in fact, he'd sugarcoated it already—calling it something as simple as a club, just as they did in Cali, just as they insisted to anyone who asked. *Stop it. Tell her the whole awful truth.* "But . . . it was really an outlaw gang. We did . . . illegal things. To make money."

She bit her lower lip, her eyes showing concern. "What *kinds* of things?"

And Lucky pressed his mouth into a flat, unhappy line. It shamed him to remember this. "We ran guns. And drugs. And we stole cars and motorcycles."

He could sense her muscles tensing merely from the way her ankles balanced on his leg now. "And you, personally, did these things?"

He sighed. "My job was . . . stealing cars. I was . . . good at it." It was strange to remember he'd once taken pride in the skill.

Next to him, Tessa stayed quiet a moment and he hated himself for who he'd been back then. "Why?" she finally asked.

The question confused him. "Why was I good at it?"

"Why did you join this club?"

He thought it over. Funny, back then, it had seemed the obvious thing to do—like some grand opportunity. "I was wandering, drifting—and it was someplace to belong. They got to do what they wanted, live how they wanted—they had a lot of power, and when I was twenty, power was appealing."

"How come?"

"I'd never felt like I'd had any before. And when you get patched into an MC, it's supposed to be like . . . a family. A family where you matter. They made me feel important. They said they'd always have my back."

"And did they?"

"No," he answered simply. An understatement of epic proportions. "All the family shit was a lie."

She simply stared at him then, for a good long time. And he wondered what she was thinking—when she finally said, "Are you gonna tell me the rest of it?"

"How do you know there's more?"

"The look on your face," she replied. And when he still didn't launch into the story, she said, "Lucky, I just need to know where you've been."

He nodded. Swallowed. He understood that. So he took a deep breath and said, "The whole thing ended . . . bad. But . . . it had been bad for a while already."

"Go on," she prodded.

"Not long after I was patched in—"

"What's that mean?"

In that moment, drawn back to an existence he'd long ago left behind, he'd forgotten the whole world didn't know MC terminology. "It's when you're made a full member. You go through different stages before you get the club's whole emblem to wear. You're tested in different ways, made to prove your loyalty, and your usefulness."

"Tested how?"

He sighed. It sounded so stupid now, juvenile. "Steal something maybe, do something against a rival gang, find a way to score some drugs for the club."

He heard her pull in a slow breath, let it back out. "Did you, um, do drugs?"

God, he was in Destiny—no one in Destiny did drugs. She'd think he was slime, but he wasn't gonna lie. "If you wouldn't do coke with the other guys, they thought it meant you were a cop. But I found out pretty fast I didn't like not having full control of myself when I was with them—I figured out it was best to stay alert. So I got good at faking it, at acting like I'd done it and, when nobody was looking, just brushing it away."

"Have you . . . done anything like that since then?"

He shook his head. "It wasn't for me. I was happy to leave it behind with the rest of that life."

"Tell me the rest," she reminded him.

It made him let out another long, shameful sigh. "Almost as soon as I was made a full patch, I started seeing maybe it wasn't as great as I thought. I mean, I knew they were dangerous—but what I didn't catch on to until too late was that they were dangerous even to each other. One minute we were swearing we were brothers to the end—and the next, guys were getting drunk or high or both, and then starting fights over nothing, or making threats, and you felt like you were gonna be stabbed in the back any minute.

"Duke hooked up with the Assassins around the same time as me, and we got along, and figured out pretty quick that it was good to have an ally. I think we both wanted to leave the club a while before we did, but the thing is—you can't just decide to go. Once you're in, it's for life. So to even talk about leaving would put a target on your back.

"Anyway . . . how things ended." He returned his gaze to hers. "You sure you wanna hear this, hot stuff?"

She nodded. "Not want to. Have to."

He sighed once more—then just tried to barrel forward. "The president of the Devil's Assassins was a guy named Wild Bill Murphy. And I didn't realize it at first, but he was . . . fucking crazy. He could be the nicest guy you'd ever want to meet or the meanest bastard on the planet, and he could switch on you in a heartbeat." Just remembering the cold look Bill could get in his eye made Lucky feel a little sick.

"So Bill's old lady was a girl named Vicki. And she . . ." Shit, this shouldn't be the hardest part, but with Tessa, it kind of was. "She had a thing for me. And there was . . . chemistry between us." He sensed Tessa tensing further beside him in the dark, but he couldn't help that—right now he just had to keep going. "It was only physical, but it was strong, and she egged it on. She was always flirting with me, and whenever Bill wasn't around, she was coming on to me, rubbing up against me and shit."

"And you . . . didn't respond?" Tessa asked.

Thinking back, he said, "Flirted some maybe, but that was it."

"Why not?"

He looked her squarely in the eye. "I valued my life. I told you, Bill was a crazy bastard, and real possessive. She was putting us both in danger doing the things she did. Truth is, she wasn't the brightest girl—she didn't seem to get that she was playing with fire. Or . . . maybe she did. Maybe that was part of the thrill for her." He just shook his head, remembering. "Either way, late one night, I finally gave in. We had sex in a back room of the Assassins' clubhouse. I was drunk, and too stupid to realize there were still a few members out front who could guess what was going on. They told Bill the next day."

He appreciated the fear in her voice when she said, "What happened?"

And this part was hard to say because even though he knew he wasn't to blame, he still felt responsible. His throat went dry. "Bill beat Vicki to a pulp. Put her in the hospital. I went to see her and it was . . . pretty damn awful."

Tessa had already moved on from that, though, asking, "What did he do to *you*?"

Lucky caught his breath and tried to quit recalling Vicki in that hospital bed with her eyes blackened, her throat and arms bruised, one lung collapsed, and all sorts of tubes coming in and out of her. "You remember that guy, Red, you met at my place?"

She nodded. "Yeah."

"During my last year with the club, he'd gone from being a hang-around to a prospect." And sensing she was about to ask, he explained, "A hang-around is somebody who tries to hang out and get in good with the club. They get bossed around, made to do stuff like get beer, stand guard outside meetings, shit like that. After that, you're made a prospect—kind of a member-on-a-trial-basis.

"So anyway, me and Duke were both steering clear of the club's usual hang-outs—but Red found us at a little run-down bar up the street from Duke's apartment. Wild Bill had sent him looking for us with a message . . . to steer clear of his woman from now on."

The fact was, Bill's message had been much more detailed than that. But there was no need to scare Tessa with that now that he finally felt assured this all lay in the past, ten years and two thousand miles away. Even if he could still hear Red telling him in that Texas accent of his, "Wild Bill said it's simple—you screw with his old lady, he'll screw with yours. Wherever you go, dude, any woman you value—her ass belongs to him and she'll be beggin' for mercy before it's over." It still gave him chills.

But he went on with the rest of it. "So I asked Red if that meant Bill was kicking me out of the MC. But Red—being Red—didn't know and said he'd have to ask." The memory left Lucky shaking his head some more—leave it to Red to screw up a threat.

"What happened then?" Tessa asked.

And—God, he didn't want to tell her the rest. If only he'd followed his instincts then. But he hadn't. And that had changed everything.

"Well, I should've left that night—should've just got on my bike and rode, as far and as fast as I could. Duke and me even talked about it. But we were afraid it would make things worse, that Bill would reach out through other chapters and ally clubs and find us somehow. We decided that staying and riding the storm out was the smartest thing to do."

After that, he stayed quiet for a minute, until Tessa's

voice sliced through the haze of memory. "Tell me the rest, Lucky." And he could almost hear in her tone now that she'd begun to understand the kind of man she'd gotten herself involved with—and he only hoped like hell she knew he wasn't that man *anymore*.

Only—what did it matter? Because when she heard the next part, she wouldn't want anything more to do with him. He couldn't see this ending any other way. And even feeling the finality of that deep down inside, he still couldn't *not* tell her. He'd come too far here, and now it was like . . . purging his sins or something. He suddenly didn't think he'd be able to live with himself if he didn't go on with the whole story, even the part that sometimes still gave him nightmares.

"The next night, Wild Bill sent another messenger to the bar—but this time it was a full-patch member of the club, a big bald dude called Hammer. Me and Duke were the only people in the whole place—when Hammer walked in, even the bartender disappeared out the back." As Lucky spoke now, he began to sweat—he no longer saw the shadow of Tessa next to him or felt the calm of the night around them. Instead he could almost smell the stale air of the bar, could almost hear Three Dog Night singing "Mama Told Me Not To Come" on the old jukebox in the corner, could almost feel the stark fear coursing through him when Hammer said in a low growl, "Bill sent me to say you're *never* out of the club, asshole. And now I'm gonna teach you the same lesson he taught that bitch, Vicki."

"Next thing I know," he heard himself tell Tessa, "the guy was coming at me with a blade."

She flinched—yet he went on, now filled with old fear, old desperation. "So Duke attacked him, from behind— hit him over the head with a bottle. But it didn't even faze him. He just turned on Duke and started slashing through the air between them, backing him into a corner.

Duke had a knife in his boot, but he couldn't get to it, and I was . . . hell, I was scared shitless. I think that's when I really understood just how good a friend he was."

Lucky felt out of breath now. He'd been sure Duke's blood was gonna flow any minute and he was gonna lose his best friend. He swallowed back the lump in his throat. "So I picked up the heaviest thing I could find—this big, antique beer stein sitting on a windowsill—and I brought it down on Hammer's head as hard as I could."

He stopped then, overwhelmed by the memories, by his own words. He'd never told anyone this before. He'd never said it out loud.

"Lucky?" she said softly. But her voice seemed to come from somewhere far away—it sounded muted, distant. At some point, she'd drawn her feet down from his lap and now leaned forward to touch his knee. "Are you okay? What happened after you hit Hammer?"

"He died," Lucky said, his own voice sounding small to him now, as well. "He hit the floor, and a big pool of blood started growing around his head. I killed him."

. . . soothe him; save him; love him; tell him you love him and will be his.

Charlotte Brontë, *Jane Eyre*

Fifteen

Christ. He felt his own words like a punch in the gut. They seemed to echo inside him now. *I killed him. I killed him. I killed him.*

Beside him, Tessa's voice shook. "Oh God. What then?"

He sought out her gaze in the dark, took in the glint in her eye. Felt as he had for years after that night, as if he wasn't sure he deserved to be alive, living a normal life. Damn, that hadn't hit him quite so hard in a while— maybe he'd even thought he was over it. And now his eyes felt wet, and a tear rolled down his cheek. "We ran. We got on our bikes and rode like hell, like the devil himself was chasing us. And he probably was—for a while anyway."

Lucky stopped once more, closed his eyes, willed away the damn tears. "We rode east, day and night. And we dumped our colors—our vests with the club's emblems—

in a trash can somewhere in Nevada. And we lived in fear for a long time, because a gang's reach can be long and far. But that was the end of it." He paused, drew in a deep breath, and tried to quit feeling everything so much.

"So now you know," he finished. "I killed somebody. And I ran away from it and never looked back. Except in my head."

"It was self-defense," she pointed out. "And in defense of your friend, too."

"Yeah, but . . ." He looked down, not quite able to face her right now. "I took somebody's life. And it wasn't mine to take. And yeah, the guy was a scumbag. But I was a scumbag, too, at the time, and . . . it's possible for people to change. So *he* could have changed, too—and . . . I took away that chance. I mean, everybody counts, don't they?"

When she reached for his hand, he looked back up at her. God, she was beautiful. Even in the pale light of a crescent moon, he could see that, drink it in. At the moment, it seemed . . . too nice a thing for him to have, to look at. He didn't deserve something that good. "Listen to me," she said. "You didn't have a choice."

"But I had a lot of choices *before* that. And if I hadn't made all the wrong ones, I never would have ended up there." He shook his head, the shame oozing like a freshly reopened wound inside him. "When I think of all the shit I did in those days—from stealing cars to fights with rival gangs to what happened with Hammer . . . damn, babe. The world can be pretty fucking ugly sometimes. And I just hate that I added more. And . . . if you don't want to be around me anymore, I would understand."

She stayed quiet for a minute, and despite her comforting words, he began to fear—to know—that he'd been right; she didn't want him anymore. And he couldn't blame her. Sometimes it was easy to forget just what a bad person he'd been for a while, what hideous things he'd done—but when forced to put it out there, to lay it on the table, it was a lot. He'd been the kind of man he wouldn't want anyone he cared for to be around. How could she feel any different?

Finally, she began to speak and he braced himself. "Maybe I should be afraid right now. Maybe I'm crazy to still be sitting here with you, holding your hand. Because, yeah, you just told me some pretty terrible stuff. But . . . it's hard for me to imagine the man I know doing those things. So . . . I have to believe you're not that guy anymore. I have to believe you're a changed man."

He swallowed past the tightness in his throat. "I am, Tessa—I swear it. I swear it on everything I have."

"I believe you," she whispered.

And he was amazed at her. Amazed at her faith. Amazed because right now, more than ever in his life, he felt like his nickname made sense: He was one hell of a lucky guy if a woman like this was willing to stand beside him after what he'd just dropped on her. "Why?" he asked, a little dumbfounded.

"Because I can see it in your eyes."

And Lucky just said, "Come here to me, babe—please," and opened his arms to her. A few seconds later she was sitting on his lap, wrapped in his embrace, and he was burying his face in the soft spot where her neck curved into her shoulder, and drinking in the feminine scent of her, and knowing once again that he didn't deserve her, but he was so, so thankful she wasn't running away from him.

And he realized in that moment, Tessa didn't do that—she didn't run. She had a health condition she couldn't run from; she just toughed it out like a bruiser. And she could have run from him on the very first day they'd met or lots of times after that when he knew he'd made her so nervous. But she'd stood her ground—that's who she was. And it was probably one more reason he'd fallen for her.

After that, he told her the rest. How he and Duke had ended up in this area on sheer instinct since they both had family in the region. And Duke had liked Crestview enough to stay—while Lucky had decided to move on, not only because he didn't want to face his family but because he was afraid he'd endanger them. They'd also been scared enough then—paranoid maybe, but who could say?—that they'd decided it was safer to just split up. And they'd both had different ideas of what they wanted anyway—Duke had sought a quieter existence someplace small, while Lucky had felt it would be easier to blend into the woodwork of a city.

"What do you want *now*?" she asked him softly. And God, it felt good just to hold her. There for a few minutes he'd been sure he'd never get to again.

He thought her question over and said, "Now that I'm older, and hopefully wiser, I'm starting to think being in a small town's not so bad after all. And getting back with my family . . . that was hard, but the truth is, it's made me feel more . . . *human* or something . . . than I have in a real long time."

"I'm glad," she whispered.

"But Tessa, I gotta tell ya . . . leaving the gang the way we did was dangerous—that's why we went so far. And by coming home—by coming in to Johnny's life, and yours . . . well, I wouldn't have done it if I thought there was still any real risk, but it's only fair to tell you—the last contact I had with the Assassins, they were trying to hurt me, bad." He thought of Vicki—dead now.

"I'm sure it's long in the past," Tessa assured him, kissing his cheek, and he kissed her sweet, soft mouth in return.

"And one more thing," he said, his gut pinching up all over again. "If Mike ever found out the things I've done . . . I'd be in big trouble with the law."

"Don't worry," she assured him. "I would never say anything."

He pulled back slightly to look at her, still a little astounded. "And so . . . after everything I've just told you, you're really not afraid of me now? Even a little?"

She leaned her forehead over against his. "Want to know a secret? When we first met, I *was* kind of scared."

He let a soft grin unfurl, their faces still touching. "That's not a secret, babe."

"But now I know what a good man you are. So no, Lucky—I'm not afraid of you."

Tessa held Lucky's hand as they walked quietly through the woods near Whisper Falls. Nothing much was different since he'd told her about the Devil's Assassins—except that now she knew. And it truly didn't matter. His smile was still just as sexy. His love for his new son was just as endearing. And his concern and care for her remained just as powerful.

Sitting on her deck listening to his story had felt almost surreal—she didn't know people who went through things like that; she'd never been near such danger. But what had stayed with her the most was his honesty, and also his remorse. The shame had practically dripped from him—and even as she respected him for feeling so strongly about it, it also broke her heart a little. Lucky's life had taken some unfortunate turns, and that didn't excuse him—but she could understand, and she could also forgive.

And maybe she *was* insane—as she'd told him, maybe she *should* be running from him. But she felt his love so strongly now, covering her as warmly as any blanket—and didn't that count for a lot?

As promised, she'd kept it all to herself. Maybe it would have been nice to use Rachel and Amy as sounding boards, but on the other hand, even if she could have, they'd both think she was nuts for staying with him. She couldn't expect anyone who didn't know Lucky the way she did now to understand it. They didn't know about the boy he'd been. They knew even less of the man he'd become.

And so as they strolled through the forest, now filled with warm shades of green—from the leaves above to moss-covered tree roots below—it was almost as if he'd never told her. And yet, everything was different, better, because there were no more questions. She no longer had to fear the mysterious and wonder where Lucky had been. Now she knew and she was making peace with it so that, hopefully, both of them could move on to something better.

As they reached the top of Whisper Falls, where the surface of the water was smooth as moving glass, Lucky said, "Let's try out that legend, see if it's true."

"About whispering across the falls? How? You'd have to be on the other side."

He just shrugged. "Water's shallow here, and . . ." He looked upstream a little. "I can jump from rock to rock up there. See?" He pointed to where a few large rocks littered the creek bed.

But she was skeptical. "What if you fall in and go over the edge?"

He just laughed. "If I fall in, I'll be lying in water about six inches deep. Don't worry, hot stuff—I don't risk my life that easy anymore." And off he went—releasing her hand, he hiked up the creek and skipped across, as effortlessly as a kid playing hopscotch. Then he jogged back down the opposite bank until he stood across the water from her.

"All right, babe," he called. "You ready to whisper something and see if can hear it?"

"Okay," she yelled back. But she knew it wasn't going

to work. As she'd told him before, most people had concluded that it was either an old wives' tale or that you both
had to be standing in precisely the right spot.

And since she was so sure he wouldn't hear her anyway,
she shielded her mouth and said what she'd been thinking
but just hadn't found the right time to tell him yet. Softly,
she whispered, "I love you, too, Lucky."

And then she lost her breath, because she saw the look
in his eyes—he appeared positively stunned. And shockingly vulnerable.

He'd heard her.

And she understood more than ever before that this
big, strong man with the tattoos running up and down
his arms perhaps hadn't felt loved by very many people
before. It made her sorry she'd waited so long to say it.
But glad she'd said it now. Her heart missed a beat just
peering across the stream at him. And she fell more in
love with him than she already was.

The first time Lucky drew his eyes down to the water,
she thought it looked as if he was wondering if maybe
he could actually walk across it. But then he took off,
running back to the shallow area with the rocks, again
skipping comfortably back to her side. And she began
to move toward him until they were both running just to
reach each other a second or two sooner.

They fell into each other's arms and she basked in his
warmth, his strength, the hardness of his body against
hers. He ran his hands through her hair and spoke low
in her ear. "I don't know the right way to say this stuff,
Tessa, but . . . you're the best thing that's happened to me.
I've never felt like this before, I've never . . . been happy
like this."

She pulled back to smile up at him. "For a guy who
doesn't know how to say this stuff, you're doing pretty
damn good."

"Yeah?" he rasped.

"Oh yeah," she promised him, and then his mouth came down on hers and she forgot all about talking and words altogether. She closed her eyes and let Lucky's kiss consume her from head to toe.

Then she let him draw them both to their knees on the ground.

Just before he laid her down on a carpet of ivy.

Unlike the last time they'd been like this outside, neither of them went slow. She shoved his T-shirt up, then helped him yank it off over his head just before reaching for his belt buckle. She worked at that as he unbuttoned the summery blouse she wore, just before unsnapping the center clasp on her lacy white bra. She undid his jeans as he undid hers, and once their clothes were off, he shoved his T-shirt beneath her back to keep her from lying directly on the ground—but it hardly mattered since they were soon rolling around there in each other's arms.

As soon as Lucky was inside her, he pressed her to the forest floor, and she loved the frame the foliage made around his handsome face, loved the powerful rush of the waterfall nearby. It echoed the excitement coursing through her veins.

And when she later got on top, straddling him, she felt wild, like some kind of untamed animal. She knew leaves stuck to her sweaty skin and twigs adorned her hair. She wiped at a smudge of dirt on Lucky's face, only to make it worse, and realized they were both filthy—and then she leaned back her head and laughed.

"What's so funny, babe?" he asked, his grin wicked as sin.

"This is grabbing life," she told him gleefully. "You make me feel like I'm experiencing every wild, wonderful thing there is!"

"There's more where that came from, hot stuff," he informed her darkly.

She raised her eyebrows "Oh?"

And he answered only by thrusting firmly upward inside her.

"Ohhh," she said.

When he did it again, she braced her dirty palms on his chest and he reached up to mold and massage her breasts. Moving on him, letting her body take over, Tessa knew a freedom she'd never known before. She wasn't sure if it had come from telling Lucky she loved him, or if it was about Lucky being so honest with her, or if it was because she felt as if they were one more wild part of nature right now. Or maybe it was all of that together, but she rocked her body on his with utter abandon, without a care in the world, losing her inhibitions as she never had.

And as the orgasm built inside her . . . oh God, the intensity of the pleasure, the passion she felt for the man beneath her, it all filled her with pure, unadulterated joy. And when the climax hit, it rushed over her with all the power of a waterfall, crashing through her being with a maddening force that nearly buried her. Her body jolted with a pleasure that made her cry out, again, again, until finally she slumped to Lucky's chest in pure exhaustion.

He hugged her tight, and she whispered, "I love you," once more, into his chest.

"Aw, babe—I love *you.*"

And when she finally gathered the strength to sit up a little, to look down into his eyes, she confessed to him again, "I feel . . . *wild* out here with you, Lucky."

"You're a mess," he informed her with a teasing grin. "But a sexy-as-hell mess, and I like it."

And he must have known, must have seen in her gaze that she wanted to get even wilder, because he didn't even look surprised when she disconnected their bodies, peered into his brown eyes—no longer smiling, then positioned herself on her knees to begin kissing her way down his chest, his stomach.

Soon, though, she drew her gaze from his face. She instead studied the flesh she kissed—the olive coloring of his skin, the smattering of black hair that narrowed into a thick line on his torso which led her farther, farther . . . until her hand curved naturally over his erection, until she was gently licking at the tip.

His deep groan pulled her eyes back to his and she realized that even if he wasn't *surprised* by the move, he seemed . . . well, more deeply affected than she'd anticipated. It fueled her, made her feel powerful, exciting. And it pushed her not to hesitate, but to kiss him there, to rain kisses up and down the length of him, listening as his breath came rough, catching at times, other times stretching into a low moan.

"I love you," she whispered against the silky skin stretching so taut over this hardest part of him. And she felt the love physically in that moment, felt it gathering into a tight, lush fist in her stomach as she licked her way back to the end of his penis and lowered her mouth over it.

"Aw—Jesus," he muttered, his eyes falling shut.

It had been so long since she'd been with a man before Lucky, and even longer since she'd felt compelled to get this close, this intimate—but suddenly it seemed easy, natural, right. She slid her lips up and down on him, basking in the pleasure of his response, and in the even purer pleasure of giving, of loving, and of being wild and free with him.

When finally she stopped, she met his gaze and he drew her briskly back up, kissing her mouth, rolling on the ground with her some more, murmuring that she was beautiful and perfect and telling her, "That felt so damn good, babe—even better than I imagined."

Their eyes met. "Imagined?" she asked.

He just nodded, eyes half shut and sexy.

And she bit her lip. "You fantasized about me?" The very notion made her feel more desirable than ever. "Before we got together?"

He nodded vigorously. "And after. Still. All the time."

The concept moved through her like a hot breeze. She knew Lucky loved her, but given her health issues, somehow she'd begun to feel he couldn't possibly see her the same way he'd see some . . . more perfect girl, some model or centerfold, someone unreal and therefore without flaws. He'd always said all the right things, but somehow, this shored them up in a whole new way. "Is there . . . anything else you fantasize about that we haven't done?"

A slightly depraved grin slowly unfurled on Lucky's handsome face. "Babe," he rasped, as if the question were silly. "It'll take us a while to get to *all* of it."

"Oh . . ." She felt his words in her chest. And gave him a naughty smile of her own. "Then we should probably get started."

At that, his amusement faded into something hotter, smoldering. "Are you sure?"

She nodded and asked, "Why?"

"Well . . ." He hesitated just slightly, then his voice came low. "I don't always like to be gentle."

"Believe it or not," she admitted, "neither do I."

Fresh heat darkened his gaze and he said no more. Instead, he rose to a kneeling position and pulled her up before him the same way, her back to his front. Then he bent her over until she was on her hands and knees, facing the falls—just seconds before he gripped her hips and reentered her that way.

"Ohhh!" He felt even bigger, deeper in this position, and it was almost hard to take. Almost. Because it was also *incredible*.

When he began to plunge into her, she felt it *everywhere*—her scalp tingled and the very tips of her fingers and toes pulsed with the driving pleasure he brought her. She cried out with every stroke, lost in the power Lucky delivered, lost in the scent of him combined with that of the woods and the water, lost in the sight before her: the smooth stream gently dropping over the edge to become something new, something wild and raging.

She had no idea how long they moved together like that, but when Lucky finally came inside her, it was with a mighty groan she could have sworn she heard echoing through the trees. She sensed his pleasure, almost felt it rolling through her own body—until they collapsed gently together on the ground.

"I was just thinking," he whispered in her ear.

"Yeah?"

"That we've probably scared the shit out of all the animals in the woods."

A burst of laughter erupted from her throat, and she rolled to her back to smile up at him.

"You really are a mess, hot stuff," he said, pulling back to look her over.

"You're not exactly fresh and tidy, either, Romo."

"Come on," he said, pushing to his feet and holding a hand down to her. Then he carefully led her to the water's edge. "Let's clean up."

Tessa raised her eyebrows. "In there? You've got to be kidding. Besides the waterfall factor, it has to be freezing."

But Lucky just shrugged. "We'll get used to it. And I keep telling you, the water's ankle deep—you're not gonna go over the falls, silly." And when she continued to stand there, still naked and skeptical, he added, "Do you wanna grab life or not?"

"Oh hell," she said, scrunching up her nose. He knew that was her weakness now.

And so they found a good place to ease down into the water, Lucky going first to make sure the footing was solid—then he helped her step in. "God, I was right—it's cold!" she screeched, drawing her hands into fists as she shivered.

"Hell, you're right," he admitted on a laugh, climbing

right back out of the water and helping her, too. "I like to think I'm a tough guy, but I'm not hypothermia tough."

After that, they just sat on the edge of the creek, and though some soap would have been nice, they still managed to get most of the dirt off of each other just using the crisp, clear water and their hands—and despite the cold splashes involved, Tessa began to appreciate how sensual and natural it felt to share this with the man she'd fallen in love with.

Afterward, Lucky pointed out a big, wide slab of rock a short distance behind them at one side of the stream, situated at a spot where the sun broke through the trees to shine down on it. Soon, they both lay on their backs there, drying.

Tessa still basked in that same sense of freedom she'd noticed earlier—after all, she was lying naked outside with Lucky in the light of day like it was a perfectly normal thing to do. Just a fifteen-minute drive away, the little town of Destiny was bustling, and no one there would ever believe what was taking place right now next to Whisper Falls.

She also found herself studying Lucky's body. She'd seen it so many times before, but usually at night, in dimmer lighting—so it was hard not to want to look. And Lord, it was a sight to behold.

"How come no tattoos below your chest?" she asked, curious.

He shrugged. "Guess I wanted 'em to show. And I'm not really a shorts-wearing guy."

Made sense, she supposed. "Did you get them all when you were in the Devil's Assassins?"

He shook his head. Pointing to Anna's name on his chest, and then the Live To Ride, Ride To Live crest, he said, "Got those after I left home, but before I ended up in California. The rest, though—yeah, they were mostly about trying to look scary enough to fit with the club."

Then she asked him something she'd been wondering about, especially lately. "So the dead man's hand and the grim reaper . . ."

"They're not about Hammer if that's what you're thinking—I got 'em long before that night. They're about . . ." He stared upward, through the trees, and she thought about all he'd seen—things she'd *never* see and never wanted to. "I guess they're about me feeling like . . . maybe I wouldn't last too long. Once I got into the MC and realized I felt kinda trapped, I wasn't real sure what my future held. Guess the tats were just . . . me getting ready to die young or something."

The thought made her shudder, and she reached out, gripped his arm. And that's when her gaze was drawn to something else she'd only seen in much dimmer lighting, and had never before asked him about. "Is that where you got your scars?" she asked softly. "While you were in the club?"

"Mostly." He sounded somber yet matter-of-fact. "It was . . . a pretty violent time."

Maybe her curiosity came back to her need to know about him. She knew the big stuff—but now maybe she needed the details. So she pointed to a small scar just above his rib cage. "How did you get that one?"

He kept the answer simple. "Bar fight."

She then touched a longer mark that slashed down the side of his torso. "This one?"

He glanced down at it. "Didn't get out of Wild Bill's way fast enough once when he was on a drunken rampage."

Most days, the red, angry-looking scar at his temple was hidden by his hair, but was visible now while he lay on his back. "And this?"

"Fight with a rival gang. Some asshole's ring cut me open."

The biggest scar was faded, lighter than the others, but still prominent. "And the one on your knee?" she asked.

His tone remained just as solemn when he replied, "Bicycle wreck when I was nine."

And she smiled a little—mainly liking to think of him at nine much more than she liked thinking of him being a Devil's Assassin.

Though *that* thought doused her smile as quickly as it had come. All those other scars still remained, and she knew Lucky carried a lot of scars *inside* him, too. "I'm so sorry you had to go through all that," she said, gently running her fingertips across his muscular stomach.

"Yeah, that bike wreck was a bitch. Had to get stitches and everything."

She grinned, and he cast her a sly, teasing expression—but it, too, faded quickly, his expression gone serious again. "Don't be sorry for me, babe," he said. "It's my fault, all of it."

She was surprised to hear him say that so adamantly. After all, she knew he blamed himself for the decisions he'd made in California, but she also knew what had originally driven him to leave home. "You don't blame your parents anymore?" she asked.

Next to her in the warm rays of the sun, Lucky sighed. "I blame them some for making me feel so . . . invisible. But the way I dealt with it, the lengths I took it to—that's all on me. I have to face that."

She pressed her palm to his chest now, then leaned over to kiss his cheek. "Sounds like you have."

On the day before Mother's Day, one of Destiny's eldest citizens, known to all simply as Miss Ellie, hosted a spring picnic at her house out on Blue Valley Road. Of course, it was really Miss Ellie's two daughters, Linda Sue and Mary Katherine, who orchestrated the event, because Miss Ellie was in her eighties now. But she had a lovely English garden to the side of her white gingerbread house just across from Blue Valley Lake, and she was a sweet old lady, so Tessa always enjoyed attending her garden parties.

Of course, getting Lucky to go was a little challenging, but he'd finally agreed, making it clear that "I'm only doing this for *you*, babe." And that was good enough for her.

"This will be a good opportunity for you to see my mom again, and meet my dad and the rest of my friends."

He'd simply offered a slight scowl from where he'd stood grilling up chicken breasts for them and Johnny, who been inside playing a computer game at the time. "Yippee," he'd said very dryly.

But now they were pulling up in front of Miss Ellie's place in Lucky's Jeep and he was being okay about the whole thing—even if a little quiet.

Soon after walking through the latticed arch that led to the garden, holding Lucky's hand, Tessa spotted Amy and another of their friends, Sue Ann, and dragged Lucky over to meet them. Amy was predictably cheerful but came off a bit nervous, so Tessa couldn't have been more thankful when Sue Ann gave Lucky's arms a long once-over and said, "Nice tats, dude."

"Uh, thanks," he replied, clearly caught off guard.

Tessa flashed Sue Ann a big smile, appreciative that her small-town friend with her small town life didn't always have small-town attitudes. "Where's Jeff?" she asked of Sue Ann's husband. The two of them had been together forever, since high school.

"He had to help a co-worker move today," she said, looking slightly bummed. Progressive thinker that Sue Ann might be, Tessa knew that at heart, Sue Ann appreciated the simple things in life—even things as simple as attending a community event with her little family. "And

Sophie is running around here somewhere, playing with Adam Becker's little boys."

A few minutes later, Tessa saw her parents and went to greet them with Lucky in tow. "Mom, you know Lucky. And Dad, this is Lucky Romo, Mike's brother. You probably remember him from years ago."

And—oh crap. The look on her usually mild-mannered dad's face was . . . one of pure shock. That's when her mom said, pointedly, "Tom, this is the young man I told you about, who took such good care of Tessa when she was under the weather recently."

And that—thank God!—changed everything about the moment. Both her parents put a great deal of stock in anyone who looked out for their children. So now her father, obviously still trying to adjust to Lucky's appearance, offered his hand. "We appreciate you helping out our Tessa."

Lucky took it, shook it, and replied, "She doesn't always *like* having help, but that's too bad, since I give it to her anyway."

Her dad laughed knowingly, and Tessa couldn't believe this had been so easy. She'd actually been nervous about introducing Lucky to her father, but had decided to just barrel straight ahead and not put it off, since it had to be done. And she nearly collapsed with joy when she heard her mom say to Lucky, "Tessa's been telling me about your little boy. We'd love to have the three of you over for dinner soon."

"Have you said hello to Miss Ellie yet?" her dad asked her a minute later.

"No, but we'll go now while she doesn't have a big crowd." Part of attending any get-together including Miss Ellie was making a point of finding her to say hello. Since she could no longer walk well, she was always seated in some pleasant spot where everyone could locate her, and when at *her* house, it was always in the picturesque white gazebo just a few steps away.

"Hello, Miss Ellie!" Tessa said loudly as she and Lucky approached the old gray-haired woman who was hard of hearing.

She smiled up at Tessa, the lines of her face deepening with the gesture. "Tessa Sheridan—how are you, dear?"

"Very well, thanks!" Then she turned to her date, who—it just dawned on her—she hoped wouldn't scare the old lady to death. "This is my boyfriend, Lucky!" she yelled.

Yet to her surprise, Miss Ellie didn't look the least bit daunted as she gave him a long, thorough looking over. "He could use a haircut, dear, but yes indeed, you *are* lucky with a fella like *that* for a boyfriend."

Tessa and Lucky simply exchanged grins, and Lucky leaned down to say, "Nice to meet you, ma'am." Tessa figured Lucky had probably met her as a child, too, but that likely neither one remembered.

Miss Ellie put a hand to her ear. "What's that you say?"

"You kinda have to yell," Tessa told him.

So Lucky yelled. "Nice to meet you! You have a real nice place!"

And then Miss Ellie actually blushed a little, glancing in Tessa's direction to say, "You tell your boyfriend he's got himself a real nice face, too."

Tessa and Lucky both smiled, but then Tessa turned on her heel to go, since other people were waiting to say hello to Miss Ellie behind them now. That's when the old woman said, "Why, look at that! You've got daisies painted on your ankle!"

Whoops. Tessa had worn one of her usual long, flowy skirts, but the tattoo had shown when she'd spun around to leave. And now her parents, along with everyone else in the vicinity, were staring at her feet.

"Uh, you want to lift that skirt up, Tessa?" Sue Ann

asked, as wide-eyed as everyone else. Other than her friend Jenny's husband, Mick Brody—who, like Lucky, had also come back after a long absence—people in Destiny didn't *get* tattoos. Until now, anyway.

So, not one to avoid the inevitable these days, Tessa pulled up her skirt just slightly, revealing the daisy chain.

And obviously feeling all eyes upon them, and thinking ahead, Lucky spoke up to say, "Uh, for the record, I had nothing to do with this. I was just as surprised as the rest of you."

Lucky sat with Tessa at a tiny table in the garden, sort of glad it was too small for anyone to join them. All this had gone okay so far, but meeting so many people—some he remembered from when he was a kid and others he didn't but probably should—was exhausting. Plus people stared a lot. At his ink. And his hair. But he'd expected that, and the important part, he supposed, was that Tessa's parents had been cool to him, and so had her friends, and he knew that was important to her.

Now everyone was eating—some at the various tables scattered around the garden, and others stood with plates in their hands. As Lucky popped the top on a can of beer, he found himself surprised people in Destiny even *drank* beer, *and* feeling damn thankful for it.

"Who's that?" Lucky asked Tessa a minute later, after shoveling a bite of potato salad into his mouth. He'd just spotted a familiar-looking face across the garden—but the person he was thinking of seemed about as likely to be at this party as *he* was. He pointed to the guy, who stood with a pretty girl in a pink dress, along with . . . was that Destiny's old police chief, Walter Tolliver, who'd once given him a ticket when he was a teenager?

Tessa followed his eyes and smiled. "Oh, that's my friend, Jenny—with her father, and her husband, Mick Brody."

"Son of a bitch," Lucky murmured, stunned. "That's Mick Brody?"

She nodded, clearly surprised by his reaction. "Why?"

"We used to be friends—back in school." In fact, Mick and his brother Wayne had been Lucky's *only* real friends as a teen—because they'd been just as reckless and hell-raising as him. But he'd been closer to Mick than Wayne, and when Lucky had left town, Mick had been about the only thing he regretted leaving behind.

"Really? I'll go get him." And quick as that, she was on her feet and across the garden—and a minute later, his old buddy was crossing the grass toward him, squinting a little as he approached, probably in disbelief. His one-time friend looked good even if older, with broader shoulders, like him—and also like him, Mick sported some ink on each arm. Lucky stood to greet him.

"Lucky Romo," Mick said with an amused grin. "I'll be damned. When the hell did *you* get back in town? You're the last person I expected to see at a Destiny picnic."

Lucky couldn't help chuckling. "Same here, dude. You couldn't be any more shocked than me."

They shook hands and gave each other a slap on the back—about as close as Lucky ever came to hugging a guy.

"I sure as hell didn't think *you'd* still be here," Lucky told Mick.

"Oh, I was gone for a good long while. But I ended up back by accident, I guess you could say—and then I married Jenny Tolliver."

"The police chief's daughter, huh?" Lucky said, still trying to wrap his head around it.

"Yep."

"Damn, bro. That makes no sense at all," Lucky said on a light laugh.

And Mick just chuckled along with him. "*You're* tellin'

me. Life can hold surprises when you least expect 'em, that's for sure."

Lucky understood *that.* "Yeah, mine has held . . . quite a few lately."

Mick glanced toward Tessa, who now stood talking with Jenny and the police chief. "And I'm betting that's one of 'em."

Lucky just nodded, still not quite sure how he'd ended up with a girl as out of his league as Tessa.

Without warning then, Mick's expression went a little darker, more serious. He dropped his voice. "Listen— after you left town, I, uh, heard you might've got into some bad shit. You okay, man?"

Tessa had told him there'd been rumors about Lucky being in a motorcycle gang. For now, he just kept it simple. "Yeah. Mostly. That's all in the past. What about you?" Given that Mick hadn't exactly been a poster child for good behavior, Lucky couldn't imagine his life had been a walk in the park, either.

"Went through some stuff I'll tell you about over a beer sometime," Mick said, confirming it, "but came out good on the other side."

Lucky cracked a grin. "And now you come to Destiny picnics with all the pretty people." Only now, seeing so many Destiny residents together, did Lucky remember just how perfect and prim everyone in Destiny had always been: All the ladies wore spring-colored dresses, looking tidy in every way, and most of the men had paired golf shirts with khaki. No *wonder* Lucky had felt so out of place here as a teenager. Not to mention now, at this party.

Yet Mick just laughed and said, "Believe it or not, they're not half bad if you give 'em a chance."

"We'll see if they give *me* a chance," Lucky said—yet even as the words left him, he realized that if Mick could fit in here, so could he. He supposed he'd slowly been figuring that out for a while now—it had started with Tessa, and Mike's fiancée had accepted him easily enough. And hell—today, despite how different he looked from the rest of them, no one here had been rude to him, unless he counted their stares, and he supposed he had to give people a chance to get used to his tattoos. The truth was, when he thought about it, the only person in this town who'd been a jerk to him was his own brother.

When the cell phone in Lucky's pocket buzzed, he pulled it out to see a text from Johnny—confirming a pick-up time for later tonight, when Lucky was taking him to a movie, then bringing him back to his place while Tessa had a girls' night out with Amy and Rachel. His relationship with his son was becoming a big part of his life, going smoother than he could have anticipated.

"Just a message from my kid," Lucky explained.

And Mick said, "Whoa."

"Yeah," Lucky replied on a laugh, "I know. Shocked me, too. I just met him, actually."

Mick arched one eyebrow. "Another one of those surprises?"

"You got it."

Just then, Lucky looked up to see Mike and Rachel walk through the archway that led into the garden. "Christ," he muttered. For some reason, he hadn't even thought about his brother being here, but now he felt almost as if his thoughts about Mike a few minutes ago had been some kind of bad omen.

Mick glanced toward Mike, then back at Lucky. "Problem with your brother?"

"A big one," Lucky bit off, angry all over again.

Mick looked a little introspective, and his voice went softer than at any point so far as he said, decisively, "Bud, you wanna get that worked out."

"What you do mean?"

Then Mick told him his brother Wayne was dead.

"Aw, damn," Lucky said, his stomach dropping at the news. He probably hadn't thought about Wayne in years, but still, they'd once been friends. They'd ridden around town together; they'd picked up girls together—or at least they'd tried. He suddenly remembered a hot summer day when he, Mick, and Wayne had floated around the lake just across the road from them now in an old rowboat. "I'm sorry, man."

But Mick just shook his head. "It's okay. I mean . . . I've dealt with it. Cancer," he added, making it so Lucky didn't have to ask. "I'm just saying—you never know how long you have with people. You think it's forever, and sometimes it's not."

Lucky shifted his gaze briefly toward Mike again, who now stood talking with Rachel, Tessa, and their other girlfriends. "It's not me, man—it's him."

And almost as if he'd sensed them talking about him, that's when Mike broke away from the girls and came striding briskly toward Lucky. "Jesus Christ, what now?" Lucky muttered to no one in particular.

Mike stopped not more than a foot away from him and looked Lucky in the eye. "We need to talk. Now."

But Lucky was in no mood for this. "Look, man, I'm just trying to have a nice day with Tessa, okay? Don't worry—I won't be doing anything to corrupt the good citizens of Destiny, so how about you just leave me the hell alone?"

"No," Mike said. "This can't wait."

And Lucky just sighed. Why the hell did his brother have it in for him? Was this about the Devil's Assassins? Had he found out about them somehow? Ever since Tessa had told him about the rumors, he'd figured that must be part of Mike's problem with him—and if Mike *did* find out the ugly truth about his past, there'd be hell to pay. And jail time to do. Shit. "Look, man, what the fuck do you want from me?"

"I wanted to do this in private," Mike bit off through slightly clenched teeth. "But if you're gonna make me do it in public, fine—have it your way."

Jesus—was Mike about to accuse Lucky, right here, right now, of being a criminal? Or of God even knew what else? He braced himself, preparing for the worst.

And that's when Mike said, "Lucky, I'm sorry."

Lucky waited for the rest. *Lucky, I'm sorry, but I hate your guts. Lucky, I'm sorry, but you're an asshole.* And when it didn't come, he finally said, "Huh?"

Mike looked perturbed as usual, and Lucky realized his brother thought he was giving him a hard time. Then Mike replied quietly but pointedly. "I *said* I'm *sorry.* For everything."

Life appears to me too short to be spent in nursing
animosity or registering wrongs.

Charlotte Brontë, *Jane Eyre*

Sixteen

Appearing dumbfounded, Lucky said, "Uh, let's take
a walk." And Mike followed his brother from the garden
into the front yard, then across the narrow road to stand
next to Blue Valley Lake in the sun.

Finally, Lucky stopped and turned to face him.

Mike didn't speak at first, because this was hard. Damn
hard. Maybe that part was about pride. He'd punched
Lucky in the face the first time he'd seen him after more
than fifteen years—that's how right, how justified he'd
felt in his opinion. And it wasn't easy to admit now that
he'd been wrong. At least in some ways.

But he took a deep breath and tried to be the good man
Rachel was always assuring him he was. "Thing is, I been
doing a lot of thinking," he began.

"Yeah?" Lucky looked cautious, and Mike guessed he
couldn't blame him.

At moments, it still felt weird to peer into the face of this big, muscular guy covered in tattoos and realize it was the same person he'd wrestled with as a kid, the same person he'd stuck up for on the playground or taken care of after a skinned knee. But that's where Mike had to go back to again—back to those days when Lucky had been innocent, as innocent as Mike had been then, too. "And I started remembering some stuff that happened. And I just wanted you to know that . . . I get it. Kind of."

"You get what?"

"That maybe after Anna was gone, nobody paid you very much attention—like even when you did good things, like when you won that art award at school."

Lucky just gave a brief nod, and Mike realized Lucky knew exactly what award he was talking about. It was maybe the only thing Lucky had ever won, one of the only times he'd ever excelled at school, and nobody had even acknowledged it at home. "I'm sorry if I was an asshole," Mike told him.

Lucky's expression didn't change—his mouth painted a straight, unemotional line across his face. But Mike could see in his brother's eyes the hurt that still resided there when he thought back, and shit—it made him mad at himself that he'd been too stubborn to really even look *in* to Lucky's eyes until now.

"It wasn't you," Lucky said, though. "It was Mom and Dad. I was just jealous of you because they loved you more than me after Anna was gone."

Mike started to say that was crazy—but he stopped, because now he understood why it had felt like that to Lucky. He tried to approach it more logically. "I can see why it seemed that way, but since coming home . . . surely you know now that they loved you."

Lucky let out a sigh that made Mike's chest feel heavy. He felt stupid to have been so blind to Lucky's feelings back then, no matter what *he'd* been going through at the same time. He'd suffered a lot, too, in different ways, but he'd never had to doubt his parents' love.

"I know," Lucky said, his voice suddenly softer than Mike had heard it before. "I just *didn't* for a long time, so I guess I'm still getting used to the idea."

Now it was Mike who sighed, long and hard, because he still had more to apologize for—being sorry for being wrong wasn't enough. "I'm sorry I've been an asshole since you came home, too, man."

"It's not like I'm blameless," Lucky said, his expression darkening.

And that surprised Mike, a lot. That Lucky would even open that door.

When Lucky turned and sat down on the bank above the lake, balancing his forearms on bent knees to look out over the water, Mike silently joined him. They stayed like that for a few minutes, the only sound the vague noise of the party across the road, until Mike finally asked Lucky what he really wanted to know, what he'd wanted to know for years now. "Lucky, what happened out west?"

"I told you already—"

"No," Mike cut him off. "The part you didn't tell us."

Lucky stayed quiet for a long time, and for the first instance since he'd come home, Mike felt a little sorry not only for Lucky the boy, but also Lucky the man. What had his brother seen, been through? Up to now, he'd just been angry about Lucky's bad decisions. But what if . . . what if Lucky had gone through really awful things? What if he'd *done* really awful things that haunted him? He was just finally starting to think of Lucky like a real brother again, like someone he cared about. He'd spent so long without a sibling, he must have forgotten how, but now it was coming back to him.

When Lucky didn't answer, Mike pushed the issue. "Lucky, just tell me."

And at last, Lucky shook his head, peering out over the

placid lake, his expression tired. "Bro, if you care for me at all, don't ask. It's just shit I'd rather forget. Shit I try to forget every day."

Mike let out a sigh. He wished it were that easy. "Thing is, Luck, I been wondering where you were for fifteen years. And I know about your business now, and about your kid, and all that's great—I'm proud of you for turning things around. But there's still a big void there, a big gap. And I wanna move past these bad feelings between us, I wanna move past it so damn bad—but I'm not sure I can until you give me some idea what I'm missing."

Lucky stayed quiet again for a time, until finally saying, "Problem is, Mike, you're a cop."

And Mike let that hang in the air a minute as he took it in and began to understand. Just as Lucky added, "And probably a good one. The kind with a lot of integrity—am I right?"

Shit. He made a good point. But then Mike remembered. "Weren't your days out west a long time ago?" He quietly told Lucky, "There are statutes of limitations on things."

Finally, Lucky said, "I did some bad stuff, Mike," his voice strained, and Mike felt . . . God, he felt transported, back to a place in time when he wanted to protect his little brother, take away anything bad that happened to him.

But he only said, quietly, "Go on."

Lucky kept his sullen gaze on the water. "What you heard is true—I got mixed up with a biker gang."

And Mike's chest tightened—not in anger, but in worry.

"And I . . . broke laws."

"What kind?"

Lucky glanced over at him, but didn't answer.

"Almost anything you could have done is past being punishable if it was over ten years ago."

Lucky didn't manage to look him in the face, though, when he said, "I stole cars. And I did some drugs—but not many. I made the world a worse place for a few years, and it's not something I'm proud of."

Mike gave a slow nod. "Is that the worst of it?"

And he waited for Lucky to say yes—and his gut clenched when his brother didn't reply.

Finally, Lucky's voice came in a whisper, his expression completely morose as he stared at the ground between his feet. "Mike," he said hoarsely, "I'm telling you this as a brother, and I'm asking you not to hear it as a cop, okay?"

Shit. Shit, shit, shit. He *was* a cop. But he also felt, in his gut, that he needed to be a brother to Lucky right now. He needed to be the big brother he hadn't been in a very long time. "Okay," he let out softly.

Lucky released a long, almost painful sounding breath and said, "Mike, I killed a guy."

The words hit Mike in a hot wave that nearly flattened him, leaving him light-headed.

"But it was in self-defense—guy pulled a knife on me. And then he turned it on my best friend."

Mike steeled himself. Tried not to feel emotional. Tried to just think clearly. "Anybody see it happen?"

"Only my friend Duke. The guy who owns Grave-diggers—the one you were about to fight when I came in that night."

Mike nodded shortly. "He trustworthy?"

"True blue. He got in the fight trying to save *me*."

"Anybody else know about it?"

Lucky hesitated slightly. "Other guys in the club knew it was me or Duke or both of us. But we got the hell out of there and never looked back. And we never heard from them again."

Mike thought it through a little more, then said, "Sounds like manslaughter at best. I'll look it up to be sure, but I think the limit on that in California is probably seven years, ten at most. It's been more than ten, right?"

Lucky nodded.

"That's good enough," Mike said, indeed more brother than cop right now.

They both peered back out over the lake again, and Mike felt a little sick on his brother's behalf, finally asking, "You okay? About that happening?"

"No," Lucky answered without missing a beat. "But better than I used to be."

In response, Mike just sighed, gave his brother a pat on the back . . . and then he let his hand stay there, same as he would have when they were kids and Lucky needed him.

Tessa stood over her desk at the cabin, Amy and Rachel flanking her, as she showed them the sketches she'd done for Duke's bar. "Wow," Amy said, "you're going to hang an entire motorcycle from the ceiling?"

"Yes, and it's gonna be *so* cool." Tessa was utterly excited about the idea. "Duke has this perfectly good bike, other than the fact that it doesn't run and he doesn't feel it's worth repairing. So Lucky's going to paint it—although he doesn't know this yet—and it'll be the centerpiece to Gravediggers' new look."

Just then, the doorbell rang, and Tessa went to answer it, finding Jenny and Sue Ann on the other side. "Hey, come on in," she said merrily. They hadn't been part of the original plan, but Tessa had invited them both at Miss Ellie's today. "I'm so glad you guys could come on short notice." Then she turned to Rachel. "Break out the wine coolers, Rach."

"Mick never minds if I have a night out," Jenny said. "And believe it or not, he's partnering with my dad for a euchre tournament at the Dew Drop Inn tonight." When Jenny and Mick had first gotten together, he and her dad had been like oil and water, but things had changed. In the same way Tessa saw things changing for Lucky right now.

"And I decided Jeff could do the daddy thing tonight," Sue Ann reported. "He's been out all day, and working late a lot, so Sophie's been missing him. And frankly, I could *use* a night out—*and* a wine cooler. Hand it over, Rachel," she said, heading to the kitchen on Rachel's heels.

"Trouble in paradise?" Rachel asked Sue Ann loud enough for all to hear.

"Girls," Sue Ann said, helping Rachel with the coolers, "in marriage, you go through great times and 'eh' times. But that's what it's all about. Fortunately, for me, the great times always come back, so it's no biggie."

Ah, even *that* warmed Tessa's heart. To know that, come what may, people like Sue Ann and Jeff would always be together—that true love really did exist.

"And speaking of great times," Amy said, turning her attention to Tessa, "you're madly in love with Lucky Romo. I saw it written all over your face today, so don't deny it."

As the warmth of a blush climbed her cheeks, Tessa said, "Fine, yes—despite my quest for sex, it's progressed to being a pretty big deal."

Rachel and Sue Ann re-entered the living room to dole out strawberry coolers, and Rachel gave her a smile. "And I'm sure Lucky told you that he and Mike finally made up today. How great is *that*?"

What was also great, in Tessa's book, was to suddenly have her friends being so supportive of her relationship with Lucky. A couple of months ago, she couldn't have dreamed all this.

"Mick was thrilled to see Lucky," Jenny announced.

"He said that?" Rachel asked, skeptical.

"Well, no," Jenny admitted. "Mick never acts *really* excited about anything—except maybe sex, and me. But I could tell because he talked about him a lot. I'm really glad he has an old friend to reconnect with."

"I'm glad for Lucky, too," Tessa told her.

"And speaking of Lucky," Sue Ann said, "can you say yowsa? No offense, Jen, but visually speaking, that man makes Mick look like a choirboy."

From there, the banter went on, with lots of laughter and fun. By the second round of wine coolers, they decided to take the party out onto the deck. Tessa turned on the radio, loud enough for it to blast through the window, declaring this was one perk of not having any neighbors. Besides Lucky, of course, who was out tonight with Johnny.

And when "Whoomp! There It Is," a party song that brought back memories of high school dances, suddenly burst through the window, Tessa followed her slightly intoxicated instincts and began to shake her hips a little.

"You go, girl!" Sue Ann said—and she began to "go," too, dancing to the fast hip-hop beat with wine cooler in hand.

Soon, all five girls were singing and dancing on Tessa's deck in the light of citronella candles. And in that fun, carefree moment, Tessa had to acknowledge to herself that life was good. A few months ago, she hadn't felt that way. She'd refused to see that, despite all she'd lost, she still had so much. Her family. Her friends. Her health a lot of the time—and it was much better than it had been a few years ago. And now she had a man she loved, too. The least likely man she ever would have picked for herself, yet now she couldn't imagine anyone more perfect for her.

There was something special, and utterly joyful, in letting herself go this way, in sharing such silly, easy fun with her girlfriends. And it hit her then: *Without all you went through the past few years . . . you never would have reached this moment in time.*

She wouldn't be moving to this fun song, doing the bump with Rachel now; she wouldn't be laughing as she watched Sue Ann dancing atop her patio table. She wouldn't have this opportunity to realize how dear her friends were to her, or to remember all they'd been through together over the years.

And . . . whoa. Then something even bigger and grander hit her—hard.

In this moment, she was experiencing everything that made up what she'd come to think of as the Ellen Philosophy: Laugh. Dance. Think Positive. And she suddenly realized that those simple tenets held all the answers she'd been seeking all this time.

She'd been searching for ways to get past the limitations her disease had imposed on her, searching for ways not to let life pass her by—in tattoos, motorcycles, sex, the idea of skydiving. And before all that, she'd seen doctor upon doctor, not to mention holistic healers, herbalists, and more. And she *liked* her tattoo, and she *liked* Lucky's motorcycle, and God knew she *loved* sex with Lucky—but in the end, it turned out the secret to happiness was much simpler than any of those things. Laughing, dancing, finding the joy in life; learning to expect the best instead of the worst. That was all it really took.

Of course, having Lucky enter her world had helped, but even before him, she'd had so much, and she'd spent so much time feeling as if it wasn't enough—and it *was*. And now, having Lucky's love on top of it . . . well, that was just the icing on the cake of her life. Really *delicious* icing. The kind that made every bite so much sweeter.

A few nights after his father-and-son outing with Johnny, Lucky sat on his usual stool at Gravediggers, drinking a beer, thinking through all the recent changes in his life. He grew more attached to Johnny every time he saw him, and still couldn't believe such a good, sweet kid had come from *him*. But then again, once upon a time he'd been a good kid, too. He just hoped to God nothing ever happened in Johnny's life that would screw him up the way it had Lucky.

And now even he and Mike had mended fences as well. Shit—it was still hard to believe he'd told Mike everything. He'd planned never to do that, under any circumstances, and yet, suddenly, there it was, coming out of him. Somehow, in that strange moment, it had felt almost like they were little kids again, confiding in each other in the dark.

He'd felt like an idiot as soon as he'd told Mike; Mike could have easily turned on him, statute of limitations or not—but he hadn't. And just like when he'd told Tessa about his time with the Devil's Assassins, getting it off his chest yet again had felt even more freeing. It was like each time he got brave enough to tell the tale, it stripped away a little of the anguish still left inside him.

Last night, he and Tessa had even met up with Mike and Rachel at Dolly's Café, right in the heart of Destiny, for dinner. They'd talked about normal things and Lucky had felt like a normal guy. They'd rehashed some good memories—and a few bad ones—but overall, he'd come away feeling closer to Mike, and like they were both really ready to put the past behind them. And Lucky had nearly fallen out of the booth when Old Mrs. Lampton, a little old lady who'd *already* been old when he was a teenager, passed by on her walker and, nodding to each of them, said, "Mike, Rachel, Tessa, Lucky," as if he'd never even been gone.

"Hey, bud—how's it going?"

He looked up just then to see Mick Brody pulling up the stool next to him. Before leaving the picnic on Saturday, they'd made plans to get together and catch up. "It's going good," he said. Because it was. It was going better than it had for just about as long as he could remember.

Lucky introduced Mick to Duke, who brought him a

beer, and before long they were reliving old times. Both were forced to admit that their high school days hadn't really been *good* times, but they'd had some fun together, and they'd looked out for each other a time or two.

Soon enough, Mick was confiding in him, admitting to Lucky that he hadn't always been on the right side of the law, particularly in the years after Lucky had left Destiny. Lucky shared just a little about the Devil's Assassins, since it sounded like both of them had come through some tough shit to get where they were now. "Getting into the MC, and then managing to get out of it, was a wake-up call," Lucky told him.

Mick nodded. "The wake-up call for me was when Wayne was sent to prison."

Lucky felt his eyebrows shoot up. "Prison, huh? I didn't know that."

"Armed robbery," Mick said. "And I realized I didn't want that to be me, so I turned things around."

They both stayed quiet for a minute, pondering, Lucky supposed, how easy it would have been for either of them to have ended up there, too. A sobering thought. And one that didn't make Lucky feel very proud.

Fortunately, Duke chose that exact moment to step up and say, "What's the problem over here, brother? You got a chick you're crazy about, a kid you dig, a family who forgave you, and a healthy business—thanks to me." Then he turned to Mick. "Did he tell you that? Guy comes back here after something like sixteen years, with some paint guns and a garage, and I've sent him about fifty customers this spring. And I give him free beer half the time, too. Guy oughta be buying *me* beer."

Duke's boasting made Lucky let out a laugh, and he was glad to have the mood lightened.

He didn't point it out, but Duke had left something off that list: Lucky also had a damn good friend in him. And it had been good to find Mick back in Destiny, too. Before the night was through, Mick even invited Lucky to bring Tessa over to the home he shared with Jenny on Blue Valley Lake for a cookout sometime this summer.

As Lucky put on his helmet and revved up his Harley, soon hitting the pavement toward Whisper Falls Road, it was hard to believe the loner's life he'd lived a couple of months ago had turned into this. And it was hard to believe he felt so damn . . . good. Yeah, it was hard when he had to watch Tessa struggle with illness, and sure, there were still moments when he felt a little overwhelmed by it all, but when he imagined leaving this all behind *now*, turning the bike away from Destiny and never looking back—he knew he wouldn't even make it to the county line.

He'd finally stopped running, for good this time.

Tessa remembered nights like this—she used to have them often. She was up late, working—joyously! It was almost midnight, but she'd gotten on a roll creating more designs for Gravediggers and hadn't been able to make herself stop. For dinner, Lucky had made grilled cheese sandwiches and heated up some soup in her kitchen, then he'd watched TV while she'd worked in the same room.

About an hour ago, he'd said, "Babe, I'm gonna head up to my place and go to bed. You wanna come up when you're done?"

She'd taken the time to stop, stand up, and give him a kiss. "Absolutely. And sorry I kind of ditched you tonight."

He'd simply squeezed her hand and said, "No worries. I know how into your work you are and I get it."

Ah, Lucky. He'd been a huge part of turning her life back into something that felt vital and productive lately. And he'd made her feel not only human again, and like a woman again, but like a very *hot* and *sexy* woman. And in that moment, a part of her wanted to drop everything and go hop into bed with her man—but she was excited about the changes she kept coming up with for the bar, and she was afraid if she stopped without getting them down, she'd lose them. So she worked, happy in the knowledge that when she finally ran out of inspiration, she could ease into bed next to him, snug and cozy, the perfect ending to a satisfying night.

Well, maybe hot sex would be the *perfect* ending. But they were reaching that comfortable place in their relationship where sometimes snuggling quietly felt "just right." She smiled at the thought—then looked up upon realizing a vehicle had just stopped outside.

The cabin's windows were open and the two houses were so isolated that when a car passed by on Whisper Falls Road this late at night, you noticed. And you also noticed if it didn't keep going.

Walking down the hall into her bedroom, she peeked out at her driveway, yet all was quiet and empty but for her Nissan. Moving to a window at the rear of the cabin, she pulled back a toile curtain and looked up toward Lucky's house—where, indeed, an unfamiliar car sat in his driveway.

Or *was it* unfamiliar? A bright moon shone down and, peering up at the older Camaro, she thought it looked like the same one that had delivered that guy, Red, to Lucky's house to pick up his bike. And then the moon gave her a glimpse of Red himself, walking around the car, opening the trunk. Was she imagining it or was he purposely trying to be quiet? And what the hell was he doing at Lucky's this late anyway?

She watched for a moment longer and though it wasn't easy to see, she sensed the scraggly older guy skulking around Lucky's garage in the dark. It was enough to make her heart pound painfully against her rib cage. Enough to make her pick up the phone. Then, on pure instinct, she even rapped on the window once, hoping maybe it would scare the guy off. After all, if he was here for a valid reason, he'd be knocking on the door. And she knew Lucky sometimes let people drop off and pick up bikes at odd hours, but he always waited up for them. Something wasn't right here.

She was just about to dial Lucky's number when a burst of light drew her attention back out the window—up to Lucky's place. And—oh God!

It was a fire! One side of the garage had just burst into flames.

. . . what mystery, that broke out now in fire and now in blood, at the deadest hours of night?

Charlotte Brontë, *Jane Eyre*

Seventeen

Her hands began to shake now and she could barely breathe, and instead of calling Lucky, she dialed 911. Then watched as the Camaro suddenly went backing recklessly up the driveway and out onto the road.

"9–1–1. What's your emergency?"

"My boyfriend's house is on fire!" she said as the car went speeding away. "On Whisper Falls Road! Just up the hill from the bridge! Please hurry!"

"We're sending help right now, ma'am. Are you in the house? If so, can you get out?"

"I'm not inside. I live next door."

"Is anyone in the house?"

"Yes!"

But she had no idea what the 9–1–1 lady said next because that's when she dropped the phone and went sprinting out the back door, barefoot, up the hill. The last time she'd gone dashing up through Lucky's yard like this, she'd been chasing Mr. Knightley and met up with a big, scary biker. Now, that biker was the man of her dreams and she was running to save him.

"Lucky!" she screamed frantically. *"Lucky, wake up! The house is on fire!"* Cool dew made her slip and fall as she ran, but she picked herself up without thought and kept going. The bright flames at the garage began to grow higher, licking at the roof now, and she could hear the fire hissing and cracking as it spread. *"Luckyyyy!"*

Thankfully, the front door was unlocked since he'd been expecting her to come up—so she yanked it open and raced inside. In her rush, she tripped over the coffee table in the dark, falling, yelling out as the pain sliced into her knee, but pushed back to her feet and ran down the hall into Lucky's bedroom, yelling all the way. *"Get up! You have to get out! The house is on fire!"*

Within seconds, she was shaking him awake and finally his eyes bolted open. Just in the short time they'd been together, she'd noticed he was a sound sleeper, and now he was disoriented. "Huh? What? What's wrong?"

"Get up!" She pulled on his arm. "The house is on fire."

Finally, this jolted him fully awake. He rolled out of bed in a pair of boxer briefs, snatching up a pair of blue jeans on the floor as they exited the room. Blood pounded in Tessa's ears as they jogged back toward the front door.

Once outside, where Lucky could see the flames, he said, "Jesus Christ—I gotta call the fire department."

He made a move back toward the door, but Tessa grabbed his arm. "They're on the way."

Lucky just stared at the burning garage, nearly half of it engulfed now, his expression a mix of bewilderment and horror. Still sounding a little out of it from sleep, he murmured, "How the hell . . . ?"

Still watching the fire, too, Tessa took his hand and held on tight. "I'm pretty sure it was that guy with the scraggly beard, the one you don't like—Red. I heard his car and saw him out my window."

Lucky turned to her then, jaw dropping. "Are you sure?"

She blinked, trying to replay it in her mind. "I think so. I remembered the car he came in to pick up his bike. It was the same one."

Fortunately, only moments later, a siren split the night air, growing closer each second. Lucky stood hand in hand with Tessa in only a pair of blue jeans as the big red fire engine came into view, screaming up the curvy, hilly road and into Lucky's driveway. Several fireman jumped down, hoses in hand, and Tessa recognized one of them as Logan Whitaker, Mike Romo's lifelong best friend. "You guys need to step back further," he yelled in their direction.

Lucky could barely make sense of what was happening— it felt surreal. This . . . this was the kind of shit he'd expected to happen ten years ago, but it never had. And Red had done it. And that meant . . . oh God. God damn it to hell.

He just swallowed, trying not to think, not to feel. But Jesus—what if Johnny had been there? What if Tessa hadn't seen what was happening out the window and called for help so fast? What if it had spread more quickly by the time she'd come in to get him? What if they'd both been there, fast asleep?

Lucky's blood ran cold. The worst had finally happened—his past had come back to haunt him. Red had lied—that sneaky little bastard had *lied* to him, *fooled* him for Christ's sake—and was obviously still doing Wild Bill's dirty work. Son of a bitch! To think they'd been looking for him all these years! And now they'd found him. Here, of all places. Where his son was, where his girl was. And his brother. His grandmother, for God's sake. He'd endangered them all by just being here.

He watched—a weird sense of numbness disguising his rage—as the Destiny Fire Department blasted thick, powerful torrents onto the flames, which were beginning to die down. He realized his heart beat violently fast.

Okay, so maybe the house isn't gonna burn. That's good. But what about the rest? How much of his equipment would be ruined? What about the three customers' bikes inside the garage? He had business insurance, but . . . shit, this was still bad.

His own beloved Harley was down at Tessa's—and he suddenly felt damn thankful he'd pulled into her driveway instead of his this afternoon when they'd come back from a ride. As far as he knew, the helmet he'd painted for her still sat on the bike's leather seat. A little thing to be worrying about now, but his mind was racing, and he didn't like the idea of his gift to her being burned up by the Devil's Assassins.

Although the very thought struck fresh fear and outrage into his heart. The Assassins knew where he was. Jesus fucking Christ.

He blinked in surprise when a police car pulled in behind the fire truck and Mike and Rachel got out, both with messy hair, dressed in jeans and T-shirts, clearly having gotten out of bed for this. They headed straight for Tessa and Lucky, and Mike met his gaze. "You all right, man?"

Lucky just nodded, still in shock.

"How did you . . . ?" Tessa asked, clearly confused.

"Logan called me on the way," Mike replied, then looked to Lucky. "An officer on duty is coming to do the official stuff, but Logan knew I'd want to know."

"Thanks," Lucky said. "For coming."

Mike simply gave a short nod, yet Lucky still felt it— that new, shockingly thick reconnection with his brother. He hadn't expected it when it had happened—and he definitely couldn't have predicted it would run so deep. But it just plain made him feel a little better that Mike was there.

Soon, another squad car came—and as Mike had promised, it brought another Destiny cop, Raybourne Fleet, to investigate.

When Tessa was questioned, she explained all she'd seen. And when *Lucky* was questioned . . . he didn't tell the entire truth. He described Red as someone he'd known socially many years ago, keeping the Devil's Assassins completely out of it. Mike sat in on the interview, and Lucky could pretty much feel Mike's doubt when he got to that part, but he just kept going.

"Well, reckon that about wraps it up," Officer Fleet said, finishing up notes on a clipboard. "We'll try findin' this fella's sister tomorrow and see if we can't track him down." Then the tall, buzz-cut cop looked back to Lucky, his eyes narrowing slightly. "You sure you don't know what beef this guy has with you, why he'd want to do somethin' like this?"

Lucky shook his head and gave the same answer he had a few minutes ago. "Other than the fact that my buddy and me weren't very friendly to him at Gravediggers, nope. When I painted his bike, I thought we'd left things on good terms. But like I said, he's always been a little . . . off. That's all I know."

Just then, Logan Whitaker approached the small group of men and Lucky saw that the fire appeared to be completely out now. "Been a long time, Lucky," Logan said, compassion in his voice. Lucky had known Logan as a kid—he'd lived just up the road and had been at their house a lot when they were young. "Sorry to be seeing you for a reason like this, though."

Lucky gave him a nod, shook his hand. "I appreciate that. And it's good to see you, man." Then he motioned toward the garage. "How bad are things?"

"Well, the good news is that the house is fine. The door

connecting to the garage is a solid fire door, with good seals on it, so no smoke got inside your living space. The other good news is that less than half the garage burned and some of the stuff in it is salvageable." Then he sighed and shifted his weight from one fireman's boot to the other. "The bad news, though, is that it looks like some of your painting equipment was destroyed, and there's significant smoke damage to the motorcycles and other stuff that didn't burn. Tell me you have good insurance."

Lucky nodded somberly. "I do."

Logan smiled, clearly trying to lighten a bad situation. "Good. Now tell me whoever owns those motorcycles aren't the scary kind of bikers who are gonna wreak havoc over this."

Lucky thought through the rides he was currently working on. "Nah," he said. "They won't be happy, but they won't hold me responsible."

"Weird thing," Logan said, looking back at the garage. "We'll have to get an arson investigator out here, but best we can tell, for this being arson, this guy did a pretty crappy job of setting a fire. There are signs of an accelerant, but only around one corner of the garage. This could have been much worse if he'd been even a little more thorough."

Lucky took that in, thought it over. "Tessa said she banged on her window when she realized he was probably up to no good. Maybe he heard it and cut the job short."

Logan nodded, and Mike said, "Makes sense."

As Mike walked the other guys back to their vehicles, Lucky sat down by himself in the grass on the hill, looking toward Tessa's house, exhausted by it all. Tessa and Rachel stood over by his deck and he could have joined them, but he just wanted a few minutes alone—to think.

It didn't surprise him that Red would fuck up an arson attempt. The guy was generally inept, a screw-up. But that created a big question in Lucky's mind. Of all the bad-ass bikers in the Devil's Assassins, why the hell would they send *Red* to do a job like this?

Maybe . . . his first assumption upon seeing the fire had been wrong. Maybe the Assassins hadn't been following him, watching him, after all. Because if they'd known where he was for any length of time, why wait until now to strike? So maybe part of Red's story was true—maybe he really *had* just stumbled onto Lucky and Duke that night at Gravediggers. He'd surely reported back to Wild Bill about it—but if Red was the one out doing the dirty work, it might very well mean that Bill and the rest of the club were nowhere near Destiny. At least not yet. Which meant he had a little time to puzzle through this before being forced to deal with Wild Bill himself or any of the other Assassins.

By the time Officer Fleet's cruiser pulled away, Lucky saw Logan and the rest of the firefighters reloading their equipment, soon climbing back up into the fire truck, ready to leave as well. A glance beyond to the charred black remains of half his garage, now strung with yellow police tape, made him cringe—both in anger and dread. The pungent scent of burnt materials filled the air.

When he saw Mike walking back toward him, he stood up. And Mike's eyes dropped to his chest. He looked stunned. "God, how did I not see that until just now?"

Lucky glanced down—to the tattoo of their sister's name over his heart. "Got it after I first left home. I was thinking a lot about her then, more than usual."

Their eyes met again and Mike said, "You okay, man? You look upset."

"Somebody just tried to burn my fucking house down," he pointed out.

"I know. But . . . who's this guy *really*? Part of the MC?"

Lucky nodded. "More or less. Once upon a time."

"Why the hell didn't you say so?" His brother sounded put out, and Lucky guessed he couldn't blame him—

being a small town cop, Mike probably expected honesty, and from most people, he probably got it.

"Look," Lucky said, "the less people who know this might be related to the club, the better. I'll figure out how to deal with it."

But Mike lowered his chin, his look mired in doubt. "How the hell will you do *that*? These guys have had you hiding out for years and you suddenly think you can beat them on your own if they're after you?"

Lucky shook his head. "I don't even know for sure how firmly this guy is still associated with the club. He's mostly a weasely tag-along who looks for attention. So I need to find out more before I jump to any conclusions." Then he looked Mike in the eye. "And the other reason I didn't mention it is . . . I don't want my kid to know I was in a gang. There's no reason he *should* know. All it could do is upset him and make him afraid of me."

He then motioned to where Tessa stood with Rachel. "Can you do me a favor? I know it's late, but can you and Rachel take Tessa home with you for a couple hours?"

"Why?" Suspicion laced Mike's tone.

"Just need to go on a fact-finding mission, like I said. I won't be long, but I just need to guarantee she's safe—just in case he decides to come back while I'm not here, you know?"

"Of course," Mike said. "But for the record, I don't like this. I don't want you getting yourself in any more trouble."

Lucky gave his brother a piercing, honest look. "Too late for that—I'm already in it. Now I just need to figure out how deep, and how to get back out of it."

As Lucky's bike sped down Whisper Falls Road a little while later, Molly Hatchet's "Flirtin' with Disaster" pounding in his ears, he again suffered the gut impulse to run. To just keep riding and not look back. His presence was putting the people he cared about in danger and it suddenly seemed safer if he just got the hell out of their lives.

But it was a fleeting thought, only momentary. An old habit, maybe—the idea that running solved things. It took only a second to realize that if he were to leave, the people in his life might *still* be in danger because of him—and besides, he had way too much here now to willingly leave it behind. And way too much to take this lying down.

Despite what he'd told Mike, Lucky felt he had to assume the worst case scenario here—that Red had done this on behalf of the Devil's Assassins. It was the only logical explanation.

But before he did anything, he had to talk to Duke. And that was where he was headed.

When he pulled in at Gravediggers, the place was still open for business—but it was late and the parking lot was mostly empty. Lucky pushed through the door to see a few leather-clad bikers shooting pool and a dude with a bad scar on his cheek making out with a blond biker babe in one corner.

And that guy wasn't the only one getting lucky at Gravediggers tonight—as Lucky approached the bar, Duke was leaning across it, delivering an open-mouthed kiss to the very same girl he'd suggested fixing Lucky up with a month or two back. The sexy girl with ebony hair hanging to her ass moaned a little against Duke's mouth.

But Lucky didn't have time to be polite here, so he stepped up and cleared his throat with purpose. When Duke glanced over, looking surprised and a little pissed off, Lucky said, "We need to talk. Important."

"Stay put, hon," Duke instructed the girl, then followed Lucky to the opposite end of the bar to tell him, "This better be damn good."

"It is. Well, damn *bad*, actually."

Duke's expression shifted from irritation to concern. "What is it, brother?"

Lucky proceeded to tell the whole story, and when he was done, Duke just lowered his gaze for a minute and let out a deep sigh. Lucky knew exactly what he was feeling, since he felt it, too: *You finally think it's over, you finally think you're safe—and then you're not.*

"The way I see it," Duke said when he looked back up, "is that, first things first, we need to take care of Red. Nobody else from the club is here, at least not yet, so we deal with Red now, before we have a whole crowd breathing down our necks."

Lucky nodded. He didn't like it—not one damn bit—but his biggest concern at the moment was protecting Tessa, who Red had seen with him a couple of times, and Johnny, in case Red knew about him, too.

"So I'll go after him," Duke went on then, like it was nothing.

And Lucky barked, "What? No way."

"You got a lot more to lose than I do," Duke pointed out. Which was damn noble of him, and just the kind of friend he was. But that reasoning wasn't good enough for Lucky.

"If it wasn't for me, *neither* of us would be have to deal with it," Lucky reminded him. "I should be the one to do it." And though Lucky nor Duke said what going after Red really meant, they both knew what they were talking about. Lucky, for one, just didn't want to put a name on it. The whole idea made him sick, in fact. Yet he didn't feel they had much of a choice. He hung his head and muttered, "Shit, I hate this. This isn't my life anymore—I can't go back to living that way."

But Duke didn't respond to any of that. "Smart thing," he said instead, "might be to track him down *together*. Outnumber him."

Lucky gave another nod, deciding Duke was right to keep it simple, stay focused—this was no time for something as useless as emotion. But in the end, he replied, "I'm fucking exhausted—I can't think straight anymore. I'm gonna go home, get some sleep, clear my head." Then he motioned to the hot brunette still waiting patiently, playing with the straw in her drink. "And you got business of a better kind to take care of."

Sighing, Duke said, "Maybe you're right. We should both sleep on it. We'll talk again tomorrow."

If Lucky hadn't *already* felt like an asshole, he would have by the time he stopped at Mike's in the middle of the night to get Tessa. These were good people—and because of him, the lights in their house were burning bright at three A.M. When Mike came to the door, he just said, "Sorry. For keeping you guys up. For everything."

Mike looked tired, but mumbled, "It's all right," as he let Lucky in.

He found the girls in the living room, drinking coffee, and when Tessa saw him, she stood up, anger blazing in her hazel eyes. "Where have you been? What the hell's going on?"

Jesus. This night just kept getting better and better. He tried to speak calmly. "Can we just go home? Talk there?"

She sucked in her breath, appearing to weigh the request, and finally said, "Fine."

Lucky only had one helmet with him, so he insisted Tessa wear it. And the wind on his face gave him the sensation it was clearing away the cobwebs in his brain so he could sort through this thing logically.

Was there any other way to deal with this besides the one he and Duke had discussed? *Damn*, how he wanted there to be another way.

But no matter how he examined it, he came to the same conclusion: He'd caused too much trouble for everyone,

Duke included, and he *should* be the one to end it. His fault, his mess to clean up. He was *tired* of running from shit. This was the only way to protect the people he loved.

And he needed to take action quickly, before Duke figured out he was going Lone Ranger.

When Lucky pulled the bike into his driveway, the sobering sight of his charred garage met him, one whole wall and half the door gone—everything inside either burned to a crisp or blackened by smoke. And while he didn't look forward to what he had to do, the sight was like a punch in the gut, reminding him he had no choice.

Walking inside, it relieved him to see Logan had been right—everything in the house seemed fine. He'd shut the windows before he'd left, and turned on the A/C, and after closing the door he couldn't even smell the remains of the fire anymore.

"Are you gonna answer my questions now?" Tessa asked. She sounded a little less upset than she had at Mike's, but not much.

In response, Lucky took her hands and led her to the couch—and he sat them down there, facing each other, cross-legged. He might be deceiving Mike a little, and maybe even Duke, but that was for their own protection. And when it came to Tessa, he owed her the whole truth. "Babe, there's . . . some stuff I need to tell you."

"Like what was so important you went dashing off in the middle of the night? And why Mike insisted I go home with them?"

Lucky sighed, then began, "It's like this." She already knew about his past with Red—now he told her in detail why he suspected the Devil's Assassins were behind the fire and that there was surely more to come, whether through Wild Bill or some other member. "So I have to take care of Red before anything else happens."

And that's when—aw, hell—her look transformed into one of . . . horror. "My God, Lucky." She wore a big, warm, tie-in-the-front sweater over a tank top and jogging pants, and as she began to ball the sweater's hem in her fists, clearly agitated, she gaped at him like he'd just morphed into a monster.

Shit—after everything he'd told her about California, he'd thought she'd *get* this, thought she'd understand why it had to be done. And he didn't want to scare her, but . . . "Next time it could be you, or Johnny. And either one of you could have been here with me tonight. I have to put a stop to this *now.* "

"You just said yourself there was more to come, so how will taking care of Red stop it?"

"It's a first step," he admitted.

And she argued, "You could approach this a different way."

He raised his eyebrows, irritated that she was making this harder than it already was. "And what would that be?"

"Let the police handle it—like anyone else would! Mike told me you'd held stuff back about Red on the police report. So you could go to Mike, officially report all the rest, and trust them to handle it."

Lucky just ran both his hands back through his hair. She *didn't* get it. "There are a lot of reasons that's a bad idea."

"I'm listening," she said, still sounding as on edge as he felt. And God, he was so tired—all he'd wanted was to come back here and hold her, sleep with her in his arms. But it sure wasn't working out that way. At least not yet.

So he explained that to officially confess to being a member of the Devil's Assassins was to confess to numerous crimes. "They probably all have statutes of limitations that have expired, but still—it's opening up a big damn can of worms. And it wouldn't hurt only me. It would hurt Johnny, and you. And Mike, too."

Before she could reply, he went on. "And once I admit that, who's to say the Destiny Police are even gonna be on my side? Who's to say they'll pursue Red as hard as they should? *Mike* would, yeah—but I'm not dumping this on my brother. I'm not making him clean up my messes or defend me to the people he works with. And besides . . ." He stopped, sighed. "Mike's a small town cop. And a good one, probably. But this is serious shit. And if something happened to him because of me . . ." He shook his head, adamant. "I can't do it. There's too much at risk, and every fucking bit of it started with me, so *I* have to take care of it."

Still facing him on the couch, the girl he loved let out a big *whoosh*ing breath, then met his gaze. He could already see in her eyes that nothing had changed, that his arguments hadn't swayed her. Her voice came out softer than he expected. "So you mean to *kill* Red, right?"

Jesus. That was the part he and Duke had avoided putting into words, the part too ugly to say out loud. But he couldn't deny it. Only . . . he couldn't make himself acknowledge it, either. The way she was looking at him made him feel . . . small, ashamed. In a way he never really had before. It had been a damn long time since he cared what somebody thought of him. And a damn long time since he'd felt like he was letting somebody down. So he simply didn't answer.

But she knew what the silence meant. And her pretty eyes grew big and round in the lamplight as she said, "You can't do this, Lucky."

He found himself speaking around a lump in his throat. "Why can't I?"

"Because you're not that guy anymore. You're not the guy who killed somebody back in California. Are you? Because you've told me over and over how lost you were then and how much you regret all that and how much you've changed. And if all that's true, then you *can't* do this. You *can't*."

Lucky's muscles tensed, his teeth clenching. He had

to make her understand. "There's no other way, Tessa. The police can't take care of this problem. Best case scenario—they'll arrest Red, maybe prosecute him. But that won't make even a dent in the hell that might be coming this way."

"And killing him will?"

He simply nodded. Once. Because it was the truth. The only truth he knew. It might be a *horrible* truth, but it was beyond his control to alter it. "Yes," he said simply. It wouldn't stop the Devil's Assassins if they were gunning for him—but it would send a strong message, it would keep them all safe in the meantime, and it would stop the flow of information about him or Duke to Wild Bill.

Tessa stayed quiet for a long time, and neither of them looked each other in the eye. Lucky stayed painfully aware of the anxious rise and fall of her chest. When she finally spoke, her voice again turned quiet. "I'm asking you not to do this. For me."

Oh God. What a request.

He considered it for a moment, seriously thought it over. God knew he didn't *want* to do this. Yet the man had struck out at him, tried to end his life. Was he supposed to just sit here and wait for the trouble to escalate? "I wish I could," he began. "I wish I could *not* do it—for you. But . . ."

Without warning, she drew her hands into fists in front of her and brought them pounding down on the leather sofa cushion between them. "My God, this is nuts! Every day I have to worry about my brother over in Afghanistan. Will somebody shoot him? Will *he* have to shoot somebody? He has no choice, Lucky—he *has* to be in danger, he *has* to be willing to use that kind of force! But you *don't*."

His reply was resolute. "Your brother has people to protect. So do I. The two situations aren't so different."

Looking at him like he was insane, she beseeched him.

"What can I say? What can I do to make you change your mind?"

He let out a heavy breath and whispered the only true answer he could. "Nothing."

Tessa felt as if she were in the middle of a tornado, being whipped in crazy circles where nothing made sense. How was this happening? It was surreal enough that someone had set Lucky's house on fire—but what he planned to do about it felt impossible to her. She understood the reasons he'd given her, but . . . God.

It was one thing to know your boyfriend had accidentally killed someone in another life, years ago—that was awful *enough*, but she'd looked beyond it, she'd had faith, she'd forgiven him for being that person. It was another thing, though, to find out he was still capable of such violence, and that this time it would be—oh Lord—deliberate.

And *could* he? Could her Lucky *be* that violent? Could the man who'd been so gentle with her, so loving, so kind, really take a life? She just stared at him, trying to see behind his eyes, trying to see inside him. He *looked* like the guy she'd fallen in love with, but right now . . . she felt utterly abandoned. Emotionally.

Just a few hours ago, she'd trusted him completely, with every facet of her life. But . . . maybe she was wrong about him being reformed. Maybe all those people who'd warned her about him in the beginning had actually been *right*. Maybe once a criminal, always a criminal. After all, at the first sign of trouble, Lucky apparently reverted to gang member mentality.

It dawned on her now just how quickly all this had happened between them, and that maybe she'd been foolish all along. And that she'd *definitely* been foolish to let herself believe in him so blindly, fall in love with him so helplessly. "I feel like I don't even know you," she finally told him.

And when he reached out to take her hands, his wounded expression tugged at her heart. "Please don't say that. Of course you know me."

She peered down at her small hands in his larger, darker ones. Hands that had killed before. Was that just now really hitting her? That he'd killed someone?

She drew in a sharp breath and pulled her hands away— then got to her feet. She didn't want to let him see her cry. He'd always told her she was strong—and she wanted to stay that way right now, at least on the *outside*. "I've trusted you, Lucky, and I've loved you entirely. But if you can do this, you're a stranger to me." And with that, she rushed out of his house and ran down the hill toward hers.

"Tessa, wait!" she heard him call behind her, and sensed him following.

But she didn't want to be around him anymore. Suddenly, he wasn't the man she knew, the man she'd given herself to in so many ways. Lord, this was ripping her heart out.

"Tessa, stop. Please!"

Yet she hurried in her back door and locked it. Because she couldn't look at him without crying now—and in fact, tears already streamed down her face.

"Babe—*please*," he said through the door.

She turned around and leaned against it, then let her back slide down until she was sitting on the floor.

"Don't shut me out! Let me in! Let me just hold you."

Oh God—that sounded so, so good. Especially after all that had happened tonight. Except . . . she no longer knew who he was. And she could never let him hold her again. Because if she did . . . she might love him too much and somehow let herself be convinced this madness was okay.

The horrible fact slapping her squarely in the face right now was that she and Lucky were from two different worlds. They might have both been born and raised in Destiny, but that was where their paths diverged. She'd

known it from the start and had looked past it for the sake
of sex, never expecting it to be any more than that. And
then she'd looked *further* past those differences, letting
herself believe people could really change. And maybe
they could. Jenny's husband, Mick, had changed. But the
sad truth in this world was that, mostly, people *didn't*
change. Not in ways that big. Not in ways that went to a
person's core. And she'd been so, so foolish, seeing this
whole situation through rose-colored glasses—all because she was so drawn to him and so eager to be loved.

"Go away, Lucky. Go home," she called through the
door. Oh, crap—could he tell she was crying?

"No!" he said. "We need to talk more. I need to make
you understand."

"You can't!" she screamed at him. Then her voice
came quieter—she was too tired to yell. And just very sad
inside. "I don't know you anymore," she said. "Maybe I
never did."

I will never again come to your side:
I am torn away now, and cannot return.

Charlotte Brontë, *Jane Eyre*

Eighteen

Lucky felt like he couldn't breathe. What the hell was happening here? He hadn't seen it coming—not at all. He'd thought she'd understand everything at stake, why he had no choice but to take action.

"Tessa! Open the door! Let me in!"

But then . . . maybe he'd forgotten. Who she was. A nice girl from Destiny. The kind who didn't usually go for guys like him. For a reason. Guys like him were too rough for her, and had too much baggage. He'd known that the second he'd laid eyes on her. But he'd just forgotten it somewhere along the way.

Yet that didn't change one important fact here. "I love you," he said through the door.

Aw, shit—was she crying on the other side? He almost thought he heard her, sobbing a little but his mind was so jumbled at this point, maybe he was imagining it.

Maybe . . . this wasn't tearing her to pieces the way it was him.

He shut his eyes for a second, tried to calm down. Then tried to wish it away. But it was still happening—Tessa had locked him out. Told him he was a stranger to her.

"God, I love you so damn much." He didn't say it as loudly this time, too tired to keep yelling, and perhaps saying it more to himself than to her. "I love you more than I knew I could."

He leaned forward, rested his forehead against the glass on the door, which was covered with little white curtains on the other side. Then he clenched his eyes shut tight. He'd fucked up. He'd fucked up his whole damn life. And he had a bad feeling he couldn't fix this. Suddenly, the very idea of him and Tessa being together seemed . . . crazy. Unfathomable. And it felt like . . . she'd finally seen the real him. Part of the real him anyway. The uglier, angrier part—the bits left over from a time of living on the edge.

But as devastating as all that was, it didn't change what he had to do.

And he needed to do it as soon as possible, yet . . . he couldn't leave Tessa alone like this, unguarded, no matter how much she might hate him. Red could come back, after all. Red could have been spying on them enough to know she lived right next door—and if Wild Bill was calling the shots here, Christ. The memory of Bill's threat against any woman Lucky might ever care for made his blood run cold.

Lucky sat down on the concrete stoop outside her back door, leaning against the house. Exhaustion gripped him, but it vied with an anxious energy inside him now, an old familiar feeling from his days as a Devil's Assassin—it was the sense of knowing you had to be on alert, ready for danger; it was also a sense of wanting to step up and meet that challenge, *be* the dangerous one, win the fight, bring it all to an end so you could sleep easy for a night or two before the next ugly hazard came along. And that energy kept him awake, kept his ears open and listening for anything beyond the songs of crickets and tree frogs in the woods. And it kept him thinking through all of this—kept him feeling the hurt of what Tessa thought of him now and the frustration that he couldn't make her see things his way. And it kept the fury toward Red growing inside him, just like the flames he'd witnessed earlier, getting higher, wilder, hotter with each passing minute.

Daybreak came quicker than he'd expected, the first soft rays of morning peeking through the trees behind his house. As the air around him lightened, he stood up, looked around. In one sense, the daylight made him feel safe, a little bit protected. But a glance up toward his home—his first real, clear look at the fire damage from last night—brought back every bad feeling, even multiplied them.

He drew in a breath, let it back out.

Then he looked toward Tessa's bedroom. Red seemed like exactly like the kind of guy who would only strike under the cover of darkness—and more from cowardliness than brains—so Lucky's instincts told him Tessa would be safe for now if he left. And he couldn't stand guard over her forever—it was time to get this thing done.

Just as the police had deduced, since Red had been in his sister's car last night, his sister's place in Chillicothe was a good place to start his search. But first, he needed to pay a quick return visit to Gravediggers.

The early morning ride over to Crestview was cool and quiet. If not for the grim task at hand, Lucky would have enjoyed the fresh, crisp air, the sight of a dew-covered meadow shimmering in the sunlight, the sense that the world was brand new again. But the world *wasn't* new—in fact it felt very old to him just now, like he could *never* escape his past, like it would always be dogging him, no matter how much he wanted to be a different man than the one he'd been in California.

He tried to block Tessa out of his mind because right now he had to stay focused—it was all important, literally a matter of life and death.

He was going to Gravediggers to get his gun, the one he'd turned over to Duke a few months back, convinced—and determined—he'd never need it again. Maybe it would be *smart* for him and Duke to go after Red together, but as he'd decided last night, this was on him—all of it. And besides, he already knew the guilt and emptiness that came with the task at hand—he saw no reason for Duke to endure it, too. And Duke was right—Lucky had more to lose than Duke, and that's exactly why he had to be the one to protect it all.

Even if his stomach was churning. Even if he couldn't quite envision how all this was going to come down in a way that would let him live with himself. *Push that aside. Just do this. You have to.*

Gravediggers sat along a stretch of road lined with aging strip malls flanked by pockmarked parking lots, all empty of people at this hour. The area felt so desolate right now that as Lucky approached, he realized the noise from his Hooker troublemaker pipes might wake Duke in his apartment above the bar, so he slowed down, deciding to park at the end of the adjacent strip mall. As a bar owner, morning was for Duke what night was for most people—his time to sleep. And Lucky's plan was to get in and back out, quick and quiet, so that Duke would never even know he'd been there. The fact that no cars or bikes remained in Gravediggers' lot assured Lucky that if his buddy had gotten busy with the hot brunette, she'd since headed home.

The quiet walk across the barren asphalt lots felt like roaming a modern day ghost town. Lucky gripped his keys tight in his fist, glad he'd never bothered to take the one to Gravediggers off his key ring after staying with Duke back in the winter.

Reaching the big black building's front double doors, he slid the key in the old lock and slipped inside, quiet as a burglar. All was silent and still as he crossed the floor and walked down the short hallway. Duke's office was unlocked, as Lucky had known it would be—Duke sometimes secured the room during business hours, but after locking the outside doors and stowing the night's take in the safe, he tended to leave the office open.

The safe sat on an old metal file cabinet in the corner and Lucky went straight for it, turning the combination lock to 36, then 24, then around again to 36. It gently clicked when he pulled downward and the steel door released. Inside were two shelves—on one rested a zippered money bag from last night, on the other lay three handguns. He drew out his Glock from between the other two firearms Duke stashed here in case of trouble. Checking the clip, he found his friend had kept it loaded, so he jammed it back in place, a step closer to completing the mission at hand.

Closing the safe back up and giving the lock a spin, Lucky paused, looked down at the gun, tested the weight of the G19 in his hand. It had been a while since he'd held it, fired it, but he'd visited a shooting range in Milwaukee on a fairly regular basis before heading south to Ohio, and now he had to trust that it would be like riding a bike. With the safety still on, he stepped into an open area in the office and assumed a shooting stance, legs spread, arms stretched straight in front of him, both hands on the weapon. The very position tightened his chest a little, geared him up for action. Yeah, he could do this. He could be the bad-ass he'd once been for a little while longer, to protect the people he loved.

It was as he pulled Duke's office door shut behind him,

stepping into the hall, that he heard a loud noise from out-side, just out the back door a few feet away—like metal scraping on concrete. And any other time, he'd assume there was some logical explanation—but right now, his muscles tensed and he instinctively clicked the Glock's safety off. Just in case.

Pausing at the door just long enough to feel ready, in one swift motion he turned the lock, opened the door, and aimed the gun outside even while protecting as much of his body as he could with the building.

And—shit. Part of him had expected to see nothing and feel relieved. But instead, right in front of him, not ten feet away, stood Red Thornton pouring gasoline around the bar's foundation.

Red looked up with a start, and Lucky said, "Don't move a muscle, Red, or I'll take you down."

Red froze, wide-eyed, appearing appropriately scared, and it pleased Lucky in an old, familiar way. That had been the good—even if shameful—part of being in a gang: feeling powerful, invincible, when people feared you. And now that strange, gripping satisfaction perme-ated Lucky, delivering an even firmer sense of control.

Red dropped the gas can on the gravel beneath him and put up his hands. "Now don't go shootin' me, Lucky. This ain't like it seems."

Christ, Red was an idiot. First, he'd failed to succeed in burning Lucky's place down, and now the numbnuts was pouring gas around a building constructed of cin-derblock.

And he actually expected Lucky to believe any of this wasn't like it seemed?

But Lucky used the moment to take in more than just that. Red's sister's Camaro sat nearby, trunk open—which explained why he hadn't seen it out front. And Red looked about as worn out as Lucky felt. So it would be smart to use Red's exhaustion against him, to get as much information from him as he could before he ended this.

"If you're gonna tell me you didn't torch my place last night, save it, asshole. I saw you." The small lie avoided putting it on Tessa, and besides, this would scare Red more.

And it did—the scraggly-bearded man began to tremble slightly. Then he stuttered a little, but no real words ever came out.

"The only thing that surprises me is to see you doing this in the daylight," Lucky said, his eyes spewing venom. "I figured a rat like you only came out to do Bill's dirty work in the dark."

Red just scowled. "Had to wait all damn night for that girl to leave so Duke would finally turn out the lights and hit the hay," he muttered.

Good—he was no longer denying it. That would make getting information from him easier. "When's Bill comin' for us, Red?" Lucky asked.

To his surprise, in response, Red turned belligerent, even boastful. "Bill *ain't* comin'. Not yet anyway. He don't even know yet."

Now that Red was getting a little bolder, Lucky concentrated harder on staying alert, keeping the gun trained on him. "He doesn't know *what* yet?" And when Red didn't reply right away, Lucky raised his voice. "I'm pointing a gun at you, you son of a bitch—*answer me.*"

"All right, all right," Red said, clearly trying to calm Lucky down. Then he let out a sigh. "Fact is, I was gonna call Wild Bill after I took care of you and Duke, was gonna get back in his good graces that way. I—I was gonna be like . . . a hero."

Lucky narrowed his gaze on the other man, beginning to get the picture now—finally. "So what you said about no longer being with the club—that was the truth."

Red nodded, swallowed nervously. "Never *did* get patched in, and Bill kicked me to the curb about five years ago."

Lucky simply shook his head. "And you're just like a little puppy, still tryin' to get Bill's attention. God damn— that's fucking sad, Red. This was bad enough when I figured you were his errand boy, but this makes you even more pathetic than I thought."

Red defended himself. "Way I see it, it's you and Duke who're pathetic, runnin' the way ya did. Well, looks to me like you can run but ya can't hide. 'Cause Wild Bill mighta gave up lookin' for ya, but as soon as he finds out where you are, you're as good as dead."

A thick anger gathered in Lucky's gut, and when he spoke, the words echoed lower, meaner, than before. "You're forgetting something, you stupid little prick. *I've* got the gun. *You're* the only one here who's as good as dead."

Red's eyes changed then, and Lucky realized Red had forgotten his predicament for a minute, too busy trying to be the big man he'd never been—and would never be. Now his voice came out nicer—hell, he even tried for a smile. "You wouldn't kill me, would ya, Lucky?"

"I've killed before," he reminded him.

And Red blinked nervously. "But listen, like I said, Wild Bill don't know nothin' about where you are yet. So we can just let all this go. I won't call him—I promise."

Lucky just shook his head. Idiot. "You tried to burn down my house, Red, with me inside it. You're trying to do the same thing to Duke right now. If you weren't such a screw-up, we'd both be dead. So if you think you're walking away from this, you're wrong."

That's when Red's features contorted in a way that made Lucky think he might cry.

"If you got any prayers to say, now's the time," Lucky

informed him, then steadied his finger on the trigger, his heart beating a mile an hour.

Red swallowed visibly, and his voice trembled. "Come on now, Lucky—don't do this. Take mercy on me. I'll do whatever ya want." Then Lucky's eyes were drawn downward as a dark spot spread over the denim between Red's legs and descended one thigh. Christ, he was pissing himself.

Lucky said nothing. Because it was time to stop talking and do the deed, end this. And it came with the satisfaction of knowing that taking Red out really *would* be the end—that was all he had to do to bring this to a conclusion, for all of them.

Shoot him now. Squeeze the trigger. Drop him.

It was easy. So easy. One tiny movement of his finger. *Just do it.*

Red stood before him, gone blessedly quiet, just awaiting his fate, it seemed— so now was the time.

But . . . Jesus Christ. Why wasn't he pulling the trigger? Why couldn't he make that last necessary move?

Aw, shit. Was Tessa right? *You're not that guy anymore. You're not that guy who killed somebody back in California.* And he knew that. But he'd thought he *could* be that guy, one more time, now.

"Come on, man, just do it!" Red yelled suddenly, voice quivering, his whole body shaking.

Damn it. Lucky felt Red deserved to die. And how the hell else could he keep them all safe? Yet his arms felt so heavy suddenly, as if the Glock weighed a hundred pounds. And slowly, his muscles began to give out and the gun drifted slowly lower, until it was aimed at the ground between him and Red.

That's when Lucky's focus shifted, just slightly . . . to the old, broken down Monte Carlo sitting among the debris Duke had let build up out back—the car Lucky had lifted Tessa onto that first night they were together. And somehow the brief but powerful memory jolted him, reminded him what he'd come here determined to save and protect. *What the hell am I doing, being so weak?* Something fierce and new gathered inside him, and he told himself to raise the gun again—just as Red lunged for him.

Lucky pulled the trigger and a shot rang out through the early morning air, but it missed Red completely and the next thing Lucky knew, they were both on the ground, struggling for the Glock. His moment of hesitation had cost him the upper hand.

They rolled in the gravel, fighting, grunting, and Lucky hadn't felt such a rush of adrenaline since the night Hammer had come after him. He was suddenly battling for his life again and he knew it, and he wasn't sorry to be risking it for Tessa, Johnny, Duke . . . his only regret was that damn moment of weakness. He used the fresh burst of energy to knee Red in the gut. But when a door opened up above—the one to Duke's apartment—and Lucky heard Duke say, "Son of a bitch!" somehow Red managed to kick him in the face, hard.

It knocked him to his back in the gravel and when he opened his eyes, he found Red standing over him, pointing his own gun at him. "Who's tough now?" Red spat. Then he glanced briefly at Duke, still on the stairs that led from his apartment. "You just stay where you are, Duke, understand?"

"Police! Drop your weapon!"

Lucky lifted his head—to spot Mike standing behind Red, gun drawn. Jesus.

In response, however, Red spun, turning the Glock on Mike, and the two stood face to face, gun to gun. Shit. The last thing in the world Lucky had wanted was to put this on his brother, who—like Duke—had surely never killed anyone, cop or not.

"Drop your weapon, damn it!" Mike demanded.

And now that Red was distracted by Mike, Lucky knew he *finally* had to end it. With fresh strength and a renewed sense of purpose, he got to his feet, glanced around Duke's debris, then picked up a steel bar lying in the weeds sprouting up alongside the building. "Red!" he said. "Over here."

Panicked and jumpy now, Red spun back around, but he didn't seem to know where to point the gun anymore—there were suddenly too many enemies around him. And Lucky smoothly, firmly pulled back the bar like a baseball bat, ready to defend his brother—when Mike gave one more warning, this time to them both.

"Drop your weapons, for Christ's sake!" he yelled, and Red fired off a wild shot at Lucky that hit the gravel a few feet away.

And Lucky was just about to swing that steel bar for all he was worth—when another shot rang out, striking Red from behind to knock him a step forward before he slumped to the ground. Mike had shot him.

They all stood silent, watching, until it was clear Red was dead. Then Lucky lifted his gaze to Mike, who said, "You okay?"

Lucky gave a short, concise nod. Then let the bar clang to the ground before turning to look up at Duke, now descending the stairs barefoot in only blue jeans. He came to stand by Lucky as they both peered down at Red Thornton. "I'll be damned," Duke muttered. "What the hell happened?"

"Caught him trying to burn your place down," Lucky said on a sigh.

Duke's gaze found Lucky's, his eyes wide with the gravity of the moment. "Shit. Thanks for showing up, man."

But Lucky just shook his head, dazed by it all. "I almost blew it." Then he glanced back and forth between his brother and his best friend and told them the truth.

"When it came down to it, I couldn't do it. I couldn't pull the fucking trigger."

Duke gave him a consoling slap on the back. "It all worked out. Thanks to your brother."

"Yeah," Lucky breathed, realizing he owed Mike his life.

And Mike was already busy doing the cop part of this: He'd whipped out his cell phone to call in the shooting, speaking strong and authoritative, as he always did.

But Mike had just killed somebody. For the first—and probably last—time. And Lucky didn't care how tough his brother was—he knew Mike was in shock, and that as soon as it passed, he'd be torn up inside over this. And that it was something that didn't go away. And it was all Lucky's fault.

It was two hours later before things settled down, but after Red's body was taken away, along with his car, and after all the interviews were conducted and the police reports filed, Lucky and Mike parted ways with Duke and were walking around to the front of the bar toward Mike's 4x4 pickup. It felt like a different world than when Lucky had first arrived here—most of the stores and restaurants in the strip malls were open for business now, and cars whizzed up and down the straight stretch of highway that ran between them all.

As for the interviews with Mike's colleagues, Lucky had stuck to the same version of the truth about Red that he'd told after the fire. And he'd claimed he'd come here to talk to Duke about the situation and had only gotten a gun from the safe after hearing a noise out back. The way Lucky saw it, there was still no reason to fill anyone in on their one-time involvement with the Devil's Assassins. It would only scare people, and more now than ever before, it felt far in the distant past.

"Sure you don't want to hit the emergency room?" Mike asked.

Lucky had gotten a little beat up—some scratches and cuts—but had declined medical treatment when it was offered. "I got Neosporin and Band-Aids at home that'll work just fine," he said. Mainly, he wanted to go home and get some sleep—he'd been up for more than twenty-four hours now and needed to crash, bad.

Mike had offered to drive him home and bring him back for his bike later, and as they climbed in Mike's truck, Lucky said, "I never heard during the interviews—how'd you know something was going down?"

"Tessa heard you leave and called me, worried," Mike replied as they slammed their doors shut. "And I just figured your buddy might know where you were—I had no idea what I'd be walking in on."

And that's when Lucky saw it—subtle, and fast, but Mike's expression had gone a little hollow, and then he'd pushed it away just as quickly to put back on his usual sturdy-cop face.

God, Lucky hated this. He should have been strong enough to do it himself. And because he hadn't, because he'd hesitated, he'd put his brother in the position of having to take a life. And yeah, Mike was a cop, he'd signed up for that—but right now, that didn't matter. Right now, it felt like it always had when they were kids—like Lucky's big brother had been looking out for him again.

Lucky continued watching Mike as he started the truck, his jaw set; he sensed Mike's muscles clenching as he reached for the gearshift.

So Lucky reached out, closed his hand around Mike's wrist.

When Mike looked up at him, he said, "Thanks for what you did today, bro. I was two seconds from bashing that guy's head in. But . . . you kept me from killing him, and maybe going to prison before all was said and done. And you kept me from . . ." He stopped, lowered his gaze—this part was harder. His voice softened. "You kept me from feeling that way again, the way I did the last time—you kept me from taking another guy's life and suffering all the guilt that comes with it." Pulling in his breath, Lucky raised his eyes back to his brother's face. "But I'm so damn sorry *you* have to know how that feels now."

As Lucky might have predicted, Mike just kept acting tough and invincible. He said simply, "It's my job."

Lucky released Mike's wrist, yet dug a little deeper. "You ever have to do that before?"

And, hand still on the gearshift, unmoving, Mike gave Lucky a look that dropped the cop façade, edging all the way into vulnerability, then shook his head. "Hell, it was only the third time I ever had to draw my gun. First time I ever shot it outside the firing range." Finally letting go of the shifter, Mike sighed and slumped down in his seat, staring at the steering wheel. "Shit."

"You don't have to be strong with me, Mike," Lucky told him. "I know how hard it is, what you just did. And you did it for *me*."

Mike locked his gaze on Lucky and spoke low. "I'd do it again in a heartbeat."

"I'd do the same for you, too."

By the time Lucky climbed out of Mike's truck, he couldn't wait to hit the bed. Screw the cuts and scrapes—they'd keep 'til after he got some rest.

But as he walked past the yellow tape across his blackened, burnt garage toward the front door, there was one more thing, just one more, that he had to do first. He had to see Tessa.

Their fight last night had been a bad one, but now he could tell her she'd been right—he *wasn't* the same guy he'd been in his Devil's Assassins days. Surely that would make things right between them again. And now that the worst was over, feeling her arms around him seemed all-important. So even as exhausted as he was, every muscle in his body begging for sleep, he started down the hill and—shit, that's when he noticed her car was gone.

Turning back toward his place, he suffered a strange sense of loneliness just in knowing that talking to her would have to wait—and damn, *that* was new: the loner feeling lonely.

He was a few steps from his front door when he saw the piece of paper taped there—a sheet of Tessa's business stationery—and his chest tightened. Maybe she was sorry, too, that they'd fought. Maybe she was as eager to make up as he was.

Rushing forward, he found a letter scrawled in messy ink—blurred in spots, like maybe she'd been crying when she'd written it. *Aw, babe, I wish you were here. I don't like to make you cry.* He hurriedly grabbed down the letter.

Dear Lucky,

I've barely slept for thinking about you, about us. What we've shared has been amazing—you've given me back a sense of joy and confidence I'd thought I'd lost forever. But last night scared me. Not the fire—your reaction.

I still love you, but I can't be with a man whose response to something is violence. I know you're doing what you think is right, and best—but it's made me realize that we're far more different than I've wanted to believe, and that those differences are too big to overcome. I knew the risk I was taking with you from the start, but now I think I was naïve.

We're still neighbors, and maybe someday we can even be friends again. But I can't see you anymore, I can't love you anymore. Please don't call me, or come to my house—I need you to respect my wishes on this. My heart feels too fragile these days to keep taking chances with it.

I wish you all the best, and please tell Johnny I'm sorry I won't be around any longer. You've got a good kid there, Lucky, and I hope being a father will help you continue to change into the man I know you can be.

Tessa

Lucky just stood there, staring at the piece of paper in his hand, feeling like he'd been sucker punched.

Well, at least this answered *one* question. He'd been right in his fears all along. When put to the test, Tessa really *couldn't* accept him for who he truly was. They really *were* too different for her to ever get past it.

It was only a shame he'd quit worrying about that at some point or maybe this wouldn't be hitting him so damn hard. It was only a shame he'd been stupid enough to believe she really loved him.

Lucky focused on his work—at the moment airbrushing a candy blue skull onto the pearl black gas tank of a Harley Shovelhead. When he was done, he'd add realistic white lightning bolts shooting out from behind it.

It had been two weeks since the fire and it was still a difficult time. Insurance was paying for the repairs and a builder Mick Brody had recommended was scheduled to start rebuilding the garage tomorrow. Lucky had replaced his damaged paints and equipment—Johnny had joined him for the drive to a supply store in Cincinnati just a few days ago to pick up what he needed to resume work. For now, and while the garage was under construction, he'd draped large sheets of clear plastic from the ceiling, sectioning off a small area where he could get back to painting and get some money rolling in again. He had some in the bank, but now that he was paying child support, plus the fact that he was using this opportunity to expand the garage into a more proper paint shop, he needed all the money he could earn. And he was thankful the jobs were still coming. As he'd hoped, word-of-mouth was starting to make its way around the area and he was getting calls from bikers in Chillicothe and beyond.

As for Johnny . . . God, what a great kid. Lucky was thankful to have him around, especially right now, although he got the idea the boy missed seeing Tessa almost as much as Lucky did, given that much of the casual, just hanging-out time he'd spent with Johnny around the house had included her. And as always, he was full of questions—never afraid to ask anything—and Lucky was glad Johnny felt that comfortable with him.

"Why's she mad at you?" Johnny had asked on the ride home from Grandma Romo's house last weekend. She'd hosted a big family cookout, complete with all the Romo cousins, and his Mom and Dad had come up, too, especially to meet their grandson. Johnny had handled the attention well, but the second they were alone again, rather than ask questions about his new extended family, his thoughts had gone straight to where Lucky's usually were: Tessa.

"It's complicated," Lucky had tried to explain. "But when the fire happened, I got so angry it made her feel like she didn't know me anymore." That was the simplest way he could put it into words for Johnny right now—it had been tough enough just explaining the whole ugly mess to a nine-year-old kid in a way that wouldn't scare him, so any details beyond what had been in the local paper had been strictly out of the question. When Johnny got a little older, Lucky would sit him down and talk to him about his past—parts of it anyway—but for now, he and Sharon had agreed it was too much to lay on a fourth-grader. Hell, he felt fortunate Sharon was still letting him *see* Johnny after this.

"Can't you just make up with her?" Johnny had suggested.

And Lucky had cast his son a sad smile. "I wish it was that simple, dude." But it wasn't. Tessa had asked him to respect her wishes, so he had. And beyond that, her letter had . . . aw hell, it had pretty much completely shattered him.

On one hand, he saw where she was coming from—she had enough problems in her life without being involved with a killer. But the idea that she could actually fear him now tore him up. And it wounded him that she would desert him so quickly. She'd been the first person to really believe in him, and over the course of their relationship, he supposed she'd started making him believe in *himself*, see himself in a way he never had before—she'd made him believe he was a good man. Yet now that she'd failed to stand beside him when he'd needed her most—it felt like . . . betrayal. He'd screwed up, yeah—but she'd been gone, that fast. One more little abandonment in his life.

Maybe you should ignore what she said in the letter. Maybe you should go talk to her, make her listen, make her see. But something kept him from it, something he couldn't quite put his finger on, even now. Missing her stung like hell, almost constantly—yet he couldn't get past that invisible apprehension that wouldn't let him go knock on her door.

As for Mike, he seemed to be doing okay after the shooting. Departmental rules had stipulated he see a counselor and stick to desk duty until the investigation was complete. He'd been more agreeable to the counseling than the desk duty, but he'd called Lucky last night to say he was officially back on patrol today. As expected, he'd been cleared of any wrongdoing, having shot only after Red refused to surrender his weapon and had begun discharging it.

Lucky had spent some time at the Romo family picnic talking with Mike and Rachel about Tessa, and it had made him feel good to find out they both wished Tessa would give him another chance. When Rachel had walked away to talk with Mike's mom, Mike had said to Lucky, "It's not that I like how you handled the situation, but I think if you had it to do over, you'd figure out another way."

And Mike was right. Lucky wasn't sure *how* exactly he'd deal with it if something like this ever happened again, but he'd learned something about himself that morning behind Gravediggers: that he really *wasn't* a killer. When it had become about self-defense in the end, that was different—but he'd been unable to take the life of an unarmed man, even after that man had tried to take his.

"You doin' okay about Tessa, bro?" Mike had asked. They'd been sitting atop a picnic table, looking out over all the festivities, kids running and playing all around them.

And it hurt—because in a better world, Tessa would have been there with him, *should* have been there with him. He'd confessed to Mike, "It's tearing me up." Sure, he went about his business, tried to act normal . . . but his gut clenched just telling his brother. He'd let out a cynical laugh. "To think, a few months ago, I was this bad-ass loner who didn't care about anybody—other than Duke anyway. And now . . . hell, a loner's the last thing I wanna be. I never knew how empty my life was until . . . I had something to fill it. And I still have the kid, and you and the family, but there for a little while— for just this short little blink in time—I had it *all*. She made it all work for me."

"You done anything to try to get her back?" Mike asked.

And Lucky had just sighed and told Mike the truth. "I . . . can't. I don't know why."

"Is it pride?" Mike asked. "Because if it is, you gotta get past it."

Lucky had shaken his head in reply. "Naw, it's . . . bigger than that. The things she wrote in that letter . . . I don't know—every time I think about it, I figure she's just happier without me, so why should I try to convince her she's not?"

Lucky knew from Duke that Tessa was busy working at Gravediggers a few days a week now, making over the bar bit by bit. Duke said she was taking his hole in the wall and giving it some serious biker class, turning it into just the kind of place he'd dreamed of when he'd first bought the building almost ten years ago.

And he also knew that every time Duke brought up Lucky's name, Tessa said she didn't want to talk about him. " 'End of subject,' " Duke told him. "That's what she always says—'end of subject.' She's kind of a tough little chick sometimes."

And Lucky had muttered, "Don't I know it." He missed that, that toughness about her. Just as much as he missed the sweetness in her, too. He missed all of her.

Duke had also informed him, just a couple of days ago, that a bar patron who owned a steakhouse in Crestview had been watching Gravediggers' transformation and had called Tessa for an estimate on redecorating his restaurant. And in addition to that, Duke knew a biker-chick-by-night/real-estate-agent-by-day who was interested in hiring Tessa to consult with homeowners preparing their houses to be sold—staging, she'd told Duke it was called. It had done Lucky's heart good to hear all this. Even if things had turned to shit between him and Tessa, at least something promising had come out of it for her.

When he finished the skull, he set down his paint gun and stencil, then pushed through the plastic curtains for some fresh air. It was June now—officially hot out, and the plastic was practical in some ways, but it trapped in the heat. Stretching his back as he stepped from the garage, he adjusted the bandana he tied around his head to hold back his hair and caught a glimpse of Tessa's cabin.

And—God, there she was. In a cute little pair of shorts and a tank top, dragging her garden hose all the way out to her mailbox to water the daisies he'd seen blooming there last week. His heart nearly stopped at the sight of her. And his whole body ached with wanting to hold her—or hell, just talk to her, just look back into those gorgeous hazel eyes.

He stopped himself then, shook his head to clear it. *Hell, who are you, man? What happened to the dude who appreciated her mainly for the way she looked in a bikini?*

But then he answered himself. The fact was, he'd been an entirely different guy then. That guy hadn't been *bad*, but Lucky had changed. A lot. Because of her.

As he stood watching her, unable to push down that gnawing ache—more physical than he'd known such an emotion could feel—he considered once more the notion of walking down the hill, trying to talk to her, trying to make her believe in him again.

But he still just . . . couldn't. Damn, that had been the one good thing about being a loner—no one had the power to hurt you, to let you down.

But he'd let her down, too—he had to remember that. And maybe . . . maybe he just didn't want to scare her again, ever. And maybe she had a *right* to be scared, in a way. After all, he'd actually told her he was setting out to kill a guy. Weeks later, that almost sounded impossible to him—but that was what he'd done, what he'd actually expected her to accept and go along with like it was an everyday occurrence in Destiny.

And it was in that moment, as he watched Tessa, her form beginning to blend in and disappear among the trees that stood between him and her daisies by the mailbox, that Lucky finally understood why he hadn't been able to go to her after the breakup.

It was more than being let down or abandoned. It was because, deep down inside, he was afraid . . . she was right.

He let out a tired sigh, leaned back against his Jeep, let his gaze drop to his feet. Shit.

What if he really *wasn't* worthy of her faith, her love? What if he *didn't* deserve her or any of the other good things in his life?

Hell. No wonder he hadn't been able to face this—it was too ugly and it hurt too damn much.

But maybe when all was said and done, she really *was* better off without him. And maybe Lucky was just as undeserving as he'd always felt.

I have little left in myself—I must have you.
My very soul demands you.

Charlotte Brontë, *Jane Eyre*

Nineteen

*O*n a quiet afternoon at the bookstore, working alone, Tessa found herself glad for Brontë's company. At the moment, the kitty stood directly in front of her on the counter by the cash register, meowing up at her and lifting a paw to gently bat at the long necklace she wore.

She used both hands to scratch behind the cat's ears. "Yes, I know—I like you, too," she said. "And I wish I could take you home with me, but what happens when I get sick? What if I neglect you?"

Continuing to pet Brontë, her own words made her think of Lucky, and of his parents neglecting him after the loss of his little sister. She supposed they'd been sick, too, just in a different way.

And neglected things just didn't grow. She knew that now more than ever because since summer was finally upon them, all the things she'd planted in early spring were suddenly thriving. She'd occasionally dabbled in flowers before, usually unsuccessfully—because she hadn't put much work into it. But all the care and watering she'd provided this spring was paying off. The zinnias and snapdragons on her deck were ready to bloom, and she'd set her first tomatoes on her windowsill for ripening. Her daisies were blooming already—a bit low to the ground, but she'd read to expect that the first season, and they still made her feel happy whenever she saw them.

And she *needed* some help feeling happy these days, so every little thing helped. The truth was, every time she thought of Lucky, her heart broke all over again.

She was so glad he had his family back, and good things in his life. But she still couldn't reconcile the guy she'd fallen for with the one who'd told her he was going to kill someone. She simply hadn't seen that coming. And it had relieved her more than words could express that, in the end, he *hadn't* been the one to pull that trigger. She knew from Rachel that what happened hadn't been easy for Mike, but at least he'd been trained to handle it, and he could justify it as a professional duty and not a personal decision.

As for Lucky—she knew he'd been in danger, too, that according to Rachel, he'd almost died. Her stomach plummeted every time she thought about that—the very idea of it left her heart in shreds. And yet as happy as she was that he'd come out unscathed, in a way, it just made everything worse. To know he'd put himself directly in the line of fire. To know his life had almost ended because he'd gone seeking that Red guy out.

She missed Lucky madly, but how could she go blindly on, pretending they were the same inside—had the same values, the same way of viewing life—now that she knew it wasn't true? How could she ever believe in him the way she had before?

When the door opened, ringing the bell above, she looked up to see a police officer walk in—and it happened to be Mike. "Hi," she said. "Rachel left a few minutes ago—headed to the orchard."

Mike stepped up to the counter, looking as serious as usual. "Not looking for Rachel," he informed her. "I need to talk to *you*."

"Oh?" At this, Tessa lowered Brontë to the floor behind the counter.

"About Lucky," Mike added.

Instantly uncomfortable, she let her gaze drop to the cash register. "Oh."

"Tessa, it's none of my business, but the guy's hurtin'."

Crap. Talk about things she hadn't seen coming. But she'd gotten to know Mike pretty well lately, so now she forced herself to lift her eyes back to his face. "Well, I'm hurting over him, too, but how can I trust that he won't . . ." She stopped then, though, not sure how much Mike knew about Lucky's original plan to go after Red.

"I know why you broke up," Mike said quietly, answering the unspoken question. "And trust me, I get it. But I guess I'm just here to say . . . I believe in him. And that didn't come easy. When that fire was set, he responded out of fear, out of habit—he went on the defensive by going on the *off*ensive. That's how he's protected himself all these years."

Tessa let out a sigh. "I understand that, but . . . how do I know he won't *always* respond that way? After all, you yourself didn't want me to have anything to do with him just a few months ago."

"I know. And I was wrong. And admitting *that* doesn't come easy, either—just ask Rachel." When he began to back away, it relieved Tessa that he wasn't going to stretch this out. "Look, ya gotta do what ya gotta do," he said, "but for what it's worth, he was protecting more than just himself that night. He was trying to protect *all of us*—he was trying to protect *you*. So I'm just saying that if you still love my brother, maybe you could just talk to him, give him another chance."

Tessa thought that over for a minute. Because she'd considered the same thing herself many times. Yet she always came back to the same conclusion. "I'm not sure my heart could take it, Mike."

Mike just offered an acceptant nod, then gave her a short wave as he departed.

She'd never expected to fall for Lucky, to love Lucky, and on the night of the fire, it would have been *so* easy to go back into his arms—but she'd feared becoming one of those women who lived in denial, who turned a blind eye, who couldn't see the truth about the person they loved. What if he did something *else* scary and she didn't have the strength to make herself leave next time? What if he did something rash and dangerous and, next time, got himself killed? To give him another chance felt like taking the ultimate risk—with her life, and her heart. And didn't she already have enough to deal with, like her health, and her money concerns? Even if the money part *was* looking up these days, thanks to Lucky.

So Tessa told herself the same thing she'd been telling herself for over two weeks. It was time to look forward, not back. Even if there wasn't a whole lot of laughing and dancing going on in her world these days, she still had to think positive, expect the best from life. No matter how hard that felt at the moment—and no matter how badly the very thought of Lucky made her stomach clench and her soul ache.

As tears threatened, she stooped down to scoop Brontë up into her arms, seeking comfort, and she turned to one of her favorite Ellenisms, because she needed it desperately right now.

Just keep swimming. Just keep swimming. Just keep swimming.

* * *

A quiet Saturday had been a good day for Lucky to take Johnny on a long—slow, cautious—motorcycle ride in the country, Johnny wearing the new helmet Lucky had painted for him using the usual NASCAR theme. And Lucky couldn't deny that it had felt good to have his kid hold onto him while they rode and to share with him something he loved.

But when Lucky put Johnny to bed that night, it was dark out, late, and as he walked into the living room by himself, he couldn't deny he felt empty inside, still missing his girl. Life had been easier back when he'd known how not to care about people very much, but now that those floodgates had opened, he couldn't seem to close them up again.

He tried to relax with a little TV, but when relaxation wouldn't come, he found himself turning it off, then reaching into the drawer on an end table where he'd stuffed Tessa's letter. He'd kind of wanted to throw it away so he wouldn't ever have to see it again, but for some reason, he hadn't been able to—and he'd just stuck it into the nearest out-of-sight place handy at the time.

He read the letter over—once, twice. It was still painful— it still pointed out all the flaws he feared in himself now that she feared them, too.

Shit, should a guy like him even *have* a kid, be a dad? Did he have a chance in hell of setting any good examples for Johnny? Was Johnny safe with him? Thinking through just a few of the many questions he'd been forced to ask himself lately, he let out a sigh.

But on the third reading of the letter, he realized there was one particular line that kept resonating in his head, the only *good* part. *I hope being a father will help you continue to change into the man I know you can be.*

The man she knew he could be.

That meant, despite everything . . . she still had a *little* faith in him. *Right?*

Maybe he hadn't quite caught that the first time because he'd been too busy getting crushed by the rest of it. Maybe he hadn't quite caught it until . . . right now.

He glanced down the darkened hall toward Johnny's room. What if it were Johnny who was shutting him out? Would he just back away like this? Would he just give up? Someday, Johnny would find out the truth about his father—and when that day came, if Johnny turned away from him, would he just accept that?

Hell no. Lucky knew in a heartbeat that even as hard as it had been for him to take that first step with his kid, now that he had something good going with him, he'd keep fighting for a relationship with his son no matter how much time or effort it took. He'd do his damnedest to convince his kid that he'd changed and was truly a better man now.

The old Lucky, on the other hand—yeah, he'd have probably given up. He'd given up on a *lot* in life, early on. But as Tessa had told him, he wasn't that guy anymore. He just wasn't.

So why the hell was he giving up on Tessa? Wasn't that just proving her point by accepting this the same way the old Lucky would have?

That last line in the letter was about fatherhood—but maybe what it was *really* saying, if he read between the lines, was that he had to get over his past and prove himself to her. He had to find a way to show her he *was* that good man already, that she'd been right about him in the first place and that he wouldn't let her down again.

And the more he thought about it, the more he realized that if he didn't try to fix this, if he just let the relationship go—it would be sort of like running away all over again. He had to face this the same way Tessa faced her disease—with courage, and heart. He had to be that man she wanted him to be, once and for all.

* * *

Tessa walked from her mom's car toward the front door, tired but otherwise feeling better than she might have expected after a morning at her doctor's office. Nothing was wrong, but she'd undergone some annual tests that generally left her unwell for a few days afterward. So far so good, though.

"Doing all right?" her mom asked.

"Fine, Mom."

"I'll stick around awhile," her mother said anyway. "I have a little time."

But Tessa protested. The tests had fallen on the day of her parents' vacation departure and it was bad enough that she'd taken up her mom's whole morning. "Nope—no way am I going to risk you missing your flight. And I can take care of myself, *really*."

She was preparing to battle her mother on the topic further when she heard her front door open—and looked up expecting to see Rachel and Amy, and also completely ready to yell at them for being there. They knew about the tests, and that her mom was leaving on a trip, and they were worried. But she was sick of making people worry about her.

So she couldn't have been more stunned to instead see Lucky exiting the cabin—as calmly as if he lived there. And—oh God—tired or not, the mere sight of him sent a hot tingle rippling down her spine.

"Sorry," he said, "I let myself in."

She just blinked. "Huh?"

"Rachel gave me her key."

Then she flinched, stunned. *Note to self: Kill Rachel. And never be stupid enough to give your friend a key to your house.* "Why?"

"Because when I heard you might not be feeling too good the next few days, I insisted."

She let out a breath, growing more irritated by the second. "Again, Lucky—why? What are you doing here?"

"I'm here to take care of you," he announced.

And her blood began to boil. How dare he? It was bad enough he'd pushed his way into her home the *last* time she'd not felt well, but *now*—it was unfathomable!

And all of that must have shown on her face, since he said, "Before you start yelling at me, just let me talk to you for a minute, okay?"

Tessa sucked in her breath. She still wanted to yell. When it came to anything having to do with her condition, or being taken care of, she had a very short fuse. But then she recalled that Lucky already knew that and it hadn't ever stopped him. So finally she snipped, "Fine."

"Um, I'll just excuse myself into the house," her mother said.

And Tessa flinched. Yikes. The truth was, at the mere sight of Lucky, she'd practically forgotten her mother was even there.

Once they were alone outside, the thick billow of full, green trees seeming suddenly to cocoon them somehow, Lucky said, "I know you don't like to believe you ever need to be taken care of, but I can't stand the idea of you being sick and alone. I need to be here for you, babe."

"But—"

"I wasn't done," he interrupted her.

She pursed her lips, perturbed—not only at him, but also at herself for still wanting him so much. Yet she shut up because . . . well, if he had more to say, maybe it was best to just let him say it, and then it would be over. Maybe it would provide the sense of closure she hadn't quite reached despite three weeks apart from him.

"The thing is, hot stuff," he said, "I've spent my whole life running. I've run from my family and this town, I've run from danger, and from fear, I've run from caring about anybody—and the last few weeks I've been running . . . from proving myself to you. But I'm not running anymore. Tessa, you're about the best damn thing that's ever happened to me. So how can I let you go without fighting for you?"

Tessa felt a little dizzy, not from anything health-related, but from Lucky's plea. The raw emotion in his voice ripped a hole in her heart. And there was a part of her, the part that was still just as in love with him as she'd ever been, that wanted to let him back in—into her house and into her life—wanted to let him *fill* that hole, that void he'd left. But it wasn't that easy.

"Lucky, I'm sorry I ended things the way I did, without even talking to you—that was wrong." She let out a sigh, sad about how she'd handled it. "But what it comes down to is this. A person's life, their history, makes them who they are. And . . . you and I are just too different to be together."

His voice came out soft but sure. "I made a mistake, Tessa. You're basing our whole relationship on one bad choice. And I get why it upset you so much—it upsets *me* now, too. But I never got to tell you what happened that night. I never got to tell you that when it came down to it, I couldn't do it. Because you were right—I'm not that guy anymore."

He lowered his voice even further then, to a whisper, probably because her mother was nearby. "I couldn't pull that trigger, babe. And I almost got killed because of it, and I ended up drawing my brother into it in a way I never wanted to—but I still couldn't do it. See, it turns out I've changed even more than I knew. Maybe it's about wanting to be a man my son can be proud of. Or maybe it's about wanting to be good enough for *you*, deserving of you. Or maybe it's just about coming home and finding parts of . . . of the guy I could have been if I'd never left. But *whatever* the reason—and even though I've had my fair share of doubts since you left me—I know I *am* the man you want me to be, Tessa."

Tears welled behind Tessa's eyes and she still didn't

know how to feel. *This* sounded like the Lucky she'd come to know and love. His words began to fill up that dark hole inside her with a fresh ray of light—and hope. Was it possible her faith in him hadn't been misplaced, after all? "But . . ." she began around the lump in her throat, "how can I know for sure? I can't see inside you, Lucky. I once thought I could, but I was wrong. So how can I be sure all the dark parts of you are completely gone, for good?"

Just then, the front door opened, and Tessa's mother leaned out. She wore a strange expression Tessa couldn't read and said, "I don't mean to interrupt, but Tessa, maybe you should come inside and see this."

"See what?" What could be so important right *now*, when she was having such a crucial talk?

"Just come in, honey," her mom said.

So she let out a sigh, then went into the cabin. And then she understood what was so important. Her living room had been transformed.

The room bloomed with daisies—vases of them sat everywhere: on the mantel, on her bookshelves, on the end tables and coffee table—it was like summertime had come indoors. And where there weren't daisies, there were words—wonderful, inspiring, strengthening words, which Lucky had clearly found in her little journal—they'd been written out on banners in bright colors and seemed to wallpaper the room:

Think of all the beauty that's still left in and around you and be happy.
    Anne Frank

If God sends us on strong paths, we are provided strong shoes.
    Corrie ten Boom

Keep your face always toward the sunshine—and shadows will fall behind you.
　　Walt Whitman

And, of course, the one she fell back on so often:

Just keep swimming.
　　Dory, Finding Nemo

And then came the one clearly inspired by Ellen, proving he'd been paying attention when they'd watched her show together:

Laugh. Dance. Tessa

It all left her speechless, almost overwhelmed. That Lucky had done this for her—that he'd known how much joy and comfort it would bring her, that he'd gone to all this trouble—*amazed* her. And began to make her think that maybe it *was* true—maybe he really *was* the man she'd believed in so fervently.

She had yet to utter a word when she heard a soft *meow* come from somewhere—and turned to Lucky, who'd followed her inside. "What's that?"

He glanced over his shoulder toward the closed bathroom door. "Oh, I put the cat in the bathroom—I was afraid she'd tear up the flowers. I didn't think through that part very well."

"Huh?" she said, confused.

"I got the little bookstore cat from Amy for you."

And she was touched, but . . . "Lucky, you know I'm not sure I can take care of a cat."

Yet he just shook his head. "*I'll* take care of her. She makes you happy, she makes you smile—that's all that matters."

Tessa simply stood there gaping at him, this man

who . . . almost seemed to know her needs better than she did right now. Which maybe meant she should try to trust him. Again.

Gazing down into her eyes, Lucky took her hands in his, and his voice came low. "Tessa, you gotta have a little faith in me now, faith in *us*. You gotta believe you were right—I'm not that guy anymore. Now I'm the guy you made me into. I'm a way better man than I was the day I met you, babe. And I plan on staying that way. I love you, and I'll do whatever it takes to prove I'm worthy of you."

Tessa's heart fluttered in her chest. "I think you just did," she whispered up to him.

Then watched his warm brown eyes change, almost seeming to deepen in color. "I did?"

She nodded. "I love you, too, Lucky. I've just been . . . so afraid."

He lifted a hand, cupped her cheek. "I know, babe. And I'm so, so sorry. I won't make you afraid ever again—I promise."

And Tessa believed him. She prayed she wasn't being naïve, but he was right—sometimes you had to take things on faith. And right now, she trusted in everything he was telling her, every promise he was making. He'd given her all he had to give in this moment, and it was enough.

"I'm, uh, gonna take off," her mom said then, from a few feet behind them—almost startling Tessa. Crap, she'd kind of forgotten she was there again.

So she moved to give her mother a quick hug and a goodbye, and on the way out the door, her mom said, "I'm glad you have Lucky to take care of you. Be smart and let him."

When the door closed behind her and Tessa turned back to her big brawny biker, he asked, "Are you gonna?"

Again, she just nodded.

And the look that came over his face reminded her of the very first time she'd seen him, how beautiful she'd thought his eyes were, how soft they'd seemed compared to the rest of him. They were that way now.

"What can I do?" he asked. "To start taking care of you?"

"Maybe you could bring Brontë to me," she said. And when he looked puzzled, she smiled and explained, "The cat."

"Oh—sure thing."

And as he walked to the bathroom to retrieve her, Tessa lay down on the couch, still tired, and when he returned with Brontë in one large hand, and his eyes locked on hers, she said, "Will you lie down with me? I want to just lie here and look at the room. And snuggle with you and my new kitty."

"You got it, babe," he said with a small grin, then passed her the cat before stretching out alongside her.

When Lucky closed his arms gently around her, it felt like coming home. And that was the *real*, *true* moment when she knew this was right. She nuzzled against him, took in the happy flowers all around them, and knew she was back where she was meant to be. But she didn't get to look at the daisies for very long because she found herself kissing him then, long and sweet and as intense as any kiss they'd ever shared. And then she was telling him, "I'm sorry I got scared, Lucky. I should have waited, I should have known, I should have—"

That's when Lucky pressed one finger to her lips to quiet her and said, "Just tell me one thing. Do you believe in me again, Tessa?"

She nodded profusely. "With all my heart."

"That's all I need to know."

. . . and I am yours, and you are mine.

Charlotte Brontë, *Jane Eyre*

Epilogue

*S*ummer had turned to autumn and the woods along Whisper Falls billowed with vibrant reds, oranges, and golds that seemed to shimmer in the sun. Wrapped in warm clothing, Tessa and Lucky walked quietly along the stream, holding hands and exchanging occasional kisses.

Since June, more than just the seasons had changed.

Lucky's new workspace had long since been finished and business was booming, and now that word of Tessa's interior decorating prowess had finally gotten out in the community, she had plenty of jobs coming in, as well.

Brontë had settled into her new home, and Tessa was thankful Lucky had made the bold move of adopting the cat for her. And though he'd never admit it, he seemed just as attached to Brontë now as she was.

For her birthday last month, Lucky had surprised Tessa by taking her skydiving. Although, by that time, she'd pretty much forgotten all about the idea and had been much more frightened than she'd originally expected. But Lucky reminded her how brave he thought she was, and they did it together, and it had turned out to be just as exhilarating as she'd originally anticipated. Again, as always, Lucky was helping her grab onto life and live it to the fullest.

And he kept life just as exciting in the bedroom, too— and occasionally out here in the woods, as well.

"Let's see if the whispering trick still works," Lucky said as they reached the top of the falls. "But this time, *you* go across to the other side."

Tessa glanced downstream to the crossing point, and since the water was low right now, decided to go for it without making a big deal of it. "All right."

"Where exactly did you stand the last time we did this?" Lucky asked, and she positioned him where she thought she'd been.

Then she made her way up the creek, soon stepping across the rocks that led to the other bank. Once she reached the spot opposite him, she said, "Okay, I'm ready. Start whispering."

From across the falls, Lucky gave her a sexy smile, and then she heard his whisper in her ear as clearly as if he'd been standing right next to her. "Will you marry me, hot stuff?"

Her gaze widened on him as the blood drained from her face. But then she found her voice and screamed out, "Yes! Yes, yes, yes!" And then added, "But I could kill you for asking me when you're so far away!"

He just grinned. "Come back across, babe, and I'll show you how happy you just made me."

And as Tessa did just that, careful not to trip or slip even as she rushed, anxious to be in her big, bad biker's arms, she knew with certainty there was no place on earth she belonged more. Not in the city. Not having a sophisticated interior design career. Nowhere. The time for that part of her life had come and gone, and now she was exactly where she was supposed to be. Laughing. Dancing. And surrounded by love.

Next month, don't miss these exciting new
love stories only from
Avon Books

Scandal of the Year by Laura Lee Guhrke
Julia always knew that Aidan Carr, the oh-so-proper Duke of
Trathen, had a bit of the devil in him—a devil who secretly
yearned for what he could not have. So when she decides she
needs to be caught in a compromising situation, Aiden is the
answer to her prayers.

Night Betrayed by Joss Ware
The Change that devastated the earth did not destroy Theo
Waxnicki, it made him something more than human—
eternally young…but not immortal. When he dies on a
mission, he's lost in darkness…until a miracle lady
brings him back.

Burning Darkness by Jaime Rush
Fonda Raine, a government-trained assassin, has her sights
locked on her latest target: Eric Aruda, a rogue Offspring—a
pyrokinetic who can create fire with just a thought. But Fonda
has awesome powers of her own—and her ability to be in two
places at one time enables her to put herself exactly where she
wants to be…in Eric's bed.

Tainted by Temptation   by Katy Madison
To escape the cruel false gossip of London, Velvet Campbell
accepts a governess position in remote Cornwall. But when she
finds, to her dismay, that her new employer—the darkly handsome Lucian Pendar—is himself the subject of whispered
insinuations, she wonders: *has she found a kindred spirit, a
destined love…or placed herself in peril?*

*At Avon Books, we know your passion
for romance—once you finish one of our
novels, you find yourself wanting more.*

May we tempt you with . . .

- **Excerpts** from our upcoming releases.

- Entertaining **extras**, including authors'
  personal photo albums and book lists.

- Behind-the-scenes **scoop** on your favorite
  characters and series.

- **Sweepstakes** for the chance to win free books,
  romantic getaways, and other fun prizes.

- Writing **tips** from our authors and editors.

- **Blog** with our authors and find out why they
  love to write romance.

- **Exclusive content** that's not contained
  within the pages of our novels.

Join us at
www.avonbooks.com

An Imprint of HarperCollins*Publishers*
www.avonromance.com